A SILVER WOLF CHRISTMAS

D0877922

TERRY SPEAR

sourcebooks
casablanca

Published by Sourcebooks Casablanca, an imprint of Sourcebooks, Inc.
P.O. Box 4410, Naperville, Illinois 60567-4410
(630) 961-3900
Fax: (630) 961-2168
www.sourcebooks.com

Printed and bound in Canada.
MBP 10 9 8 7 6 5 4 3 2 1

I dedicate A Silver Wolf Christmas *to Maria McIntyre, one of my beta readers and friends, whose name inspired my heroine's name. All my best to you, lassie.*

Chapter 1

CONNOR JAMES SILVER, BETTER KNOWN AS CJ, couldn't believe it had been a whole year since he and his brothers rejoined their cousin Darien Silver's wolf pack. Though his oldest brother was still butting heads with Darien at times, CJ was glad they had made amends and returned home to Silver Town, Colorado. His ancestors had built the town, which was still mostly gray wolf run, and he envisioned staying here forever.

Especially now that three lovely sister she-wolves had joined the pack and were remodeling the old Silver Town Inn. In two days' time, they would have hotel guests. CJ smiled as he strode up the covered wooden walkway in front of the tavern and glanced in the direction of what had been the haunted, neglected hotel across the street, which was now showing off its former glory. The windows were no longer boarded up, the picket fence and the fretwork had been repaired, and a fresh coat of white paint made the whole place gleam.

"CJ!" Tom Silver called out as he hurried to join him. Tom, the youngest of Darien's triplet brothers, was CJ's best friend.

He turned to watch Tom crunch through the piled-up snow, then stalk up the covered walkway. He had the same dark hair as CJ, although his eyes were a little darker brown. Tom was wearing his usual: an ecru wool sweater and blue jeans. The toes of his boots were now sporting a coating of fresh snow.

Tom pointed at the hotel, evidently having observed CJ looking that way. "Don't even *think* about going over there to help with the final preparations before their grand opening."

CJ shook his head. "I know when I'm not wanted." But he damn well wasn't giving up on seeing the women—well, one in particular.

Tom smiled a little evilly at him. "Come on. I'll buy you lunch. Darien has a job for you."

Even though CJ was a deputy sheriff and took his lead from the sheriff, everyone stopped what they were doing when the pack leader needed something done. Pack took priority.

He and Tom headed inside the tavern, where the fire was burning in a brand-new woodstove in the corner, keeping the room warm. The Christmas tree in front of one of the windows was decorated with white lights, big red bows, and hand-painted ornaments featuring wolves. The aroma of hot roast beef scented the air, making CJ's stomach rumble. Sam, the black-bearded bartender— and now sandwich maker—was serving lunch without Silva, his waitress-turned-mate. She was now down the street running her own tearoom, where the women ate when they wanted lunch out. The men all continued to congregate at Sam's.

The tavern usually looked a lot more rustic, less… Christmassy. Sam loved Silva and tolerated her need to see that everyone enjoyed the spirit of Christmas either at her place or his, though he grumbled about it like an old grizzly bear.

CJ glanced at the red, green, and silver foil-covered chocolates in wooden Christmas-tree-shaped dishes on the center of each table. Those were new. Silva had also draped spruce garlands along the bar and over the long, rectangular mirror that had hung there since the place opened centuries earlier. She'd added lights and Christmas wreaths to the windows and had put up the tree, though Sam had helped. He looked rough and gruff, and was protective of anyone close to him, but he was a big teddy bear. Though CJ would never voice his opinion about that.

"We'll have the usual," Tom called out to Sam.

He nodded and began to fix roast beef sandwiches for them.

"Staying out of trouble?" Tom sat in his regular chair at the pack leaders' table in the corner of the tavern. This spot had a view of the whole place, except for the area by the restrooms.

"I haven't been near the hotel." CJ glanced around the room, nodding a greeting to Mason, owner of the bank; John Hastings, owner of the local hardware store and bed and breakfast; Jacob Summers, their local electrician; and even Mervin, the barber—all gray wolves who were sharing conversations and eating and drinking. It was an exclusive club, membership strictly reserved for wolves.

CJ looked out the new windows of the tavern—also Silva's doing, now that the hotel was quite an attraction instead of detracting from the view. The new sign proclaimed Silver Town Inn, just like in the old days, as it rocked a little in the breeze. Only this time, the sign featured a howling wolf carved into one corner. CJ loved it, just like everyone else did.

The pack members couldn't have been more pleased with the way the sisters had renovated the place, keeping the old Victorian look but adding special touches. Like the two wrought iron and wood-slat benches in a parklike setting out front, with the bench seats held up by wrought iron bears.

Tom turned back to CJ. "Darien said—"

"I know what Darien said. My brothers and I were getting under the women's feet. They didn't want or need our help. Don't tell me we can't participate in the grand opening." Even though CJ would be busy directing traffic for a little while, he intended to stop in and check on the crowd inside the hotel to ensure everyone was behaving themselves.

Sam delivered their beers in new steins, featuring wolves in a winter scene etched in the glass, along with sandwiches and chips on wooden Christmas tree plates. He gave CJ a look that told him he'd better not make a comment about the plates or steins. CJ was dying to ask Sam how domesticated life was, but he bit his tongue.

"I'll be setting up the bar for the festivities," Sam said. "Silva is bringing her special petit fours, and she's serving finger sandwiches. The hotel had better be ready to open on schedule."

"Do you think any of the guests will run out of there screaming in the middle of the night, claiming the place is haunted?" CJ asked. It was something he'd worried about. He wanted to see the sisters do well so they could stay here forever.

Sam shook his head. "Blamed foolishness, if you ask me."

Sam didn't believe in anything paranormal. Some

might ask how he could feel that way when they were *lupus garous*—wolf shifters. But then again, their kind believed they were perfectly normal. Nothing paranormal about them.

Someone called for another beer, and Sam left their table to take care of it.

"When you were over there getting underfoot, did you see anything?" Tom asked, keeping his voice low.

"Nothing unusual." Even though they'd been best friends forever, the ghostly business with the hotel was one thing CJ really didn't want to discuss with Tom. Neither of them had, not once over all those years.

CJ took another bite of his sandwich, hoping now that the hotel was opening, he could finally start seeing Laurel MacTire in more of a courtship way. He would never again make the mistake of mispronouncing her name. Who would ever have thought that a name that looked like "tire" was pronounced like "tier"? He couldn't know every foreign word meaning "wolf." But he did love that she was a pretty redheaded, green-eyed lass. She had been born in America, but she still had a little Irish accent, courtesy of her Irish-born parents. He loved to listen to her talk.

The problem was that she and her sisters, Meghan and Ellie, acted wary around him and everyone else in the pack. In fact, they didn't seem like the type of proprietors that should manage a hotel, since they were more reserved than friendly or welcoming. He wasn't sure what was wrong. Maybe they'd never lived with a pack before. He had to admit that everyone had been eager to greet them, so maybe they felt a bit overwhelmed.

The pack members were so welcoming because

fewer she-wolves were born among *lupus garous* than males, and many of the bachelors were interested. The women in the pack were also grateful that they had more women to visit with. Besides that, the wolf pack's collective nature was such that its members openly received new wolves.

After eating the rest of his sandwich, Tom leaned back in his chair. "The two painters working on the main lobby left prematurely yesterday after demanding their pay for what they'd finished. They said that when they returned from a lunch break, their paint cans had been moved across the room, their plastic sheeting was balled up in a corner, and an *X* was painted across the ceiling in the study."

CJ frowned. "None of the sisters saw or heard anything?"

"The sisters had returned to their house behind the hotel to have lunch."

"Could it have been kids? Vandals?" CJ figured that what had happened wasn't the result of anything supernatural.

"Who knows? If we discount the ghostly angle, could have been." Tom finished his beer.

"Did the women smell the scent of anyone who had been in there earlier?"

"Not that they could say. So many people have been traipsing through the hotel, finishing up renovations, that maybe somebody else just moved the stuff. The electrician and a plumber were in earlier."

"About that... I've seen that they've hired humans for a number of the jobs. Except for Jacob, the electrician. I would think everyone, even if they're new to the pack, would hire wolves."

Tom shrugged. "They've never been in a pack before.

It'll take a little getting used to. Maybe no one gave them a list of who could do the jobs for them. We all know who does what in the vicinity. The sisters wouldn't have a clue."

CJ nodded, but he was already thinking about how the painters had left the work unfinished. Maybe the women could use his help in painting the rest of the place. As long as the town or surrounding area didn't require him to get involved in any law enforcement business, he was free to help out. And eager to do so.

"Of course, that doesn't explain the *X* on the ceiling," Tom said.

"Most likely vandals."

CJ wasn't afraid of any old ghost in the hotel. He hadn't been since that day when Darien and Jake had tried to scare him and Tom when they were all kids. CJ told himself it had just been them. But neither of the Silver brothers had said anything about what CJ had witnessed, confirming or denying it. He was still telling himself the apparition he'd seen was only a figment of his imagination. That, as a kid, he'd been so scared, he could have imagined anything. That the darkened shadow of a woman was nothing more than dust particles highlighted by moonlight shining through the basement door's window.

Tom sat taller in his chair. "If visitors ask about the hauntings, Darien wants everyone in the pack to tell them the stories are just rumors."

"Right. Ghosts don't exist."

Tom let out his breath. "But you know differently. We both know differently."

That made CJ wonder what Tom had experienced.

But if CJ admitted to even one soul that he believed the hotel was haunted, there would go his best-kept secret of all time. Besides, Tom had never shared what he'd experienced either.

Tom straightened a bit. "Okay. Well, as I said, Darien has a job for you."

If it had to do with helping Laurel MacTire, CJ would jump right on it. He was certain that she *really* didn't mind that he'd been so in the way when she was trying to get the place fixed up. She was just overcautious about everyone in the wolf pack.

"Hang some Christmas lights on the hotel?" Then again, the job could have nothing to do with Laurel, her sisters, or the hotel. CJ finished the last of his beer.

Tom tilted his chin down. "*No* helping the women with the hotel. Unless they change their minds and ask you to."

"All right," CJ said. "What then?"

"We have some ghost busters in town."

"That's just what we need." CJ was ready to protect the three sisters from anyone who might try to ruin things for them.

"For now, they're staying in the Hastingses' bed and breakfast, both tonight and tomorrow. But they have reservations at the hotel, and they will be moving over there as soon as it opens. They've been grilling Bertha Hastings and everyone else about the hauntings."

"That's not good."

"Of course, we're worried they might stir up trouble for the ladies by reporting the place is haunted to discourage people from staying there. But what we're really concerned about is that they'll learn that something a lot more serious than ghosts exists in the area."

"*Lupus garous*."

"Yes. Us."

"You want me to get rid of them?" CJ asked, surprised. Not that he thought Darien wanted him to kill anyone, but keeping their wolf halves secret was paramount to their well-being.

Tom chuckled. "No. But you're assigned to watch over them. If they see anyone shift when they shouldn't, then we'll have to take care of it."

CJ's whole outlook brightened. "Right. They're staying at the hotel." And if he had to really watch them, he'd have to stay there too! That meant he could see Laurel more.

"Can you handle it?"

"Hell yeah."

"I mean..." Tom glanced around the tavern where pack members filled nearly every chair at the wooden tables. The room was humming with conversation. He leaned forward. "Because of the ghosts."

"That don't exist."

"Right."

"Yeah, I can handle it." CJ smiled. He would do anything to be able to spend more time with that wickedly intriguing she-wolf. Though he hoped he wouldn't be running out of the hotel and breaking out into a cold sweat—again.

More than that, he knew something else was going on. The women didn't just buy the hotel because it was a beautiful building or a great investment opportunity, or because they desperately wanted to join a pack. They'd been reservedly friendly. Like they didn't trust anyone. And they hadn't joined in any pack functions during the six months they'd been renovating the hotel. Not once.

Of course, they said it all had to do with getting the place ready, and they were too busy or too tired afterward to participate. But he'd noticed the looks between the three sisters when he'd asked them why they had chosen this hotel to buy. It was as if they had some deep, dark secret, and they had to keep it that way.

So yeah, he was definitely interested in Laurel, but not just because she was a hot she-wolf. He wanted to know what she and her sisters were *really* doing here.

Laurel MacTire's luck hadn't been so hot lately. Tomorrow, both her sisters had to go out of state to ensure the shipment of furniture had arrived from Paris and then was safely transported here. When she and her sisters had tracked down the auctioned highboy and blanket chest that had belonged to their aunt Clarinda, they were afraid something bad had happened to her. In her will, their aunt had promised the furniture to their mother—her twin sister, Sadie.

If their mother had died first, then the furniture and their aunt's belongings would have gone to the girls when she died. *If* their aunt had died. But they'd learned from their mother six months earlier that Clarinda had vanished fifty years ago. Someone had auctioned off the furniture around that same time. After searching for several months following their mother's death, the sisters had finally located and purchased the pieces.

Clarinda had said in a letter to their mother that the furniture was unique, with an added feature. Their mother thought one or both of the pieces might contain a secret compartment. Maybe a clue hidden in a secret panel in a drawer would help them learn what had become of their aunt. Pictures documenting the initials of the furniture designer, *ELS*, and the fact that each piece had been made specifically for its owner, had helped the sisters to prove the items had belonged to their aunt.

No matter what else happened, the sisters wanted to keep the furniture in memory of their aunt.

That meant Laurel had to manage everything on her own for a couple of days, starting early tomorrow morning—and including the grand opening ceremony and the first hotel guests' arrival. What made it worse was that, according to Darien Silver, three of the men who had booked rooms for a week were supposedly ghost busters. That was *all* they needed!

What if the three men told the whole world the hotel was haunted? There would go the business. They'd either not get any guests or they'd have a bunch of paranormal thrill seekers wanting to stay there. Maybe even a well-known author like Stephen King would stay there to gain information and use the setting for a new book. Well, on second thought, she supposed that could be a boon.

She opened the buffet drawer in the lobby and pulled out the fifty-year-old postcard, the last communication that her missing aunt had sent to Laurel's mother. Laurel reread the note for the millionth time, as if she'd miraculously get more clues from it.

Silver Town Inn. Miss you. Falling in love. Kiss girls for me. See you at Christmas. Love, C

Ellie was headed for the stairs, a box of blinds in hand, when she saw Laurel reading the postcard again. "Hey, no matter how many times we look at it, it's not revealing anything new. We know for sure these were our aunt's last words to our mother—that she was staying at the Silver Town Inn. And she sounded like she was involved in a romance. When she failed to show up at Christmastime, Mom got worried. But though she investigated, she didn't find any sign of her sister. We were too little to really understand what was going on. Just that our aunt wasn't coming to play with us. She was always so much fun."

"Right." Laurel tucked the card back in the drawer. "I wish Mom hadn't waited until she was dying to tell us this about Aunt Clarinda."

Meghan came around the banister with a drill and a couple more boxes of blinds. "Are we talking about the postcard again? Mom was worried that something sinister might have happened to her sister—and that we'd learn about it and go looking for her, which could get us in trouble. But in the end, Mom wanted us to discover what happened to her sister. It was her last dying request. You know it had to have weighed heavily on her mind all these years."

Laurel agreed. "I hope we can learn the truth sooner than later." She closed the buffet drawer as her sisters headed up the stairs to hang the faux wooden blinds in the windows.

So far they didn't have anything to go on but the postcard and a lot of supposition. What if one of the Silver Town pack members had something to do with Aunt Clarinda's disappearance? He could still be here. That was one of the things about the wolves' longevity.

Their aging process was so much slower, or at least it had been. Recently, something had changed the dynamics and now their life spans were closer to humans'.

That meant anyone could be suspect—even CJ Silver, who was so eager to please her in his own way. She'd caught herself a ton of times letting down her guard with him. She needed to remember that she couldn't trust anyone but her sisters.

Now Darien was assigning CJ to watch the ghost busters? She'd never expected that to happen.

As soon as CJ walked in the door, all six feet of him, his amber eyes immediately sought her out as she worked on varnishing the countertop of the check-in desk. His sable hair complemented his tan face, and his muscular but wiry build had definitely turned the head of more than one she-wolf. She reminded herself that getting involved with any of the wolf pack members could be a bad idea.

"Did Darien tell you that I'll need to stay here when that ghost-busting crew arrives?"

"Yes."

"I heard you had trouble with the painters. Do you want me to finish the painting for you?" CJ looked perfectly willing.

Against her best judgment—because she was feeling a bit overwhelmed with all that still needed to be done—she nodded. "Thanks. You're…not afraid of ghosts?"

CJ smiled. "They don't exist. I'm ready to paint when you are. Just let me know what I need to do."

"The painters left the paint, brushes, plastic, everything, and won't return. So it's all over there." She pointed to the corner of the lobby.

"Great. I'll get right on it."

He was cute, but he looked so restrainedly pleased, she smiled. But then she saw her sister Meghan walking down the curved stairs and staring at CJ. Meghan shot her a look, as if to say she shouldn't have invited him to paint. Laurel hadn't even had a chance to tell her sisters that Darien wanted CJ staying with them to watch over the ghost busters.

"What's Ellie doing?" Laurel asked.

"She's finishing up the blue room, still hanging the new blinds in there. *We* were going to finish the painting down here, I thought."

"We have to decorate the whole place for Christmas next. We don't have time to finish the painting too. Not with the two of you leaving tomorrow to take care of other business," Laurel said. "Plus, we sort of have an issue."

Meghan narrowed her green eyes at her sister. "What *sort* of an issue?"

"You know the three men who were the first to rent rooms?"

Folding her arms, Meghan nodded.

"Darien learned they're self-professed ghost busters. They even have a TV show."

"*Great.*"

As if they hadn't had enough problems. A frozen, then broken water pipe that flooded the basement, the painters getting spooked by ghosts, and half of the windows arriving in the wrong size were only a few of the minor disasters they'd had to deal with.

CJ had already started painting one wall. It was white, but the pictures that had previously been hung there had left rectangular shadows on the walls. Even with the start of a fresh coat of paint, it looked better. "Darien is checking our guest list to make sure we're not going to have any other trouble. That's how he discovered who these men are and why they wanted rooms. He's concerned about them."

Meghan frowned. "Darien won't be doing background checks on all our guests forever, will he?"

As if Laurel and her sisters were staying in Silver Town forever. This was their business—buying, renovating, and selling hotels. They never stayed long. "He's the pack leader. If he thinks we might have any trouble, or that the rest of his pack might, he'll keep a close eye on the hotel. So with regard to that, he wants CJ to stay with us until the men leave."

Openmouthed, Meghan stared at her. Her gaze switched from her to CJ to Laurel again. "*You're…kidding*. Stay with *us*?"

"Yep. Darien gave him the job of watching the ghost busters to ensure they don't see anyone shifting. If they do, then the pack will handle it."

"*Just great*."

"Yeah, I know. Tell Ellie, will you?"

"Sure. So which room is he staying in?" Meghan smiled a little evilly. "The maids' quarters?"

"No way. He can have the attic room. Hopefully nothing will bother him up there." Laurel frowned as she stared at the center of the wall that CJ had already painted over. "Do you see a letter in the center of the wall?"

Meghan studied the wall. "I was hoping I was just imagining it."

They moved closer as CJ considered the section he'd just painted.

"Okay, so your name is CJ and you're being cute

by painting a *C* on the wall?" Meghan asked, her voice sharp and on edge.

Laurel knew very well CJ hadn't done it. Not considering how much he seemed to want to please her and her sisters, if he was going to initial his paint job, why not make it *CJ*? The letter was a foot and a half tall, maybe a foot wide, about six inches thick, and whiter than the white wall he was painting. It hadn't been there before he started painting, and he was using a paint roller. It would have been impossible for him to paint the letter without using a paintbrush and a guideline, a stencil, or something, considering how crisp and clean the lines were.

CJ stepped back from the wall and stared at it. "If the letter is still there after I paint the wall and it dries, I'll use some special paint that covers water stains and the like."

Laurel pointed to the corner. "A can of that kind of paint is over there."

"Okay, I'll take care of it."

Meghan headed for the stairs. "I'll tell Ellie about the trouble we might have with the ghost-hunter TV personalities." She glanced warily at CJ.

Laurel went back to work varnishing the old oak countertop while her sisters put the finishing touches on the rooms. The Silver pack had planned a grand opening ceremony, and all eight rooms were booked, now including the attic room. It only had a small table, a chair, a three-drawer bachelor chest, and a twin-size bed. They'd fixed it up but hadn't really thought they'd have anyone staying there—unless someone desperately needed the lodging, was single, and wasn't overly tall. Which made her realize that CJ would be too tall for the bed.

Where else could they put him? The basement had four rooms and a shared bathroom for the maids' quarters, but Laurel and her sisters had put off renovating those until later because of all the other plumbing, painting, and electrical problems they'd had to deal with. They lived in the guesthouse out back, a lovely four-bedroom home with gingerbread trim to match the hotel.

"*What?*" Ellie said, her voice elevated as Meghan talked with her upstairs in the blue bedroom.

Laurel didn't know if Ellie was outraged about the ghost busters staying with them or one of the members of the Silver pack lodging here, or maybe a little of both. In any event, they had to deal with it.

She and her sisters felt like they were walking on the edge of a cliff. One wrong turn and they would fall off, without a safety net to catch them. She was certain the pack wouldn't be happy if she and her sisters discovered that one of its members was involved in their aunt's disappearance.

Laurel looked up from her varnishing work and saw that CJ had started painting over the *C* with the stain-killing paint—three feet out in every direction to hide the letter.

Morbidly fascinated, she watched as the whole area became one block of white. As the paint began to dry, the letter reappeared as bold as day—white on white, as if it was meant to be there. Or Clarinda O'Brien was trying to tell her nieces she had been here.

Maybe she still was here.

Chapter 2

CJ TRIED TO TELL HIMSELF THAT PAINTING THE WALL had revealed someone's old stencil job. Yet he knew that wasn't so. The walls hadn't been painted in forever. Everything else disappeared underneath the fresh coat of paint—the shadows where the pictures had hung, the plaster filling the picture hanger holes, everything but the letter that hadn't been there when he started painting.

It didn't bode well that he was going to be staying in the attic. Even so, he would do anything to make it up to Darien and the pack for allowing him and his brothers to return after they had left their family behind. And he would do anything for Laurel and her sisters to ensure they didn't have any trouble. For now, that meant watching the ghost busters. He paused to look at the letter on the wall, the huge block of fresh paint making the letter show up even more.

Maybe at night under the chandelier lights it wouldn't be noticeable. Or maybe the women had a big picture they could hang over it. If the letter was still there in the morning.

"He's staying in the attic?" Ellie said from the room upstairs and laughed. "Better him than any of us."

He smiled a little. He wasn't afraid of any ghosts. He turned to see Laurel watching him, done with her job, it appeared. She was frowning, her soft green sweater bringing out the emerald of her eyes, her gaze capturing and holding his attention. As an alpha wolf, she didn't drop her gaze but instead arched a brow in question.

Despite trying to deny it, she seemed to be as interested in him as he was in her. She lowered her chin a little, waiting for him to say something. If she truly couldn't have found the time or inclination to bother with him, she would have looked away and done something else. But more than that, she had allowed him to stay and help. Hell, maybe she'd only asked Darien to tell CJ and his brothers their help wasn't needed because there had been too many of them underfoot. Eric had been a bit bossy, telling the ladies how he thought they should do things.

Maybe Laurel was perfectly happy to have CJ help them by himself. He assumed things were changing between them now and for the better.

"The paint dries quickly. Two hours tops. I'll paint over it again in a couple of hours. Tom said that an X was painted on one of the ceilings. Did you need me to paint over that too?"

Laurel pushed a lock of curly red hair behind her ear, maybe not in a flirtatious way, but it sure was sexy. "We actually painted over that ourselves and it worked out fine."

"That's good." He felt a bit of relief that they didn't have another mark that they couldn't get rid of. Maybe the same thing would happen here. "Did you want me to help you hang some Christmas lights next or do anything else?" He wasn't leaving if he could help it. He wanted to prove he really could be of service and not a hindrance. And to get to know her better.

She hesitated, then let out her breath. "With my sisters

leaving so early in the morning, I'm afraid I won't get it all done before the grand opening. If you don't mind, I'd appreciate your help."

Thrilled, he smiled, trying not to look overly enthusiastic and make her change her mind. "Not at all."

About that time, Meghan and Ellie headed down the stairs, both eyeing him with suspicion. Then Ellie saw the wall. Her face paled a little. CJ looked back at the letter, imagining that droplets of blood were now dripping from it. But the letter was just…white. And still there.

"What's next?" Meghan asked, as if the *C* was of no importance.

Laurel lifted a piece of paper off a marble-topped sideboard buffet. "You said you'd hang the garlands and red bows on the fence and the garland on the mantel. Ellie, you said you wanted to decorate indoors."

Meghan made a disagreeable face. "If I had known how cold it is here in the winter, I would have opted for Ellie's job." She attached some evergreen garlands to the fireplace mantel.

Ellie lifted a cardboard box and headed back up the stairs. "Last year, when Laurel was making up all these lists of things for us to do, I was smart and checked the weather forecast for this time of year here."

CJ smiled a little. The she-wolves were from Florida, and he suspected it might take them a while to get acclimated. Then he frowned. He hoped that they got used to it and didn't leave because they didn't like the cold weather. "Where can I wash out the paint rollers?"

"The basement has a sink for gardening stuff and the like," Meghan said quickly before Laurel could respond.

If it had been summer, CJ would have washed the paint out of the rollers with a garden hose. The basement was where he'd been scared to pieces. He had never been back. Not that he was afraid, but it just didn't feel right down there.

"I'll go with you." Laurel came around the counter.

Meghan gave her a warning look. From the stairs, so did Ellie.

For heaven's sake, he wasn't going to ravish their sister. Though in her emerald-green sweater and with her pretty red hair curling about her shoulders, she was seriously attractive. And so was her voice. The sisters all had lovely Irish accents, but Laurel's was like a siren's lure.

So why was she coming with him? To make sure he didn't steal anything? He didn't trust her motives because of the way she and her sisters were so reserved with the pack. Maybe they had their reasons. Bad wolf experiences. But surely they could bond with some of the women.

Laurel unlocked the basement door, turned on the light, and then preceded him down the stairs. The place smelled slightly damp and musty. The block walls were gray, the cement floor just as gray—and it hadn't changed since he'd come down here with Tom so many years ago.

"Maids' quarters." Laurel led him to where a gray utility sink stood. A small bathroom with a sink, commode, and shower stood next to that.

A door led outside, the window letting in a little gray light. The weather had turned overcast and snowy again. He couldn't imagine having to live down here.

"Are you going to fix these up so you'll have additional guest quarters?" He began to run water over the paint rollers.

"Maybe later. The hotel is booked to capacity right now. But would anyone want to stay down here?" Laurel shivered and rubbed her arms.

"Maybe with some fresh paint to lighten up the place, tile floors, and a bigger window in the door, or even a glass door to let in more light. Add lots of lighting and a dehumidifier to take the moisture out of the basement, and it could work."

"Great for vampires—if we painted the window black and left everything as it is."

He smiled.

She leaned against a wall and watched him. "Is there any way you can ensure that the ghost busters don't report the place as haunted and ruin our chances at renting out rooms?"

He wished there was, but he couldn't lie to her. "I don't think so. People will believe what they want. If folks want to stay here to see if they experience any hauntings, they will."

Looking contemplative or maybe a tad worried, she chewed on her lower lip. Which made him want to pull her into his arms and kiss away the concern.

She took a deep breath and let it out. "Are there any other buildings that are supposed to be haunted in Silver Town?"

"One of the silver mines nearby and one of the miners' huts. And a ghost wolf is seen in the woods on the drive out to Darien and Lelandi's home from time to time."

"But nowhere that is inhabited?"

"No."

"Do you believe in ghosts?"

CJ finished wringing the excess water from the last paint roller. "Do you?"

She raised her red brows. "For the sake of our guests, no. For your sake, yes. And a warning. The attic *is* haunted."

The hotel *was* haunted, truth be known. At least, paranormal happenings had occurred in every room in the hotel since the sisters had been here. Nothing bad, except for the appearance of the letter *C* on the wall downstairs, and that was more annoying than anything. It ruined the whole look of their new decor.

Laurel wanted to warn CJ so he'd be prepared and not let the ghost busters know that the hotel was haunted. Thankfully, he didn't seem to believe in ghosts, and the notion that his room was haunted hadn't caused any kind of reaction.

CJ set the rollers aside to dry. "After I repaint the wall, if the letter is still there, did you want me to hang a painting over it?"

"Yes. I hadn't planned to hang one there for now because my sisters and I couldn't agree on one. But we do have a painting hanging over the fireplace mantel in our house that we could use in the interim. It's a lovely rendition of a field of purple daisies with a backdrop of the Rocky Mountains and a forest of pines. It'll look fine there." Except that it would leave a blank spot over their mantel.

"My cousin Jake does beautiful photography. I'm certain he wouldn't mind offering a photo so that you could showcase it. No charge to you."

She appreciated the offer, but since *Jake* hadn't offered, she didn't want him to feel obligated. Mostly though, for the Victorian feel, she thought a painting would fit in better than a photograph. Someday, they might find something that would suit the period that they could hang there.

"Thanks. Does…does anyone know why any of the places are haunted? The silver mine, and so on?"

"Over a hundred years ago, a mine collapse killed several miners. Some speculate that a few of their spirits are trapped down there. As to the miner's shack? Fight with another miner over a card game. One pulled out a revolver and shot the alleged cheater, fatally. The wolf? Hit by a car. That's pure conjecture though."

"Was it a real wolf or *lupus garou*?"

"Supposedly one of our kind. Rumors are that sometimes she's seen as a naked woman and at other times as a wolf. Truthfully, I haven't seen her or anything ghostly in the silver mines or the miner's hut either."

"Maybe you're not as sensitive to their presence. That could be a good thing in your case."

He smiled a little, as if he truly didn't believe in the paranormal. "What are you going to do if the ghost busters learn you *do* have bona fide ghosts living here?"

She headed up the stairs. "The only thing we can do. Advertise it as Silver Town's only haunted hotel." Smiling at the notion, she glanced over her shoulder at him.

He followed her up the stairs too closely, showing

his wolfish interest in her. Sensing him so close on her heels, she should have given him a look to back off. But she couldn't do it. She liked his persistence. Most wolves that she'd discouraged as much as she'd tried with him and his brothers would take a hint. CJ wasn't buying it. And she liked that.

She and her sisters hadn't had time to do any investigating into why the place had ghostly occurrences. Not with all their renovation troubles that had nothing to do with paranormal activities. Nor had they found anything in their investigations into their aunt's disappearance.

"What about this place? Any rumors as to who haunts the hotel and why?" She wanted to know if others had seen their aunt "haunting" the hotel. She and her sisters hadn't witnessed any apparitions here. Just lights going on and off when no one was there and things moving from place to place before they returned to work on the hotel the next day.

"No." He held her gaze.

Laurel wasn't sure she believed him. She sensed he might be hiding something from her.

"What made you come here? And not go somewhere else?" he asked.

She hadn't expected that line of questioning, so it took her aback. She and her sisters had carefully rehearsed the reason. "We heard the hotel was for sale and that a wolf pack ran the town. We're in the small-hotel renovation business—Victorians are our specialty—and we like quaint towns with a resort feel like this one. We liked that you have a ski resort close by and not much lodging available. And…the pack is an added benefit."

She hoped that would satisfy his curiosity, but she

wondered why he'd asked. Had she and her sisters given themselves away somehow? She changed the subject. "Why hasn't anyone bought it before this?"

"Rumors that it's haunted. And Darien has been picky about who buys it. All of the businesses in town are run by our kind, and he wants to keep it that way. A couple of big out-of-town developers were interested in buying the hotel, giving the song and dance that the place was in such bad shape it would have to be torn down, that the area wasn't developed enough to really bring in business, and so on. They were just trying to get Darien to come down on the price. But he kept the price up, making it so unreasonable that no one would have invested in it unless the investor was a wolf, looking to settle down with the pack.

"Folks around here knew he'd bring the price down if any wolf members thought they could renovate and run the hotel. No one had any experience at it though, or any desire to give it a try. When you and your sisters showed some interest, Darien and Lelandi were thrilled. So he gave you a real bargain price to make it work."

And that they happened to be she-wolves? She and her sisters had noticed that more of the population was male than female and there were lots of bachelor males. "Ahhh. Okay. I wondered about that. We worried that maybe more people had died in the hotel recently, scaring off prospective buyers. Then Darien suddenly dropped the price way down because of too many hauntings, and it really wasn't a good bargain at all."

CJ grinned, but then his smile faded. "You say 'more' people died in the hotel recently. What made you believe anyone died here in the past?"

She ground her teeth. This was one of the reasons they had avoided having much to do with the pack. Hiding the truth was damned hard. "I assumed it since the place is haunted and had been abandoned for so many years."

"Ah."

She couldn't tell if that satisfied him, not as indecipherable as his expression was. She made a mental note never to play card games with him.

As they climbed the basement stairs to the main floor again, one of the rollers rolled off the roller tray in the sink where CJ had left them to dry. They both looked back at it. "I must have set the roller too close to the edge of the tray and it rolled off."

"Right." Laurel wanted to believe him, just like she tried to explain away anything that seemed supernatural. "So how long have you lived in Silver Town?"

"Since I was born."

She was afraid of that. If any wolf was new to the area, she could scratch that person off their list of suspects in their aunt's disappearance. Darien had given her a list of the pack members' names so she and her sister could get to know everyone. But she was really using it to narrow their list of suspects by determining who couldn't have been in the area when their aunt had been living here.

Then again, the person—wolf or human—who might have had a hand in their aunt's disappearance could be dead or maybe had just been passing through.

Even so, this was all she really had to go on, and she hoped to cross a lot of the people off the list since it totaled nearly three hundred wolves. They definitely could eliminate newly turned wolves, children, and those who had moved here more recently. She really needed a local wolf who could help her with this. Someone they could trust. But they couldn't really trust anyone. At least not yet.

When she and CJ reached the lobby, both of their gazes were trained on the freshly painted wall to see if the letter had disappeared. It hadn't. "I'll bring the painting over in the morning if the *C* is still there after you paint the wall again in a couple of hours," she said.

"How do you know the attic's haunted?" CJ suddenly asked.

"Since you don't believe in the supernatural, I'm sure you'll find nothing that will go bump in the night up there." Surprised he'd asked, she figured there was no sense in telling him what they'd seen or heard. It was better to let him experience it for himself and come to his own conclusions.

He glanced back up the stairs, but he didn't look concerned. "So how did you want me to help with Christmas decorations?"

"Could you hang the Christmas lights along the roof of the hotel and some around each second-floor window?"

"Sure. I'll call my brothers and see if one can help out too. That will make it go a lot quicker."

"Thanks." She felt guilty about asking him to do all this when she had said no before, but he was so eager.

Meghan gave Laurel a chiding look, then put on her coat, hat, and gloves. She gathered up more garland and red bows, but couldn't manage all of it on her own. Laurel hurried to dress in her warm clothes so she could help. They carried the garland and bows outside, and CJ followed them out.

"Okay, Brett. See you in a few." CJ pocketed his phone.

To Laurel and her sister's surprise, CJ took one end of the garland and stretched it out along the white fence railing. Laurel held the other end, and Meghan began securing red bows around the garland and the fence.

"So what do your brothers do?" Laurel asked. She knew that CJ was a deputy sheriff because she'd seen him in uniform.

"Eric, my eldest brother—only by a few minutes, but it's enough to make him think he's the boss of all of us—is a park ranger. The next oldest is Sarandon. He's a trail guide, nature guide, whatever kind of guide his clients want him to be. He and Eric love the great outdoors. Not that the rest of us don't, but they could spend weeks in the wilderness and be perfectly happy. Brett is a reporter for the pack's new newspaper. He's always looking for a story—as long as it's not wolf-related. Unless it's to showcase wolves in a good way."

"Full wolves or our kind of wolves?"

"Both, actually. Humor, human interest, special goings-on. He's the one assigned to do a feature on your newly renovated hotel and some of its history."

Laurel perked up at the sound of that. "So he's done some research on it?"

"Yeah. Anytime you want to see any of the old documents, pictures, information on who owned the hotel over the years, any of that, feel free to ask. Darien has more old data—census records, tax information—stored at his house."

"Thanks. I will. I'm fascinated with the old place and it'll be…fun to see pictures of it back in the day." More than fun. Maybe CJ's brother or Darien had the clues

they needed to solve the mystery. And pictures of their
aunt at the hotel to learn if she had been a guest or a
maid, if they were lucky.

Meghan paused from tying bows on the garland and
fence. "And you're a deputy sheriff."

He smiled. "I'm one of them. But we all are available
to help new members establish their businesses as long
as there's no trouble brewing anywhere."

Meghan tied off another section of the garland.
"We've heard it's a fairly safe place to live."

"We've had a few problems. But nothing we couldn't
handle. It does help to have both human and wolf protection. We run everything here from the jailhouse to the
clinic, so we're all set for any trouble we might have."

Meghan had been the most excited about moving to
a location where wolves ran the town, and she'd already
made several comments about setting down roots here.
The problem was that Ellie was in total agreement with
her. Laurel wasn't used to that. Usually, her sisters
agreed to whatever she said.

CJ wasn't wearing his uniform, just jeans, a pale blue
wool sweater, and cowboy boots. Laurel had to admit
that he looked warm and accessible. In his uniform, he
seemed friendly but more…official.

As if reminding Meghan why they were here, Laurel
said, "So about the mine collapse or other things like that—"

"Ghost-related, you mean?"

"Yes. Do you have newspaper clippings about that?"

"Unless another town reported on it, probably not.
We didn't have a newspaper here until recently."

"Why not?" Meghan sounded skeptical.

"I guess no one was interested in running one. I don't

know. Sure, there were some rags printed in the early years, but none of them survived."

"Would there have been police reports? Surely some kind of documentation exists." Laurel stepped back to consider what they had done. It looked really nice, perfect for the time period of the hotel.

"We have a cemetery full of headstones giving the names, dates of birth, and dates of death, in addition to a note that the miners had lost their lives in the silver mine. Also, we did census reports like any other law-abiding citizens, but we had to change some of the particulars to hide our true ages."

That still wouldn't help her and her sisters learn the truth about their aunt or the hotel.

"Brett's getting together all the information that he can and bringing it over to see if you'd like to look at it and add any comments for the article—"

"Now?" Meghan looked way too eager.

"Tomorrow. He hadn't finished gathering it when I last saw him, and for now, he's dropping everything to help string lights along the roof of the hotel."

Now Laurel wished they hadn't sidetracked Brett. But they couldn't tell CJ to call his brother back and say that the history of the hotel was more important than decorating the place for the grand opening.

Once they'd finished hanging the garland on the picket fence, they moved to the railing around the front porch.

Within twenty minutes, a man drove up and parked. Brett Silver got out of his car, dressed casually in a royal-blue-and-tan-striped sweater and jeans. His hair was a lighter brown, and his smile infectious.

"You remember Brett?" CJ asked.

"Yes," Laurel said. Between Eric telling them what to do, and Brett taking pictures for posterity's sake before they could remodel, the men had been a hindrance. "CJ was telling us you're doing a story on the hotel. We'd love to learn all there is about it."

"Yeah, sure. I'm getting a bunch of stuff together for you, old photos and the like, that I can bring over tomorrow."

"Thanks," both Meghan and Laurel said at the same time.

"We have the job of putting up the lights along the roofline and around the windows," CJ told his brother.

Brett smiled at him, since CJ wasn't letting go of the garland as Meghan secured the last bow to hang it on the porch railing. It really was nice having the men's help. Although she and her sisters had meant to keep their distance from all of the pack members, Laurel decided they needed to have the brothers over for dinner to thank them.

"Darien said that ghost-buster crew made reservations at your place for tomorrow," Brett said.

Laurel heard the annoyance in his voice right away. As far as she was concerned, the ghost busters were most likely frauds. Ghosts did not make scheduled appearances for TV shows. They appeared when they appeared.

Then again, it was too bad that she and her sisters couldn't have contracted them to paint, since they most likely wouldn't have been spooked by any ghostly happenings like the others were.

"Darien's worried about them being here," Brett set up the ladder to begin hanging the lights.

Laurel held the first wreath up to the window while CJ secured it for her.

"Darien figures these guys might witness something more paranormal than ghosts."

"Can you usually run safely as wolves around here?" Meghan asked.

"Sure we can. In the forests. After the ski resort is closed for the night, we often also run through that area. Snow graders plow in the morning, grooming the trails but also hiding the evidence of the wolf tracks in the more heavily used areas. If you and your sisters would like to run with us any time, let me know. We'll show you the sights," CJ offered.

"Tonight? Before the hotel opens? It'll be the last time we can all run together. Someone will always have to be on duty at the hotel otherwise," Laurel said before she could stop herself. Meghan's mouth gaped as she stared at Laurel.

Laurel figured they needed a fun break before the hotel opened. She and her sisters deserved it. What harm could there be in that?

"Tonight would be great," CJ said.

"I'm game," Brett said. "Because of the fresh snow-fall, a lot of wolves will be out there tonight. We'll have a great time."

"We're glad you decided to open up the place." CJ hooked up the last of the lights on the windows. "It's a beautiful hotel and has been neglected for far too long."

Laurel and Meghan exchanged looks. This was the hardest part to deal with—that everyone was genuinely happy to have them here. But only until they learned why they were truly here.

Before long, Laurel and Meghan were hanging garlands on all the upstairs balconies while CJ and his brother strung the lights along the edge of the roof. Meghan's cheeks and nose were red, and Laurel imagined hers were just as rosy.

"Jake said he'd take some professional photos, free of charge, of the hotel in all of its Christmas finery to add to his photography website. And he'll give a copy to the newspaper to run a free, full-page ad," Meghan said.

Now, Laurel felt guilty that she hadn't jumped at the chance to hang some of Jake's photography over the letter *C* in their main room.

She spoke softly for Meghan's ears only. "I can't believe how everyone's going all out to make us feel welcome."

"Yeah, they're glad we're improving the look of the place and bringing in more income. And it probably doesn't hurt that we're single females."

"Did you want to go in and tell Ellie we're going to take a wolf run tonight?"

"With pack members? She'll be shocked and thrilled." Meghan headed into the hotel to give Ellie the news.

Laurel hoped the plan wouldn't backfire.

Chapter 3

By the time they'd finished decorating the roofline with white lights, the ski resort was closed for the night. CJ drove the ladies to the base ski lodge. Though he'd asked if anyone wanted to ride in Brett's truck, everyone had wanted to ride with him. He thought it was because they were shy about getting to know any of the other bachelors.

The resort had a restaurant, restrooms with changing areas, and rentals for skis, poles, snowboards, and ski boots. But skiing wasn't on the schedule. About twenty adults were there, ranging in age from twenty to eighty-five in human years. Some were already wearing their wolf coats and waiting outside for the rest of their friends or family to join them. Others were still disrobing at lockers and shifting.

A group of three teens were also there watching them. Cody, Minx, and Anthony now worked at the resort. Minx's twin sister, Caitlin, was with her twin toddler boys and her mate, Trevor, the other deputy sheriff standing nearby.

Cody smiled at Laurel and her sisters, his jester hat moving and jingling as he talked. "We're working here at the ski resort, so if you need any help, just let us know." He motioned with his thumb to the other teens, and they all smiled at the sisters.

"Thanks," Laurel said. "We appreciate it." She and her sisters went inside to strip off their clothes and shift.

Cody joined CJ and asked, "So are the sisters all taken yet?"

CJ raised his brow. "Don't tell me you're interested in one of them."

He laughed. "Nah, I'm still trying to make some headway with Minx, and so is Anthony. But we got bets going that you and two of your brothers will beat out the other guys who are interested in the sisters."

CJ shook his head and sighed dramatically. "They all came in the truck with me tonight."

Cody grinned. "Yeah, we were all talking about that. Who would have thought that you, the youngest of your brothers, would get all the girls?"

Laurel and her sisters loped out of the building as wolves, and CJ felt his cheeks heat a bit despite the cold, certain the ladies had heard Cody's comment.

"I'll be right out," CJ said, then went in to change.

Laurel and her sisters were delighted with the prospect of running over the snow-covered ski slopes as wolves—as a pack. She was surprised to see so many of the pack members here, even though it was really only a small portion of the Silver pack. But it seemed like a huge group to her, because their previous pack had consisted only of the three of them since they lost their mom. Their dad had died when they were young.

The wind was whipping the snow about, but Laurel's fur coat kept her nice and warm. It was so different from running in Florida where the cold wasn't nearly this brisk. Their coats had thickened up considerably while they'd been living here.

As soon as CJ joined her, she and her sisters followed his and Brett's lead. This felt so good. Everyone else was smelling the air, learning the sisters' scents as Laurel and her sisters tried to memorize as many wolf pack members' scents as they could. They'd met a few people already in the pack and had cataloged their scents, but not nearly enough.

CJ and Brett stayed nearby and watched to make sure the sisters didn't get lost, which Laurel appreciated. Two other wolves joined them, and recognizing their scents, she realized that they were CJ's brothers Sarandon and Eric. The brothers led the way, and she and her sisters followed them into the backcountry away from the ski resort.

She realized then that it was good that they hadn't participated in any other pack activities, because having fun with these wolves wasn't in the cards. She was afraid that the more they enjoyed being around the pack, the more they'd want to stay. Then what would happen if they learned about foul play related to their aunt?

For now, she was having the time of her life. In Florida, they had explored some of the more than one million wooded acres—in the thirty-five state forests— when they ran in their wolf coats. They really had to watch out for humans though. Living there, they never got to play in snow. Ellie glanced her way. Meghan wore the same devious expression. Laurel knew they were considering tackling her.

Ellie was closest to her, so Laurel pounced on Ellie first, and Meghan leaped on top of Laurel after that, making a pileup of three gray she-wolves in the pure white snow. They were so busy playing with each other that they didn't realize until they shook off the snow that several wolves were watching them and smiling.

Wolves loved to play. But this kind of play was a lot different from what she and her sisters were used to. She loved how big the pack was and how it could be the perfect place to raise a wolf family. *For others*. Not for them.

———

After the run in the snow, Eric, CJ's oldest brother, took him aside while the women were in the timber lodge getting changed.

"Be careful, little Brother." Eric was the most serious of the brothers, the one who had made decisions for them when they were younger, but no longer.

"The ghost busters won't give me any problems. Even if they're well-known for their ghost-busting show." CJ attempted to keep the irritation out of his voice. He was a deputy sheriff now. No professed ghost busters were going to give him any trouble.

Eric raised a brow at him.

CJ let out his breath in exasperation. He and Tom would never live it down that Darien and Jake had scared them to pieces at the hotel when they were kids. "There are no ghosts," CJ added.

"I'm not referring to ghosts or ghost busters." Eric shoved his hands in his jeans pockets. He was the tallest of the brothers at six one, and his black sweater made him look especially formidable. His dark gaze turned to the lodge where Laurel and her sisters were exiting the building, laughing and talking.

A couple of women intercepted them and began chatting. The sisters looked like they'd had a grand time. CJ smiled to see them in such great spirits. All of the pack members had gone out of their way to speak with the ladies about doing something fun, sure that they had needed the break from the renovations. He couldn't believe they'd finally agreed to do this.

"They're not staying long," Eric warned.

"How do you know?" CJ couldn't help feeling defensive. He was certain they were here for some purpose other than joining the pack. But he believed that if enough of the pack members made them feel welcome, the ladies would make this their home. "Because they've done the same with the last couple of hotels they've renovated? There were no wolf packs in the area." At least that he and his brothers knew of. "If they're not used to living around wolves, give them a chance. They'll get used to us. Before you know it, they'll feel as though they've been members of the pack forever."

"It's more than that. They're here for some other purpose. Mark my word."

CJ suspected that too, but he refused to believe that the women would decide to leave after a while. At least in the case of the other hotels, the sisters had waited a good year after they renovated them and got them into the black before putting them up for sale. That meant they'd be here for another year.

Unless this one became profitable too quickly and they found another hotel they needed to buy pronto. Then he had a thought. What if one of the she-wolves really became interested in one of the wolves of his pack? The sisters wouldn't leave without her, would they? Then again, maybe the male wolf would leave with the women.

"Maybe you should…court one of the ladies," CJ said.

"Laurel?" Eric asked, and CJ tried to hide how growly he felt at the mention of her name.

Eric smiled knowingly at him. "She's in charge of her sisters. If anyone's mind needs to be changed, it's hers."

"If either or both of the other sisters decide to mate a wolf from our pack, Laurel won't be leaving." CJ let out his breath in annoyance. From what he'd seen of the way she interacted with her sisters, she wouldn't want to leave them behind.

Eric slapped his brother's back with his gloved hand. "You have the best chance at making that happen."

CJ studied his brother, wondering why he thought that. He was only interested in Laurel, and he suspected her sisters were leaning toward staying, but Laurel wasn't.

He and his brother grew quiet as the ladies drew near.

"That was fun," Ellie said to them. "I'd love to do it again soon."

"Anytime," Eric said, smiling a little. But he didn't seem interested in any of the sisters.

CJ wasn't sure what was going on with his brother. He knew he'd been butting heads with Darien, as alpha as both were. Eric still believed that their father, and not Darien's, should have run the pack. And when their father got into the mess he did, Eric would have led the pack. CJ really thought they'd resolved that issue to some degree.

He was happy with Darien's rule. He was a fair and just leader, and CJ was close to Darien's brothers and many others in the pack. He was afraid Eric would leave the pack again. Only this time, CJ wasn't leaving. He wasn't sure about Brett and Sarandon, but he didn't want to see any of them go.

"I'm glad you had so much fun," he said to Laurel as they returned to his truck, her sisters' snow boots crunching on the snow behind them as they talked about treats and Christmas drinks they wanted to serve each night as the guests came in from skiing.

"It really was nice. You can't know how much we enjoyed that—such a difference from running as wolves in Florida," Laurel said.

"I couldn't imagine running in the heat there. Not that it doesn't get hot here in the summer, but I love the fall and would miss that there."

"The fall colors were beautiful here," Ellie agreed.

Before long, they were parking at the house behind the hotel. It was nice that they had a parking lot back there and another out front so that guests could come in either way.

"Even though it's getting late, do you mind if I check and see if the letter *C* is still visible?" CJ asked Laurel. "If so, I'd like to paint it again right now. That will give it a chance to dry overnight."

"It's so late," Laurel said, trying to talk him out of it, but he was determined to do it.

"Night," Ellie and Meghan said and headed to the house, not bothering to see which way this would go.

"You really don't have to do this," Laurel said again. "I could do it even."

"No, that's okay. It's bugging me and I hate leaving a job unfinished."

"Thanks then. I appreciate it."

When they entered the hotel, she turned on the lights in the sunroom and then the hall before they walked into the main lobby. The letter was as prominent on the wall as before.

She folded her arms and shook her head. "It's persistent, if nothing else."

"So am I." This time he painted with brushes instead of the roller, hoping that a thicker coat would make a difference. When he was done, he said, "I'll just clean this out and then let you get some rest."

"Come on. I'll go with you."

"I don't believe in any ghosts."

"That's all right. I do." Not that Laurel had seen any. Just what a ghost had supposedly done. She walked with CJ down the stairs and noticed that nothing had happened while he was there—except for the appearance of the letter on the wall. She hadn't experienced cold spots, other than what would be normally there because of seepage around the windows or pipes. But nothing unusual since CJ had begun helping them out this time.

While he washed the brush, he asked, "So when is a good time for me to come over and paint again?"

"Anytime in the morning is fine with me."

"Eight?"

"Sounds good. Meghan and Ellie will be gone by then."

He smiled a little at Laurel, and her cheeks warmed considerably. Why was it that a guy typically turned everything into something more intimate? Like they'd be alone together…to do what?

And that had her blushing furiously all over again.

After that, they said good-bye, and she locked the hotel up and headed out the back door to the house.

Her sisters were both watching out the window, sipping mulled wine from Santa mugs. Tomorrow, Laurel still had to decorate the yard and gazebo, but everything else was ready. The gazebo, fountain, and gardens were perfect for guests during any season, though the fountain couldn't run until spring now. For winter, they were decorating everything for Christmas. That way the rooms that had a garden view would see festive touches everywhere.

The house was toasty warm, a fire crackling, the divine aroma of mulled wine—honey, wine, cinnamon sticks, cloves, and oranges—scenting the air as she walked inside. She breathed a sigh of relief.

"Well?" Ellie headed for the dining room where she and Meghan had put grilled cheese sandwiches, pickles, and chips on Santa plates.

Laurel was delighted that they'd made something to eat.

"Did it go away?" Ellie asked.

"No." Laurel hated that it hadn't. But at least they could cover it with the painting. What would happen then? Hopefully, the painting wouldn't vanish and allow the letter to still be seen.

"That's good news about Brett finding information about the hotel. When are we going to take a look at it?" Ellie asked.

"He's coming over in the afternoon. He has something else he's doing in the morning, and then he said he'd gather up all the stuff and bring it over," Laurel said.

"Wish he'd wait until we got home." Ellie poured Laurel a mug of mulled wine, then added an orange peel on top. "That means if you find anything important, you have to call us right away."

"I will."

"It's truly beautiful, don't you think?" Meghan looked out their front window at the lights strung along the back side of the hotel, the white lights flickering like diamonds. Green wreaths adorned with red bows hung in each of the windows, making it Christmas-card perfect.

"It is." Laurel admired the beauty of the place. "But we're sure our aunt vanished from there. Once we solve the mystery and can prove what happened to her, if there was foul play, the pack will have to handle it. Then we're out of here."

Ellie pursed her lips. "What if she was murdered and the killer wasn't part of the pack? Or was and is long gone? I'm tired of moving. We've never lived with a wolf pack, and I like all the people we've met so far. I had the time of my life tonight."

"How do you think they're going to feel, knowing this is why we bought the hotel? That we're only pretending to be loyal pack members?" Laurel shook her head.

Meghan took her seat at the middle of the table, Ellie across from her, and Laurel at the head of the table. They began to eat their grilled cheese sandwiches. The extra-sharp cheese added the perfect tanginess, as did the dill pickles.

"I'm with Ellie on this." Meghan got the bag of chips out again and poured more. "I'd like to settle down. We could just manage the hotel and leave it at that. CJ and his brothers are sexy as all get-out. Plus that sheriff is hot, and the pack has any number of other bachelor males. And they're all interested in us. I'm really tired of moving. I'm ready to set down roots for a few years—at the very least."

"And really run a hotel for the long term? A haunted hotel? Solving our aunt's disappearance is our primary drive." Laurel brushed the crumbs off the table. "Just remember, anyone in the pack could be responsible for her disappearance. So don't go thinking any of them are charming and your real friend because none of them are—not until we resolve this. Even then, if we uncover anything sinister, we're bound to create hard feelings when we reveal the truth."

Ellie nodded. "As much as I hate to agree, I do. It's not on your list, but Rosalind McKinley is coming by with the poinsettias from her greenhouse early in the morning, and I'll put those out before we leave. Did you know that her sister-in-law, Carol, is a psychic? I wonder if she might have a clue. She's newly turned and wasn't living here at the time. So she should be scratched off the list."

"Already done. I heard she has future visions, so I don't think that would help us," Meghan said. "If she could sense entities or speak with them, that would be different."

"Future visions?" Laurel took another sip of her wine, breathing in the fragrance again.

Meghan speared another pickle. "Yeah, well, she might be one of those frauds, you know. But they say she saw Darien Silver's pack members shifting in her visions. And she told Darien's mate. Anyway, she was turned and that solved that problem."

Finished with supper, Laurel gathered up their plates and carried them into the kitchen.

Meghan grabbed the bag of chips, and Ellie began to put away the bread, cheese, and jar of pickles.

Laurel turned to look at Meghan and frowned. "Still no sightings of our aunt? None of your strange sensations?"

Meghan shook her head. "I figured the renovations

would stir things up. But other than the shadowy figure of the woman, who I couldn't recognize, nothing else."

"Except for the stuff that happened to the painters' equipment and to CJ. Hopefully nothing awful will happen while the guests are there." Laurel turned to Ellie. "Have you sensed anything?"

"Just what you have," Ellie said. "I tried incense when the two of you were shopping for throw rugs, but nothing more."

"Maybe you used the wrong kind for this entity," Meghan said. "We'll have to be more careful now that we're opening the hotel. I really think we should have waited until we had communicated with her."

"You know that it can take a long time to make any connection. And sometimes it doesn't ever happen," Ellie said.

"What if the ghostly figure isn't of our aunt? What if she died there, but she's moved on?" Meghan posed the question none of them had wanted to consider.

"If she has, we'll still need to learn what happened to her, make the place profitable, sell it, and move on." Laurel removed her boots.

"I wonder if Carol would know of any ghost mediums." Meghan yawned.

"We don't believe in most mediums. Many are fakes." Laurel rose from the sofa, walked over to the window, and eyed the attic window of the hotel. She really hoped nothing would bother CJ there.

"Is he afraid of ghosts?" Ellie joined her at the window.

"He says he doesn't believe in them," Laurel said.

"What about that letter on the wall?" Meghan asked.

Laurel bit on her lower lip. "He's a deputy sheriff,

and I doubt he's inclined to assume any mysterious happenings are the result of a ghostly presence. He probably considers anything out of the ordinary to be the result of someone creating mischief. Yet, I wouldn't want to be him sleeping in the attic room for the next several days."

She really hoped CJ wouldn't have any trouble. He appealed to her in so many ways. He'd always been nice and polite to her sisters, which had also made her appreciate him. But he had eyes only for her. Yet, she couldn't let him get close.

At least, not yet.

Meghan took a chip and crunched into it. "The letter on the wall—it's got to be a sign from Clarinda, don't you think?"

"I don't know. Why wouldn't it be something more…irregular? If I tried to draw my name on the wall, it wouldn't be totally straight or with curved lines or perfectly even in width," Laurel said.

"It looks like it was stenciled on the wall," Meghan agreed.

"The three of us always try to explain away mystical happenings. To uncover the reality, rather than conclude that what we've experienced is supernatural. Even though we believe in things we can't explain or that others don't witness. It doesn't mean that what we see, feel, or hear isn't valid," Laurel said.

Ellie was so quiet that Laurel assumed she had a different opinion. "Ellie?"

Ellie looked up at her. "Mom said Aunt Clarinda loved to quilt."

"So?" Meghan took a bite of another chip.

Laurel swore her sister could eat a whole bag of them at a sitting and never gain an ounce.

Ellie frowned at Laurel. "Neither of you was interested in sewing. But I took it up when I was a kid. Hooking rugs; cross-stitching; embroidery work; making dolls, bunnies, and bears; and I quilted."

From their puzzled expressions, neither Laurel nor Meghan was following Ellie's logic.

"In quilting, I used stencils."

Chapter 4

CJ HAD JUST REACHED HIS HOUSE IN THE WOLF PINES subdivision, a cozy development where the homes were spaced out on pine-tree-covered, five-acre lots to give everyone privacy and a woodland feeling. A park had also been created to give the wolves a place to really run. That's what he loved about the wolf developments. The prices of the properties were kept low for *lupus garous*, but way overpriced for humans to keep them from living there.

It wasn't that the wolves in the pack didn't like humans. They just wanted to give their own people the freedom to run in their wolf coats without worrying about their neighbors seeing them or having to erect huge fences to keep their wolfish nature secret. That felt too much like being confined to a zoo, so except for a couple of neighbors two streets over who had fences for their dogs, everyone kept a naturalistic, open setting.

He was entering his one-and-a-half-story, French provincial home when he got a call. "Yeah, Brett?" In the kitchen, CJ pulled out some leftover spaghetti and heated it up in the microwave.

"I have to cover another news story tomorrow afternoon, so I don't have time to share the information about the hotel with Laurel and her sisters. Since you're going to be staying with them for a few days, do you want to fill them in on the details?"

"Yeah, sure. I'm actually going back to the hotel tomorrow to help a little more before they open. Ellie and Meghan are leaving early in the morning on some errand that's taking them out of state. I'm helping to paint because their painters got spooked."

"Oh. Okay. Well, what if I run by your place and drop this stuff off tonight?"

"That would be great."

"Have you eaten?"

CJ looked at his warmed-up spaghetti. "Not yet."

"I'll drop by Pizza to Go and grab us a meat-lover's deluxe."

"Sounds good to me. See you in a few." CJ put the spaghetti back in the refrigerator. He and Brett were only a couple of minutes apart in age and had always been the closest of the brothers, pairing up against their older brothers when they gave them grief.

While he waited for Brett to arrive with the pizza, CJ packed a bag of clothes for his stay at the hotel. Brett used the spare key that CJ had given him and called out, "Pizza delivery!"

CJ came out of the bedroom and joined his brother in the dining room. Brett had already placed the pizza box on the table and yanked off a couple of paper towels to use as plates. At the end of the table rested a purple-and-yellow polka-dot photo box. It looked suspiciously like one that Lelandi had given her brother-in-law Jake.

"Why does that box look familiar?" CJ asked.

Brett opened the lid, lifted out six large manila envelopes, and placed them at the end of the table. "Lelandi gave it to Jake for his photos last Christmas. But he either takes digital shots or makes them into large canvas pictures for art galleries, so he doesn't need it. I thought I'd run over there to get copies of photos he had taken of the hotel over the years." Brett paused, then smiled. "Okay, so yeah, he did have some that weren't digital. Anyway, he quickly offered the box to carry the photos in. I'm sure it was a way to get rid of it without offending our pack leader."

CJ smiled.

"I organized the photos by date."

"I'm sure the ladies will be thrilled to get all the information. After they finish looking at all this stuff, they can give you their thoughts about the hotel for your article. As for the polka-dot box? Not sure they'll want it either."

Brett chuckled. "Surely the women will like it better than Jake does. I should have asked. Are the paper towels all right for plates?"

"No sense in using dishes for just the two of us." CJ grabbed a couple of beers for them.

"Where are you staying in the hotel? I heard it's already booked, and I know the women didn't renovate the maids' quarters yet."

"Attic room."

"Did you go up there? Turn on a light and leave it on?"

Wondering what Brett was getting at, CJ took a seat opposite him and grabbed a slice of pizza. "No, I've never been up there. Visited the basement though."

Brett's eyes rounded. "See anything?"

"Just the paintbrushes and rollers I had to clean."

"Well, I went over to take some pictures of the hotel all lit up in Christmas lights. I had taken some earlier before the light faded. But the light on in the attic made the hotel look a little spooky. I'll take more shots tomorrow night before the guests all arrive. I'll just ask the women to turn on the lights in all the rooms at the front of the hotel."

CJ finished a slice of pizza and reached for another. "They're also decorating the backyard tomorrow, so maybe you can get a few shots out there."

"I will. And some inside the hotel, showing some of the old features and how the lobby looks now."

"Have you looked at all that stuff?" CJ motioned with his bottle of beer to the envelopes.

"Yeah. Interesting place. What do you think of staying there?"

"Works for me. I just hope we don't have any real trouble with the ghost busters."

"You're a deputy sheriff. Throw them in jail if they do anything illegal."

"I will. Believe me."

"So…" Brett finished his beer, sat back on the chair, and raised his brows. "How's it going with Laurel?"

CJ smiled. "Is it that obvious that she's the one I'm interested in?"

"Hell, yeah. Since you'll be over there tomorrow, her sisters will be gone, and no guests will be there yet, you'll have her all to yourself. Is she warming up to you? She seemed to have fun running with the pack tonight, but she still stuck close to her sisters. It was fun watching them tussle in the snow. They've been so subdued that I didn't think they even knew how to play as wolves or otherwise."

"Maybe they're just getting used to the rest of us. We've been so thrilled they've joined us that I'm sure it's been a little much. Then, too, they've been under a lot of stress in getting the hotel ready for the grand opening."

"Agreed. When do you think the backyard will be decorated so that I can take pictures?"

"Tomorrow morning. I'm going to repaint a wall, and then I'll help Laurel hang the lights or whatever she plans to do there. I'll tell her that you want to get some pictures of the place with all the lights on."

"Good deal." Brett finished the last slice of pizza. "Anything going on over there? Anything…paranormal?"

"Yeah, but I'm sure there's an explanation for it." CJ explained about the *C* on the wall.

"You're kidding." Brett sounded like he knew something about it.

"What?"

Brett began emptying the folders on the table. "Here's a note that Darien's dad kept from a pack member who was concerned because a letter *C* appeared after the hotel's lobby was repainted thirty years ago."

"Thirty years ago. Huh. Well, apparently it disappeared after that. So here's hoping when I paint over it again, it'll disappear."

"That's what you've been painting?"

"Yep. And it's not going away."

"Did you try that stain-killer paint?"

"Yep."

"No blood dripping from it, right?"

CJ chuckled and shook his head.

Brett helped clean up and pulled out his keys. "Okay, I'm out of here. I'll see you later tomorrow."

CJ said good night to him, then started reading through all the documents and examining the pictures

of the old hotel, which were mostly of the lobby and
front of the hotel, some with the owners standing on
the covered veranda. He recognized one of the Silvers'
friends from the old days, Jonathon Bowling, who built
the hotel in 1871, plus his wife and two daughters. All
of them had long ago died, though the *lupus garous*
until fairly recently had extended longevity. That had
changed drastically though, according to a *lupus garou*
geneticist, Dr. Aidan Denali. He had come into town and
taken blood samples from all the wolves, looking for the
reason that their longevity had morphed into a time span
more similar to humans.

As to Jonathon Bowling, after he and his family died,
the hotel was sold off to three more owners. The last
owner before the MacTires was Warren Wernicke, who
bought the hotel in 1953. He was a bachelor who never
married. At least as far as anyone could tell. He might
have lost a mate earlier and never found another, which
often occurred among *lupus garous*.

Owning a hotel as a single entrepreneur was a little
unusual. Wernicke's sister lived in the house with him
and managed the hotel for a brief while, according to
Darien's dad's notes. Then as far as reports could tell,
twelve years after he bought the place, Warren Wernicke
left one night and never come back. His sister, Charity
Wernicke, vanished shortly after that.

A police report filed by Sheridan Silver, CJ's father,
as acting sheriff, said Warren seemed to have run off
with a maid. His sister then left because the hotel was
in financial ruins.

CJ had to let the sisters see all this, but he really
didn't want to. As unafraid as they seemed, he worried

that this might disturb them more, particularly since his father had never located the Wernickes to verify that his suspicions were correct. Still, the sisters had every right to see the information about the hotel. Besides, they could obtain the information themselves anyway.

Looking at everything Brett had gathered about the hotel, CJ realized his brother was the perfect match for his job. He was really good at research, and he'd included old deeds, an auction listing of furniture and other incidentals, and pictures of some of the lovely carved pieces of furniture that were sold off when the hotel closed down after Charity Wernicke disappeared.

After that, no one had the funds or the know-how to run the hotel. Or the desire. He remembered how kids would dare each other to spend a night in the old place, swearing ghosts floated about the hotel, moaning and crying and wreaking all sorts of havoc on anyone dumb enough to stay there.

He noticed a photograph of a hand-pieced quilt with a stenciled letter *C* right in the center. The letter was the approximate size of the one on the wall. CJ stared at the picture, wondering why Charity had disappeared. And her brother too.

Chapter 5

THE NEXT MORNING, ELLIE AND MEGHAN TOOK OFF before CJ arrived, both warning Laurel not to get too involved with him. And yet, she thought they really didn't mean it. Not when they gave each other secret smiles. They probably hoped *he* could convince her to stay.

They had to know her better than that. She was totally focused on getting their hotel up and running. No time to play with a male wolf.

Laurel had to admit she'd thoroughly enjoyed playing in the snow with her sisters last night and taking a long moonlit run across the snowfields with the rest of the pack. She wasn't ready for any other pack activities, but she would remember last night fondly.

This morning, she hadn't wanted to check the wall in the hotel's lobby, afraid of what she'd find. She carried the painting over there, just in case, and sure enough, the *C* was still as big as day.

She leaned the painting against one of the perpendicular walls so that CJ could paint over the *C* again.

When she heard knocking at the door, she felt a little thrill of excitement at seeing him again and immediately scolded herself for feeling any such thing. She hurried for the door, paused, put on her more professional face, then unlocked and opened the door. But it wasn't CJ. Instantly, she became wary. Three men stood on the hotel's porch, and she suspected they were the ghost busters.

"We're not open yet," she said, trying not to growl like she wanted to. She had to remember that she was in the business of welcoming guests, and they *would* be her guests tomorrow.

"I'm Stanton Wernicke," the darkest-haired man said, his blue eyes hard. "These are my brothers, Yolan and Vernon. We're your guests tomorrow, but you might have heard that we have a TV show—"

"*Ghost Busters Extraordinaire*, yes," she said. "But we're not open today."

"We thought maybe we could look around before everyone arrives. That way we won't be in everyone's hair."

Already Laurel didn't like Stanton Wernicke. He was pushy and acting as if his business was more important than hers. And that she should welcome the great TV personalities. *That* would be the day.

"I'm sorry, no. You'd be in *my* hair, and I'm busy."

She heard a vehicle park out front, and though she couldn't see around the three hulking men, she hoped CJ had arrived. If these men wouldn't take no for an answer, they'd change their mind when they learned CJ was a deputy sheriff.

"We promise we'll stay out of your way and—"

"I said no. Beyond that, I didn't know who you were when you booked your reservations. I have no intention of allowing the hotel to be part of your show. Furthermore, you haven't asked permission to photograph or videotape the hotel for the purpose of sharing with the public."

"Slight technicality," Stanton said. "I thought one of my brothers had received permission." He gave them a condescending look. They gave him the slightest knowing smiles back.

She knew he was lying, and she really didn't like these men.

"What seems to be the trouble?" CJ asked, coming up behind the men so quietly that she hadn't even heard him. But his voice wasn't the least bit quiet. It was darkly baritone and stated he meant business.

Except that he was carrying a purple-and-yellow polka-dot box that ruined the tough-guy image. She hoped he wasn't bringing her a gift now that her sisters were gone.

"No trouble." Stanton glanced down at the colorful box, a slight smile appearing on his thin lips, as if he thought CJ was a joke. "We're staying here tomorrow, and we wanted to get some readings before everyone else arrives because we have a TV—"

"Show. We know." CJ's dark expression told the men they had no business here. Even so, he waited for Laurel to say if she agreed.

She appreciated CJ's gesture.

"You may not have permission to film or photograph the hotel or properties while you're here," she repeated in front of the deputy sheriff, so that he could share that with Darien and the sheriff in case these men ignored her rules. "I don't want you disturbing other guests with your paranormal equipment. You're welcome to come tomorrow and check in after the grand opening like everyone else and to use your rooms. *For sleeping*. If you aren't happy with the rules, I will gladly cancel your reservations without penalty." She folded her arms and managed a small smile. "Sorry. We really need to get some things done. Hectic day before the grand opening tomorrow."

Stanton looked like a bulldog, and he and his brothers

weren't budging from the porch. He finally said, "All right. But you're making a mistake."

She raised a brow. Was he threatening her? CJ took a step toward him, though she wasn't sure what he was going to do if things got physical, since he was still holding the polka-dot box.

Stanton held his position. "I mean, because we could do a lot of good promo for your hotel."

She narrowed her eyes. "What? Saying the place is haunted? Or not haunted? I don't think so."

"Whichever way works best for you."

She snorted. "And here I thought you were the real deal." *Not.*

Stanton smiled a little. "Believe me, we're the real deal. But we could slant it one way or the other, whichever way you preferred. No one but us would be the wiser."

"Tomorrow, gentlemen. Rooms are for overnight guests only. Deputy Sheriff Silver, would you like some breakfast before we get to work?"

The men's expressions changed subtly from pushy to surprised.

She was glad they hadn't ignored that revelation.

"Yeah, sure. See you tomorrow at the grand opening." CJ waited for the men to clear out.

"You think he really is?" Vernon asked the others under his breath. He was blonder than his brothers and a little shorter, but just as muscled and serious.

They looked back at CJ, still standing on the porch. He'd moved closer to Laurel, and she felt safer with him around. Not that these men would really pull anything, but they seemed to think their TV-show fame gave them rights that no one else would have.

When the men drove off in a blue van, CJ and Laurel entered the hotel, and his gaze shifted to the wall and the letter *C*.

"I'm glad you told them up front that they couldn't film here. That will give me better leverage in kicking them out if they do anything you don't like." CJ didn't care for those guys already. "Are you fixing breakfast here or at your place?" He didn't smell anything cooking in the kitchen, and he doubted that she would be making a meal here since they didn't plan to have a restaurant. Maybe in the future. The kitchen could be used for special refreshments for their guests though, just like they were using it tomorrow to serve Silva and Sam's food and drinks at the opening.

"At the house. I only have a few things in the kitchen here for the big opening tomorrow." She released a relieved breath. "I don't know why I didn't think about it before, but it suddenly occurred to me that the ghost busters hadn't asked permission to do any ghost busting here. And I have every right to limit what they do in the hotel." She led him outside, and they walked along the stone path that meandered around the fountain and gazebo on its way to the house.

"Looks like they could be trouble. Brett might have informed you already, but he couldn't bring the information about the hotel over until much later today, so when he learned I was coming here this morning, he sent it over with me."

She eyed the purple-and-yellow polka-dot box. "That's great. Colorful box."

He shook his head. "Not that I have anything against polka dots or colorful boxes, but I could have used something a little manlier when I was facing down the ghost-buster crew. I don't think they took me very seriously."

She laughed. "Was it Brett's idea?"

"No, Lelandi's. You know Darien's brother, Jake, the photographer. Lelandi, Darien's mate, gave him the photo box. I'm sure he couldn't wait to pass it along to Brett when he was gathering all this information for you."

"And now *I* have it."

"Don't tell Lelandi, but Jake doesn't want it back."

"What about Brett?"

Smiling, CJ shook his head.

She chuckled. "Do you like French toast?"

"Sounds great."

While she fixed them breakfast, CJ spread out the pictures and copies of other documents on the table for her to look at when they were done eating.

It wasn't long before she'd served the French toast, and he was smothering his in maple syrup. He noted she was reading one of the documents when he asked, "Would you like to go skiing some time with me?" He figured he'd start this courtship right away since the ladies were ready to open the hotel. No more excuses for not having time to let down their hair a bit.

"Ohmigod. One of the people who owned the hotel was named Wernicke. And his sister ran it for a time, but they both vanished," Laurel suddenly said.

Surprised, CJ frowned at her. "Did you know them?"

She looked up at him. "No, but the ghost busters said they had the same name. What are the odds?"

CJ closed his gaping mouth. "Hell." He got on his cell and called Darien. "Hey, Brett gave me some information about the old hotel. Do you know anything about the Wernicke family that owned it?"

"Not really." Darien's voice darkened. "Wait, isn't that the name of the ghost busters?"

"Yeah, same name. Too much of a coincidence, don't you think?"

"It sure as hell is. Are they wolves? They're staying at Bertha's bed and breakfast, but she didn't say anything about them being wolves. She would have informed me right away."

CJ watched Laurel pull over another document to read. "I didn't smell any wolf scent on them. Were the Wernicke sister and brother wolves?"

"I don't know. My father was in charge of the pack back then. I thought he was concerned about keeping Silver Town as wolf-run as possible, just as I've been since I took over. Maybe he'd sold it to the Wernicke family just so that someone was operating it."

Laurel set her fork down on her plate, only half of her French toast eaten, and began to look at the pictures in earnest. Her face blanched a bit, and CJ noticed that she was looking at the picture of the quilt bearing the letter *C*.

She began to look quickly through the rest of the documents, and he wondered what she was searching for.

"Is there any way to find out?" CJ asked Darien. "If the ghost busters are human, and the previous owners weren't, they're not related."

"We'll ask some of the old-timers to see if anyone knew for sure."

"Agreed. And these men might be trouble. They were over here this morning, wanting to see the place before the other guests arrive tomorrow. Laurel said no, but they weren't buying it. Not only that, but she told them they didn't have permission to use their ghost-busting equipment to videotape or photograph the hotel."

"Good. Then you've got grounds to charge them if they give you or the sisters trouble. Keep an eye on things then. Let me know if they get out of hand."

"Will do." CJ ended the call with Darien and shook his head at Laurel's questioning glance. "Darien doesn't know if they're related to the ones who ran the hotel, or even if the earlier owners were wolves."

"They have to be related. Maybe they think they can lay claim to the place."

Laurel seemed so disheartened, CJ reached over and grasped her hand and gave it a squeeze. "They'd have to have proof they were related. We'd have to ensure that the former owners didn't die of unnatural causes. And that they had willed the properties to these men." Hell, he'd thought the problem was that the men might discover werewolves existed. Now this? Then again, the men didn't smell like wolves, so if they saw someone shifting, the pack would still have trouble.

"Wait. On second thought, though I don't know the situation entirely, if they disappeared and no one paid the taxes, Darien's father, as pack leader, would have paid them to keep the property with the pack."

"Okay." Laurel took their plates into the kitchen, though she looked visibly upset and hadn't finished eating her breakfast.

CJ wanted to ask about the similarity of the *C* on the hand-quilted comforter and the one on the wall, but he figured Laurel was probably more worried about the ghost busters now.

"Are you going to tell your sisters about the men and the former owners?" CJ asked.

"No. Not while they're trying to take care of other business. When they get home tomorrow night, I will. I can show them the pictures and the documents, and we can discuss it."

CJ and Laurel returned to the hotel, and he headed for the basement. She unlocked the door for him but didn't go down this time. He hurried to retrieve one of the rollers and the paint tray and climbed back up the stairs.

Laurel was carrying a box of Christmas lights out to the sunroom. "I'm going to start hanging lights around the gazebo. I'll see you out back when you're done here."

"Sure. Oh, one thing. Brett said he wanted to take pictures of the backyard once it's decorated for Christmas. And he wanted to get a picture of the hotel with all the lights on in the front windows tonight."

"Okay, super. Thanks so much to you and your brother for helping out. And…for all the promo. We'd like to invite you over to dinner some night."

"We'd love it. I was thinking… Since this is your last night before you open, would you like to go for another wolf run? We could go to the tavern, have drinks to celebrate, and eat supper there."

"A run would be nice."

"But no on the tavern?" He could see her reluctance. She shook her head.

He wondered if she felt it would be too intimate. Too much like a date.

"Supper tonight at my place?" He wasn't giving up

on the idea of eating with her. She was alone. He was alone. They had to eat. It couldn't be more perfect with her sisters away for the night.

"How about if I fix supper at mine?" Laurel finally said.

"Okay, works for me. What can I bring?" He was thrilled she'd go for it. He hoped he didn't sound overly eager.

"Wine? Dessert?"

He smiled a little.

"Chocolate," she clarified.

"Sure. Sounds like a winner. I'll join you outside in just a bit." But it was still hours before supper and he had to come up with another plan to spend more quality time with her.

He went to work on painting the wall, again, and once he was satisfied that he'd covered the entire area, he washed the paint out of the roller in the basement. He didn't sense anything spooky or see anything that made him feel the basement was haunted. Just that wall he'd been painting. He walked upstairs and into the room where the X had appeared on the ceiling, but there was no sign of it.

The painters would have had a ladder set up in one of the rooms. It would have been easy for someone to enter through the unlocked door and paint an X on the ceiling after everyone had gone.

CJ walked outside into the brisk morning breeze. The air was chilly, but the sun was shining today, and with the snow all over the backyard, it truly looked like Christmas.

Lauren looked just as festive in her sparkly white sweater, with her red hair curling about her shoulders and her jeans showing off her curves as she stretched up to hang white lights on the top edge of the gazebo.

"Here, let me help you. Unless you want me to do something else."

"Sure, you can do this and I can hang the garland on the lower railings." She climbed down off the ladder, and he changed places with her while she hung the garland. "Is the letter still on the wall?"

"Yeah, it is."

She let out her breath in the frosty air.

"Hey, do you want to decorate that tree out here too?"

She considered the silver spruce. "Sure. I hadn't thought of that. What do you think? Just lights or red bows and lights?"

"Why don't we decorate it with lights, and if it looks like it needs something more, we can add red bows."

"Okay." She smiled up at him as though she really appreciated the suggestion. He was glad he'd made it.

He glanced up at the attic window. It was dark, but it reminded him of what Brett had said about the light being on in the room when he went to take pictures. "So did you...leave the attic room light on last night?"

Laurel stopped hanging the garland and looked up at him. "No, why?"

"Brett said it was on last night when he went to take a picture of the hotel all lit up in Christmas lights."

"Maybe one of my sisters left it on by mistake."

"And turned it off this morning?" CJ finished hanging the lights on the gazebo and went to work on the silver spruce.

"Right." Laurel didn't sound sure of herself. She finished the garland, then pulled her phone out of her pocket and called someone. "Hey, Ellie, did you leave a light on in the attic last night? Okay, if you didn't, ask Meghan, will you? If she did, maybe she turned it off this morning before you both left. All right. Thanks. Everything's fine here. I told the ghost hunters that they weren't allowed to photograph anything inside the hotel. They were not happy." She smiled.

"Yeah, they looked a little shocked." She glanced in CJ's direction. "The letter *C*? Even after the paint dried all night, the letter was still there this morning. CJ painted over it again just a few minutes ago. Yes, I told CJ the room was haunted. Thanks." Laurel ended the call and pocketed her phone.

She moved over to help him with the lights. "No one turned on the attic-room light that they remember. Both know for sure they didn't turn it off this morning before they left."

"Burned-out bulb, probably," CJ said.

"Right."

"Would you like to go skiing with me sometime?" CJ unraveled more of the light string.

"I've never skied before."

"Easily remedied. I'm one of the best ski instructors there is. I can give private lessons."

She laughed. "I bet you can."

"I can. Free of charge. I'll pay for your lunch at the ski lodge and—"

"I have a hotel to run."

"On your days off."

"Okay, I'll take you up on it."

"Hot damn!"

She smiled.

"Oh, and by the way, Darien will look further into the ghost busters' backgrounds. He'll try to find out if they're related to the previous owners."

"Good. I just can't believe they wouldn't be related."

When Laurel and CJ were done stringing the lights, they stepped back and looked at the tree.

"I like it just like it is. No red bows," CJ said.

"I agree. The tree looks lovely."

All spruced up in Christmas finery, the hotel and grounds were beautiful. Not modern gaudy, but reminiscent of an older time—even nostalgic. Evergreen garlands and red bows trimmed the white fence, and evergreen wreaths decorated with red bows hung at each of the nine windows of both floors. The gazebo and spruce out back sparkled with white lights.

"You and your sisters have done a beautiful job. It's really going to be great having the additional lodging for visitors to the area. Bertha's place gets packed and some of the bigger homes have started to rent bedrooms, but this will be nice for a few more guests."

"I agree." She turned to CJ. "Not to change the subject, but why do you think the Wernickes left and never came back?"

CJ was afraid she'd been worrying ever since she heard about the disappearing brother and sister. Though she seemed to enjoy decorating the backyard with him, and he was glad he could help her while her sisters were gone.

"I don't know. But I'm all for uncovering what went on," he said. "I'm sure that the situation was investigated as thoroughly as it could be at the time. But it certainly doesn't hurt for us to see if we can come up with anything new." He wished his father was still alive so they could ask him what he'd learned but hadn't specified in his report.

"What are your sisters doing?" CJ didn't want to pry, but it seemed odd that they'd left when there was still so much decorating to be done and then the grand opening was tomorrow.

"We located…" Laurel paused. "Um, we purchased a couple of antiques, and when they didn't arrive on time, we were afraid something had gone wrong. We just want to make sure we get them all right."

CJ was instantly suspicious because of the abrupt change in what Laurel was going to say, the way he smelled her concern, and how she seemed afraid to tell him the truth—but also because he couldn't imagine a couple pieces of furniture being so important that Laurel was left to deal with the hotel's opening on her own.

"Is there a special place where the furniture is going to be displayed?"

She snorted. "Maybe in front of the letter on the wall. Then we can rehang our painting in the house."

That didn't answer his question. Why had her sisters needed to leave? "We have a long time before supper. Why don't we run up to the slopes and get some afternoon skiing in?" he asked.

She looked a little unsure about that.

"You're done with the place. Nothing else to do unless you want to watch a movie at home or something. But we could go skiing, have supper, then go for a night run if you'd like."

"Okay, but I'll warn you now, I went ice skating

once, and I'm not the most graceful skater. So don't expect much of me for my first time on the slopes."

"That's why having your own personal trainer is the only way to go."

She smiled a little, then headed for the stairs. "I'll get my ski pants and jacket. I picked them up on sale when we first got here, just in case. What about you?"

"I have mine in the truck. I always have a bag packed for emergencies in case I have to run to the ski resort."

"Oh, okay, super. Be right down." She disappeared upstairs.

CJ immediately retrieved his bag of clothes and changed in the guest bathroom.

When she returned, she was wearing formfitting black ski pants that showed her curves, a pale blue sweater, and a matching jacket. She looked scrumptious. He hoped she loved skiing as much as he was going to enjoy teaching her.

He grabbed his jacket and she slipped on a ski hat and gloves, then they locked up her house and climbed into the truck. As he was backing out of the parking area, something at the hotel caught his eye. His gaze shifted upward.

The light in the attic room was on...again.

Chapter 6

LAUREL KNEW THAT KEEPING SECRETS FROM CJ OR anyone else would be difficult if she and her sisters spent much time with any of the pack members. She couldn't believe she had nearly made the slip about her aunt's furniture.

She climbed into CJ's truck. He hesitated to drive out of the parking lot and was looking at the hotel. She turned to see what caught his eye. The light was on in the attic room.

"Told you it was haunted," she said. He smiled, shook his head, and drove off to the ski resort.

To get her mind off being apprehensive about skiing, Laurel thought about her mother trying to find out what had happened after that long-ago Christmas when she didn't receive word from her sister. Despite going to Silver Town, Sadie hadn't learned anything. A couple of local residents claimed Clarinda *hadn't* worked for Warren Wernicke. And they'd been adamant about it.

Sadie had even spoken with Sheridan Silver, the sheriff. Laurel and her sisters had hoped to question him further but had been sorry to learn he was dead. Laurel wished she could ask CJ if his father had said anything about their aunt or mother.

He might not know anything about it. In any case, she didn't want to alert CJ as to why she and her sisters were here.

She looked out at the pristine expanse of snow, broken up by pines laden with the white stuff that sparkled in the noonday sun. Beautiful. She tried to put thoughts of her aunt out of her mind for just this afternoon, but she couldn't help thinking about her.

After Laurel and her sisters heard their mother's suspicions concerning her sister's disappearance, they began investigating it. In an old chest, Ellie had found a photo Aunt Clarinda had sent their mother to help document her ownership of the highboy and blanket chest. All of the furniture at the hotel had been auctioned off at one point, and it had taken Laurel and her sisters months to finally track her aunt's things down at another auction. The fact that Aunt Clarinda's furniture had been sold at the hotel auction proved that she had lived there.

Now that the furniture had been returned from Paris, Laurel and her sisters wanted to keep track of it because of what might be hidden in secret compartments—if there were any. Laurel just hoped that no one had emptied what might have been hidden there.

"Here we are," CJ said cheerfully as they arrived at the ski resort.

Several pack members waved at CJ…and at her. She wasn't used to so many people, wolves, treating her like she was a good friend. She hadn't considered what it would be like to be up here with him. Alone. Without her sisters to quash some of the speculation.

Despite knowing it was not the best idea to appear as though she and CJ were a couple, she felt good about it. Relished the notion that she *was* with the hot deputy sheriff. That he was well liked, and for the afternoon, she was with him.

—·~·—

As soon as Laurel was fitted for ski boots and skis, four instructors descended on her, offering to give her private ski lessons. Arms folded across his chest, CJ just smiled at them.

"Don't tell me that *you're* giving her lessons?" a blond named Cantrell said. Another man, Robert—obviously Cantrell's twin—silently stood by, nodding. They both looked like Viking gods—blue eyed, muscled, tanned, and grinning broadly.

"I tell you, those Silver wolves always get the women," Robert said.

"We've got to learn their secret."

Laurel laughed. She'd never expected to see such lighthearted wolf rivalry over a woman. She'd been a little concerned about male wolf fights over eligible she-wolves, so she was glad there was none of that here.

"Are you ready?" CJ asked, giving her a wink.

"Yeah." She just hoped she wouldn't do too badly. She could do a lot of things well, but when it came to new adventures like this? She could see herself falling down more than standing up, breaking something before she barely got started, and generally embarrassing herself in front of all the pack members. It would be easier if she and CJ were doing this at any other ski resort where they didn't know anyone.

Yet, everyone's friendliness encouraged her.

Out of the way of any skiers, CJ showed her how to put her skis on. He demonstrated how she should point her skis to form a V. "Slightly incline your knees inward so that you can dig your skis into the snow a bit. Relax your arms and hold your poles with the tips pointing outward so that you're less tense."

She realized then how tense she was and willed herself to relax. He could probably hear her wildly pounding heart. Hopefully, he just believed she was excited.

"Then you'll turn, planting the tips of your poles into the snow behind you and pushing off gently." He demonstrated. "To slow down, widen your V and zigzag down the slope. You can traverse more of the slope to the side and then turn to go down the slope, and again turn to the opposite side, digging into the slope."

He showed her how to take off her skis and then walked her to the beginner's ski lift for the bunny slope. She couldn't believe how heavy the boots were or how difficult it was to walk in them. She'd thought it would be easier to just ski over to the lift, but then she watched a kid of about ten years old flying by, pushing out with his skis to get over to the lift. And another, sliding over the snow, expertly using his poles to push him along. She definitely didn't have that skill yet.

Skiing just didn't seem like a wolf sport. Yet she loved the outdoors and the fresh air, the smiling faces, and everyone looking like they were having so much fun. She was glad she'd come here to take a much-needed play break before opening the hotel.

By the time she reached the ski lift, Laurel was thinking that she would be good and tired tonight. She wished her sisters could be here, but she liked that she got to try skiing first.

She managed to get her skis on without any trouble, then slid them across the packed snow to reach the lift line. Talk about unwieldy! She crossed the tips of the skis twice and nearly fell. If CJ hadn't grabbed her arm and kept her upright until she could get her skis uncrossed, she would have landed on her butt. Talk about a lifesaver! Not that she was in terrible peril, except for risking embarrassment if she fell in front of everyone.

Wearing his mirror sunglasses, his kissable mouth smiling up at the corners just a tad, CJ looked so hot and cute that she fell in love with him a little. Not as in a mating. He was so sweet to offer to teach her and didn't seem to mind that she was a klutz. Not all men would want to bother. Most would rather show off their hotshot skiing skills than babysit a novice.

"You can teach me for a little while, then I can practice while you ski on your own." She didn't want him to feel obligated to stay with her all afternoon. She could just imagine how bored he would be. And she was sure that if she just practiced, she could get better without him having to watch her.

"Are you kidding? Not only am I looking forward to having fun on the slopes with you, but there's no way that I'm leaving you alone for a second. There are way too many hungry bachelor wolves on the slopes this afternoon."

He looked so serious, she laughed. He just smiled back.

Before she knew it, she and CJ were sitting on the ski lift, her skis swinging a bit, which seemed hazardous. She was afraid she'd fall off because there was no bar to keep a body secure.

At the end of the ride, when she had to get off the ski lift in a hurry, her heart was pounding with worry that she'd fall right in front of the lift. One of the two male teens in front of them had just fallen, and she could see herself doing the same thing. Thankfully, the teen was up and gone before she hopped off. She managed to stay on her feet, or skis, and skied a little out of the path before she slid to a stop.

"Okay, we'll go this way. Blue trail over there is for intermediate skiers. The green signs always mean easy, and this one over here is the easiest of the six easy slopes. To get moving, just push off with your skis, one and then the other. As we ski down, remember to form your wedge."

When they started to ski down, he reminded her, "Keep your weight mostly on the downhill ski as you go across the slope, keeping your skis parallel, and always form a wedge when you're turning downhill. If you find yourself falling, fall toward the upper slope."

They headed down the slope, which looked incredibly tall and steep. It probably wasn't, but for someone who wasn't used to this, like Laurel, it looked that way. She began to pick up a little speed, more than she was ready for, and quickly widened her wedge. That slowed her down right away, and she began to gain confidence, realizing she did have some control over her movements. This wasn't so hard after all.

And she was having fun as she moved down the hill. Getting tired too, as she used muscles in ways she hadn't before.

Little kids zipped past her, making her wish she'd taken up skiing a long time ago, though she and her sisters hadn't lived in snow country for some time. And when they had, they hadn't lived near a ski resort.

Besides, she didn't imagine she would have had private wolf lessons anywhere else. So this was really enjoyable.

After going up the ski lift and skiing down the slope a number of times, CJ smiled at her when they reached the base. "You're really getting the hang of it."

All along, he'd been saying things like that. She loved how encouraging he was. She guessed she wasn't too bad for a beginner. In the beginning, getting used to the trail was important so that she could learn its nuances and concentrate more on her form. After a couple of runs, she knew where the top of the snow had crusted over and was more slippery, where it widened and where it narrowed, where there was a tiny bump in the snow, and how long it would take her to reach the base where everyone coming down off other slopes converged and headed for the ski lifts.

"Looking good, Laurel," someone said, skiing past them. Someone else echoed the man's compliment.

She smiled. She hoped her sisters would take up skiing too. By next season, they could all be halfway good at it. "Do you think you're ready to go down the next slope, or do you want to keep skiing down this one? The next one is a little steeper, still a green, really easy to navigate, and with a much longer slope so you have more time to practice turning. It's up to you."

He had to be bored coming down this easy slope, she thought.

After about an hour of the green slope, she was eager to try out another trail. Especially if he thought she was ready for it.

If it turned out to be too difficult, she could go back to the easiest slope. "Yeah, I'd love to."

"Good show." He looked proud of her. "You're a celebrity, you know," CJ said as they rode up a different lift.

"What do you mean?"

"The Wernicke brothers think that their show has so much appeal, but you have everyone watching you today."

"Great. I'd really rather that no one noticed me falling down a hill."

"You're doing super. And you have to remember it's your first time."

"I see these little kids skiing like they've been doing it for years, and it makes me wish I had been."

"They *have* been doing it for years. Parents put them in ski school at three years of age. Ski bunnies. By the time they're seven or eight, they've already been skiing for a number of years."

"Wow. Do you ever teach them?"

"On occasion when I'm off-duty. I'm usually up here during the duty day, if Peter needs me for deputy sheriff duties. I've taught the kiddies in a pinch. You're really doing well, Laurel. Some people can't get the hang of it right away. You're having fun, aren't you?"

"Loving it." She couldn't envision CJ teaching the little ones, but she would love to see it.

"Loving it is all that matters."

With all his encouragement, she felt she was doing really well. She was learning how to fall and get back up, which was a lot harder than it looked. Ski poles and skis just seemed to get in the way. And when she was on a slope? She couldn't decide if it was harder or easier than when she took a spill on level ground.

Taking a different ski lift meant seeing a different view of the trees and slopes from up above and, for her, exploring a new virgin trail. This one curved more and was steeper. Although still wide, it wasn't as wide as the bunny slope. Attempting a different slope was scary, but after she had gone down it, she was ready to sample another and another, which she did until she'd tried them all.

CJ even took her on the easiest intermediate slope. It was much steeper with a few moguls, but she skied around them. She loved it, although her legs were becoming weary. Running, walking, and swimming kept her in great shape as a wolf, but skiing worked her muscles differently. She fell more on the intermediate slope, maybe because of the steepness of the slope, and panicked when she hit a mogul and flew over the top of it rather than cutting sideways across it. She quickly turned into the slope and maintained control. Thankfully.

When she skied down the last time and reached the base, she wasn't sure what happened next. She turned to stop, but an out-of-control skier nearly ran into her. CJ came in behind her, his skis on either side of hers, and moved her in a forward motion out of the skier's path. But the skier who sliced past them startled her, and Laurel lost her balance, while the skier crashed and burned a few yards away.

Laurel felt herself falling. And taking CJ with her.

Skis and poles and legs tangled, he landed on the ground hard, softening her fall. She was sitting half on his lap and half off. They looked at the wiped-out skier, who was getting up, dusting off snow, and heading out to confirm that he was fine. Then CJ and Laurel's gazes collided. They both burst out laughing.

He dropped his poles, cupped her face, and kissed her.

Letting go of her poles, she kissed him right back,

tongue for tongue, mouths locked, the cold wind no longer noticeable as he heated her blood right up.

She kept telling herself that the way she was feeling was just gratitude for him being such a trouper in teaching her to ski. Yet, she couldn't help wishing the kiss would lead to more. A deeper relationship, maybe.

They still had so much other stuff to resolve. But in this instant, half sitting on his hot lap and half off, wearing the unwieldy skis on her heavy ski boots, and feeling his mouth hot and hungry against her lips, she was leaning a lot toward yes!

CJ pulled his mouth away from hers first, his eyes darkened to midnight, his hands still cupping her face, as if trying to sense how she felt about this jump in their relationship.

She smelled the testosterone fired up between them and smiled a little. "I bet when you're teaching new students to ski, this doesn't happen often."

He smiled a little. "I *never* give private lessons."

She chuckled.

"But for you, just say the word and I'll bring you up here for more."

"I'd love it. I need to do it again soon so I don't forget all that you taught me." She sighed. "What are we going to do about getting up?"

He was fully aroused, and she figured he was going to have a time of it. So was she.

"I don't think there's any way to do this gracefully. Just do whatever you have to. And then, did you want to get a drink at the lodge?"

Leaving at this point would be less embarrassing, but she wasn't a cowardly wolf. A hot drink sounded good.

"Yeah, I'd love that."

Somehow, she managed to swing her leg around, despite wielding the long ski, though he groaned a little as her buttocks pressed against his arousal. All she'd accomplished was to move her leg off his. She was still sitting squarely against his crotch. She leaned forward to try and stand, and he gave her rump a little boost. Startled to get some help from behind, she nearly fell but managed to stabilize herself. She looked back to see how he was managing.

Despite being so good at skiing, he took a moment to rise to his feet. He squirmed a bit as if he was trying to re-situate his gear to get more comfortable, while she was trying not to smile. Then he skied with her to the baseline lodge.

They left their skis and poles outside, leaning against a wooden rack where he looped his pole straps around her skis and his as if claiming her—or stating they were together. Which she found amusing.

Little things like that might not mean much to some people, but they were a big deal to *lupus garous*. He was telling other wolves to keep their paws off her. She didn't mind, because she really liked CJ, and, well, she could see them going further with this, if she could resolve the business with their aunt's disappearance and not upset the pack in the process.

Inside, they looked for a free table to sit at. Many were filled with skiers stopping to get a drink. At one of the four-person tables, the Viking brothers, Cantrell and Robert, waved them over.

"Do you mind sitting with them?" CJ asked.

She really appreciated his thoughtfulness, ensuring she liked the men before she agreed.

"Sure. That would be fine." She glanced up at CJ. "We have only a half hour left to ski before the resort closes. I thought this would be a nice end of the day. What do you think?"

"Hell, yeah." He grinned from ear to ear.

She laughed.

"But," he said very seriously, "we still have *supper* plans."

"Yeah." She wouldn't give them up for the world. It would be a lovely way to conclude the evening, especially since her sisters weren't around and she knew she would be lonely.

When they sat down with the brothers, both were grinning at them. "I should have known you'd take your cue from Tom," Cantrell said, directing his comment to CJ, who smiled back a little. To Laurel, he explained, "His cousin Tom and Tom's mate, Elizabeth, were caught on video kissing up by one of the ski lifts before they were mated. The video went viral in the pack."

Laurel frowned at them. "Don't tell me anyone took pictures or a video of *us*."

Robert pulled out his phone. "I don't know if anyone else did, but I got a shot."

She wouldn't have cared if she and CJ were truly courting. But they weren't, and worse, she didn't want her sisters to learn about it like this. In this case, a picture was worth more than a thousand words. It would cause all kinds of speculation.

"But, of course, you didn't share it with anyone," she said, putting Robert on the spot. Didn't the pack members need permission?

"Not me. My shot didn't turn out all that great."

Robert gave her another cocky smile, then handed his phone to her.

She saw twenty-three other pictures posted of the kissing scene. Some from a distance, so it was hard to tell who was kissing whom on the slope. Others, close-ups. And one was a really short video from one of those helmet cams as someone skied past.

Shaking her head, she handed the phone back to Robert. But she was amused. She'd never expected that to happen.

"So how did it work out for Tom and his mate after they earned all that fandom on the ski slopes?" she asked, curious if that had led to their mating shortly thereafter.

"She left him," Cantrell said.

Laurel laughed.

"But obviously she returned," Robert said. "We knew that would happen."

"We have to get back to ski rescue. If you need rescuing from CJ, just let me know," Cantrell said.

"But call me when you do." Robert slapped CJ on the shoulder. "See you later, man."

"Yeah, see you." CJ waved to a waitress. Then looking a little worried, he asked Laurel, "Are you okay with the pictures? I can ask Darien to have everyone take them down, if you want."

"I'm okay with it. I'm just not used to pack dynamics, and I wouldn't want everyone to think…" She hesitated. She didn't want to say their kissing didn't mean anything to her, because it sure did.

"I understand," CJ said quickly, as if he didn't want her to say she wasn't interested in him the way she knew he was interested in her.

The waitress hurried over to the table. "What would you like to drink?"

They both ended up having hot rum toddies before they left the lodge and dropped by a liquor store. When CJ picked up a bottle of champagne to see if she was agreeable, she raised her brows at his selection. She suspected this had to do with something other than just some holiday cheer.

He was officially declaring he wanted to court her.

Chapter 7

"TO CELEBRATE YOUR FIRST LESSON ON THE SLOPES," CJ said to Laurel as he paid for the champagne. And their first kiss and, as far as he was concerned, their first date. After that kiss on the slopes, he was moving this courtship business along.

Her wicked smile indicated that she knew he meant a lot more by the gesture than he was letting on.

Afterward, they dropped by the grocery store, and she picked out a seven-layer chocolate cake. She wasn't kidding when she said she loved chocolate. He'd had to smile when she first saw the cake and her eyes lit up.

When they arrived at her house, it was still only four in the afternoon. She excused herself to run up and change out of her ski clothes. He ditched his ski jacket and pants on the arm of the couch.

She came downstairs wearing jeans, her peach sweater, and a pair of suede slipper boots. Something about the way she was so casually dressed made him feel right at home.

"Do you want me to open the bottle of champagne now?" he asked while she started to roast slices of beef, tomatoes, and garlic in a pan.

"Do you want me to do something extra special with it? Make it a Christmas drink?" she asked.

"Sure." He opened the bottle for her.

"This will be poinsettia champagne. Just mix a little

orange liqueur and cranberry juice, then add the champagne." She mixed it up, poured them each a glass, and offered one to him.

He clinked his glass against hers. "To first lessons and much more." He wanted her to know that this wasn't just another day, but an important beginning for them.

She smiled and sipped her champagne. "And to kissing on the slopes—without an audience next time."

He laughed and drank to that. He was glad she was all for it. "Still on for a run tonight?"

"I sure am. It'll be the last time before the hotel is open. Do you want to look at this stuff again? See if we find anything that might tell us who was there about the time of the owners' disappearance?" She motioned with her glass to the photos and other items that Brett had gathered for them.

"Yeah, sure." He really just wanted to enjoy the time with her. But since learning what had happened to the owners seemed important to her, he'd do whatever it took to help her learn the truth as quickly as possible.

"I don't see anyone labeled as Warren Wernicke's sister in these pictures. Unless she was a mated wolf and took her husband's name. Is there any way that we can get some of these photos blown up in size but still be able to keep the detail?" She turned her attention from the photos to CJ.

"We can certainly ask Jake to give it a shot." CJ still didn't see anything that he thought would help with learning the truth about the siblings.

Laurel finally sighed, stacked all the items at the end of the table, and began to set the table.

He helped her serve the meal, and then they sat down to eat. "I'm glad you had fun skiing."

"It was great. I'll probably be a little sore tomorrow with all the spills I took, but otherwise, I had a ball. I can't wait to do it again when I have the chance. I imagine my sisters would love to try it too."

"I'm sure any number of our ski instructors would be willing to give lessons."

"Private lessons, right?" She lifted her poinsettia champagne and toasted him.

"Absolutely, but I'm only giving *you* private lessons." He didn't want her thinking he did this all the time. He ate another bite of the roast. "By the way, this is delicious. I love it."

"Thanks. Just something really simple to make that tastes great."

After they ate and put everything away, he hoped she wasn't too tired or sore from skiing to run. He was really looking forward to it.

"Are you ready?" she asked as he put the champagne flutes in the dishwasher. "I thought we could have the chocolate cake when we get back. I'm too full to eat a slice now."

"Sounds like a great idea." He was thrilled she wasn't going to bow out tonight and wanted to spend even more time with him after the run.

After she pulled on her snow boots, coat, and gloves, he drove her out to the woods on Darien's property, rather than to the now-closed ski resort, and parked. "I wanted to show you a different place that we run." He wanted to show her everything that was great for their kind here, now that she was willing to take the time to see the sights with him.

"We often run as wolves out here. This is Darien's

property—several thousand acres of forest, no hunting allowed. The title to the land is in Darien and Lelandi's names, but it's for the use of all pack members. There's a river back there where we boat, fish, and swim." He pointed in the direction. "Any of us who want to take a run out here can. It's like the ski resort at night. Our safe haven for wolves."

"That's really nice. I have to say that while we were living in Florida, we were on our own. We had to be extra careful to avoid being seen. No gray wolves exist in Florida. Lots of forests though. We always ran at night." She smiled. "This truly has been a nice change of pace."

"I'm glad you're enjoying yourself. We have a great place here. Great for raising wolf families, and you can't say that about a lot of locations. I'll take you down to see the river." To give Laurel some privacy, he left the truck, shut the door, and removed his clothes, then opened the door and tossed them inside.

She had stayed in where it was warmer, removed her clothes, and shifted. She leaped out of the truck. She probably wasn't used to shifting in the cold that much. She looked nice and warm now in her gray fur coat, her chest and face tan, her pretty green eyes alight with excitement as she looked him over. He was freezing in his naked human form, so he quickly locked the door, then shifted.

They ran side by side, enjoying the snowy breeze ruffling their fur as they made their way to the river. He could smell the sexy she-wolf, the snow, the pine trees, and fresh water. He always loved running as a wolf, but running with a she-wolf he was interested in courting?

He hadn't realized it would feel so different. Like he couldn't be himself because he wanted to impress her. With his brothers or cousins, he could run with them, tackle them, and just do whatever he was used to doing. He had loved watching Laurel take her sister Ellie down. And then when her sister Meghan tackled her next.

They were cute, but he didn't feel that he could play with Laurel like that. Not yet, anyway. He'd love to when they got to know each other better. With humans, it was easier—take her out to dinner, to a movie, a ball game, anything that the man thought would interest the woman. With wolves, courtship was much more physical. It had to be. They didn't have any other options. Yet he definitely didn't want to come on too aggressive and push her away. On the other hand, he didn't want her to think he was a beta wolf since she obviously was not a beta herself.

He got closer and rubbed up against her a little, which was definitely a show of courtship. He hadn't just brushed up against her to indicate he wanted her to go in a different direction.

She looked at him, and he thought she was wondering what he was up to. Hell, he could pretend he wanted to go in a different direction, or he could tell her what else he was thinking. He brushed up against her again and licked her cheek. Now, he had told her in no uncertain terms what his intentions were. She showed her beautiful teeth in a small smile, right before she tackled him.

He couldn't have been any more surprised or delighted. Due to his wolf's nature, he would normally give it his all, and that meant he'd tackle her and take her down. Would she see that as too aggressive? If he didn't take her down, would he look weak? He hated overthinking this.

Their mouths clashed. He touched his tongue to hers as she growled at him, purely in play, but he was taking this a human step further. In a pinning effort, she rested her chest and forearms on his chest as she continued to bite at him in play, her tail wagging vigorously, her whole butt wagging at the same time. He was on his back, his tail wagging also, and loving every bit of their interaction. He realized he didn't need to show how aggressive he could be. Just taking his time with her like this was a perfect wolf way to get to know her. He bit back in a gentler way, getting in the licks he wanted that were as much a human's interaction as a wolf's. He let her have her way with him.

Not that he was acting like a beta wolf in the least, or he would have tucked his tail against his belly, flattened his ears, and let her completely dominate him. When she looked like she wasn't getting enough of a reaction from him, maybe that he wasn't challenging her enough and acting too submissive, he changed his posture subtly. He got ready to take charge, trying to keep from revealing his intent. She was wary enough to recognize he was going to make her pay—in a fun way.

To avoid payback, she jumped back from him. He leaped from his prone position and with a quick, strategically placed lunge, he pinned *her* this time against the soft snow. She was even *more* aggressive when he brought her down. He could tell she liked it when he wasn't letting her win the confrontation too easily. They were both growling, and if any humans heard them, they would think the wolves were having an angry fight.

She was beginning to wear down as he rested on her

chest, and they began to kiss, wolf style, licking and nuzzling each other. He was absolutely in heaven. He was so glad he had suggested going on a run with her and that she was having just as much fun with him. Then he heard an unfamiliar "woof" in the woods south of them. He quickly got off Laurel, and she rose to her feet. Both smelled the breeze, but the wolf was downwind of them, which meant he or she could eventually smell CJ and Laurel.

He imagined it *had* to be one of the wolves in their pack, but he hadn't heard enough of the *woof* to recognize it. He waited and watched. A black wolf, then a gray, and finally a third wolf, also gray in color, came out of the woods. All three headed for the river, then stood at the water's edge. CJ tried to recognize them. He sniffed the air again. But he couldn't smell them, and they didn't look familiar.

They were a long ways off, looking out across the river, and weren't aware that CJ and Laurel were watching them.

Laurel stuck close to him as she observed the wolves too. Her ears were perked, her tail straight, her posture as wary as his.

As soon as the wolves caught CJ's and Laurel's scents and looked their way, CJ only hesitated a second before doing what any of his wolf pack members would do. He lifted his head and howled for the pack. He could have run with Laurel back to the truck, but that might trigger the three gray wolves' natural inclination to take chase and hunt them down, particularly if they were all wolf and were trying to establish a wolf pack here. If they were *lupus garous* and were trouble, no telling

what they might do. So his only option was to call for
the pack and to stay there with Laurel.

A few of his pack members living in the vicinity
would hear him howl—Darien and his family, Darien's
brother Jake and his wife, and a few others scattered
about in the wilderness.

The three wolves stood their ground for a moment,
as if they were trying to decide whether they wanted to
challenge the local wolf pack's authority. Then the lead
wolf turned and ran off into the woods, vanishing from
sight, and the others quickly followed.

CJ didn't chase after them. He was sticking close to
Laurel. He doubted she or her sisters had been involved
in much wolf-to-wolf combat, so he wasn't about to
leave her on her own. He wouldn't be foolhardy enough
to chase three male wolves down on his own anyway.

A few minutes later, Jake and Darien howled, letting him know they were coming. They would also
have alerted several pack members about the unknown
trouble. It hadn't been a false alarm, particularly if the
three male wolves had decided to attack them. But it was
also a way of showing pack unity and reinforcing that
this was their territory as far as other wolves or *lupus
garous* were concerned.

Jake and Darien soon reached them, and CJ shifted to
speak with them. "Three large, gray male wolves were
standing next to the river down that way. One was black,
the others gray. As soon as I howled for you, they hesitated, then took off."

Darien shifted then. "Reinforcements are coming.
We'll check it out. Why don't you and Laurel head
back in?"

"Will do." CJ was disappointed that they couldn't run farther, just the two of them. He liked exploring the wilderness and giving her a taste of what it was like living here.

He shifted and so did Darien. Then Darien and Jake loped off in their wolf forms, ready to tear into the intruders if they had to. CJ was torn between helping them or leaving with Laurel. The three male wolves outnumbered them. But he reminded himself he needed to get Laurel home safely. He'd never expected to run into any difficulties with other wolves.

When they returned to his truck, he shifted and unlocked the back door for her. This time, he climbed in with her and shut the door.

"Sorry about that." He began pulling on his briefs in the chilly truck. He tried to give her some privacy as she shifted, then began pulling on her panties. He couldn't help but notice that she was watching him too. "We usually don't have any trouble out here."

"It's not your fault. I find it refreshing to see a wolf pack come to its members' aid. If they weren't from your wolf pack, were they real wolves? Or who else might they have been?"

"Taking a wild guess? The Wernicke brothers. If they're related to the previous owners and Warren and his sister were wolves, then these men have to be. But if they are wolves, they've been hiding the fact that they're *lupus garous*, and Darien won't allow them to run here. Not until he knows what's going on. Still, I'm sorry our run was cut short."

"Maybe after my sisters return and are able to manage things without me for a while, we can do it again."

"I'd love that." He lifted her head and waited only a heartbeat for her to pull away. When she didn't, he leaned down and pressed his lips against hers, their berry-and-orange-champagne-flavored breaths mingling. His body throbbed with need, just like when they'd kissed earlier on the ski slope, making his blood burn. He felt her heart thundering against his chest. He kissed her again, feeling compelled, his hands raking through her silky, red hair, her fingers gripping his shoulders and keeping him close.

He was surprised but grateful that she seemed to have changed her mind about him and the pack. He absorbed her heat and softness, smelled her sexy pheromones. Too wrapped up in the feel and smell of her, he was powerless to stop this madness. He wanted this and her, wanted to convince her to stay as long as it would take to truly court her.

Until someone pounded on the window. Laurel jumped a little in his arms, and he turned to see the windows all fogged up. He wiped the nearest one with his arm and saw Darien, dressed now, frowning at him.

CJ opened the door. "Did you find them?"

"Yes, and I lectured them. I thought you were taking Laurel home."

"I am." CJ couldn't help feeling defensive. He knew Darien had everyone in the pack's best interests in mind when he ruled about things, but CJ really didn't want his interference in this.

"I'm calling a meeting. I talked with the wolves, assuming they were the Wernicke brothers, and told them if they want to stay in town or visit in the future, they will obey pack rules. Which means no more using hunter's spray to hide their scents."

"So we don't know for sure if it is them."

"Not for certain. They stood their ground but didn't make a move to fight or run off, so I knew they were *lupus garous*. But I couldn't smell them. None of them shifted to speak to me, only acknowledged with a slight bow of a head that I'd called a meeting and they're to be there in an hour. I wanted you to come too since you'll be watching things at the hotel."

"What about Laurel?" CJ preferred that she go with him. Not that anything bad would happen if he dropped her off at her house, but he wanted a chance to drop her off properly, not in a rush. And besides, they were nearly to Darien's house. Taking her home and returning would take too long.

"She can visit with Lelandi," Darien said, casting him an elusive smile.

Laurel shook her head. "That's okay. I can go home. I've got a lot of things to do before tomorrow."

CJ didn't think she really did. He took her hand in his. Perhaps not the smartest move in front of his cousin, but he didn't want to take her home just yet. "Are you sure? Lelandi would love to visit with you for a bit. We're almost at Darien's home. And then I'll take you home after the meeting."

He was certain Lelandi would be very welcoming, but he had another purpose in mind—he wanted Laurel to get to know Lelandi better. To make friends with her. He knew they hadn't had time to see much of each other socially because Lelandi was busy with the toddlers, the pack, and her psychology business. And Laurel and her sisters had been so busy with renovating the hotel.

"I'm sure it would be an imposition—"

"No imposition at all," Darien said.

"All right. As long as it doesn't take too long," she said.

"If it does, one of the men can take you back to your place."

"Okay, thanks."

When Darien left, CJ climbed out of the backseat of the truck and sat in the driver's seat.

Laurel moved up front too. "That was…awkward." She fastened her seat belt. "I felt like a teenager caught kissing a guy in front of the pack leader. Not that we didn't already kiss in front of a few people at the ski resort, but it's…different."

CJ chuckled. "I'm sure Darien's used to it."

"He's used to you kissing she-wolves in your truck?"

CJ laughed. "No. Other pack members getting caught at it. His brothers. My brothers."

"Tom and Elizabeth on the slopes?"

"Yeah. That was the talk of the pack."

"So what do you think Darien will say to the men?"

"He'll tell them again not to use any more hunter's spray. And no hassling you or your sisters about the hotel. He'll probably ask about their connection to the previous owners."

"Maybe I should sit in on the meeting." Laurel looked out the window as they drove to Darien's home.

"We can ask Darien when we get there." Considering how much Darien and Lelandi wanted the women to remain in the pack, CJ knew Darien would agree to just about anything where they were concerned.

Chapter 8

WHEN THEY ARRIVED AT DARIEN AND LELANDI'S house, the two-story home was all lit up with Christmas lights and looking festive in its woodland setting. All it needed was a couple of wolves sitting on the front porch to make it perfect.

Laurel took a deep breath. "It's beautiful."

"It is. They have big celebrations on the back acreage every season of the year. Since the pack has grown, they have a building now for events, parties, and pack business if the weather is inclement. But for this, we'll just meet in the conference room. If it was just four or five of us, we'd meet in Darien's office. But there'll be more than that."

"Who else will be there?"

"Sheriff Peter Jorgenson, Deputy Trevor Osgood, and Darien's brothers, Jake and Tom. Me, because I'm a deputy sheriff."

"And you're watching over the situation at the hotel." She leaned over and gave him another kiss on the lips.

He was about to lean in for more, but she turned away when she saw Lelandi coming outside to greet them. Laurel smiled. "Almost got caught—again."

CJ just laughed. He was definitely kissing her good night when he dropped her off at her place later.

Lelandi welcomed Laurel as they headed inside.

Glad the two women seemed to get along, CJ said to Laurel, "I'll ask about you sitting in on the meeting."

"No, that's okay." Laurel smiled. "I'd rather visit with Lelandi."

Right then and there, CJ felt something change between them. As if this meant she was considering staying for good and wanted to become friends with Lelandi. At least he was hopeful.

Heading into the conference room, CJ felt light-hearted about the way things were going with Laurel. Normally he would have felt somewhat annoyed that the pack had to deal with *lupus garous* who were bound to give them trouble. Only Darien and Jake were in the room. Everyone else was still on their way.

"How did they act when you met up with them?" CJ asked and took a seat at the long conference table.

Darien poured himself a cup of coffee, then sat down at the head of the table. "They were growly. Belligerent. They didn't like being taken to task. But if they're going to stay here, they'll have to get used to pack rules. Or they'll have to leave the area. Since they never shifted, just nodded in agreement, I can't say any more than that about their behavior."

Jake took a seat. "Do you want me involved in this?"

"As sub-leader, you need to know what's going on. Same with Tom. So just keep your eyes and ears open. If you learn anything about them, let me know."

Tom arrived then and smiled at CJ. "I hear Laurel's with you. And that you had fun on the slopes today with her."

CJ figured that when Darien called the meeting, he'd told Tom about CJ and Laurel running together. And apparently Tom had already heard about their kiss. CJ said, "She wanted private ski lessons."

Tom's smile broadened. "Hell, is that what they're calling them these days?"

Everyone chuckled.

"Where is she?" Tom asked.

"She's visiting with Lelandi."

Tom's lighthearted expression said he was glad CJ was making progress with Laurel. It was the first time that Laurel, or either of her sisters, had visited with Lelandi.

Laurel was too unpredictable for him to believe he was really making progress with her. It would take a while before she changed her mind for certain about staying, if she was even interested. He still felt something other than the desire to join the pack had brought her and her sisters to Silver Town.

Trevor and Peter arrived after that. Then they waited for the Wernicke brothers to show, but by the time an hour had passed, they still hadn't.

Darien never liked to be kept waiting when he'd summoned *lupus garous*—for good reason. It was a sign of disrespect, unless they had a good excuse. Of course, everyone had talked about other subjects, and at one point, Lelandi and Laurel had peeked in to see if the men had arrived yet and then gone back to visiting.

Darien tapped his fingers on the table. He was a patient man, but this business with the Wernicke brothers was already wearing thin with him. CJ knew the feeling.

Laurel had wondered why CJ and the others were taking so long to speak with the Wernicke brothers. When Lelandi saw how much the delay was bothering Laurel, she had taken her to the conference room. Laurel loved that the pack leader was so attuned to watching out for a pack member. Maybe some of it had to do with Lelandi's psychology training.

Laurel could tell Darien wasn't happy about the delay. He was tapping his fingers on the table, and the smile he offered her and Lelandi was strained. Laurel didn't blame him one bit.

She was somewhat apprehensive about visiting much with Lelandi because the pack leader was a psychologist. Laurel was afraid she was analyzing her every word and action. On the other hand, Laurel thought she might learn something important from Lelandi.

"I hope you know how much you and your sisters being here means to us." Lelandi took a sip of her Black Forest cocoa. It had chocolate sprinkled on top to form a Christmas tree in a reindeer-decorated mug. Laurel wanted to replicate the cocoa for her own guests when the hotel was open.

"At one time, Sheriff Sheridan Silver suggested we tear down the hotel because it was an eyesore. As it continued to deteriorate, it would be a hazard to anyone sneaking inside, despite it being boarded up. You know how it is when places are put off-limits."

"Right. Some want to see what's in the forbidden place."

"Exactly. And the word had spread that the place was haunted. Many wanted to see if it truly was. Including Darien and his brothers and cousins. But no one who has been in there has been injured. The consensus was that the building was part of our heritage—like the tavern and Bertha and John Hastings's bed and breakfast. Those buildings were some of the first and are still standing proud."

"I so agree. I love old buildings. And I love restoring them to their former grandeur."

"Which you have done."

"Thanks." Laurel smiled. Lelandi wasn't just trying to convince her they wanted her to stay with the pack; she truly did love what they had done with the hotel.

Though Laurel had asked CJ why no one had bought the hotel before this, she wondered if Lelandi knew of a different reason. "Do you know why it was abandoned for so long?"

"Oh, it was a boardinghouse for years before it was a hotel. Miners, drifters, a couple of women with no family stayed there. Then the silver mine closed and the drifters moved along. Eventually, it was remodeled and opened as the Silver Town Inn."

"What about the Wernicke brother and sister who ran the hotel? Didn't he vanish, and his sister disappeared after that?"

"Darien's having the sheriff and Trevor look into it. Since CJ is watching over the hotel and these men for now, he really can't do it. Darien didn't know anything about the disappearances. Or maybe he heard something in passing years ago, but his father would have been the pack leader back then so he would have dealt with it. I didn't live here at the time. So I don't have a clue."

That's what Laurel had thought. She'd already crossed Lelandi's name off the list of suspects.

They heard a commotion in the other part of the house and then some conversation that she couldn't quite make out, but it sounded like the Wernicke brothers had finally arrived. She really did want to sit in on the conversation, but Lelandi said, "So how did you hear about the hotel? And why did you decide to buy this particular one when there must be hundreds of listings of other hotel properties available all over the States? It's not advertised as a wolf-run resort and town, so we know it wasn't for that reason. We don't recall that you passed through here before. So it wasn't that you knew about us for that reason either."

Laurel never thought the conversation would end up going in this direction. And she really didn't want to keep up the charade with the pack leaders. If they were involved in a crime, so be it. If they weren't, she was certain now that they'd want to learn the truth and handle it.

"Our aunt was staying at the hotel and then she… vanished."

—⁓—

As soon as the Wernicke brothers took seats at the conference table, not explaining why they were so late, Darien came straight to the point. "Are you related to the previous hotel owners—Warren and Charity Wernicke?"

"They were our aunt and uncle on our father's side," Stanton said. CJ assumed he was the one in charge of his brothers.

Looking pack-leader stern, Darien sat up a little taller. "I see. So what is your purpose here? I don't believe it's to schedule a ghost-buster's TV show. Even if you had planned to, Laurel MacTire has said no to giving you permission. So why stay?"

"We're here to learn who murdered Uncle Warren and Aunt Charity," Stanton said, his eyes just as hard.

"They disappeared without a trace. No one knows what happened to them," Darien said. "My father was pack leader at the time. But now that the issue has been brought up again, I'm starting a fresh investigation. So again, I ask what your purpose is in coming here. To search for clues? Why do you suspect they met with foul play? And why come now, of all times?"

CJ imagined that the men were here to either seek revenge or to lay claim to the property. But like Darien, he wondered why now, after all these years?

"Someone made them disappear. Our father, Warren and Charity's triplet brother, said that someone in your pack murdered them."

The Silver brothers and cousins all stared at Stanton as if he had accused each of them personally.

Darien calmly said, "I see. And when did he tell you this?"

"A couple of weeks ago. Right before he died."

Way too convenient, to CJ's thinking. Darien's brow arched, and Jake and Tom smiled a little.

Stanton ignored their reactions and continued. "But our dear dad clasped my hand and begged me to learn the truth."

CJ considered the other brothers' expressions. They were keeping straight faces, looking somber for the occasion.

"Why did he wait so long in telling you this?" CJ asked before Darien had a chance. He knew it wasn't the proper protocol. Darien was the pack leader and he was asking the questions. But the words just slipped out before CJ could stop them. *Hell*.

Stanton switched his attention to CJ. "He and

Warren had a falling-out some years ago. Dad wanted to make amends with him. They did, but then they were busy with their own lives and didn't speak for a number of years. He didn't know the man's name, but Dad said Warren had trouble with one of the members of the pack."

Darien folded his arms. "So you don't have anything to really back up your claim."

"Dad was dying and then we had to clear up his estate. But he mentioned that Warren had been seeing a woman, another man was involved, and both were with your pack. Then Warren ended up missing, presumed dead. Their sister disappeared shortly after that. Dad thought she probably learned the truth about what happened. We've been busy with a current TV production and couldn't get away until now. Then we learned that someone had bought the hotel that rightfully belonged to our family and renovated it. When we heard it was the MacTires, we wanted to see what they knew about our aunt and uncle's disappearances."

Darien opened his mouth to speak, but CJ frowned, irritated to hell with the lies Stanton was telling, since he couldn't back any of it up, and asked, "Why would Laurel and her sisters know anything about your aunt and uncle when they only moved in six months ago?"

"Their *aunt* was at the root of all the trouble." Stanton folded his arms across his chest. "She was the woman who caused the disagreement between Warren and another male in your pack."

His brothers both nodded.

"What aunt?" CJ asked, getting a sickening feeling in the pit of his stomach. This was why Laurel and her sisters had been so hesitant to socialize with the pack before now. They believed one of the pack members had also made their aunt disappear.

Stanton snorted. "So they didn't tell you that they're looking into the disappearance of their aunt? Did you think they truly cared about the old hotel?"

Yeah, CJ knew they did. "Like you do? They renovate old hotels and make them profitable. That's their business." He couldn't help but defend the sisters. They'd proved that they knew what they were doing in that regard. Their aunt was another story, and he wanted to hear from Laurel herself what *that* was all about. If she and her sisters were looking into the disappearance of their aunt, he would do everything he could to learn the truth and help them find closure. The same as the rest of the pack would.

"So I ask you again what you're doing here," Darien said, finally taking over the discussion again. "Are you seeking to learn what happened to your aunt and uncle, or were you hoping to take over the hotel?"

Stanton sat back in his chair and smiled a little. His brothers were watching him, waiting for his response.

CJ was certain they had discussed the matter among themselves and knew just what their brother had planned to say.

"I hadn't even considered that Silver Town Inn might rightfully be ours, at first."

CJ didn't believe the man for a moment. "So you wait until the MacTire women renovate the hotel, then step in and claim it's yours? You can't. We had to pay the taxes on it. The pack owned it until they sold it to the MacTire women."

"I suppose we would have to pay them fair compensation for fixing up the place. But we never authorized their work on the hotel, so I'm not sure something like that would be legally binding. We might have just decided to tear it down and rebuild."

Darien shook his head. "You're missing the point. The hotel isn't yours to claim. If the MacTires hadn't already bought it, you might have been able to buy it, but we have town ordinances against building anything new that doesn't fit in with the look and feel of the historical district. The hotel is part of our heritage," Darien said. Which meant he wouldn't approve anything else they designed, and everyone in the pack would vote Darien's way.

"Your heritage? And that includes murder." Stanton arched his brows.

"Inconclusive. If you have some evidence, I'd love to see it."

"In good faith, we would be willing to pay for some material cost—within reason," Stanton said, referring to the hotel again.

"You would have to prove you are indeed related to the brother and sister, and that the property had been left to your father," Darien said. "And that you have a receipt for paying the taxes on the property for all those years."

CJ smiled a little.

Stanton narrowed his eyes at Darien. "So you're trying to say we're not entitled? Hell." Then he straightened a little under Darien's scrutiny. "One or more of your pack members had to do with their disappearances. We'll prove it, and that the property belongs to us. I'm sure we can find tax receipts for the property."

"As long as you don't break any laws or create problems for our pack members, you're welcome to try," Darien said.

But CJ was certain Stanton would attempt to cause trouble for them.

"What I don't understand is how your father, who was estranged from his brother, would know that Warren was seeing a woman in our pack and having trouble with a male pack member over it," Darien said.

"They talked right before he disappeared."

"Here? Your father came to see him here?"

"I don't know for sure."

"And your father's name?" Darien asked.

"John Wernicke."

"Okay, and you're from…?"

"Raleigh, North Carolina."

"And your dad died there two weeks ago?"

Trevor was taking notes, CJ realized.

"Correct."

"Now that we know why you're here, more or less," CJ said, "you don't still want to stay at the hotel, do you? I'm certain the management will refund your money and you can go about your business."

"Of course we want to stay there," Stanton said. "It's a shame we have to pay for the rooms when we by rights should be the real owners of the hotel—but we'll remedy that soon. If that's all, gentlemen, we have a long day ahead of us tomorrow. Oh, and do we have your permission to run as wolves where your pack runs? We don't want to be chased down again as if we were common criminals." Stanton tilted his chin up a bit.

Darien bowed his head a little bit in agreement. "I will permit it and let the rest of the pack know that you are allowed to run in our territory."

"Thank you."

Stanton and his brothers rose from their seats. "See you tomorrow at the grand opening." Jake quickly escorted them outside to their van.

Darien directed his comment to CJ. "Ask Laurel to join us, will you?"

CJ hurried out of the room but practically ran into Lelandi and Laurel as they headed for the conference room.

Lelandi said, "Now that the Wernicke brothers have had their say, Laurel wants to talk to you all about the disappearance of her aunt."

"Why didn't you tell me about your aunt? Or tell any of us? Darien? Lelandi? Before tonight?" CJ asked, driving Laurel home in what had become a blinding snowstorm, the windshield wipers barely clearing the glass before it was covered again. Everything was coated in white—the road, the trees, and every space in between.

"I'm sorry, CJ. I know you're angry with me now. But how could we tell anyone why we were here?"

"I'm annoyed that we had to learn the truth from the Wernicke brothers. Why couldn't you have told us?"

"Anyone in the pack could have made her disappear! Who could we have trusted?"

"Even me?" He let out his breath. "Okay, I get it. You don't know us that well, so it's easy to see how you would be wary of any of us. Sure, pack loyalty means a lot to us. But if anyone had murdered your aunt, that person would pay the price, no matter how many years have passed."

He paused, hating to tell her anything about his father's misdeeds. What if she thought that he or his brothers might turn out to be like their father? But given the circumstances, he thought it was important to tell her before she learned about it from someone else. "You might have heard that my father, Sheridan, was sheriff of Silver Town until a couple of years ago."

"My mother said he looked into her allegations that her sister died, but there was nothing to it. And that he died a while back, so we couldn't even question him."

CJ was glad that Darien hadn't told the sisters what Sheridan had done. He wanted to be the one to tell her.

"Lelandi said that he wanted to tear down the old hotel."

CJ frowned. He'd never heard his father say that. "Are you sure? I guess if Lelandi knew, then it was for certain. I never heard him say that. Not that we were real close. My dad always felt as though he should have been the pack leader. The pack decided otherwise."

"Darien seems like a fair leader."

"He is. But my dad was disgruntled about it. I've got something to tell you about my father. It doesn't reflect on me or my brothers, but I just want you to know in case you hear about it from others. I'm glad that no one has mentioned it so that I could share this with you, since he was my father."

CJ explained that his father had murdered Darien's first mate because she betrayed the pack by having an adulterous affair. There had been more to it than that. CJ felt for now that was enough to explain without overwhelming her with the details of all the people who had been involved in the murder. "Darien was forced to fight my father to the death. My brothers and I left the pack after that and only recently returned. My father was wrong in doing what he did. But it's no reflection on my brothers and me."

He waited to hear what Laurel had to say, hoping that she wouldn't see him as anything like his father had been.

They were still only about halfway to her house when she shouted, "Stop the truck."

He was afraid she meant to bolt from him. He opened his mouth to object, because he wasn't letting her out here to make her way home on her own in the wilderness in the middle of the snowstorm.

"I saw the ghost wolf! Stop the truck!"

He couldn't believe it. He'd been concentrating on the blowing snow and trying to make out the edges of the road in the low visibility. Certain she really hadn't seen anything, he pulled off onto the shoulder, hoping that no one would hit his truck. She immediately threw open the truck door, slammed it shut, and took off running into the woods.

Hell! CJ put on his truck's emergency flashers, jumped out of the vehicle, slammed the door, and raced after her. "Wait up!"

"Shh," she said, casting him an annoyed look.

What? Did she believe the ghost wolf could hear him and would shy away from them? Seriously? He was jogging next to Laurel as she ran through the powder when she did the unexpected—fell face-first in a pile of snow.

"Are you okay?" He hurried to help her up, worried she'd broken a bone or twisted an ankle.

She was breathing hard, turning away from him and looking for any sign of the wolf. "Yes," she whispered. "My boot caught on a tree root buried in the snow. But I'm all right."

"What exactly did you see?"

She was peering at the snow, looking for tracks. They could tell something had moved through the snow, but it was too deep and powdery for anything to run along the top of it and leave paw prints. It could have been a member of the pack taking a wild run in the snow.

"Did you see what the wolf looked like?"

"It was white."

He frowned. "Not an Arctic wolf."

"Or a black wolf whose color has changed. Most wolves become gray or grayish with advancing age. But sometimes black wolves will turn practically white in just a short while."

He'd never seen a white wolf in the area. "Or ghost wolf?"

"In the mix of snow, that's what it looked like."

"Okay, did it have shorter ears and legs than a gray wolf? Do you think it was a male or a female?"

"How would I know that? I only saw a glimpse of it before it took off running. And the wolf's legs were buried in the snow like ours are. You took too long to stop the truck, and I couldn't reach the wolf fast enough. Not as a human, anyway." She looked up at him, hopeful.

He raised his brows. "You want to try to track it in the blizzard?"

"Is this where the ghost wolf is always seen?"

"Supposedly this area, yes."

"Then why not?"

"As wolves or humans?"

She smiled a little at him. Then began to strip.

He had to ask. But this time he watched her as she stripped in front of him. He was only human after all and a lot wolf. Her breasts were mouthwatering as her rosy nipples puckered in the cold. Much like his were as he hurried to strip. Long, shapely legs, and lots of curves. And the curly red hair between her legs was the same color as the curls blowing around her shoulders as she called on the shift and in the next instant turned into her wolf.

He followed suit, before she raced off without him.

As they ran as wolves, he followed her lead, watching their surroundings, looking for anything else unusual, besides a ghostly white wolf. True to the nature of a ghost wolf—if it existed and the wind blowing the snow hadn't played tricks with Laurel's vision—he smelled no sign of a wolf.

They had been searching for the ghost wolf for about an hour when they came to a dirt road that led to the river where some of their people parked and hauled their canoes, rafts, or other small boats into the water during the summer. What he saw gave him pause. Fresh tire tracks in the snow, although the blowing snowflakes would soon obliterate them.

Their white ghost wolf was driving a truck? They checked the area further but didn't find anything, ghost or otherwise. Still, someone else might have parked here and run. Then again, the ghost wolf could have just vanished, as ghostly creatures were known to do.

He let out his breath in a frosty mist and glanced at Laurel, who was still sniffing around at the tire tracks. She finally lifted her head and looked at him.

Then she nodded, as if she knew what he was thinking. Time to give up the search.

It took a while to locate their clothes because the fresh snow had already buried them. He shifted and shook out her clothes first, then located his own and was digging them out when she began to dress.

"Brrr, cold."

He smiled. "Bet this is nothing like living in Florida in the winter."

"It gets chilly there, and we have to wear coats. But no, nothing like this."

"So what do you think about the ghost wolf?"

"I think he's driving a pickup truck."

Chapter 9

TRUDGING BACK TO CJ'S TRUCK THROUGH THE DEEP snowdrifts, Laurel stumbled again. CJ reached out and grabbed her hand to help her through them. He thought she must be worn out after the long day and the ghost-wolf run.

He was trying to show his thoughtfulness and gallantry and, more, to ensure she knew he was truly interested in a courtship. What if the only reason the sisters were here was to learn about their aunt, and once they solved that mystery, they'd sell the place and leave?

He had every intention of proving to Laurel that she would love it here with him and the pack. When they reached his truck, they climbed in and he drove off, thinking again about the ghost wolf, pondering how Laurel had come to the conclusion that it was white. Probably the snow had made the gray wolf appear that way.

"I'm glad it wasn't a real ghost wolf." Laurel pulled off her gloves and warmed her hands in front of the truck's heater vents. "I'd much prefer that supernatural sightings be explained away."

Like the letter *C* on the wall, CJ thought. "Agreed." He didn't want to bring up the issue of his father again, if she didn't want to talk about it further. He was fine with that.

She suddenly said, "Why would your father have wanted the hotel torn down? Maybe because the hotel harbored evidence that linked him to another, well, crime?"

CJ couldn't believe it! How could she come to that conclusion? "No." He hadn't meant to answer so harshly, but he couldn't believe she'd pull accusations out of thin air without shoring them up with real evidence.

"Lelandi said that your father told Darien he thought the hotel should be torn down because it was an eyesore," she reminded CJ.

CJ had to agree that, given the circumstances, it could sound that way. But still, it was a stretch.

Not knowing what to say, CJ drove the rest of the way to her house in silence, then parked when they arrived. He cut the engine and turned to her. "What exactly are you thinking?" He was afraid that the news he'd shared about his father was finally sinking in.

She glanced out the window.

"I'm sorry, but I wanted to tell you about my father because everything else was being discussed. I don't believe he had anything to do with any other murder. That happened to be a special circumstance. It all had to do with the leadership of the pack. Which wouldn't apply to your aunt's disappearance."

Her gaze returned to his, her jaw steeled. "What if something else was going on? And it had been just as important to him as running the pack? Couldn't this change everything? What if your father was involved in this too? Sometimes a catalyst causes a person to be implicated in a violent crime and it's a onetime occurrence. But what if the first murder that person committed wasn't actually his first? And he'd gotten away with it. He could do it again. What if he did such a great job of concealing the crime that no one ever learned the truth? Maybe he continued to kill and still didn't get caught, but then the new situation presented itself, and he did it again. Only this time he was exposed."

"You're talking about my father." CJ couldn't help but be irritated. He'd been devastated to learn about his father's involvement in the murder. He didn't want to believe his father had murdered anyone before that. But it bothered him to learn that his father had wanted the hotel torn down.

Laurel stared out the windshield. "My mother talked to some of the people who lived near the hotel, and they said my aunt had never worked or lived there. And your father, as sheriff, corroborated that."

"How do you know that she worked there for certain then?"

Laurel explained to him about the postcard. "In the basement in one of the maids' rooms, a small letter *C* was carved into the baseboard, as if the maid claimed the room as her own. Maybe she'd been a maid."

"So management lied about her working there." He pondered that for a moment, then thought about what else she'd said. "So she was seeing someone? That's what Stanton said. It sounded like a love triangle." His father and Warren Wernicke maybe? CJ ground his teeth.

"Yes, but Aunt Clarinda didn't give a name. My mother wondered if the man was a mated wolf, or if he was human and she didn't want my mother to know."

"If he was human, would your aunt have turned him if he had returned the affection?"

"My mother thought she would. Aunt Clarinda was

often reckless. She hadn't liked their father's rule and had run off on her own when she was just a teen."

"All I can say is that we'll do everything we can to learn the truth. I wanted to tell you about my father's previous crimes, but maybe in doing so, I've caused you to worry about more when there's no reason to, and for that, I'm truly sorry."

"No, thank you for telling me. Thanks for taking me skiing and for the run tonight. And"—she smiled a little—"for humoring me and helping me to track down the ghost wolf. I had fun, but I'm exhausted. The business with the Wernicke brothers is troubling too. It's just a lot to absorb."

He started to get out of the truck to walk her to the house, but she shook her head. "I'll see myself inside. Thank you."

She was out of the truck in a flash, stalking through the snow on the stone path that led to her front door. She waved good night, and he waited until she had gone inside and turned on a light.

He'd wanted this night to end differently. A kiss, maybe sharing a drink—and something more to eat because he was hungry again.

If his father had something to do with Laurel's aunt's disappearance, CJ didn't think he would ever fully come to grips with what Sheridan Silver had done.

———

Later CJ stood in his kitchen, trying to decide what to make to eat, not really caring about the kind of food when all he wanted was to make the situation right with Laurel. He yanked out the leftover spaghetti and stuck it in the microwave. His cell phone rang and he pulled his phone out of his pocket. Brett. CJ thought he knew what his brother's call was all about. "Hey, Brett…"

"Yeah, Brother. Are you free to share a meal with me? Or are you *busy*?"

CJ would have loved to have been busy in the way his brother meant. "I'm free."

"I'm on my way."

CJ suspected Brett had gotten word about the situation with the Wernicke brothers and the MacTires' missing aunt. Knowing Brett, CJ thought his brother wanted to make sure things were all right.

Feeling a bit cheered that he'd have Brett to talk to, CJ thought again of Laurel and how she was all alone. He wished her sisters were home already. Better yet, he wished that he and she hadn't ended the night on such a sour note. He took a deep breath, wishing he could say something that would make her feel better. But until they learned who had done what and resolved the issue with the Wernicke brothers, he didn't feel he could say anything to her that would help.

He pulled the container of leftover spaghetti out of the microwave and put it back in the fridge.

Within twenty minutes, Brett was at CJ's house. CJ swore his brother was over here more than he was at his own house. Though he loved Brett's company and was glad for it, especially tonight.

"How's it going with Laurel?" Brett asked as he brought in groceries—steaks, pumpkin pie, whipped cream, and a premade salad.

At least his brother always brought food. And it was good food. Though when CJ saw the pumpkin pie, he thought of how he had missed sharing some of that seven-layer chocolate cake with Laurel.

"I thought I'd come over tonight because you'll be busy tomorrow night and for however long it will be before the Wernicke brothers give up their ploy to avenge their supposed aunt and uncle's deaths and take over the property."

"Even if the hotel had been willed to them, they lost the right to it when the family abandoned it and the pack had to pay the taxes on it," CJ said.

"Unless they decide to lawyer up and fight, or use their TV program. They might still try to claim the hotel is haunted or do anything else they can to ruin it for the women. Post bad reviews, and so on. Hell, they might even air a segment on the theft of their hotel with speculation about the tryst that ended in their aunt and uncle's murders. I don't trust them."

CJ didn't want to worry about what-ifs, but he couldn't stop thinking about Stanton Wernicke's claims. CJ knew the sisters would be devastated if they had to give up the hotel due to bad publicity. Even if they planned to leave, he knew they hadn't intended to uproot this soon. And for now, the hotel was their special endeavor, not the Wernickes'.

The rest of the pack members were delighted to have the sisters living here. He doubted anyone would feel the same way about the brothers. Taking the property from the MacTires would be an underhanded thing to do under any circumstances, after the women had worked so hard to renovate it.

He had to consider how he'd feel if he and his brothers had just learned the property was theirs and... Hell,

he was certain his brothers would feel as he did. The hotel belonged to the sisters.

"I don't know. We'll have to deal with it *if* it comes to pass."

"What would you do if you learned the hotel was ours?"

Brett started cooking the steaks and grinned at him. "Hell, that's easy."

CJ wondered what Brett had in mind, but he knew from his brother's expression that he was not taking this seriously.

"Move in with them. I definitely wouldn't take over or kick them out of the place."

CJ shook his head. "If you moved in, they'd be moving out in a heartbeat."

Brett laughed. "Besides, before they can do anything about anything, you'll most likely be setting up housekeeping with Laurel. After that, her sisters are sure to fall for a couple of the rest of us lucky wolves. Even if they don't have a hotel, they won't be going anywhere."

"You know they will leave," CJ said gloomily. "This is their livelihood. Like writing for the newspaper has brought you lots of enjoyment, and solving crimes or keeping people safe has been the best thing for me. Take their business away from them and they're sure to leave. There's nothing we can do about what the ladies decide to do, but we can help them as much as possible and hope they stay."

CJ pulled out plates and began to set the table.

Brett flipped the steaks. "I heard about the situation with the aunt."

CJ tore off some paper towels for napkins and

frowned. "That's why they were being so standoffish with the pack for so long."

"That changed today though," said Brett.

"How?" CJ asked. After he had mentioned their father, Laurel had put on the brakes big-time with him.

"Hell, Brother. The news about you being on the slopes with Laurel and then running with her early this evening is all over the pack by now."

"That was before we knew she and her sisters were here because of the disappearance of their aunt."

"You didn't have anything to do with it. She's not going to blame you if one of our pack members had something to do with her aunt's disappearance."

"That was before I talked to her about Dad."

Brett stared at him in disbelief, then let out his breath. "Ah, hell, CJ. You should have let sleeping dogs—"

CJ gave him an annoyed look.

"All right. I guess if I were in your shoes, I would have told her too. Just to clear the air and ensure that if she learned from someone else, it wouldn't be a sticking point."

"Well, it *is* a sticking point."

Brett raised his brows.

CJ served the salad and brought out a couple of beers while Brett loaded the T-bone steaks on their plates.

"Okay, so tell me what's wrong between you and Laurel."

This was the part that CJ had been avoiding. He really didn't want to tell his brother what the ladies believed. "It was going great, I thought, until I had to tell Laurel about our father."

Brett took his seat at the table and so did CJ.

"Okay, we're back to that."

"Yeah. I had to tell her what happened to him because I knew, with everything else going on, she was sure to learn about it. Then she might think I was trying to cover up his ill deeds. The problem was that Laurel's mother spoke with our dad because he was serving as sheriff. Along with the hotel owner, our dad denied that Clarinda had even worked there."

"Wait, what if she hadn't? How had they come to that conclusion?"

CJ explained about the proof they had.

"Oh. Okay, so learning that our father was a murderer didn't sit well with her, I gather."

"Hell, she thinks Dad might have had something to do with her aunt's disappearance too," CJ said.

Brett stopped cutting into his meat and looked up at CJ. Apparently Sheridan had lied to Laurel's mother. So what else might their father have been involved in?

"Hell."

"Agreed."

Brett continued to cut up his steak but didn't say anything for a moment.

In the silence, CJ was processing all that he had learned in the past couple of years about their father's deceitfulness.

"Maybe Dad didn't know Clarinda worked there," Brett said. "What if she didn't join the pack and was stuck working at the hotel all the time? She might have disappeared before he even knew she worked there. On the other hand, Dad didn't have a perfectly honorable track record, as we learned too late. Laurel has nothing to go on but a few scanty records and a whole lot of inconsistencies."

"It's possible he didn't know about Clarinda, of

course. I'd considered that too. But given his previous history, Laurel has good reason to suspect that he might have been involved in more shenanigans."

"Hell. Have you talked to Eric or Sarandon about this?"

"No. She just mentioned it tonight, so I haven't had a chance to talk to anyone but you."

Brett sat back in his chair. "Why don't we wait to tell them for the time being? If Dad was involved in the cover-up of Clarinda's disappearance or—God forbid— worse, I don't want to say anything to Eric or Sarandon until we know for certain."

"Agreed. We've all taken the news about his criminal activities hard enough. I'd rather know something definite before we discuss it with them. I only mentioned it to you because you're looking into this like I am, and you need to know everything I do."

"Darien already has a number of us working on the case."

CJ frowned at his brother. "Why didn't he tell me? I should be working on it too." Though CJ planned to do that every chance he got.

"He doesn't have to tell you. He knows you're working the inside job. You're the key, the most important person in investigating this matter. You have access to the sisters and the opportunity to learn everything they know about their aunt's disappearance. You have free rein at the hotel when everyone's sleeping and can explore it for clues to your heart's content. You'll be keeping an eye on the Wernicke brothers, and who knows? During a conversation with one of them, you might learn something that will prove they're frauds. Whatever. But you are at the heart of all of it."

CJ hadn't seen it that way, but he agreed. "So I take it that you're researching more about the hotel for your newspaper article."

"And the disappearances of the Wernicke brothers' aunt and uncle and the MacTires' Aunt Clarinda. Darien has both Trevor and Peter using their law enforcement background to dig deeper. They're questioning anyone who remembers anything that far back. Anything that might trigger a memory of something that seemed odd before the disappearances. Anyone who has a recollection of a woman fitting Clarinda's description who worked at the hotel. We'll solve it one way or another. Although Darien needs to be informed about everything that is going on, he also wants you to know what everyone else learns, since you might not be able to listen in on conference calls while you're watching the brothers."

"Okay, sounds like a good plan."

"Right. So I take it that this has become an obstacle in you getting to know Laurel better."

"It could work against me if we learn Dad was involved in the disappearance of her aunt or a cover-up, yes." CJ took a swig of his beer, then asked the question that had been on his mind since Brett first told him he was coming over tonight. "Have you ever seen the ghost wolf?" They'd never talked about it, so he really didn't know if his brothers had seen it or not.

Brett finished his beer and got them another cold one. "So, I take it you saw it?"

"No."

"I haven't seen it. It's just an old wives' tale. Parents told that story to their kids to spook teens that were learning to drive, so they'd watch their driving and not run into a wolf on the road. Why mention it now? Are you sure you haven't seen it?"

"No. But when we were driving back from Darien's place after the meeting with the Wernicke brothers, Laurel thought she saw it."

"The snowstorm has died down now, but it was going full blast there for a while, wasn't it?"

"Yeah."

"So it's easy to think you see something when there's nothing. I swear I've seen deer in the middle of a blinding snowstorm. I might have, or I might have just imagined it. I've never seen a wolf in that area while I've been driving. Then again, if one was running in that kind of weather, it would be easy to believe it was a ghost wolf and not the real thing."

CJ glanced out the dining room window and watched the snow falling in tiny flakes now.

"Well, don't you agree?" Brett asked.

"We went running after it in our wolf coats." CJ looked back at his brother, who was staring wide-eyed at him.

"You chased after a phantom gray wolf?"

"It was white."

"You saw it then? You said you hadn't seen it." Brett frowned. "An Arctic wolf? I didn't think you saw it."

"I didn't. That's what Laurel said. Some gray and some black wolves have been known to turn pure white. We don't see that as much with our *lupus garous* unless they're very old. But even traumatized wolves can turn white. I remembered reading about a gray wolf that had a leg injury and his coat began to turn white. When the injury was healed, the coat returned to its grayish-tan color. So it could be a regular-size gray wolf or a shorter-legged Arctic wolf, if Laurel really saw what she thought she did."

"Okay, wait. Back up a bit. You're coming up with an explanation for why a gray ghost wolf is white when you didn't even see it?"

"Laurel saw it. And we chased after it."

Brett smiled a little, and CJ was certain his brother thought he was just buying into Laurel's flight of fancy because he liked her.

"The ghost left tracks?"

"A trail. The snow was too deep for the wolf to leave paw prints in the snow."

"Did you smell the wolf?"

"No. It's a ghost wolf." CJ smiled.

Brett laughed. "But it left tracks as it plowed through the snow."

"Right. When we reached a dirt road that led to the river, we found fresh tire tracks. Really fresh. Despite how much the snow had been blowing, the flakes hadn't yet filled up the tire tracks."

"The ghost wolf was driving a car." Brett took another swallow of his beer and smiled.

"Pickup truck, by the look of the tire treads."

"Did you tell Darien?"

"Are you kidding? Look at how *you* reacted."

Brett shook his head. "You know what Darien is like. He isn't me. He's the pack leader and he takes everything seriously. You never know… He might have learned something that ties into what you've seen that he hasn't shared with everyone."

"I didn't see anything but the tire tracks. Laurel

might have imagined seeing a white wolf in the snow. Someone in our pack might have been out fishing or running and left just before we arrived. He might have been running near the road and took off into the woods when he saw my truck, thinking we were human."

"I'd still call Darien and let him know what happened. Do you really think that Laurel imagined seeing the wolf?"

"No. We followed a trail and it disappeared in the vicinity of the truck's tire marks. I think she saw a wolf."

"Not really a ghost wolf then," Brett said. "But we don't have any pure white wolves in the pack."

"I know."

"When you saw the Wernicke brothers, they weren't white wolves, were they? I never had a chance to ask Jake or Darien what they looked like."

"One was black. I'm thinking it was Stanton because he seems to be the leader, and he was in the lead there. The other two were gray. I really think the snow colored Laurel's vision," CJ said. "If the wolf was old, he couldn't have moved as fast as he did. Though it took me a little while to park the truck, then get out, strip, shift, and take chase. Do you really believe the ghost wolf story was just told to frighten teens into watching their driving on the country roads?"

"That's what I've always heard. Nobody I've discussed it with has ever seen the ghost wolf or a naked woman. So I don't believe she exists. It's just a situation like you and Laurel experienced. A wolf out for a run that's spotted by a passerby driving in a snowstorm. Have you seen anything else? Anything to do with the hotel, beyond the situation with the paint cans being moved?"

"A letter *C* appeared on one of the walls in the main room. I've painted over it a number of times already, but it keeps reappearing."

"Huh. Any reason for it?"

"Your guess is as good as mine. Oh, one other thing. Did Dad ever talk to you about wanting the hotel torn down?"

"Not that I recall. He didn't like it sitting there, as dilapidated as it was becoming. He said it was an eyesore. But I don't remember him ever saying he thought it should be demolished. Darien wouldn't have gone along with it. He's the reason we have Victorian Days. He loves the town and everything about its history. If our dad had wanted to tear it down, even petitioned for it, Darien would have said no."

"I agree. Which is probably why, if Dad wanted that, he never said anything to the rest of us."

They finished their meal, and then Brett began to cut up the pumpkin pie, topping it with whipped cream as CJ cleared the dishes and loaded them in the dishwasher.

"Okay, so about Laurel. You're not going to let this stop you from getting somewhere with her, are you?" Brett asked.

CJ snorted.

"I'm serious. She only has eyes for you, and we all know you are totally hung up on the woman. So…how are you going to resolve this with her and make it right?"

Damned if CJ knew.

Chapter 10

ALONE IN THE HOUSE, LAUREL FELT REALLY ISOLATED. Even though their home had a feel-good aura, she hadn't realized how lonely it would be with her sisters away. She felt like a wolf missing her pack mates.

The wind was blowing and howling eerily. She considered the chocolate cake still sitting in its box on the kitchen counter and realized she'd intended to invite CJ in for a slice or two after their run.

As much as she loved chocolate and as inviting as it looked, she didn't want to have a slice by herself when she'd intended to share it with him.

Feeling drained, she finally retired to bed, pulling her handmade quilt up to her chin. She'd seen Brett taking pictures of the lights on the hotel earlier, a little after CJ left, but then Brett had disappeared around the front of the hotel again. She'd almost wanted to invite him in for cocoa and a piece of cake to thank him for helping to promote the hotel in the paper, but she didn't want him thinking she was interested in him like she was interested in CJ. And that made her feel disconcerted about CJ all over again.

She knew she'd upset him by mentioning that his father could have been involved in her aunt's disappearance or the cover-up. But she hadn't been able to let go of what CJ had revealed about his father. It all added to her unease about what had happened to her aunt. She'd felt she had to say what she thought could have happened.

Because she felt something for CJ, she didn't want to hide the truth of what she'd been feeling. Still, she felt bad about suggesting that his father could have been involved in her aunt's disappearance and that her comments had upset CJ. She should have kept her thoughts to herself and let the truth come out on its own.

She rolled from her back to her side and stared at the clock. She couldn't sleep. Tomorrow was the big grand opening, and now she was even more worried about the Wernicke brothers and what they might find, or how they might try to make her and her sisters' lives more difficult. She closed her eyes, her thoughts drifting back to kissing CJ, his warm, sensuous lips pressed against hers, his hard body tight against her body. Thinking about playing with him in the snow as wolves brought a smile to her lips. He was so good-natured to have taught her how to ski. And he hadn't dismissed her concerns when she wanted to chase down a ghost wolf that hadn't been a ghost wolf at all.

After what she'd said to him about his father, CJ probably wished he'd never kissed her or shown her any affection. Unable to stop feeling bad about it, she groaned and stared at her cell phone sitting on the bedside table. Would he be awake? Annoyed if she called him? With every intention of apologizing, she lifted the phone off the table. Thankfully, Darien had given her all the key pack members' cell numbers in case of an emergency. Which was something else nice about belonging to a pack.

This wasn't an emergency, but she couldn't sleep,

and if she didn't make amends with CJ, she'd never get any rest. She hoped he wouldn't be sound asleep and become further annoyed with her for calling him at this late hour.

She poked at his name on the phone and a tired male voice said, "Hello?"

"I'm so sorry about this evening. I shouldn't have said what I did—"

"Who is this?"

Ohmigod, in her tired state she must have punched a different Silver's phone number.

"Laurel?" There was a definite hint of a smile in the masculine voice.

The trouble was the Silver brothers and cousins all sounded similar. She had no idea which one she had called. Because of her slight Irish accent, he could guess it was her or one of her sisters. And since she was the only one here at the moment, it had to be her.

"Sorry, wrong number. I was calling Ezra Holcomb. I guess that's not you." She ended the call, her whole body warming with embarrassment as she snuggled under the covers and felt like a complete idiot.

She set her phone on the table. Sheesh, teach her to just leave well enough alone. What if it was one of the married Silver brothers? Then she had disturbed his wife too. Or one of the other Silver bachelor males, and he had the notion she was actually getting friendly. No, whoever it was wouldn't think that because she'd said she was apologizing and—oh brother, she'd never get to sleep at this—

Her cell phone rang. She stared at it, hoping it wasn't whoever she had just called. Maybe it was one of her sisters.

"Hello?" she said.

"It's CJ. Are you still wide awake?"

"Who did I call by accident?" She wanted to clear that up right away.

"Darien."

She groaned.

CJ chuckled. "He was worried. He thought it was you and that you meant to call me because I'm right above his name on the list of numbers. Unless you were really trying to call Ezra Holcomb."

She shook her head at herself.

"Is everything okay over there?" CJ sounded so nice, masculine, and comforting. She wished they'd ended tonight on a better note. "Darien was concerned because you're alone and thought maybe someone was giving you some trouble."

"Oh, no. I'm okay." She hadn't thought anyone would think she was in trouble. That made the situation even worse. "I'm fine, but…I'm so sorry about saying your dad might have had anything to do with my aunt's disappearance. I shouldn't have said anything unless I had evidence one way or another. It was totally uncalled for."

"It's all right, Laurel. He might have. We just don't know. It's important to consider any option. If he's a suspect, we need to investigate that angle further. You were perfectly right in bringing it up."

"I upset you."

"The whole issue pertaining to him has been upsetting. But none of us are burying our heads in the sand concerning his complicity if he was also involved in this."

"I didn't want to make you feel bad."

"I'm fine. I talked to Brett about it, and he's doing more investigating. Did you want some company?"

No. She needed to sleep, but what she would give to have him snuggled with her in bed at the moment.

"I'd be there in ten minutes, tops."

She smiled. She just bet he would. "I need to sleep. I just...couldn't."

"You sure you don't want me to come over? We could make a snowman in the garden, or one in front of the hotel for the guests' arrival tomorrow. Or we could build snow forts and have a snowball fight. Surefire way to wear you out and make you sleepy. Then we could have cocoa with marshmallows on top. And I've been dying to have a piece of that seven-layer chocolate cake. I can't quit thinking about it."

She laughed. He was serious! "If you're sure you're not upset over what I said to you earlier—"

"Not if you make it up to me. I'm getting dressed right now."

She chuckled. "It would be kind of cute making a snowman in front of the hotel for the celebration."

"Nothing would be better. I'll be right over."

She could hear him getting dressed in a hurry, slamming drawers, but he hadn't hung up on her yet.

She laughed. "All right. If my sisters knew what I ended up doing in the middle of the night before the opening, they'd want to commit me."

"We'll send them a picture."

"No way."

He laughed. "Be there in a few minutes."

She couldn't believe it. She was never this impulsive, but CJ really brought out the playfulness in her. More than anything, she did want to make it up to him. What better way to do so? She knew after they were done with this, she'd be able to sleep with a clear conscience.

She had barely dressed and made her way down the stairs when she saw a pickup's headlights as the truck pulled into the parking lot out back. She peered out the window to ensure it was just CJ.

He was slipping on a parka as he strode to the front door. She smiled at him. "I'm never this impulsive, I want you to know."

"Me either," he said, and she wasn't sure whether to believe him or not. But then maybe she brought out the playfulness in him too.

She pulled on a blue knit hat and her white parka and gloves, and then the two of them headed around the front of the hotel to begin building the snowman. "Oh, wait, I didn't think to get anything for the snow-man's face."

"I've got it all here, just in case we needed something." CJ patted his pocket.

It wasn't long before they were building a snowman. The Christmas lights on the hotel cast a diamond-like sheen over the front lawn where they were creating their snow art, and the old-time brass lanterns along Main Street added to the festive night with their garlands and red bows. "You look like you're experienced in the art of creating snowmen."

CJ added more snow to the base. "After a good snow-fall like this, we often have a snowman-building contest. Brett posts pictures in the paper and online, and the pack and anyone else interested votes on the best."

"And the winner receives?"

He stood back and watched to see what she was doing as she reshaped the snowman into something else.

"Hmm?" she asked.

The snowman wouldn't win any contests if it didn't look like a snowman. "The winner receives steaks on the house at the tavern."

"For...two?"

"For as many as it took to create the best snowman." He packed more snow on the base. She scooped more of it away and stacked it higher. They were definitely at cross-purposes on this project.

He began to watch what she was doing. And then he realized the shape the "snowman" was taking. Not so much a snowman as a snow sculpture—one wolf sitting ready to greet the hotel guests the next morning. It couldn't have been more perfect.

He brought more snow over, only this time he set it next to her, surprised to see her creating such a wonder. "I wouldn't think you'd ever have a chance to build a snowman where you lived."

"One of the hotels we renovated was in Minnesota. We haven't been there in many years, so we've gotten used to the hotter Florida climate. It'll take us some time to get used to the snowier weather. I guess we won't win any snowman contest though."

He continued to bring her snow as she formed the head: chin lifted, the wolf howling, calling the pack together. It was perfect for the welcoming tomorrow. He took a picture of her doing the finishing touches.

A car's lights, engine rumble, and tires slushing in the snow caught their attention. It slowed down as the driver looked at their creation and honked the horn with approval.

"John Hastings, owner of the hardware store and bed and breakfast." CJ waved at him as he passed them by on his way to the bed and breakfast.

"I wouldn't think anyone would be out this late."

"Are you kidding? We're wolves. I bet anything that Darien will change the contest tomorrow. Instead of being strictly for snowmen, it will be for snow sculptures."

"Would he do that? Doesn't seem fair to anyone else."

"I say Darien, but Lelandi will probably be the one with the final say in the matter. They know what everyone would like in the pack anyway, so no one will be upset with the changes. Believe me, when everyone sees this, you'll be the sure winner. Wolves trump snowmen any day."

She smiled. "But *we* did it. If you hadn't brought over all that snow, I'd still be moving handfuls over here. The wolf needs something more. Hold on. I've got it. Be right back."

CJ stepped back so he could take pictures of the wolf with the hotel all lit up as the backdrop. He was afraid if they had a lot of wind tonight, it might whip away some of the snow.

She was taking forever, he thought, but he reminded himself that she had to go all the way around the hotel, or through it, to reach her house out back. And no telling what she was looking for. Or how long it would take her.

When he finally saw her, she was smiling brightly, her green eyes sparkling, a green, blue, and red plaid wool scarf clutched in her gloved hands. "It is said our family worked for the Ross clan, but others say that when we left Ireland and moved to the Highlands of Scotland, we were part of the MacIntyre clan."

"Which do you believe about your roots?" He watched as she reverently tied the wool scarf around the wolf's neck. Now it had a human touch and wasn't just a wolf, but a *lupus garou* calling the pack together. If he didn't know any better, CJ would say she was reaching out to the pack, the symbolism so vivid with the wolf wearing her family's tartan. She and her sisters were welcoming the pack into their space, their home. They were ready to stay. If it wasn't for the problem with the Wernicke brothers.

"I believe that we are the son of the earth, the wolf, with allegiance to the pack."

His pack now, he hoped. "Let me take some pictures of you and the wolf."

"You should be in them too."

Another car slowed down to see their creation and CJ smiled. Then he realized it was Brett and waved to him to park.

"What are you doing?" Laurel asked.

"It's Brett. John must have called him to come by and get a really good shot of it before the wind gets to it. He can take a picture of both of us."

Grinning, Brett got out of his truck and pulled out his camera.

CJ was certain his brother would never have believed he'd be creating snow art after their conversation tonight. He was sure to suspect more was going on between CJ and Laurel.

"Bertha's husband called and said you needed me to take some pictures of the two of you. Says this has to be the winning snowman of the season." Brett motioned for the two of them to get closer to each other.

CJ was already standing right next to Laurel, and he couldn't get any closer.

"We need more energy in the picture," Brett said.

"Should we both get a snowball and throw it at him?" Laurel asked CJ.

"Great idea, only don't throw it," Brett said.

Laurel laughed. They posed a number of ways, including one where CJ wrapped his arms around Laurel and felt her trembling from the cold. He leaned down and kissed her nose, then turned to smile at the camera. "Okay, enough pictures. Laurel's cold and you'll take pictures all night long if we let you. You're as bad as Jake."

Brett smiled. "Night, folks." And then he quickly left them alone.

"Do you want some cocoa and cake before you go home?" she asked CJ.

"Yeah, it was the main reason I came over tonight."

She laughed, and he considered taking her hand as they walked back to her house, but he decided it was time to show her just how much he wanted to be with her, that there were no hard feelings about her comments concerning his father, so he wrapped his arm around her waist. He pulled her close—to warm her up too. She snuggled against him, showing she was just as happy with getting close to him.

He smiled down at her. She was the most beautiful she-wolf in the world: her nose, cheeks, and lips rosy from the cold, her red hair flying in the breeze, her green eyes bright and cheerful. And she didn't look the least bit sleepy. It was only a little after midnight.

"Do you have anything we could watch while we're drinking our cocoa and eating our cake?" He wasn't about to give up the opportunity to spend more quality time with her if she was willing.

"Yeah. How about something…Christmassy?" Laurel asked.

"Sounds good. What did you have in mind?"

She unlocked the door. "I have some oldies—but they're my favorites: *Miracle on 34th Street*, *It's a Wonderful Life*, *A Christmas Story*, *A Christmas Carol*, and some others. You choose, and I'll make the cocoa." She removed her jacket, took his, and hung them both on a coat rack.

"My brothers and I love *A Christmas Story*. It reminds us of ourselves when we were that age."

"Your father didn't want to give you a BB shotgun because you might shoot your eye out?"

"Nah, back in our day, we grew up with the real thing and used rifles for protection as young as eleven years of age."

"What part reminds you of your childhood then?"

"Doing something dumb when trying to please Dad and cursing when it went all wrong. Then Mom washing out our mouths with soap."

Laurel smiled at him as she mixed cocoa into the milk in the saucepan on the stove. "It's a wonder you didn't go blind."

He laughed. "Yeah. So we really love that movie. What about you? Which is your favorite movie and why?"

"Oh, I love all of them. Even *The Snowman*. You know, that animated one? I could watch it over and over again. I listen to the beautiful music and dream I have a snow buddy like him."

"Ah, but he was an only child and didn't have any brothers and sisters."

"Still, I missed the snow and building snow sculptures."

"Do you always create wolves? As good as you are at it, you must have made them before."

She stirred the cocoa. "A few times."

"Here I thought I was going to be teaching you how to make your first snowman."

Smiling, she poured cocoa into snowman-decorated mugs. "So what was your favorite gift ever for Christmas?" She sliced off a couple pieces of cake, put the mugs and plates on a red-and-green Christmas-tree platter, and carried it into the living room.

He wanted to say his best Christmas present was that Laurel would be here for the holidays. But what if she didn't remain here? What if he was moving a little too fast?

"My first rifle," he said instead.

She shook her head and set the tray on the coffee table. "Men and their guns."

"Having my first rifle was a sign of manhood. I helped hunt for food and protected my family. What about you? What was your favorite Christmas gift?"

She sat on the sofa and took a bite of her cake while he crossed the floor to start the movie.

"Well, a cloth doll Ellie made me. The button eyes were askew, the hair—her own real hair—shed everywhere until Missy was bald, but she was the most special doll I ever had."

"Do you still have her?"

"No. In one of our moves, a box was misplaced. I

swear Ellie got rid of it because she didn't want to be reminded of her earlier creations."

"Does she still make them?"

"No. She made one for Meghan, but she wasn't into dolls and it disappeared long before that. I think Ellie had something to do with her doll's disappearance too. She couldn't get to mine because I kept her with me always, until we moved that one time. Ellie likes to try new things all the time. She never really gets good at anything hobby-wise because she doesn't spend the time to learn any particular craft."

"What about yourself? Do you like to make things?"

"Snow wolves?"

"Yeah, that's sure to be a winner." He joined her on the couch.

"So what's the worst Christmas gift you ever got?" she asked.

"Chicken pox."

She laughed.

He loved hearing her laugh and seeing her happy. This was a much better way of ending the night. "No kidding. And then my brothers all came down with it, but after Christmas. I was the only one lying on the couch, itching to pieces and sicker than a wolf, while everyone was opening gifts."

"You poor thing."

"It was the worst Christmas ever for me. I was running a fever, and for the first time ever, I didn't even want to open gifts. What about you?"

"I don't think anything could be worse than chicken pox on Christmas, except for measles on Valentine's Day. I was dating a wolf, but he wouldn't come near me for Valentine's Day. And then I guess he felt guilty about it and couldn't face me, so he didn't come to see me for a couple of weeks after that. That was it for me. I never saw him again. My choice."

"Had he ever had measles before?"

"No."

"That's probably why he wouldn't get close to you. But the delay afterward, not acceptable. To tell the truth, I'm glad about it. You don't need to be hooked up with a cowardly wolf."

She smiled and settled back against the couch. "I guess my worst Christmas gift ever was the kitten that ran away."

"Kitten?" He pulled Laurel into his arms and got comfortable for the movie.

"Yeah. Meghan gave her to me, but the kitten was too wild and soon took off. I had the sweetest gray-and-white kitten, and then I didn't have her. Christmas gifts that run off are the worst."

He laughed and started the movie.

Snuggled together, they ate their cake, drank their cocoa, and watched the movie. Between the lateness of the hour and his unwillingness to let go of Laurel, he didn't even realize they'd both fallen asleep curled up together on the couch.

Until both their phones began to play tunes, letting them know they had calls coming in. And it was already well into the next day.

Chapter 11

"OH NO," LAUREL SAID, SOUNDING SHOCKED OUT OF her sleep, lifting her head, and looking at CJ. She grimaced. "I can't believe we fell asleep on the couch last night." She tried to get off him, and he shook his head.

"Creating snow wolves takes a lot out of a body."

She smiled.

He glanced at his phone and answered. "Eric. I'll get back to you in a minute." He wanted to get a cup of coffee before he had to deal with whatever his brother needed to discuss with him.

"My sister." Laurel sat up on the couch as she answered her call. "Hey, Ellie, what's up?" She pushed her hair behind her ear and leaned back against the couch, looking pleasantly dreamy.

He couldn't believe he'd fallen asleep on the couch with her and had held her in his arms all night long. He smiled a little. This was more like the way he had wanted to end last night's date.

"Coffee?" he mouthed. The time to just walk out of her home like none of this had happened had passed. And Laurel seemed unwilling to send him on his way. For which he was glad.

She nodded, then closed her eyes. But they popped right open, and he stayed to see what the matter was. "What? Okay, no, I haven't seen it." She looked up at CJ. "What do you mean, is he still here?" Laurel's face flushed a little red. "We're having coffee and breakfast before the hotel opening. Thanks. I'll tell him." She closed her eyes and groaned.

"What's wrong?" But he suspected someone had already told her sisters that he'd stayed the night with her.

"Well, the good news is we won the snow sculpture contest."

He smiled. "That's great news. We get to have a steak dinner on the house at Silver Town Tavern. And the bad news?"

She turned her phone toward CJ and showed him the screen. The picture Brett had featured online for everyone to see was the one where CJ was kissing her on the nose, and she was smiling up at him as they stood behind the wolf sculpture, the hotel lights glittering in the background.

He smiled.

"That's not all of it," she warned.

His smile faded. "Okay, let's hear it."

"Ellie got word that your vehicle has been parked outside the hotel all night long. The picture of you kissing me was shared online, which would have been innocent enough, except that she got word about the scene on the slopes too—like a couple dozen shots of us kissing as I was sitting on your lap—and then this other business showed we were still together late last night. Since you never moved your vehicle—"

"It's assumed we stayed together."

"That we *mated* each other."

He smiled again. "Cream in your coffee. Right?" He headed for the kitchen. "Word in a pack spreads quickly."

"We're *not* mated!"

"We could remedy that," he said, teasing her.

"I'm getting a shower. I can't believe this!" She left the couch and headed upstairs.

"We were tired. Perfectly innocent of any wrongdoing. Do you want me to fix us breakfast?"

"Cheese omelets. And ham. Hash browns too, if you can make them right. I already told my sister you were here for breakfast, so it's too late for you to sneak off now."

"I never sneak."

She chuckled. "I will *never* live this down."

Worried that he might have caused her sisters some concern over the matter, he frowned. "Your sisters aren't upset, are they?"

"No, I'd say 'shocked' would be a better word."

"Good." For that, he was glad. He didn't want them to be upset with him. If he was going to make this work with Laurel, he knew he had to have their approval. CJ's phone rang again. *Eric*. "Got to take the call from my brother this time before he drives over here to see if something's wrong."

"*Great*." But she didn't say it in a way that meant it was a cheerful "great." She disappeared into a bedroom upstairs.

"Yeah, Eric, what's up?" Though CJ was certain his oldest brother's call had all to do with him and Laurel.

"Darien called me early this morning to ask about you and Laurel."

CJ grinned. Talk about the word going viral in the pack. "Because of the picture of us?" He figured it was more like his staying overnight.

"And your truck was parked outside the hotel all night."

Pulling a couple of large baking potatoes out of

the fridge, CJ hated to break the news to him but did anyway. "We're not mated." He searched in a number of drawers and found a potato peeler and a grater.

Eric didn't say anything for a moment, and CJ realized he really must have believed they were and wanted to hear firsthand.

"Not even close," CJ added. He started to peel a potato.

"Well, hell, Brother, why not? Will you let Darien know? Lelandi's all ready to celebrate the big event and just wanted confirmation first. And next time, be more discreet, will you? Or maybe that was the plan."

"No, it wasn't in the plans. But sometimes life just happens." Though if it had worked out that way, CJ wouldn't have objected. "I've got to go."

"Yeah, you're roping off Main Street for the party and in charge of crowd control, right?"

"Uh, yeah, after I have breakfast with Laurel."

A pause followed. "So…you're still there. Good show." As if that meant CJ and Laurel still had time to mate. "Let me know first when it happens."

"When we have breakfast?" CJ wasn't about to take it for granted that Laurel and he would become mated wolves.

"When you become *mated* wolves. Talk later." Eric hung up on him.

Smiling, CJ finished peeling the second potato and began shredding them.

His phone jingled. He looked at the caller ID. Brett. CJ was certain that each of his brothers would get in touch with him now. He'd thought Eric would just tell Brett and Sarandon the news instead.

Before Brett could say anything, CJ set him straight.

"No, we're not mated. And why did you pick that particular picture out of all the ones you took to share online with the local residents?"

"Are you kidding? The pack members loved it! Not only was it a winner as far as the wolf sculpture with the newly renovated hotel decorated for Christmas as a backdrop, but there the two of you were looking as cute as could be—romance in the making. It was the perfect Christmas shot of two wolves in courtship. And the snow wolf howling in front of you, telling the pack the news? Nothing could have been better."

"What if posting the picture had upset Laurel?"

"Ha. She was looking up at you with such an adorable expression, no way could she object to it. I've been fielding questions all morning for you though. Anyway, I just had to hear it for myself. No mating yet."

"No, and you can share that. I'm sure she'd be glad for it."

"But it's happening, right?"

"No, at least not for now." Even though he'd met her months ago, he hadn't really begun to know her until more recently. Sure, he knew she was good at organizing, had her own way of doing things—as evidenced by the way she turned their snowman into a wolf—and was very take-charge. She was very tender and passionate and family oriented, and had a great sense of humor, which was especially good around him. Once she'd let her hair down, she was playful. He prized her for all of it.

"Okay, check with you later. But if you mate, let me know pronto."

"Eric wants to know first."

Brett laughed. "Make it a conference call."

CJ's phone beeped, letting him know he had another call coming in. The sheriff. "Got another call. Peter's calling."

"Probably wondering why you're not at work."

"I am. I'm supposed to be helping Laurel and her sisters out today. Only they're not here. Talk later." CJ answered the call. "Yeah, Peter. I'll be out in just a few minutes."

"Take your time. I've got enough people on it: volunteers and Trevor is coordinating efforts. If anyone learned I was impeding a mating between you and the she-wolf and didn't convince the sisters to stay here with our pack, I'd be out of a job."

CJ chuckled. He loved the pack, his job, the boss. And he couldn't have been gladder that he had returned to the pack when he did. "Okay, well as long as you're all right with it, I'll finish fixing breakfast for Laurel and me, and then I'll be out there helping with the crowds as they begin to gather."

"Breakfast, eh? Sounds good. See you in a bit."

CJ had started the omelets and then the hash browns, thinking this was the best day ever, when *Sarandon* phoned him. CJ groaned. He was glad Laurel was upstairs taking a long shower and getting ready for the big day.

"Hey, CJ. How the hell did you manage to get an invite to stay over at the MacTires' place—all night long?"

"I thought you were doing a guided tour in the woods this morning."

"Yesterday morning. I couldn't miss the grand opening or all the news about my youngest brother either. I leave you alone for a day and what happens?"

"Nothing."

Sarandon started laughing. "You're as good as mated."

CJ heard footsteps on the stairs. "Hey, got to serve up breakfast and then get to work. Talk to you later."

"Can't believe it. I'll see you at the opening or before."

"All right." CJ pocketed his phone and began slicing ham, then warmed it up.

"So…was that one of your brothers?" Laurel poured them both cups of coffee, then fixed mimosas: orange juice and champagne from the bottle leftover last night.

"Yeah, and the others all called."

She shook her head.

"And so did Peter."

"Oh." Laurel's expression turned to concern. "You're not late, are you? I should have thought of that. You must have work to do to get ready for all the people coming to town to celebrate. You're not in trouble with Peter, are you?"

"Nah, Peter said to enjoy our breakfast. And not to rush." CJ loved working with a wolf pack. Anywhere else he couldn't imagine being able to do such a thing.

"That was nice of him." She started setting the table. "So what did your brothers say?"

"That next time I should not leave my truck out in the open like that."

She snorted. "There's not *going* to be a next time. Or even if there was, which there *won't* be, my sisters will be home tomorrow and that would end any speculation."

He doubted it. She really didn't understand pack politics. Everyone wanted the ladies to stay here and run the hotel. That was much more likely if one of them mated a pack member.

"What if the Wernicke brothers cause real trouble for us?" She sat down to eat breakfast with CJ. And smiled at the way he had made the hash browns. "Oooh, these look so good." She took a bite. "Ohmigod, I haven't had fresh potato hash browns in forever. You're hired."

He laughed. "I'm all for it. As for the hotel, we'll come to that when we have to. For now, the Wernickes have to prove they had nothing to do with their aunt and uncle's disappearance. I'm curious about the furniture your sisters had to retrieve though." More than curious. He still couldn't imagine them taking off to get it and leaving Laurel to take care of everything here on her own.

She sighed. "It was my aunt's."

<hr>

Laurel didn't tell CJ anything more than that, figuring he'd assume it was important to them for sentimental reasons. She took another bite of her crispy hash browns, loving them. She could get used to having these on a daily basis—if CJ made them. They were so good.

He was drinking his coffee when he set it down and frowned at her. "Wait, the furniture has some importance, doesn't it? Like it proves something."

She sighed again. It was impossible to keep secrets around another wary wolf. Besides, she felt their relationship had gone too far not to trust him.

"We hope so. We won't know for certain until we get it home and can...really look it over good."

CJ was watching her, gauging her response. "There's something more to it than that, I suspect."

She nodded. "We thought our aunt's furniture might

have hidden compartments. We don't know for certain. Some old pieces of furniture were designed that way."

"Hell, that's great news, if something could be found to help solve the mystery."

It certainly gave her and her sisters hope that they might find some key piece of evidence that would aid them.

"Did you have any substantial reason to believe it might?"

"Only that the two pieces were special enough and our aunt said they were unique. She willed them to our mother, and they were to go to my sisters and me if my mother died early. Why would she will the highboy and chest to us unless they were special in some way?"

"Maybe just because it cost so much to have them made in the first place."

"True. It could be. But we're hopeful there's more to it than that."

They finished their breakfasts and began to clear away the dishes.

"Can I have a look at them when they arrive tomorrow?" he asked.

"Sure, but it might be really late by the time they get in."

"No problem. I'll be staying in the attic room and will hear your sister's car when it arrives. I can run over then as long as it's not inconvenient for you and your sisters."

She opened the dishwasher and began loading the dishes while he put away the food. "It should be fine. If they're too tired to stay up after the long drive, I can look over the furniture with you. Have you ever had any furniture that had hidden niches?"

"No. But it should be interesting to see. You said you have a postcard from your aunt. Could I see it?"

"Uh, sure." She left the kitchen to get the postcard out of the buffet drawer.

When she returned, CJ was scrubbing one of the skillets. She and her sisters always vied to cook the meal so they didn't have to clean the pots and pans. A wolf who did both? A dream made in heaven.

She drew close to him. "Thanks for the lovely breakfast *and* for washing the pans."

She tugged on his shoulder to get him to lean down a little, and when he obliged, she kissed him thoroughly, tasting the sweet mimosa on his lips and tongue, feeling the heat of their bodies collide, smelling his piney woods scent and male hotness.

"Hmm," she said, pulling away, then showing him the postcard.

He was looking at her, not at the card. "Did we have to stop?"

Already his eyes were darkened and more than intrigued.

She chuckled. "Yeah, we do. Opening day. Remember? I need to get over to the hotel."

This time he sighed and then looked down at the card. "Says Breckenridge, Colorado, and that's a picture of their town some years ago."

"Right, but it was mailed from here."

"Well, I kind of wondered. I didn't think anyone had made postcards of Silver Town. Though it's a great idea. Maybe Jake would like to do that. Especially now that the hotel is newly renovated. Let me finish washing this skillet, and I'll give the postcard a good look."

"Sure. I can wash the other one while you're looking

over the card." At least she only had to wash one pan and not both.

"Don't you dare. After all the trouble I caused you by staying over here last night, it's my treat." He finished cleaning the pan, rinsed it, and set it to the side to dry. "Come on and we'll look at this together." CJ eyed her as if he was afraid she'd start washing the pan while he wasn't looking.

"All right." She sighed dramatically. "Here I thought I'd found a great live-in cook and pot washer."

He laughed. "You can come to my home and that's just what I'll be."

She hadn't realized he was going to sit on the couch or anticipated his next move either. He pulled her onto his lap and looked over her shoulder at the postcard.

"See where she says she was staying here at the Silver Town Inn?"

"And hints at a romance."

She reread the note out loud, as if that would make it clearer and reveal something more. "Silver Town Inn. Miss you. Falling in love. Kiss girls for me. See you at Christmas. Love, C"

"And it's her handwriting?"

"Yes. Mom never doubted it."

"But she never came to see your mother for Christmas?"

"No. After Christmas, Mom came to see her at the hotel, to learn if anything was wrong. She had a sixth sense about her sister sometimes. She'd thought something was really wrong before this, and then she got this much brighter card and believed things were turning around for her sister. She could have thought Aunt Clarinda was just busy with a romance and hadn't had time to visit, but Mom worried that something had happened to her."

"So she came here, but no one your mother spoke to knew Clarinda worked at the hotel. And my dad, as sheriff, said the same thing. On the card, she doesn't say she actually worked here."

"Her furniture was in with the hotel furniture that was sold off at auction."

"How do you know that it was hers and not just part of the furniture that belonged to the estate?"

"She had sent Mom pictures of it. She was so proud of the highboy and blanket chest. It was the first time she'd bought any new furniture. She had to have been working at the hotel to earn both room and board and to afford to buy the furniture. She had no other income."

"Were the hotel and the home's furniture sold off at the same time?"

"Yes."

CJ didn't say anything more, and she wondered what he was thinking. "You think the furniture wasn't in the maids' quarters downstairs?"

"Here's a far-out thought. What if Clarinda was romantically involved with Warren Wernicke? What if she came here to rent a room as a guest while she was looking for work, and he became interested in her? She needed a job, but maybe he didn't want her to work for him because he didn't have romantic liaisons with his staff. Particularly because they most likely were wolves. Or maybe he already had all the maid staff he needed."

"Okay, so you're saying she moved in with him? Was living with him?" That put a whole new wrinkle on the situation.

"It's possible. And then she didn't want to tell your mother that she was living with a man she hadn't mated."

"Huh, okay. That makes sense." Laurel didn't know what to think now.

"So then Warren Wernicke hadn't lied when he said Clarinda hadn't worked for him."

"Nor would your father have lied. Maybe he was even protecting her memory. No sense in telling my mother she was living with a wolf and not mated when she had already disappeared. Wouldn't Aunt Clarinda have at least run across folks? Someone else in the pack would surely have seen her at some point and wondered what had happened to her."

"Let's say she's been traveling, searching for a place to stay. She's rather a nomad. No job. Maybe just enough money to get her to Silver Town. Or maybe someone gives her a lift, and he drops her off at the hotel. It's late. Maybe the hotel is full and Warren is interested in her. They hit it off, and he offers her one of the rooms in this house. Plenty of room. He's living alone."

"What about his sister?" Laurel asked.

"Right. She was living with him and taking care of the household duties while he ran the hotel. When Warren vanished, Charity stepped in to run the place."

"Then she vanished. Who was living here at the time who would have known the Wernickes?"

"Peter will be putting out the query to ask all pack members if any of them knew the brother and sister or anything about a Clarinda O'Brien."

"And no one has responded yet?"

"We've only known about your missing aunt since last night, and with the grand opening of the hotel this morning, folks might be a little slow to get back to us on it."

"You'll let me know if anyone comes forth, won't you?"

"Absolutely, Laurel."

She was glad she'd finally told them about her aunt. She just hoped her sisters wouldn't be upset with her for not asking them first. But the situation had been awkward last night when she was speaking with Lelandi, and it would have been a lot more awkward if she hadn't told her about their missing aunt *before* the Wernicke brothers mentioned it to Darien.

"Wait. Last night at the meeting Darien held, the Wernicke brothers knew our aunt had disappeared. How did they know if we hadn't told anyone about her and none of you knew about it?"

Chapter 12

SOMEHOW, CJ KNEW THIS SITUATION WAS GOING TO get a lot more complicated before they resolved anything. "I'll check with Peter and see if he can question the Wernicke brothers. If not, Darien will call them in again and learn how they knew when none of the rest of us did."

Laurel nodded. "Okay. What if the brothers *do* prove that the property belongs to them through no misdeed of their own?"

"The pack runs the town. They took over the hotel and paid the taxes for it all these years. When you bought it, you essentially paid for the taxes on the property." CJ leaned back against the couch and pulled her tight against his body in a comforting manner, wanting her to know in the worst way how much he wanted her here with him. He wanted her sisters here as part of the pack. He didn't want them leaving, no matter what they learned.

"What if they try to ruin business for us?"

"We'll do whatever we can to fight them legally. But if something unforeseen happens and the hotel doesn't bring in the profits necessary to keep you in the black, what about building a new place? As you can see by how fast your hotel was booked, we do have a need for rooms. You wouldn't have all the hassle of refurbishing an old place. You could make it any style you want—just as Victorian, except with some modern touches. You'd have the whole pack behind you and all the help you'd need to build it. I promise I'd tell Eric not to be so bossy if he helped with the new project."

She smiled.

"Just give it some thought if things don't work out the way we hope."

"I have to thank you and all the pack for everything you have done for us to date. I guess you know we hadn't intended to stay."

"I suspected as much when we learned that you were investigating your aunt's disappearance. I also want to say I don't want you to leave. Not you or your sisters. And neither does the pack."

She frowned at him then, and he was afraid he'd said the wrong thing.

"That's…that's not why you stayed here with me last night, is it? To try and convince me to stay?"

He laughed. "No, I'm really not that devious. You wore me out last night. I want you to know though, I *never* fall asleep on dates. Even if it wasn't a date per se."

She smiled. "Okay. I'm going to do some last-minute things before I need to start greeting guests."

"Sounds good. I'll ask Peter about the other business." When Laurel disappeared into another part of the house, CJ quickly called Peter and got to work on cleaning the remaining frying pan. "Hey, we have another issue with the Wernicke brothers. No one knew about the MacTires' Aunt Clarinda living here at one time. How did the brothers know anything about it?"

"Hell, I'll call Darien and let him get hold of them. We're kind of busy with the hotel opening."

"Thanks. Be out soon."

When CJ was done in the kitchen, Laurel joined him. "Are you ready to go?"

Before he could take her hand, she reached up and kissed him on the mouth. She might not be signaling that this was more than just a thank-you for the time they'd spent together, but he had every intention of showing her that it already meant more to him.

He cupped her face and leaned down to give her a sweet kiss…at first. But when she pulled him tight against her body, he deepened the kiss.

———

Laurel felt his growing arousal and welcomed it. She loved that she could turn him on so quickly. Already, her pheromones were raging every time she started to kiss him, prompting her to go further. Wouldn't that be a shock to the whole pack? If she missed opening day to frolic with Deputy Sheriff CJ Silver, cousin of the pack leader?

With great reluctance on her part, she pulled away. "Really got to go."

He smiled, but he slipped his hands to her shoulders and rubbed them. Clearly he was having a hard time letting go as well. "We'll work it all out one way or another."

She nodded.

She was really viewing the hotel as theirs with all the work they had put into it. All of the hotels they'd renovated in the past were labors of love, but somehow this one was different. She felt that whatever had happened to her aunt here, the hotel was still warm and welcoming. And the idea that anyone would try to ruin it for them didn't sit well with her.

Then they parted company and CJ moved his truck around the back to the parking area behind the hotel. Bertha, Silva, and Sam arrived, carrying the food they'd made through the back door of the hotel. Before long, they would be serving the finger sandwiches, drinks, and sweets from the hotel kitchen.

Because of the winter storm coating everything in several inches of fresh snow that day, everyone began to arrive slowly. In about forty-five minutes, they would have the ribbon-cutting ceremony and head inside. Laurel couldn't believe how she'd been so tired last night, and then she'd slept until way too late this morning.

Many of the townsfolk, of all ages, had gathered to talk and enjoy the revelry while the barber, Mervin, wore his barbershop quartet outfit—a black vest, a red band around the arm of his white long-sleeved shirt, a red bow tie, and a straw hat—to play a fiddle, while someone else was playing a flute. He had to be freezing!

Despite the snowstorm, nothing could dampen the enthusiasm. As soon as she began to greet everyone, Laurel was asked over and over again where her sisters were. As wary as wolves were, she was afraid the pack members suspected something was up when they learned her sisters weren't there. She still didn't want to tell anyone but CJ about the furniture. What if she and her sisters learned who the murderer was from a slip of paper in the highboy, and the murderer learned of it too? Then again, what if the murderer had been Sheridan?

CJ had been upset about his father's complicity in

a murder before, and she knew he'd be upset all over again if he learned his father had been involved in the death of her aunt. As close as she and CJ had become, she felt she owed it to him to let him know what they had hoped to find in the furniture.

But now she and her sisters had a new dilemma. Were they going to have real trouble with the Wernicke brothers? She was beginning to feel that this could be their real home. It all had to do with the wolf pack that lived here—and one special wolf in particular, CJ.

Even Carol Wood, the psychic, was there, her blond hair in a bun, her blue eyes warm and smiling. Laurel smelled that she was a red wolf. There were so few of them that she wondered how the woman had been turned. Had Lelandi, also a red wolf, turned her? Carol was there with her mate, Chester Ryan McKinley, with his dark coffee-colored hair and amber eyes, and his sister, Rosalind. She had the same color hair, except it curled about her shoulders, and her amber eyes were darker, but she and Ryan definitely looked like twins. She owned and operated the greenhouse and garden shop in Green Valley where Ryan and Carol served as pack leaders. Laurel thought it was nice that the pack members here were also welcoming to pack members from elsewhere.

She was surprised to see so many people wearing just wool sweaters. No one had gloves, though a few wore ski hats. She was bundled to the max: hat, gloves, wool scarf, wool coat, and snow boots. She was wearing jeans and they were way too cold. She truly had not yet acclimated to the weather in Colorado.

"We love your wolf sculpture," a couple of teenage

girls said as they hurried on by, their target a group of four teen boys.

Other attendees were crouched down with the wolf sculpture, having their pictures taken, which she loved.

Laurel managed to break away and tell Rosalind how beautiful the poinsettias were that she'd brought over yesterday morning. "I'd love to order live flowers for the check-in counter three times a week, if that would work for you," she told Rosalind.

"Oh absolutely. I have deliveries all over the area, including Bertha's bed and breakfast and Silva's tea-room. Silva's even making Sam keep plants in the tavern near the window and flowers for the women's bathroom. He refused to put plants or flowers in the men's room."

Laurel chuckled. She loved seeing the dynamics between the various pack members. Even though *lupus garous* were human too, their wolfish half dictated their behavior just as much as their human half influenced their actions as wolves.

She noticed Carol was staring at the attic window. Laurel didn't want to look and see what she saw or inter-rupt her thoughts. But she was dying to ask her what the matter was. Carol didn't look worried, but she was concentrating on something.

Quietly, Laurel said to her, "I understand you have some…special abilities."

Carol swung her attention from the attic window to Laurel. "Uh, yeah. The pack members know about it, but it's not something I advertise. I'm a nurse full-time and wouldn't like the word to get out to…other kinds."

"Sure. My sisters, Meghan and Ellie, sense things too."

Carol smiled then, looking as though that made all the difference in the world to her. "I see future visions."

"Do you see anything about the hotel?"

"No. Now that I'm with Ryan and his pack, and living in a different town, I often have visions about goings-on there. But I haven't seen anything here for some time."

"Did you ever see anything about the hotel? Or witness anything paranormal when you lived here before?"

Carol glanced around, but the only people nearby were other pack members. "As a human? No. I don't see ghosts or feel paranormal activities any more than others do. Just sometimes, I see a glimpse of the future."

"Ah, okay. So…what made you look at the window?"

"The woman up there, peering out."

A wave of chills crashed over Laurel as she turned to look at the window. No one was there.

"Um, no one's in the house. Could it be a future vision of yours? Someone else staying in the room at a future date?" Laurel clung to any explanation other than the obvious: the woman was a ghost.

"Could be." Carol gave her a bright smile.

"So not a bad premonition."

"No. I have good ones too."

Laurel hoped that's all it was. She looked for CJ and saw him near Bertha's bed and breakfast. He must have run home to shower and change into his uniform while she was directing where the food should go for the opening. He was busy with crowd control—mostly watching everyone. He looked sexy in his uniform, in charge, alternately frowning and smiling. Everyone she'd met in the pack seemed even friendlier toward her, if that was possible. As if they knew that she and CJ were mated or about to be.

She glanced down at the beautiful wolf sculpture they had created last night, still perfect. Just like the night had been. She couldn't see building a new Victorian-style hotel. Or watching their hotel being run by someone else. They loved renovating old hotels and bringing them to life again. But this one was special.

If they felt they had to leave, she would miss CJ most of all. She noticed that Peter and Trevor were also overseeing the crowds. Each of them slapped CJ on the back at one point, looking in her direction while chatting, then headed off to do their duty. She could just guess what they were saying.

Even his brothers had stopped to talk to him. All grins. She felt her face turn hot despite the frosty breeze.

Main Street had been closed to traffic so that everyone could walk down the street. A large gravel parking lot at the end of town had been set aside for events like this. She and her sisters had witnessed Victorian Days in the fall, an annual celebration the town held to show their thanks for their longevity and to celebrate the town they had built. She and her sisters hadn't participated, telling everyone they were too busy with renovations.

But the Silver Town wolf pack hadn't given up on them so easily. During Victorian Days, Silva had brought over tea and cakes, and Bertha had made lunch for them to ensure they enjoyed the celebration too. Several other pack members had dropped by, wearing their Victorian gowns, to say that next year would be the best ever because the hotel would be part of the celebration. Laurel had seen the guarded looks her sisters gave her. She'd noticed even then how much they hated living the lie that they were here to stay. She wished they'd remain as focused as she was on learning the truth about their aunt. Even so, she harbored a secret longing to dress up and have some fun next year.

She had originally thought they would be out of the area well before that, but she had to admit that all the outpouring of wolf camaraderie and, well, falling for CJ were seriously changing her mind.

She couldn't help but love the way the people in the pack made her and her sisters feel so welcome.

She got a call and looked at the ID. *Ellie*. "How's everything going with the furniture?"

"It arrived on time, so that part was good. We're hoping to arrive back late tonight."

"Okay. Were you able to…look for anything?"

"No. We've had movers with us, and once we inspected the furniture to make sure the pieces were in good shape, the movers bundled them in blankets and packed them in the truck. We'll have to investigate them when we get in."

"Okay, sounds great."

"How's the grand opening?"

"Everything's good. We're cutting the ribbon in half an hour. We need to figure out what's going on with the three men staying with us." Laurel looked around for them again. She hadn't seen them yet today. Maybe they slept all day and ghost busted at night, or maybe they were out looking for ghosts somewhere else right now. She didn't want to discuss this with her sisters over the phone. They couldn't do anything about it right now, so why worry them? She'd let them know what was going on when they got home.

"Okay. Good luck with everything."

"All right, Ellie. And thanks. Talk to you later."
Laurel saw the Wernicke men coming from the direction
of the public parking lot. Apparently they'd gone for a
drive. To check out the ghost woman and wolf sightings, maybe? Or the haunted silver mine? Maybe they
wouldn't hang around the hotel much. But she doubted
it. She was certain they were trying to dig up what had
happened with their aunt and uncle, just like she and her
sisters were trying to learn about their aunt.

She was dying to ask them how they knew that she
and her sisters were looking into their aunt's disappearance. She wondered if Darien had already questioned
them about it.

"Hey," CJ said behind her, and she turned around
quickly, relieved he was there, despite telling herself
she could handle the Wernickes on her own. "How are
you holding up? You must be tired, as late as we went
to sleep last night."

Her cheeks heated all over again. He smiled. She
wanted to sock him for the comment, even if he hadn't
meant anything by it. If anyone heard them, they'd
wonder just what went on last night. At least he hadn't
made the mistake of saying they'd slept together.

"I slept really well." She hated to admit that nothing
had disturbed her sleep last night while she snuggled
with CJ, and that she had felt perfectly safe and content.
No howling wind, nothing. She had enjoyed his warmth
wrapped around her, listening to his steady heartbeat
and breathing in his sexy, masculine scent of spices and
wolf before she'd fallen into a deep sleep.

He suddenly frowned and she wondered what was
wrong now.

"What about the paint job?"

"Shoot, I forgot all about that. I need help hanging the picture. I carried it over just fine yesterday, but it's so unwieldy that it takes two to actually hang it."

"We could slip in around the back before the ribbon cutting. We don't want anyone to think you're ready to let everyone in just yet. It would look a bit odd for the painting to be sitting on the floor next to the other wall. Some might think something ghostly moved it."

She glanced in the direction of the Wernicke brothers, but they were talking to Sam.

"Sure, let's do it." She walked with CJ around to the back of the hotel and crossed the patio.

She pulled her keys out of her pocket and unlocked the door. Then she twisted the handle. Locked. Confounded, she stared at it for a moment, then tried her key on it again. Only this time it unlocked it.

"You hadn't locked the door." CJ sounded like he was scolding her.

"Yeah, I had locked it. I'm fairly certain. You know how it is when you do something so automatically, you don't even think about it. Although I was in a rush to get things done, including helping to haul in all the food for the celebration. So…maybe I didn't. I don't know. But I really thought I had." As often as she'd run back to the house for something and then returned to the hotel, she had begun to leave the back door to the hotel unlocked occasionally since she was coming right back. Besides, Darien had told her the town was really safe.

"Everyone's out front, so I'm sure everything's fine." But CJ still sounded worried.

When they walked into the sunroom and continued

into the main lobby, he looked around, taking deep breaths of the air scented with Christmas spice potpourri, wassail, and mulled wine. Plus, the sweet cakes — decorated in Christmas themes from drummer boys and snowman frosting to Santas and angels — scented the air. She didn't smell any new people smells other than of those who had been here helping out recently.

When they walked through the sunroom and reached the main room, she looked at the spot where the painting had been sitting. It was gone.

Chapter 13

BEFORE LAUREL COULD SAY ANYTHING TO CJ ABOUT the missing painting, he said, "The letter on the wall has vanished."

She switched her attention from the missing painting to the wall. Goose bumps trailed down Laurel's arms. No matter how many times she'd had to deal with ghostly happenings like these, they always gave her chill bumps.

CJ smiled. "It must have been just some old shadow of a stencil-painted letter, probably from sometime after the hotel was abandoned."

"Right." She was certain he didn't truly believe that any more than she did.

He looked where the painting had been. "I…thought you had brought that painting in here to hang. Wasn't it leaning against that wall over there?"

She stared at the wall as if the painting would suddenly reappear. "Uh, yeah, it was."

He frowned at her. She didn't want to say it had vanished along with the letter on the wall.

Still, he waited for an explanation.

She let her breath out in exasperation. "I have no idea where it went. Maybe it's back at the house."

He looked skeptically at her. "One of your sisters…"

"They were gone and it was still sitting on the floor there."

"Okay. Why don't you join the revelry outside and I'll check the place out."

Now he sounded like a cop, worried someone might be in the hotel already. "I'll come with you."

"Okay." He checked out all the rooms, including the attic—where the light was still off—and then they went down into the basement. They found nothing out of place. "Let's go on over to your place and see if it miraculously appeared back home. If it did, you'll need help hanging it over there, won't you?"

"Yeah. If it's over there."

"The back door was unlocked," he reminded her.

And that irritated her. "You think someone entered the hotel just to steal one old painting? I wouldn't think so. And the painting is big. It's not that easy to hide. Or remove in a hurry."

"What about this morning when you were getting things ready? Was it sitting there?"

"It was, if I remember correctly. I definitely looked at the letter on the wall. And it was still there too. Then again, I don't specifically recall looking at the painting. Just the wall."

Feeling disconcerted, she and CJ left the hotel and walked down the stone path to the house, following tons of tracks from the parking area where everyone had been hauling stuff to the hotel. Silva and Bertha had also helped Laurel carry more things from the house. So there was no telling if anyone else had been tramping down the snow here.

When they entered the house, she looked at the fireplace first, half expecting the painting to be hanging over the mantel already. But it was sitting on the floor next to the fireplace.

She didn't move. No way had she carried it back here and not remembered having done so.

"Are you certain your sisters didn't move it?"

"*No*. They had already left, and it was still sitting against the wall perpendicular to the one you repainted so many times."

"Okay." He helped her to hang it and stood back while she straightened it. "A ghost didn't move it," he said matter-of-factly. "It's way too heavy."

She smiled at him.

"Well, I would think it would be way too heavy for a ghost to carry." He smiled back.

She had to agree. Yet she didn't smell anyone else in the house who might have done it either.

CJ frowned. "Lots of *lupus garous* carry lock picks, in case they need to find an unoccupied house to shift in if they can't stop the shift. Although if you left the hotel door unlocked, you might have also left the house door unlocked."

"And carried the painting back into the house? How would the person have known that's where it belonged?" She hated sounding so frustrated, but she couldn't help it. "Not only that, but we would have smelled somebody else in the hotel and in here. Someone new. And I didn't. Did you?"

"No. You're right. I didn't either. Would anyone be trying to spook you and your sisters? To try to get you to leave the place?"

"Like the Wernicke brothers? But if they prove that they are entitled to the property, they wouldn't need to do that. And then they wore hunter's spray." *Damn it.* If it was them, she'd kill them. What if they were trying

to scare her into wanting to give the place up? What if
their aunt or uncle had something to do with her aunt's
disappearance, and the brothers were afraid she and her
sisters would learn about it?

"Maybe it was them. I'll call Darien after the ribbon
cutting and let him know what happened."

"Do you always fill him in on the details of what's
going on?" She was curious about the pack leaders'
involvement in daily affairs.

"Yeah, when it could mean trouble. We want to
ensure that you and your sisters don't have any more of
it. Are you ready to do your ribbon cutting?"

"Yeah, I'm ready."

"Okay, good show."

"Thanks for…for all your help."

"You're welcome. We're all here for you. As a pack,
everyone's willing to help out."

To discover what really happened to their aunt? She
was certain the pack members would be upset to learn
that one of them had made her aunt go missing, if that
was the case.

As soon as they skirted around to the front of the
hotel, everyone standing there turned and smiled expectantly at her.

She wished now, more than ever, that her sisters were
here for the big event.

As the alpha mate to Darien, Lelandi gave the
speech and then helped cut the ribbon to open the hotel.
"You've done such a wonderful job on the hotel. We're
really happy to have you here."

"Thanks. We thought it really turned out well too.
And thanks to everyone for such a wonderful welcome."

Everybody cheered and then Laurel opened the door and welcomed the visitors inside.

Again, it was so much warmer than the openings she and her sisters had had at the other hotels. The people were genuinely friendly, like family, not like outsiders who were visitors to the hotel. She couldn't help that it swayed her toward wanting to stay.

Everyone began to saunter through the main room, grabbing treats off the long dining room table, slowly taking a look around the place, and commenting on the renovations and decorations. One of the focal points was the Victorian-decorated Christmas tree, with miniature lace fans, embroidered angels, lace-decorated sleighs, burgundy glass-bead garlands and white lights. Visitors were sipping from cups of wassail or mulled wine, and enjoying petit fours and finger sandwiches. Laurel sighed as visitors tromped up and down the stairs. She'd need to clean everything before the guests signed in a little later.

But she loved how everyone smiled and pointed out the refinished hand carvings on the banister, the crown moldings, the wolves' heads holding up the fireplace mantel, and even the grandfather clock with the wolf carvings on the sides and top. She thought everyone loved those best of all.

This was the first place they had lived where wolves would appreciate her and her sisters' love of wolves.

"The door to the basement is locked. Can we see what's down there?" Stanton Wernicke asked.

There was so much noise, she hadn't even heard him come up behind her. And she felt unnerved that he'd drawn so close without her being aware of it.

"No, sorry. The basement hasn't been renovated yet. So it's off-limits to everyone for now."

"Because of the work we do, you know, for our TV show, can't we get some special concession? Just to look around. No photographing anything. We're just curious."

"I'm afraid not, for insurance reasons." She noticed CJ was watching her and Stanton, looking ready to step in if Stanton pushed the issue. She wondered if he suspected there was something important down there—since it was not open to the general public.

"We'll sign a waiver. We often go into more…well, dangerous places to see what we can find. If we find anything, it'll often be in those kinds of locations."

"She said no." CJ joined them, looking hot, authoritative, and perfectly heroic at the moment.

Stanton smiled a little at CJ but not in a friendly way.

Despite so many people milling around, Laurel asked, "How did you know we were looking into our aunt's disappearance?"

That wiped the smug smile off Stanton's face. "I don't know what you're talking about."

"*No*body knew we were looking into her disappearance. How did *you* know?"

"Lucky guess. Your aunt was involved with our uncle, and then he disappeared and his sister after that. Then your aunt takes off."

"You're saying my aunt had something to do with your aunt and uncle's disappearances?"

Stanton shrugged. "Read into it what you will. You've got to admit it sounds highly suspicious."

"If you know so much, where was she staying?"

"In the house. I thought you already knew that. One

big, happy family. Except that our aunt didn't like yours. She thought she was a gold digger. And now look what happened. Not only were our aunt and uncle removed from the scene, but now her nieces have benefited from their disappearances. Sound like a coincidence?"

"I don't believe in them, any more than I believe you didn't know what happened to your aunt and uncle for so long. Or that your dad asked you to look into this before he died."

"Believe what you will. In the end, we'll learn I'm right and you're way off base. Don't worry. We won't hold what your aunt did to our family against you. We know you didn't have anything to do with it. So we're willing to do what's right here. We'll pay for the renovations and even keep you on to run the place, since you seem to do a good job at making a healthy profit, judging by the sales of your other properties."

"And the back taxes?" she asked, amused. Unless they made up tax receipts, and then there would be duplicate ones, he wasn't going to win this argument. But she realized the Wernicke brothers had been investigating her business operations. She wondered what else they were looking into. Then again, Darien was investigating the brothers.

"Our business is painting, and we're tied up with ghost-busting show commitments. So it would be a good deal for you. Stay, take a cut, and even live in the house at a reasonable rent. We can work out the details later." He ignored the tax issue.

Before she could come up with a response to his "deal," he bowed his head a little—in a signature way for a *lupus garou*—and moseyed off. Laurel stared after him as he joined his brothers. She moved closer to CJ and whispered, "I don't believe him, do you?"

"There might be some truth in it. Darien texted me that he's getting a few old-timers together to discuss what they recall about Warren Wernicke and his sister."

"Good. Do you think Stanton knows about some evidence in the basement?"

"If so, why wouldn't they have come before you bought the hotel? And revealed it to the pack or disposed of it, if that benefited them. None of it makes any sense."

"No, it doesn't. Unless they didn't know that the family owned this place until recently, like he said."

"Right." CJ turned his attention from the Wernickes, who were discussing something among themselves, to Laurel. "Did you still want me to stay at the hotel and watch them?" His orders were to keep an eye on the men to make sure they didn't see anyone shifting, but since the Wernickes were *lupus garou*, that was no longer necessary. Though he preferred to stay here and watch over things for her, he wanted to make sure she still approved it.

"Yeah. I don't trust them. And I'm sure they'll be sneaking around the place to their heart's content when I'm not able to observe them. How much do you want to bet they'll try to get down there?"

"I'm with you on that." He folded his arms and observed them again. "I thought the festivities were really nice. Great turnout."

"Agreed."

"Why didn't they just come here and say by rights they owned the hotel—through an inheritance or some such thing? Why make reservations here instead? They had ample opportunity to say something at any time," CJ said.

"They don't have any proof. What if these men aren't who they say they are? What if they're not related to the Wernickes who disappeared?" Laurel eyed the brothers with suspicion.

"Good point. I hadn't considered that. They might not even be named Wernicke. So they learned who owned the place before you, probably searching for another place to include in their TV show, and discovered the family name. And then they thought to pretend kinship to try to lay claim to the place, but hadn't realized the situation with the unpaid taxes."

Laurel frowned as she watched people moving about and visiting with each other, and heard bits of conversation about visiting the old haunted hotel when they were kids. "I don't believe in coincidences. The name is so unusual. What are the chances that they would do some kind of haunted building search and come up with this one where the owners had the same name as them?"

"I wonder who decides on the shows they do. Maybe the TV producer? What if he was looking for a different kind of place to feature and came across the name of the former owners and how they had disappeared. Then he told the Wernicke brothers. His idea might be to make it seem more personal, closer to home. Except that the brothers decided to pretend they're related."

"That's possible."

A high squeal sounded upstairs in the vicinity of the attic room. Laurel jumped a little, and then laughter followed.

A few people came down the steps and Anthony, at the foot of the stairs, asked, "What was the scream all about?"

"The light in the attic room suddenly flickered on. Must be on an automatic timer. Or someone switched the light on and off again without us noticing. Just scared us for a second," Minx said, her blond pigtails swinging as she made her way down the stairs. "I wouldn't be surprised if it was Cody. He was in the hall and could have done it."

Wearing his rainbow-colored jester hat, bells jingling, Cody joined her from the direction of the sunroom and laughed. "Should have known that was your squeal, Minx. I was downstairs by then. I thought you saw a mouse or something."

She rolled her eyes. "Get real. As if a mouse would scare me."

"Wiring," both CJ and Laurel said at the same time. She got on her phone and called the electrician who had rewired the old hotel. "Did you happen to work on the wiring in the attic?"

"I checked it and it was safe. Your sister Meghan said not to bother doing any new rewiring for the time being. She said she didn't think anyone would be staying there," Jacob said.

"Can you check it out? I think it has a short in the light switch." At least she hoped that was all there was to it. That was an easy and inexpensive fix, and it would solve one of their ghostly mysteries. "I have an unexpected guest staying there for the next few days, so when you have a chance, I'd love to get it taken care of. I'm sure he'd appreciate not having the light disturb his sleep all night long."

"I'm in the basement of the hotel right now. I'll take a look at it as soon as I can get around the crush of people down here."

"What? How did you get into the basement? The door was locked. I'm on my way." Holding the phone to her ear, she stalked that way as CJ hurried after her.

"The door was wide open, and I just followed some others going down here. Sorry about that," Jacob said.

"Thanks. Let me know what you discover about the light switch."

"I'll be up there as soon as I can."

Laurel glanced around, looking for the Wernicke brothers. None of them were in sight. She followed CJ down the basement stairs. Judging by his steely expression and angry stride, he was ready to take the men to task when he found them.

When she reached the foot of the stairs, she said to everyone exploring the basement, "I'm so sorry. Someone must have unlocked the door, but this part of the hotel hasn't been cleared for viewing for insurance reasons." Though that wasn't true at all. She just didn't want anyone down there until they did renovate it, if they renovated it.

The fifteen or so people walking through the maids' rooms and common area stopped, looking a little guilty.

"You can go out that way and see the decorated backyard and gazebo," she offered, trying to appease everyone. "When you're done, you can come into the hotel either via the back deck or around the front and have some more refreshments. I'll lock this door again after you."

The mob started to disburse, most going outside. The

electrician and a handful of men and women climbed back up the stairs to the main part of the hotel.

"It had to have been the brothers," she growled to CJ after she checked to make sure no one else was in any of the rooms before she locked the basement door again.

"I agree. Are you going to be all right?"

"Yeah. What are you going to do?"

"Look for them."

"We don't have any evidence that they did it. Their scent wasn't down here, though they could have disobeyed Darien's orders and worn hunter's spray again." Now that she thought about it, she didn't recall smelling Stanton standing close to her either.

"Or they only unlocked the door to cause problems for you and they didn't come down here. It won't hurt to question them or to just emphasize that they aren't welcome if they don't mind the rules."

"What if they say the place is horrible? Terribly haunted. Something to get people to stay away?"

"We'll end up getting a new crowd staying here."

"Paranormal seekers." She shook her head. "Let me know how it goes with talking to them."

"I will. See you in a bit."

CJ got on his phone and updated Darien. He also mentioned the picture moving from the hotel to the house.

"Not a ghost's work."

"No. I assume someone moved it while Laurel was outside visiting with the partygoers. When she went to unlock the back door, it was already unlocked. Either someone else unlocked it, or she forgot to lock it in the rush to finish last-minute stuff this morning. Too many tracks were left out back because of everyone hauling in

food and drink for the celebration to determine if someone in particular had gone that way."

"So somebody else moved the painting. The Wernicke
brothers are there, I take it."

"They were. Somehow the basement door was also
unlocked, and then visitors filed down there to look
it over."

"I looked into the Wernicke brother and sister who
ran the hotel," Darien said. "I couldn't find any verification that these brothers are related to them. Then again,
because of our longevity, we have to hide our ages and
the like, so they might have changed their identities at
some point. As to their father, it's just as Stanton said.
Their father died a short while ago in Raleigh. We
couldn't learn if he had a brother and sister though. As to
whether the Wernickes who ran the hotel were wolves,
we don't keep lists on that sort of thing, but some of
our older people that I questioned said they were, that
my dad was adamant about the hotel being sold only to
wolves and not humans."

"We wondered if they were even related. The brothers might not be kin of theirs."

"True."

"All right. I'm off to look for them and see if they're
the ones who unlocked the basement door, despite
Laurel telling them it was off-limits."

"Breaking and entering, if you can prove it. Just let
me know if you want to kick them out of town. They
can investigate their aunt and uncle's disappearance,
however they want to, from outside our pack territory."

"Will do."

"Oh, and one other thing."

"Yeah?"

"Brett said you saw a ghost wolf, or what you thought was one, running in that area of the woods where she's been spotted before. He said Laurel believed the wolf was white. And drove a pickup truck."

"Yeah." CJ had meant to tell Darien after speaking with Brett about it, but then he'd forgotten and ended up at Laurel's place, and there went any thought besides being with her. But Darien didn't seem to mind. Probably because he thought CJ was making strides with keeping the she-wolves here.

"We're making a concerted effort to look into it."

He was surprised. "Don't you think it was just a gray wolf? One of ours who saw my truck and didn't recognize it in the snow?"

"We're checking into it, just in case."

"Okay, thanks. I'll let Laurel know." CJ told him that Stanton knew about Laurel's aunt. "What about the old-timers' meeting?"

"Scheduled for tomorrow evening so that they can close up their shops for the night and have time this evening and tomorrow to gather anything they might have that helps the case. Let me know if you need me to talk with the brothers."

"Will do." Even though CJ was the law, Darien was ultimately in charge whenever it came to wolves in their territory. CJ headed outside and saw that the Wernicke brothers' van was no longer parked in the lot. He made his way to his own truck, having to stop several times to talk to pack members before he got on the road and started to do a search for their vehicle. It would be easy to spot by the sign on its side that said: Painters by Day, Ghost Busters by Night.

He called the van's description in to Trevor and Peter, in case they were free to help locate the men.

When he didn't see any sign of the Wernicke brothers' blue van, he headed out to the woods where Laurel had seen the ghost wolf. When he reached the spot where the tire tracks had been, he parked the truck and got out to explore a bit. The tire tracks had been right next to the riverbank. What if the wolf hadn't taken off in the truck? What if it had swum across the river?

He stared across the river, the wind blowing the powdery snow all over, and swore that a white wolf stood watching him in the woods before it turned and vanished.

Chapter 14

AT FIVE O'CLOCK, THE CELEBRATION WAS WINDING down and Jacob Summers, the electrician, joined Laurel in the kitchen as she finished cleaning up, though several others had helped her with the job.

"Your finding?" she asked.

"A short in the wiring. I fixed it. No extra charge. Code-wise, everything is fine."

"Thanks, Jacob."

"No problem."

Lelandi came into the kitchen to give her a hug. "Beautiful. Everything went splendidly. I'll finish up anything else you need done in here. You have some guests ready to check in. Silva was going to do it, but she wasn't sure what to do."

"Oh, thanks so much." Laurel gave Lelandi a big hug back. "I couldn't have done it all without you and the rest of the pack who helped out."

"That's what we're here for. And about winning the snow sculpture contest…it was an honest choice—and I'll say unanimous. Everyone voted for it."

"For…the sculpture," Laurel said, smiling skeptically.

Lelandi smiled right back.

"Thanks again for everything." When Laurel hurried to the check-in counter to take care of her guests, she saw the three Wernicke brothers standing there, looking a little miffed that she hadn't checked them in at once. She stood taller. "Did CJ talk to you about the basement door?"

"No, why?" Stanton asked.

"Because someone unlocked it and let everyone down there." She wondered where CJ had been all this time if he hadn't run into the brothers and spoken with them already.

"That's not good—for your insurance."

"If you're not pleased with the accommodations or anything else here, I'll promptly refund your money."

Stanton gave her a weak smile. So faked. "We just wondered who was going to check us in. Then again, we figured if we were…make that, *when* we're running the hotel, we'll have the proper staff to manage it. Though we would still be willing to hire you for the job."

Normally, she and her sisters did hire a manager and more employees to help run their hotels, but this one was so small that they had wanted to take care of it on their own in the beginning. They figured they'd have time to hire additional staff once they knew the pack members better.

"If you do end up owning it, that will be up to you." Laurel had no intention of running the hotel for these men. But from the sound of it, the brothers couldn't claim it no matter how much they thought it should be theirs. "How are you paying for your stay?"

"Since the place is really ours, it should be free of charge." Stanton smiled again.

Acting alpha-like, he was waiting for her to cower a bit. She wasn't afraid of him. Not that he couldn't be dangerous, but she just wasn't going to be cowed by him.

She tapped her pen on the countertop. He slowly

pulled out a wallet and then handed a credit card to her. She said, "And I'll need to see some photo ID."

His brothers chuckled.

"We have a TV show," Stanton reminded her.

"That I don't watch." She eyed his photo ID carefully, memorizing his address, and then began to fill in the information on her computer. "And you're staying a week and checking out on…"

"Two weeks."

She looked up from her computer. "You made reservations for a week, checking out on Saturday morning by ten."

Stanton turned to his brothers. "I thought you said we had reservations for two weeks."

"That's what I changed it to. Don't remember who I talked to, and I didn't get any confirmation number," Vernon said.

"Then you didn't get any reservation extension. We already have the rooms booked after that."

"Then when do you have the next available opening?" Stanton leaned against the counter, getting into her space.

"Not for three more months."

"I don't believe you." He tried to see her computer, and she turned the monitor so he couldn't observe it. "That's fine. We'll stay at Bertha's bed and breakfast."

Lelandi came out of the kitchen and smiled at the men. "Gentlemen, enjoy your stay here." Then she turned to Laurel. "Thanks for accommodating my brother's… friends for the coming month. They've looked forward to skiing here while my brother, his wife, and their children visit with Darien and me."

"I can't wait to meet them," Laurel said cheerfully,

then handed the keys to the Wernicke brothers. "Your rooms are the first three on the right as you reach the top of the stairs."

The brothers left then and headed to the stairs.

Lelandi whispered to her, "CJ was supposed to be back already, but he saw the white wolf you thought you had seen—only this time it was on the other side of the river."

Laurel's heart skipped a beat. "You're kidding."

"No. So he and some others are trying to reach that side of the river and track the wolf down. Trevor's coming here to keep an eye on things for you until CJ returns. I'll stick around until he arrives."

"You don't really have to." Laurel knew Lelandi had little ones to take care of.

"Someone needs to stay here with you in case you have trouble, given the circumstances. CJ would, but he had the notion to check out the white wolf and just happened to see it."

"It's not one of yours?"

"No."

"A full-blooded wolf?"

"Maybe, or one of our kind. Just not one of our pack. Anyway, we need to know the truth, and if it's one of our kind, we'll see. Oh, and about the hotel bookings," Lelandi said softly, for Laurel's hearing only, "we'll ensure your place stays booked."

"They'll just stay at Bertha's."

"It's also booked, guaranteed."

Laurel smiled. She loved this wolf pack.

CJ got ahold of Darien, then contemplated how to get to the other side of the river. A bridge crossed to the other side ten miles down the road, but he didn't want to lose the opportunity.

"I'm shifting," he said over his phone to Darien.

"Are you sure you don't want to wait until you have backup?" Darien asked. "I've had the alert roster called. Your brothers are at the top of the list, and Peter's coming."

"What about Laurel and the hotel?" He was supposed to be there, keeping an eye on the Wernicke brothers.

"Lelandi is there with her."

CJ didn't like it. Two women were no match for three aggressive male wolves.

"Trevor's joining them as soon as he can get there."

"All right."

"But about this wolf—"

"It's just one wolf. And because it's white, it could be old or injured."

"Or an Arctic wolf, healthy and strong. Could you tell?"

"No. The wind was whipping the fresh snow around and pushing the snow from the pine branches, making for a screen of white."

"Are you sure it's not a gray wolf and the snow was making it appear white?"

"I don't think so. I've stripped. Got to shift and go."

"Take care, CJ. Howl if you find anything. I'm on my way."

"Will do."

They ended the call, and CJ buried his clothes and phone underneath a pile of snow. Using his enhanced sense of smell as a wolf, he would easily locate his belongings when he returned.

He shifted, his muscles and skin heating as the welcome change came over him, the chill of the wind instantly blocked as his double coat of fur protected him from the elements—both cold and heat. Then he raced to the rocky riverbank, slipped down the rocks until he was no longer standing on the smooth stone river bottom, and swam against the strong flow of the current.

He hoped that if the wolf was older, he could reach him before long. But if this was the same wolf others had said they had witnessed—the ghost wolf that had never been located—he might be so good at evasion that even CJ wouldn't be able to locate him.

CJ struggled against the pull of the cold, black water. If the wolf had not driven off in the truck like they had previously surmised, had he managed to swim across the river that night, evading them that way? CJ wasn't sure when the first sightings of the wolf had been reported, though he'd never heard anyone say it was a white wolf. And he'd never known anyone personally who had witnessed the wolf. Or at least who had let on.

When he finally reached the other side of the river and found purchase on the slippery stones, he made his way up the bank and ran into the piney woods. He was here, ready for the chase and whatever he found, but he wished he could be in three places at once: here looking for the white wolf, watching over the hotel to ensure the Wernicke brothers didn't give the sisters any further grief, and at the sisters' home, learning if Laurel and her sisters had found anything hidden in their aunt's furniture when it arrived. He hadn't told Darien or anyone, because she hadn't wanted to divulge the furniture's secret compartments. If she found anything, she would tell him. And Darien and Lelandi if it was beneficial to the case.

But he was here for now. He wanted in the worst way to learn who the wolf was—to at least solve one of the mysteries they had run across.

He concentrated hard on looking for a wolf blending with the snow-covered trees. He was smelling for it and listening for any sign that it was moving through the woods. With the wind whipping about and the snow making popping sounds as it fell off the trees in clumps, he didn't sense the wolf anywhere.

Worse, he had just climbed on top of a snow-covered, tangled mass of fallen trees and branches, and as soon as he stepped on it, he felt it move. The timber suddenly cracked and snapped. His heart went into his throat, and before he could leap off it, the deadfall broke beneath his weight and he fell.

Laurel's sisters arrived nearly at midnight. As soon as the men off-loaded the furniture into the house and left, Laurel gave both her sisters hugs in greeting. Then Ellie said, "Okay, spill the beans."

Laurel couldn't stop worrying about CJ. No one had heard from him in hours, and Lelandi had updated her every hour on the hour. He'd taken off after the white wolf and then vanished. All Laurel could think of was the way in which their aunt and the Wernicke brother and sister had disappeared. At one point, she thought of alien abductions, which was nuts, sure, but she couldn't quit thinking about CJ and wanting to go in search of him. Lelandi had told her that they had at least forty men out looking for him now. They would find him and he'd be fine, Laurel kept telling herself.

She swallowed hard and tried not to let her sisters see her eyes again fill with tears. If she hadn't seen the white wolf, CJ wouldn't be missing now. She was certain he wouldn't have vanished without a trace unless something bad had happened.

She tried to concentrate on searching one of the highboy's drawers for hidden compartments while her sisters worked on others. Worrying about CJ wouldn't help anyone.

"Spill the beans about what?" Laurel asked, certain that Ellie and Meghan wanted to know all about her and CJ. But if that wasn't the topic her sister had in mind, Laurel had no intention of bringing it up.

Both her sisters had stopped looking at the drawers and were waiting for her to answer Ellie.

"What do you mean, about what? About CJ, of course. Here you are telling us not to get too friendly with anyone in the pack, and what do you do? Get *really* friendly with one of them. And he's not just a member, but the pack leader's close cousin." Ellie teased.

Laurel hadn't thought they'd be upset about it, but hopeful that she'd want to stay. She hadn't been sure until now.

"*Really* friendly," Meghan said, nodding.

"I have some bad news." Laurel hated that she had to tell them now. She didn't want to mention what had happened with regard to CJ, unless that turned out to be really bad news.

"Don't tell me you've already broken up with CJ.

Ahhh, how could you go and do that?" Ellie asked. "Here I thought after you and he were caught in that scandalous photo—"

Immediately, Laurel defended herself. "He just kissed my nose."

"And the one where you were sitting on his lap? Then he stayed overnight." Ellie looked up from the drawer she'd pulled out and had been inspecting. "And more?"

"We just watched *A Christmas Story* and fell asleep on the couch."

"Ohmigod," Ellie said, poking Meghan, who was staring wide-eyed at Laurel.

"What did you think?" Laurel was afraid they thought she was mated.

Meghan smiled. "Wow. We thought he'd fallen asleep on the couch and you'd gone to sleep in your bed. You slept together on the couch? Together?"

As if she hadn't said the word "together" enough! "You've fallen asleep on the couch while watching a movie any number of times," Laurel said.

"Not. With. A. Wolf." Meghan raised her brows.

"For heaven's sake, that's not what's important."

"It is too," Meghan said.

Well, yes, it was. Wolves didn't have sex unless they planned a mating, and it sure sounded like they could be headed in that direction. But now she wanted more than anything to join the search teams out looking for CJ. If something terrible had happened to him... She shook her head at herself. She couldn't think of it. He was fine. They'd find him soon, and he'd be fine. But her gut instinct told her it wasn't true.

"Okay, so what's the bad news then?" Ellie ran her fingers over the bottom of the drawer, searching for a hidden compartment. "Ow."

Laurel and Meghan looked up from examining two more drawers to see what the problem was.

"Sliver."

Meghan rolled her eyes.

"The problem is that the Wernicke brothers claim they're related to the hotel owners who vanished. And now they're alleging that the hotel belongs to them."

"Holy crap. No way," Meghan said. "Are they still staying here at the hotel as guests?"

"Yes. But they thought they should have free rooms."

Meghan put down the drawer and headed for the front door of the house.

Grabbing her arm, Laurel intercepted her. "Where are you going?"

"They can't stay here if they think they're going to take the hotel away from us." Meghan's eyes glistened with tears.

Feeling her distress, Laurel pulled her into a hug. "Darien and everyone else in the pack will help us to uncover the truth. And the unpaid taxes meant that the pack took over the property, so the brothers wouldn't be able to claim it. But they could cause other trouble for us, trying to ruin our business and forcing us to lose money. We could face financial ruin."

"And if that happened?" Ellie looked just as distraught.

"CJ suggested we build a new hotel. It can be Victorian, small, exactly how we like our hotels."

"But we love this one. Meghan and I were talking

about it while we were away. How much we loved this hotel and how beautiful it is."

"Right, but we may not have a choice."

"Wait," Meghan said. "You want to build a new hotel here?" She wiped away the tears trailing down her cheeks. "You'd do that to stay here? To stay with the pack?"

"I don't know. We still have to learn why our aunt disappeared and all the rest. The pack may not even want us here after we learn the truth. Would you even want to build a new place? CJ said they'd help us, but is it even something we'd want to do?"

"We love the old buildings," Ellie admitted. "But to stay with a wolf pack? Especially as welcoming as this one is? I'd be willing."

"I agree with Ellie. I like the charm of old buildings. But if it meant staying, I'd do whatever it takes," Meghan said.

Then Ellie smiled deviously. "The pack would never allow the Wernicke brothers to buy the hotel, or if they did, they'd run them out of business."

"I agree. So in the meantime, we fight them tooth and claw if they try to ruin our business. Even though they have a TV show, which could give them some clout, we have a pack to back us," Laurel said. "But that's only contingent on the pack still wanting us here if we discover one of their beloved pack members had anything to do with our aunt's disappearance."

"Are you kidding?" Meghan set her drawer aside and pulled out another. "Poor CJ would have no one's nose to kiss on a cold, snowy day."

"Or a she-wolf to snuggle with on our sofa while

watching Christmas movies." Ellie ran her fingers under the top edge of the highboy.

"If his father was involved in our aunt's disappearance?" Laurel asked, trying to be pragmatic about it. "Family is family, after all."

"He's not going to stick up for his father if he was involved in murdering Clarinda or covering it up." Meghan gave up on the highboy and started to search the blanket chest for a false bottom.

Laurel was hoping that would be the case. Her phone rang and she hurried to answer it, her sisters watching her.

She frowned when she saw it was Darien calling, not Lelandi. Her stomach clenching with dread, Laurel feared the worse. CJ had been found.

And he was dead.

Chapter 15

WHEN CJ CAME TO, HE WAS STILL IN HIS WOLF FORM, thank God, or he would have frozen to death. He was lying on his side at the bottom of a twelve-foot-deep killing pit, with leaves, twigs, and pine needles cushioning his fall. A few wooden stakes pointed skyward at the black night, waiting to skewer their victims. The pit had been used to kill animals—and had been here for years, he suspected, as he considered the weathered age of the stakes. He couldn't see all that well in the dark, as deep as he was, but he would have been able to smell new wood that had been carved into stakes.

His head throbbed where he was certain he'd cut it, and minor bruises, scratches, and a few ligament strains made him ache all over. An animal or two must have fallen into the pit earlier, and the unfortunate beasts had broken a few of the sharpened stakes. Thankfully, the broken ones hadn't been replaced, and CJ hadn't been gored.

Unsteadily, he sat up and tried to get his bearing in the darkness, some of the deadfall still covering the hole. He had to warn anyone else not to take a misstep and fall into the pit. The snow-covered trees looming above hid the sky from his view.

Nothing on the sides of the pit could help him climb if he shifted. There were a few exposed, gnarled roots, but they wouldn't be strong enough to hold his weight. Remembering that Darien was coming and also sending men, CJ lifted his chin and howled. Maybe someone would hear him. His howl sounded strange and unreal to his ears. Maybe because he was surrounded by earth and sitting so deep in the pit. He hoped whoever had built this pit wasn't still around to finish him off.

Off in the distance, howls rent the woods and he was cheered to hear his brothers and cousins calling. He howled again in greeting and in relief.

Everyone was everywhere, combing the woods for him, he realized. But they would be in their wolf forms. No one could get him out of here without shifting and using ropes. And for that they needed a phone. He was destined to stay down here for who knew how long.

Worse, he worried about Laurel being alone and hoped Trevor was keeping an eye on things. CJ wished he had her in his arms, snuggling with her on the couch again, breathing in her sweet she-wolf scent, listening to her steady heartbeat, feeling the heat and softness of her body.

Everyone had stopped howling. He knew they wanted to hear from him again, to pinpoint his direction. He suspected they wondered why he sounded like he was buried alive. He howled long and low, letting them know just where he was again. His head splintering in two, he collapsed on his side and waited for his rescuers to come for him.

Then a wolf woofed down at him. He wanted to warn the wolf to watch out for the deadfall covering the hole. That it could still be dangerous. When he looked up, he stared at a white face, ears as long as a gray wolf's, and legs just as long. The white wolf. The ghost wolf. He or she was very real.

CJ didn't remember anything after that, didn't hear anything for a long time. When he opened his eyes later, he realized he must have passed out. He expected to see the white wolf peering down at him, but it was gone.

Then barks and woofs grew close, and again he managed to sit up and howl.

Darien howled back. He was nearly there. His brothers howled in unison. They were close by. He loved the sound of the wolves' calls to gather the pack, to warn, to share camaraderie. A wolf howled again, right above CJ's location, and peered down at him. Then several more. Darien, his brothers, others. CJ wanted to tell them to watch that they didn't fall into the pit, but he knew they would be careful. He felt like an idiot for falling into it himself.

Darien shifted, crouched to stay warmer, and quickly said, "As soon as you howled and sounded like you were buried, Peter and others went back to get ropes and gear to get you out of there. Is anything broken? Are you injured?"

CJ shook his head, his skull splintering into a thousand fragments before he heard Darien calling his name from what sounded like a million miles away. "Hell, CJ. You are too injured."

As wolves, the pack gathered, his brothers lying down next to the pit. Darien shifted into his wolf form and remained sitting upright, waiting, watching, his ears twitching back and forth, his nose sniffing the air.

Then his brothers sat up. CJ heard the other men coming before they got there. Men were so much noisier moving through the woods than wolves.

"Which way do you want to do this?" Doc Mitchell asked. "Bring him up as a wolf or a human?"

Hell, they had called the vet? CJ *wasn't* injured!

Lanterns were sitting all over the place, and someone threw a couple of glow sticks into the pit. They landed near CJ and he glanced over to see what kind of animal had fallen and broken the stakes that had saved his hide. The bones of a wild boar and an elk. But what chilled him to the marrow of his bones was a human skeleton lying among the rest of the bones scattered in the pit.

"Human skeleton," Doc Mitchell said. "Hell, CJ, we thought you were searching for a ghost wolf, not a human skeleton. Good job."

Yeah, as if CJ had jumped down here, risking life and limb, to get a look at a skeleton! But then he worried that it could be Clarinda O'Brien. That made him feel ill. He really didn't want to have to be the one to tell Laurel that her aunt had died this way.

Staring at the remains—a stake between the ribs of the human skeleton—he just couldn't believe it. Brett and Eric disappeared and reappeared a few minutes later, wearing their clothes. Each of them carried a backpack, then hooked themselves into climbing gear, getting ready to rappel down into the pit.

When they were standing on the ground beside CJ, they made sure they didn't step on any of the bones. Others in the pack would need to gather the evidence to determine who had died here and how. Instantly, CJ wondered if they'd had any other cases of missing wolves over the years. The problem was that sometimes wolves left the pack, no reason given, and there were always drifters and loners, so just about anyone could have made the mistake—like he did—of stepping on the deadfall and plummeting into the pit.

"Do you want us to take you up as a wolf or as a human?" Eric asked, crouching next to him and running his gloved hand over CJ's head.

CJ hated to shift because it was so cold and it might take him a while to get dressed. He decided to run as a wolf. He woofed.

Eric smiled. "A wolf it is." Before he put CJ in a harness to lift him out of the pit, Eric removed his gloves and checked him over, looking for broken bones or other injuries.

As a forest ranger, Eric was trained in first aid—which even meant caring for wounded animals. All the brothers and several members of the pack were trained in search and rescue and first aid. It was best that way so they didn't have to call in humans to help find and take care of their kind.

Eric's hand touched a tender ligament in CJ's foreleg, and he yelped. Eric's already furrowed brow deepened. He checked his foreleg again.

"Broken? Chipped? Torn muscle?" Doc Mitchell called down.

"Maybe just bruised," Eric said, sounding relieved.

Then Eric and Brett carefully cinched CJ into a harness and gave the go-ahead to lift him. His body scraped against the exposed tree roots, and he gritted his wolf's teeth until they hauled him up to the edge of the pit. Several hands grabbed for him, lifting him and placing him on a litter. He had every intention of running with them as a wolf, but he could see Darien and Doc Mitchell had other plans.

Three men strapped CJ down, while others went back into the pit with more lights to photograph and document the evidence and then to retrieve the human remains.

CJ growled. Wolves didn't like confinement and he really wanted to run, to prove he was just achy and nothing was really wrong.

Brett soon joined him as the men carried him on the litter. "Trevor is watching the Wernicke brothers. While you're getting checked out at the vet's, I'll let Laurel know we've found you and you're all right. You might need to stay at the clinic overnight, depending on what Doc Mitchell says. We've got men locating your clothes and cell phone. They'll give them to me so I can bring them to the clinic, and they'll also drive your vehicle back to your home."

"Doc Mitchell says CJ's staying at the clinic tonight. Unless someone watches over him." Doc Mitchell stalked up beside him, wearing his usual vet attire—leather vest, denims, well-worn cowboy boots, and a weather-beaten Stetson—and smelling of horses. He smiled.

Why couldn't they have sent Doc Weber? Though he was even older than Doc Mitchell. Maybe Darien had been afraid that making the trek would be too much for the elderly doctor. But at least he worked on humans. Not that CJ was human at the moment.

CJ growled again at being strapped down. Brett and Doc Mitchell chuckled.

As soon as Lelandi called Laurel with word that they'd found CJ and he was getting checked out at the vet's office, Laurel collapsed on the sofa, her body feeling numb, the blood draining from her face. "Thank you. I'll tell my sisters, and I'm headed over there."

"Brett asked if you'd wait and let him pick you up."

"Thanks. I'd like that." Laurel was so anxious, she wasn't sure she could drive on the icy roads, but she was relieved that CJ would be okay. At least she hoped he was. They ended the call, and she looked up to see her sisters' anxious faces. She explained what had happened, and her sisters gave her grief for not telling them beforehand.

"Do you want us to go with you?" Ellie asked, taking Laurel's hand.

"No...he's okay. He's at the vet's office."

"Vet's office?" Meghan asked. "Remind me never to get sick or injured here."

Laurel managed a smile. "Yes. They brought him in as a wolf, and the vet took him to the clinic to check him over. Brett's coming to pick me up and take me there."

"Good. We'll keep trying to find any hidden places in the highboy and blanket chest." Ellie looked at the highboy. "I don't know. Maybe neither of the pieces of furniture has secret compartments."

"Maybe not. Or we might have to find a furniture refinisher or cabinetmaker and see if he can locate a hidden compartment," Laurel said.

"Are you sure you're going to be all right?" Meghan asked. "You looked like a ghost when the color drained so quickly from your cheeks."

"Yeah. I'm just worried about CJ."

"From the sound of it, he's fine. We'll let you know if we locate anything." Meghan frowned. "Is he going home tonight?"

"I don't know."

"Well, if he needs someone to stay overnight with him, I'll volunteer you." Ellie smiled. "Don't think about *me* doing it." She glanced at the old grandfather clock. "Speaking of which, I need to go to bed."

Meghan agreed. "We can look these over again tomorrow. It's time to sleep. We'll take care of the hotel in the morning, so don't worry about rushing home from CJ's place."

"He may not even be going home." And since when did Laurel's sisters decide what she was going to do?

A knock on the door sounded, and Ellie hurried to get it. "Your chariot awaits," she said, then opened the door. "Hey, Brett, I hope your brother is all right."

Laurel stared at Ellie. Her voice sounded sweet and demure, and Laurel swore her sister was looking coyly at Brett, like a she-wolf who was interested. Laurel wondered if that had anything to do with her involvement with CJ. Maybe Ellie felt it was okay to start dating a wolf too.

"CJ will be fine. Kind of growly, but he wants to go home," Brett said. "If Doc releases him, he'll want someone to watch over him."

"That would be Laurel," Ellie said, nodding sagely.

"I'm certain one of CJ's brothers will be vying for the task." Laurel joined them, giving her sister a look to behave. Ellie just grinned back at her. "Night, Ellie, Meghan. I'll see you in the morning." After making sure that CJ was okay, she would return and retire herself. To her *bed* this time.

Brett escorted her out to his car.

"*Will* the doctor release him?" Laurel climbed into Brett's car.

"Yeah, if someone will watch over him."

She really thought one of his brothers would.

Brett shrugged. "Between you and me, if he has a choice, he's going to ask for you to stay with him. He'll be on his best behavior. Believe me. With me, he'll be a growly wolf to live with. Especially if you won't go home with him."

She chuckled. "I doubt it."

"Yeah, well, he won't show that side to you. Just to his brothers."

"Is he really all right?"

"He was knocked out when he fell, bruised, and scraped up, but all that will heal in the next few days. He'll be fine. The doc just wants him watched overnight."

"What happened exactly? Lelandi said he saw the white wolf across the river and then told Darien he was going after it. She just said you all had found him."

"He did go after the wolf. He swam across the river and then started searching for the wolf, but before he found it, he stepped on top of snow-covered deadfall rigged to cover the top of a killing pit."

She felt her stomach drop. "How'd he survive?"

"Other animals had broken off the stakes."

"Thank God for that. So he never found the white wolf?" Not that the wolf was as important as what had happened to CJ. She couldn't imagine anything more terrifying.

"No, and neither did we, but then we began to search for CJ instead because none of us had run across him. Then he howled, and we knew he'd either found something or he was in trouble."

"But he's really okay."

"Yeah. Just grouchy."

She smiled, glad he was just ill-humored. That could be resolved with a little tender loving care.

Chapter 16

WHEN LAUREL AND BRETT ARRIVED AT THE VET CLINIC, Brett went to see CJ while Doc Mitchell took Laurel into his private office and told her what he wanted her to do in case CJ began feeling bad. She hadn't even said she was going to take care of him! She'd been torn between wanting to and not letting on that she wanted to while she let one of his brothers take care of him instead.

After Dr. Mitchell talked with her, he led her to a pet exam room where CJ was sitting in a chair in his human form, fully dressed, his eyes closed. As soon as CJ smelled her scent in the room, he opened his eyes. Brett was quietly leaning against the wall, waiting for her and Doc to get there. CJ smiled a warm, loving smile. Some of the knots in her belly untangled. He immediately stood, but wavered a little.

She rushed to steady him, and he wrapped his arm around her shoulders. He wasn't clinging to her as if he needed help standing, rather like he wanted to feel her touch and hold her close. Vastly relieved, she realized how much his disappearance had affected her when she had been trying so hard not to jump to conclusions. She slipped her arm around his back and gave him a squeeze, looking up at his darkened eyes and assuring herself he truly was fine.

"Sorry that we don't have wheelchairs here. My patients don't normally need them." Doc Mitchell gave CJ a broad smile.

"I can walk," CJ grouched, and Brett immediately winked at Laurel.

She smiled a little. She understood why CJ was irritated, probably feeling emasculated in front of her.

"Come on," Brett said. "I'll help you out to the car, and Laurel can get the doors for us."

She thought she could have managed to help CJ all on her own. Then again, if CJ suddenly collapsed, Brett would be better able to handle him.

Once CJ was settled in the backseat of Brett's car, she climbed into the front and Brett said, "I didn't think to mention it, but we better run by your place so you can pack an overnight bag."

"Uh, yeah, I guess so." Laurel should have considered it, but then again, she hadn't wanted anyone, her sisters included, to believe she had planned to stay with CJ all along. Yet, witnessing his bright smile when he saw her arrive, she had felt her heart flutter with happiness. How could she have done anything but agree to stay with him?

When they arrived at her place, she hoped to slip into the house and not wake her sisters, but being wolves, they both heard her shut the front door and had to investigate. She wasn't certain if they wanted to ensure it was just her returning to the house, or if they wanted to know *why* she had returned and not remained with CJ.

As if choreographed, both of them opened their bedroom doors and peered out, frowned, and said, "What are you doing back here?"

She almost laughed at *their* growly looks.

"Don't worry. I won't ruin your plans. I'm grabbing an overnight bag."

Instantly, their expressions brightened. "Oh good,"

Ellie said. "Here I thought I'd have to go over there and stay with CJ instead." As if Ellie would even consider such a thing!

They followed Laurel into her bedroom.

"You both can sleep. No need to keep me company. I'll only be a second." Laurel hurried to grab a change of clothes and some pajamas.

"Those?" Meghan started rummaging through Laurel's sleepwear drawer. "What about this?" She held up a see-through, lace shorty nightie that Laurel loved.

"I'm not sleeping with him. And I'm not wearing that around him. And it's for summer, not winter."

"You'll get hot. If I was sleeping with him, I'd get hot." Ellie smiled.

"He's bruised and skinned up. I'm not sleeping with him."

"Oh." Meghan pulled another pajama set out. "How about this one?"

Laurel grabbed it from her, shoved it in the drawer, shut it, and headed for the bathroom. "They're waiting in the car for me, probably wondering why I'm taking so long. And you are not helping. CJ needs to rest so he can heal quicker."

"He'll heal quicker when you're in his bed, guaranteed." Meghan leaned against the bathroom doorjamb while Laurel grabbed some of her personal items, ignoring her sister's comment.

"Even agreeing to stay with him probably cheered him tremendously." Ellie moved out of the doorway to let Laurel leave.

Laurel jogged down the stairs, hoping her sisters wouldn't follow her. She made a detour into the kitchen and grabbed the box of chocolate cake off the counter. She wasn't certain it would lift CJ's spirits, but if she were him and feeling like he was, the cake would definitely lift hers.

"You're taking the chocolate cake?" Ellie said from the top of the stairs.

"We didn't even get a piece of it yet," Meghan teased.

Laurel knew they didn't care or they would have gotten a piece already.

"Night!"

"Give him extra tender, loving care from us," Meghan said.

"Pleasant dreams," Ellie said.

Laurel shook her head at her sisters, then returned to Brett's car. CJ was sound asleep, for which she was glad. She climbed in as quietly as she could, hoping that closing her door wouldn't wake him. Brett just smiled at her and drove them to CJ's house, located past a treed park and several walking trails. She thought how lovely it would be to run as a wolf there at night when everyone had gone to bed. She imagined that the park had been designed for wolves who lived close to town and still wanted a place to run.

When they arrived at CJ's home, she thought how beautiful it was. French provincial style, fashionable, elegant, a big circular drive with a stand of birch trees in the center. She had thought his house might have had a simpler design. She loved it. And she couldn't help thinking about living there—with him. She knew that was far-fetched, and yet a little thrill of excitement welled up in her at the thought. A real home. Roots. A pack. CJ. Yeah, she could see it.

As soon as Brett parked his car in the drive and shut off the engine, it was as if CJ's wolf senses were awakened and he knew at once that he was home. He sat up, groaned a little, and then smiled to see her sitting in the front seat, as if he'd forgotten she was coming home with him.

Even though he objected to Brett helping him into the house while she carried in the cake and her bag, his brother reminded him, "I told Laurel you'd be on your best behavior while she stayed with you."

She smiled at the brothers and unlocked the door. As they entered the house, the lights turned on immediately.

Brett told her the security code and where the alarm was located while he helped CJ in. She quickly disarmed it, then set the cake in the kitchen. It was all done in blue and white tile, and she loved the color scheme. Then she found Brett helping CJ to his bed in a large master bedroom suite, complete with private bath, wide-screen TV, and sitting area. She wondered what he watched in bed. She could envision seeing Christmas stories on the TV as she snuggled with him.

Everything in the room was decorated in forest greens and burgundies, making it look like a hunting lodge, very masculine and wolfish, yet really appealing to her nature too, probably owing to *her* wolfish side. It had a Victorian feel, not new age, and she loved that too.

"I'll check on you both in the morning." Brett patted her on the shoulder in a brotherly way. "Don't let him give you a hard time."

"I heard that," CJ said, frowning at him.

"He'll be fine." Laurel walked Brett to the front door, said good night, then shut the door and locked it. She thought about getting CJ a slice of cake, but figured it was so late now that he'd probably rather just sleep. She had every intention of sleeping on the velour couch in his living room, if he didn't have another furnished bedroom.

Tired, and ready to go to bed herself, Laurel returned to CJ's bedroom. "Do you want me to remove your clothes?"

"Hell, yeah," he said, and the growly expression immediately vanished. He held his arms out to her, his smile stretching from ear to ear.

"You're hurting," she said, drawing closer.

"Hell, one of the techs swabbed down all the insignificant scratches, just to look like he was doing something. I look great for getting a she-wolf's sympathy, don't I?"

She chuckled, loving his sense of humor, but then she frowned, unable to imagine him falling like that and surviving. "You could have been killed."

"I wasn't. I'm fine." He let out his breath. "Thank you for staying with me tonight. Staying at the vet clinic *wasn't* an option."

She laughed and began untying his boots. "I would never have thought that an injured pack member would be taken to the vet clinic. What would they have done with you for the night? Put you in a cage?"

"No way. If I'd been injured that badly, Doc Mitchell would have transferred me to the human clinic. Doc Mitchell was called to come out since he's more used to trudging through the woods. I was hurting at the time, so I didn't want to shift in the cold and have to try to get dressed in a hurry."

She sighed. "I really worried about you. Everyone was."

"I'm sorry. I had no way to get ahold of you."

"Darien and Lelandi kept me informed."

"I'm glad. And Trevor was watching over things there."

"Yeah."

"I think more than a third of our pack members were out hunting for me. If any bunnies were around, they must have been quivering their little tails off."

Smiling, she shook her head. "I'm glad the men found you okay." She pulled off a boot and dumped it on the floor, and then the other. Once she'd slipped off his socks, she moved to unbutton his blue flannel shirt. He wasn't wearing a sweater, but she supposed that was because he hadn't wanted to wear anything else over his cuts and bruises.

When her fingers touched his top button, he wrapped his hands around hers. "No matter what we discover," CJ said, his voice dark and serious, "I want you to stay here. With me, the pack. You and your sisters."

She looked up at him. He was frowning at her, appearing a little anxious.

"Because of what we might discover about how our aunt disappeared?"

"Because I want you in my life."

She took a deep breath and let it out. He was talking of mating with her? But she didn't want to assume that's what he was saying and make a fool of herself.

"What do you want, Laurel? Beyond learning what happened to your aunt? Do you always want to move to new locations and remodel old hotels? Do you feel that's your calling? Or is it just something you love to do, but given a choice—like staying here with the pack, with me—you might consider just running the hotel and still be happy?"

"What if we learn your father was involved in my aunt's disappearance?"

"Then he was involved. It won't come between us."

"What if it was someone else, someone close to you in the pack, and you felt resentful that we discovered the truth and upset everyone?"

"We can't allow pack members to murder people without paying the price, no matter how long ago it happened or who they are or how well they're liked. If it was due to extenuating circumstances—not saying that it was in your aunt's case, but just an example, if someone was defending himself and fatally injured the one attacking him, then we would have to take that into consideration." He ran his hands down her arms as she worked on his buttons again. "Did you find any secret compartments in the furniture that your aunt owned?"

"No. Not yet at least. Maybe they don't have any. Do you have any cabinetmakers in the pack?"

"Jacob, the electrician. He's made furniture on and off. We could have him take a look at the pieces. When you were looking over the old photos, did you see if your aunt was in any of them?"

"Aunt Clarinda didn't look like us, unfortunately. She was darker haired than Mom, finer boned, taller. I didn't see anyone in any of the photos that looked like her. That doesn't mean she wasn't there. Just that she wasn't photographed in those particular photos."

"I agree. Here, let's take off your snow boots," CJ said.

She gave him a look like she knew where this was headed.

"It's late. You have to sleep. You can't sleep in your boots."

She smiled, sat down on the bed, and removed her boots and socks. Then she stood and helped him out of his shirt, though she was certain he didn't need her help and was just enjoying her touch and the closeness it afforded him.

"Did you see any sign of the white wolf?" she asked.

He hesitated to say.

"You did. Brett didn't say anything about it."

"Yeah, I did. Though the thought briefly crossed my mind that the wolf was not really there. That I had imagined it."

Surprised, she stared at him. "Why?"

"My head was hurting, and when I looked up again, he or she was gone. The wolf had to be one of us, or he wouldn't have come to check me out. He had to be worried about me, or he wouldn't have risked discovery."

Laurel couldn't believe that he had actually seen the wolf. "Did he howl for anyone to come to help you?"

"No. The next time I looked, he was gone."

"Did you tell anyone?"

"No."

Her lips parted as she studied his serious expression. And she realized he was treating her like someone special. Someone he felt comfortable enough with to share the secrets that he didn't want to divulge to anyone else. Something a mate would do.

She sighed. "I was hoping he wasn't afraid of you and might allow you to approach him and learn who he is."

"I believe he was concerned about me, but I doubt he would have come near me if I had been above the hole."

"If he was concerned about you, that's good news. Was he a gray wolf or Arctic?"

"Gray wolf. His ears were too big to be those of an Arctic wolf."

"Then he has to be old."

"Or an injured or stressed wolf. Though I don't know how in the devil he made it across the river without us catching up to him if he was either old or injured."

"You mean the first time? Maybe he let the river carry him downstream so that we wouldn't see him getting out of the river and where he ran after that."

"Possibly."

"Are you sure it was a he?"

"No. It could have been either. All I saw were his head and forelegs. Not the size of his body. And it was dark."

She touched CJ's skin where it wasn't bruised, glad he would heal quickly and that he hadn't been severely injured. "Could the truck have belonged to someone else?"

"Might have, but it seems like the person in the truck would have seen the wolf and reported him."

"Unless the person was afraid to mention it to anyone, worried the pack members would think he was seeing things. *Or* he might have been human."

"Could be either possibility."

Laurel straightened and considered CJ's belt buckle with a brass wolf's head engraved on it. She was putting off removing his jeans. Not that she was embarrassed, but because she was afraid CJ would take it as a yes for connecting in a deeper way—a mating that would bond them together for life. Yet, he might not be ready for anything of the sort, and maybe she was thinking too much into the situation.

He needed rest, to sleep and to heal his injuries. Most likely his ligaments and muscles would be sore from the fall.

She unbuckled his belt and then began to unzip his jeans, her hand unintentionally brushing down his arousal. She saw the tension in his face and his body, the way he was trying hard not to react to her touch. But it was too late for that. She fought smiling.

"We've only known each other for around six months," she reminded him, as if they might want to take this…situation between them slower.

"That's all? Hell, we should have been mated long before this. I don't think I've known any wolf couple to wait this long before they mate. Except Silva and Sam, but even they finally agreed on it." CJ took Laurel's hand and pulled her on top of him.

She stiffened, worried she was hurting him. "Your bruises and cuts—they have to be painful."

"That's nothing compared to the thought of you packing up and leaving town. And that *is* killing me." His arms wrapped securely around her, implying that even if he was sore, he wanted the intimacy between them more. Wanted to show her just how much he needed her in his life. How he didn't want to wait.

She sighed and snuggled against him, and he began to stroke her back. She loved breathing in his musky male scent and feeling his hard body beneath hers, the way he was already aroused—all because of her touch.

"What if we never learn the truth about your aunt?"

he asked gently, his touch just as tender, not pushing to go further if she didn't wish it.

She had been afraid of that—not finding out the truth quickly enough. Of putting her life on hold when she could really build something here with CJ, her sisters, the pack. Especially because Meghan and Ellie both wanted to stay. In the past, they'd been just as eager to move on to the next project as she had been. Uprooting them now would be wrong. She couldn't ignore their happiness.

Yet if she truly did want to leave, she was certain they'd follow her. She realized it must have been that way with CJ when Eric left the pack and CJ and the others left with him to show their support of their brother, even if in their hearts, they hadn't wanted to leave the pack behind.

"Not as a have-to-or-die mission, but would you continue to help me search for clues about my aunt?" She had made the decision, right or wrong, feeling in her heart that she belonged with CJ, with his pack, no matter what happened to the hotel or what else they discovered. Being with him felt right.

In one swift and powerful move, CJ managed to turn her onto her back and pin her down with his half-clothed body. He might have had some muscle strain from the fall, but if so, he sure was hiding it and showing that he was pure alpha-male wolf. "It's a given and it's my priority, because not only do we want to solve that dilemma, but we have to learn the truth about the Wernicke brothers and what's going to happen with the hotel."

She ran her hands up CJ's chest in a soft caress,

avoiding the bandaged areas and bruises. "What if they do manage to sabotage our sales? Ruin our business? Where would my sisters and I—"

"With me—this will be your home. I have plenty of room for your sisters too."

"You only say that—"

He frowned at her. "Because I mean it. I care for your sisters as if they were like my brothers."

She laughed. "I'm sure they'd love to hear it."

He smiled. "I care for you in a whole other way—as my mate. Loving you and only you until the end. Say yes and you can show me how to create snow wolves and we can watch Christmas stories and…"

"Make love." She pulled him down for a kiss.

She wasn't being impulsive, she told herself. For half a year, she'd avoided any intimate entanglements with CJ, knowing he'd had an interest in her from the beginning that was more than just friendship.

It was obvious from the way he looked at her with wolfish interest and how he had gone out of his way to tell her how glad the pack was to have her and her sisters there and how beautiful the hotel looked. He also admired her for her dedication and tireless work despite all the troubles they'd had while renovating the hotel. He'd always been eager to help her.

She'd avoided getting in too thick with the pack members, even going so far as to ask Darien to tell his cousins she and her sisters didn't need their help. Sure, in part it was because they feared how the pack would react if they learned the sisters were trying to discover what happened to their aunt, and the fear that anyone could have had something to do with her disappearance.

But Laurel realized some of it was because of her concern that taking a mate would change her life forever, and that of her sisters. And yet, her sisters had wanted that all along.

She'd even considered that she might be dishonoring their aunt's memory by even thinking of mating a wolf from the pack, when one of its members might be connected to Aunt Clarinda's disappearance. Then again, Laurel knew in her heart that CJ hadn't had anything to do with it. There was no sense in denying she wanted this and wanted him.

He was looking into her eyes, caressing her hair, his gaze heated and lustful, but he didn't make a move to go any further, as if he was afraid she still had doubts.

So she threw herself into the kiss, into the feelings she'd been trying so hard to hide. And onto a path of no return.

"It's forever," he murmured against her ear, his hot breath tickling her.

She nodded, wanting this more than anything.

He kissed her then, his arousal pressed against her mound, his tongue tangling with hers. She wanted out of her clothes, now.

"We're too dressed," she managed to say.

"Easily remedied." CJ shucked off his jeans and boxers in the time she'd managed to sit up on the bed and grab the bottom edge of her sweater. Then he pulled off her sweater and ran his hands over her pale blue lace bra. The rough lace against her nipples made them all the more sensitive and eager for his touch.

"Are you sure?" she asked, breaking off the kiss.

"Hell, yeah." Her words seemed to trigger his need, and he quickly removed the rest of her clothes.

Then there they were—body to body, naked, man, woman, he-wolf, she-wolf…ready to do it.

He didn't ask if she was sure, just started kissing her again, his hot body working against hers, rubbing his stiff cock against her mound, showing her he wanted this.

She spread her legs, forcing him to fall between hers. She felt the smile on his lips against hers before she wrapped her legs around the back of his, claiming him, securing him to her.

He dipped his head and kissed along her throat, his breath hot as her skin tingled and her blood felt like it was on fire. His hand cupped a breast, and then his mouth was on it, his tongue licking her nipple, his lips closing in and sucking. She was wet for him, ready, throbbing with need, her fingernails caressing his scalp as she groaned with pleasure.

She had imagined being like this with him when he'd caught her eye, his gaze heated. But she never could really envision how it would feel to recline on her back on his soft bed, her legs secured around his, his cock grinding against her clit.

The intoxicating feel of him—the hot, and sexy smell of all-male wolf—felt better than right. This was it. And she wanted it, him, all of it. She slid her hands down his muscled arms, stroking him like he was stroking her breasts. Then he moved over and began to apply his fingers to her feminine bud, coaxing her into orgasm. He kissed her mouth, inserting his tongue in wickedly masculine domination.

She sucked on his tongue. He groaned and smiled a little. So much for him being totally in charge. She smiled back, and they began kissing again. She savored the way his touch aroused her and felt the climax teasing her, just out of reach, so close she could almost taste it.

He was driving her crazy with his touch, the scent of him, the raw, primal desire. She was carried away on a rough sea of pleasure, and she cried out his name. He didn't wait to see if she was ready for him or not.

CJ was ready for her. He knew she wanted this too. His throbbing need dictated his haste as he slid into her warm, wet sheath and filled her to the max.

He began to pump into her and kiss her, while her hands stroked every bit of his skin that she could touch. Gone was any hint of muscle strain or the feel of bruises as he claimed his she-wolf. He thought of how he would soon fill her belly with his progeny and loved her for it.

She thrust her hips upward as he drove in, the sensation pumping him up even harder. God, he loved her. Loved what she did to him. Loved her for just being her.

He was tense, so on the verge of relief, he growled his pleasure in a male-wolf way. Her green eyes were hot with passion, and she smiled a little at him right before he released, filling her with his seed, mating her for now and forever.

He collapsed on her, wanting to stay right there for the moment, his cock still inside her, craving the maximum intimacy between them before he separated from her and pulled her into his arms to sleep.

"Love you," he said, kissing her mouth, and she tightened her hold around him.

"Love you too." She wondered why she had avoided entanglements with him for so many months when tangling with him like this was the best thing ever.

She realized then she wasn't wearing anything to bed—forget pajamas or summery nighties. He finally moved over and pulled her against him. She wasn't certain that he'd want to sleep that close. On the couch—sure. There hadn't been room for them to move apart. But in his king-size bed they had plenty of room. He didn't let her go though, and she was just as happy to snuggle against him all night long.

Before she drifted off, she wondered how her sisters would react. Then she frowned. "I'm not hurting you, am I?" He might be feeling sore again, and she didn't want him to feel any discomfort. She could snuggle with him later, when he was all healed up.

He snorted and held on to her tighter. She smiled and snuggled closer. "Love you." And she meant it with all her heart. As sleepy as she was, she couldn't stop thinking about the white wolf he'd seen though.

"I want to search for the white wolf," she said, but CJ was so quiet, his heart rate slow, his breath soft against her hair, that she figured he had fallen asleep. She repeated softly, "I want to find the white wolf." Because she was certain the wolf was reaching out to them in some way, and she wanted to offer friendship in return. If her sisters could manage the hotel, and if CJ was feeling healed up enough to go with her, she wanted to search for the wolf first thing tomorrow morning.

Chapter 17

EARLY THE NEXT MORNING, CJ WAS UP FIXING COFFEE and crepes filled with eggs, ham, and cheese, feeling that everything would be right with the world if they could only solve the disappearances of Laurel's aunt and the other hotel owners. But he also wanted to learn who the white wolf was.

He hoped he had done the right thing last night in not telling Laurel about the human skeletal remains in the pit. He hadn't thought about it until waking this morning, and then he'd worried. He hadn't even known if the remains were male or female. And he didn't want to upset Laurel with what could be when it might not be at all.

Because of the fall he'd suffered, he realized his thoughts hadn't been focused enough to really examine anything in the pit. Not that he could have seen all that much that night, as dark as it had been. Even after they'd tossed down the glow sticks and he'd seen the human skeleton, all that he'd been aware of was that the skull was a human's, and that two of the ribs had framed one of the stakes. Which had reminded him of how damned lucky he'd been.

The doorbell rang and he stalked through the living room to see who was visiting at this hour. Normally, anyone coming to see him would call to let him know ahead of time. One good thing about living here: no solicitors, so he knew it wasn't a salesperson.

What he didn't expect was to see when he opened the door was Ellie standing on his front porch, looking distraught. "Ellie, come in."

"You found a body."

Her words felt like an accusation and hit him hard. Her gaze shifted to a point behind him, and fearing where this would lead, he turned to see Laurel, her expression one of disbelief, lips parted, red brows slightly raised. Then she frowned. "You found a body? Whose? Where? When?"

She looked so pale, he wanted to comfort her, but he suspected she'd be ready to slug him when she learned just when and where they'd found the remains.

"Docs Weber and Mitchell will be examining the area and the skeletal remains. We don't even know if it's male or female, one of our kind or strictly human," he said, speaking the truth.

"Did they find clothes? Remnants of clothes?" Laurel asked.

"I was kind of out of it last night." CJ hated admitting that.

Laurel narrowed her eyes at CJ. "Wait. *Where* were the remains found? And *when*?"

Ellie was wringing her hands, looking like she really wished she hadn't opened the can of worms.

"In the pit where I fell."

Tears filled Laurel's eyes. "You *knew* and you didn't tell me last night?" Her words were almost whispered, as if she didn't have the strength to give them any more power.

CJ took a deep breath. "Laurel, it could be anyone. Nothing to do with your aunt. There wasn't any reason to upset you when there could be no reason to do so."

"You were afraid to tell me last night because I might be too distraught and not have agreed to a mating!" Now Laurel's face was red with anger, her lips pursed.

He wished Ellie wasn't here to witness all this and that he could deal with it in private with Laurel.

Ellie's jaw dropped. "You're *mated*?"

Ignoring her sister's comment, Laurel stormed off in the direction of the front door. "I'll ask Darien to keep Trevor at the hotel to watch our guests. You don't need to be there."

CJ stalked after her to stop her. "Wait, Laurel, damn it. There wasn't any reason for me to mention—"

She gave him a dagger of a look. "Can you tell me honestly that you didn't consider that it might have upset me so much I wouldn't have mated you? At least not last night?"

He couldn't lie about it. "Of course, I considered it. But—"

"*Fine*. If we can't share important issues with each other…" She again headed for the door.

He reached out and grasped her arm. "Laurel, *wait*. I'm sorry. I didn't mean to withhold anything from you so that you'd mate me last night. I swear it."

She nodded, but he could tell she didn't believe him. Then she pulled away. "If you need to see us in an official capacity, have Peter send Trevor to talk to me."

There was no way in hell Laurel was cutting him out of her life. CJ smelled the crepes burning, and smoke started to curl into the air. "*Shit*. Wait, let me get the pan off the burner before I burn down the house." He bolted for the kitchen but heard the door slam on the sisters' way out. "Damn it to hell."

He turned off the heat on the burner, then moved the pan to the back of the stove top. He yanked out his phone and called Doc Weber. "What did you learn?"

"Good morning to you too. Feeling any better after your fall?" Typical Doc. Current medical issues had to be addressed first and foremost. Dead bodies were of secondary concern. Especially when the case was so old.

"Yes, sorry, Doc Weber. Good morning. So what did you learn about the remains?"

"White, male, approximately forty years old, can't tell if he was one of our kind since we don't leave any traces of the wolf in us. The stake he fell on gouged at one of the ribs, had to have penetrated the heart and broken another rib. The fabric left behind appears to be of the kind worn around the time that Mr. Wernicke disappeared. I'm sending out what's left of some of the fabric to a forensics lab to have them date it. It's deteriorated so much that I'd say the gentleman has been down there for years."

"Can you prove it was Warren Wernicke?"

"The dead man was wearing a diamond stickpin. It was found attached to a remnant of the clothing. If we go over the photos we have of him, we might see that stickpin. Then we'd be more assured it was him. Unless someone stole it from him and was wearing it. Or he gave it away. Or there was another like it."

Too many other scenarios. "Can you tell if he was murdered or just came across the pit by accident like I did?"

"If he had been struck, it wasn't anything that would

have killed him or caused severe injury. No sign of blunt force trauma. It looks more like he just fell and the stake piercing his heart killed him."

"Someone had to have covered the pit over with deadfall. Two other animals had fallen through."

"A wild boar and an elk. Yes. And someone had to have covered up the hole three times. The boar was off to the side, but one hind leg was beneath the human's left fibula—shinbone. The elk had landed on the other side, but the hindquarters were resting on top of the human's pelvic girdle. It's impossible to tell whether the man just fell in or was lured there on purpose."

"Who could have dug anything that deep?"

"The movement of groundwater created the natural pothole in the limestone. It's been there forever, but someone set it up as a natural trap for animals."

"Or humans. Was the meat carved off the boar? Was someone actually using the pit for hunting purposes at one point?"

"Yes, on the boar. No, on the elk."

"Then we need to know if someone actually set it up to kill a particular person, or if the one who died met his death there accidentally."

"Agreed."

CJ's cell beeped at the same time that someone began knocking on his door. "Gotta go, Doc. Call you later."

"I'll let you and Peter know if I learn anything more."

"Thanks. Out here." CJ answered the other call and headed for the front door. "Yeah, Peter? I was just talking to Doc Weber."

"I have a copy of his initial medical findings and a picture of the stickpin. Are you feeling all right enough to return to the hotel and watch what's going on over there?"

CJ answered the door, found Eric standing there, and motioned for him to come in.

"There's been a slight change of plans," CJ said to Peter as Eric walked into the house and shut the door. "Laurel wants Trevor to stay there instead, if it's all right with you."

"Anything…wrong?"

"Hell, yeah. I didn't tell her about the skeleton we found in the pit last night, and now she's pissed off at me."

"We didn't even know who it was, and it didn't turn out to be her aunt." Peter sounded annoyed with her.

"Right, but…well there's more." Hell, CJ hated to admit any of this, but he'd rather his boss and his brothers know what happened than for them to think Laurel was being completely unreasonable. "We're mated."

Dead silence.

Eric shook his head, but he was smiling. And heading for the kitchen.

"So she's pissed because… Okay, got it. I'll have Trevor stay there, and you can try to run down who our dead man is."

"Thanks. I'll get right on it." CJ ended the call and followed his brother into the kitchen.

Eric stared at the blackened pan. "Looks like breakfast didn't go over too well either."

"I've screwed up everything this time." CJ poured hot water and dish soap into the plugged sink and shoved the cooled pan into the soapy water to let it soak.

"Hey, it wouldn't be the first time and it won't be the last."

CJ frowned at him. "Thanks. I know that. But how do I fix it?"

"If it were me? I probably would have done the same thing. And been in the same bind the next morning. Have you told Darien that you're mated to Laurel yet?"

CJ let out his breath. He really didn't want to do this now. But he made the call to Darien and said, "Okay, Laurel and I are mated wolves. Just needed to let you know."

"Hot damn, CJ. That's good to hear. I'll tell Lelandi, and we'll let the pack know."

CJ wanted to groan out loud. "Okay, I've got to talk to Eric about the case."

"Good show. Talk to you later." Darien ended the call with CJ.

"Darien's glad, I take it," Eric said.

"Yeah, he is. I just didn't want to let him in on the latest development."

"Understand. The two of you will work it out. So what was Doc's finding?"

CJ showed him the findings Peter sent him over the phone, including the picture of the stickpin.

"Send the picture to my email, will you? I'll forward it to Brett since he's digging into all the photos of that period. Maybe he'll see a man wearing that pin." Eric frowned as he studied the picture. "Why would a man be wearing something so dressy when he's running around in the woods?"

"That was one of my thoughts too. Was he chasing after someone? Lured there? I'm guessing he wasn't just out for a Sunday stroll in the woods when he fell into the pit. It's too far from any road."

Eric read through the report. "And since his clothes were there, that meant he hadn't been in wolf form. Okay, what else did you need me to do? Don't ask me to fix things between you and Laurel though. You're on your own there. Oh, and by the way, congratulations."

CJ snorted. "I think that was the shortest mated relationship in history."

"You're mated for life."

"I know. But I don't think she'll have anything further to do with me."

"She'll come around. Give her time. First, the skeleton wasn't her aunt. And second, you didn't mention it because you didn't want to worry her unnecessarily. Which was heroic."

"But then I mated her."

Eric smiled. "Good move."

"Hell, Eric, now she doesn't want to see me again."

"Learn what happened to her aunt. Then maybe she'll realize why she wanted you to be her mate in the first place."

"And if I learn her aunt was murdered?" CJ shook his head. "Somehow I don't see how that's going to get me out of hot water with Laurel anytime soon."

Chapter 18

"OHMIGOD, I CAN'T BELIEVE YOU MATED WITH CJ AND didn't tell us! You can't seriously be thinking of breaking up with him. You can't as a wolf. He didn't tell you about the skeleton because he didn't know anything about it and didn't want to unnecessarily upset you," Ellie said. "He was devastated. I wanted to give him a hug and tell him everything would be all right between you, since you have such a forgiving nature, but I was afraid you'd turn all wolf on me and bite me."

Laurel fought smiling at her sister. Ellie could always brighten her outlook, even during the darkest moments of their lives.

"Jeesh," Ellie continued, "he burned the breakfast he was fixing—and just the fact he *was* cooking breakfast should clue you in that he's a keeper. It was killing him that he had to run to take care of the dangerous mess before he had a fire on his hands and couldn't stop you from leaving. You know when he heard us shut the door, he had to have been really shook up. He probably would have carried you off to bed and made it up to you right after that if I hadn't been there."

"He didn't tell me about the skeleton, Ellie! Don't you get it? He didn't want me delaying a mating with him last night! He might not have wanted to upset me, sure, but it was the business of the mating that makes the difference." Laurel's cell rang and she saw that it was

CJ. Her heart skipped a couple of beats. She couldn't help it. She really did love the wolf.

Ellie glanced at her. "If it's CJ, *answer* it."

Laurel gave her sister a dark look. She wasn't going to ignore him. She was far too alpha for that. "What?" she snapped at CJ.

Ellie smiled.

"I'm sending the official police report to you, but I'll give you a brief synopsis." He told her about the skeleton found in the pit. The skeleton was a *male*. Instantly, she felt her eyes fill with tears.

She was relieved that it hadn't been their aunt, but she still felt bad that someone else had come to such a gruesome end. She thought again about CJ and how it could have been him. She quickly wiped away tears. Before her sister got the wrong idea, Laurel held her hand over the mouthpiece of the phone. "The skeleton didn't belong to our aunt."

"Thank God for that." Ellie sounded as relieved as Laurel was.

"This is what we're looking for now. A man who was wearing this diamond stickpin," CJ said, sending her a photo of the jewelry.

"Mr. Wernicke," Laurel said, barely getting his name out. "There's a picture of him standing in front of the hotel with a lot of other folks. It appeared to have been his grand opening."

"Are you sure?"

"They had a close-up photo of him."

"Hell, if the pin is his and he was wearing it at the time of his death, then that was him in the pit. I'm on my way over to your place. I spoke with Jacob, and he said he'd meet me there so we could look over your aunt's furniture."

Laurel should have suspected that CJ wouldn't take her at her word. "All right. We're just pulling up at the house now. Ellie's going to go to the hotel. Trevor and Meghan are taking care of it for now. I'll see you in a few—" She raised her brows to see CJ's truck pull in beside Ellie's car. "Now."

Ellie shook her head. "He's your mate, and you're his. Looks to me like he's not letting you go. That's a good sign. I'll see you later. Oh, and you're not planning on keeping your mating secret, are you?"

"I doubt it's a secret any longer."

"Good. I'm telling Meghan before she gets pissed off because she's the last to know. You think you have it rough with CJ. You don't want to offend Meghan over this." Ellie hopped out of the car. "Later." She gave CJ a small smile.

He looked like he was in the doghouse, which was infinitely worse than anything a wolf could imagine. Wolves were *not* dogs.

Laurel almost took pity on him, but she wanted him to realize how underhanded she felt he'd been last night.

Ellie hurried off, crunching through the snow when CJ shifted his attention to something in the drifts. Laurel glanced down to see what he saw. Wolf prints.

"Who was running around your property as a wolf last night?" he asked, sounding accusatory.

"I was with you last night. How would I know?"

"Someone was. And you have human guests."

He crouched down and looked closer. "Definitely a wolf's from the size and shape." He followed the tracks, while Laurel hurried after him, until they reached the street that had been recently plowed. "Looks like the wolf ran along the road after that. Then the snowplow scraped the rest of the paw prints away."

"Or the wolf got into a vehicle and drove off."

"Right."

Jacob drove up in his electrician's van and greeted them both. "You needed me to look at some furniture for hidden compartments? Every carpenter has his own method. That's what makes them truly secret."

"Thanks, Jacob, for coming over on such short notice," CJ said.

"No trouble at all for the Silvers and their mates." Jacob smiled at Laurel.

Great. She so hoped that Meghan hadn't heard from Trevor that she was mated to CJ.

Before they reached the house, she heard the sunroom door slam and saw Meghan headed her way, red-faced.

"Why don't the two of you go in and take a look at the furniture? They're the highboy without any drawers and the blanket chest sitting in the middle of the living room. I'll be inside in a moment."

The two men headed inside as Laurel steeled herself for Meghan next.

Meghan frowned at Laurel and stalked right past her!

Laurel hurried after her. "What's wrong?" She was afraid her sister intended to slug CJ, when Laurel and CJ had to work out their own differences. She didn't want her sisters' or anyone else's interference.

"One of the Wernicke brothers and Trevor are having a disagreement. I thought *your mate* could help out."

Just great. All Laurel needed was trouble with the Wernicke brothers right now.

"All right. I'll tell him. Wait, you tell him and I'll head over there. You stay here with Jacob and see what he learns about the secret compartments in the furniture."

Laurel hurried off to the hotel, and when she reached it, she heard the door to the house slam. "Hold up!" CJ called out to her. As if he was going to be her knight when she was perfectly fine on her own. And she had to let him know that right away. She wasn't some little beta wolf he had gone and mated.

She headed inside but before she shut the door, she heard him racing across the snow to catch up to her. She smiled a little, shut the door, and hurried to reach the main room where Stanton and Trevor were arguing.

Ellie was on the phone, standing behind the check-in counter taking a reservation and typing away at the computer.

"All I said was we wanted our reservations extended because we know there's more time available and…" Stanton stopped speaking when he saw Laurel enter the room.

"I already told you it was booked," Laurel said.

"And I already told *you* that the hotel belongs to us."

She folded her arms. "Do you have proof?"

"We do. We've sent for it."

She didn't believe him. She felt CJ draw close to her, smelled his sexy scent, felt the heat of his body, and in that instant, no matter how crazy the thought was, she wanted him to pull her into his arms and give her a hug.

"We heard a body—or skeleton, I should say—was

found in the woods. Was it our aunt or uncle? Her aunt? When do we get to ID the body?" Stanton asked.

"That might be kind of difficult, given that only a male skeleton was found. We're awaiting official verification on who the individual was," CJ said.

"Where exactly was it found?"

"In the woods. But the area is a crime scene for now. So no access to civilians. You wouldn't happen to have ever hunted prey using a deadfall trap, would you have? Or your brothers?" CJ asked.

Stanton smiled a little at him. "Like now I'm a suspect? Or my brothers are? Anything to ensure the MacTires keep our rightful property? It won't work."

"The hotel has been sitting vacant for years. Why come now and try to lay claim to it? Because it's newly renovated? Because you couldn't have managed it on your own? Or because now it has some value?" CJ asked.

"Hell, we could have fixed the place up on our own and cut the cost of renovation in half. First, we didn't know our aunt and uncle had owned it. And once we learned they had and then disappeared, we were so busy with our successful TV show that we didn't have time to prove we owned it."

"And before, it wasn't worth a whole lot and now it is? Besides, it wouldn't have been free and clear for you to just take over anyway," CJ said, bringing both issues up again.

She suspected the same. Maybe they realized that it could be a profitable venture after all, even if they had to pay for the hotel like she and her sisters had.

Stanton shook his head. "Fine. I'll talk with the sheriff." He and his brothers stalked out of the hotel.

"He's got to realize he's not getting anywhere with Darien running the pack and the town," Trevor said, "unless it benefits the rest of us."

"They must not be with a pack. Stanton is used to throwing his weight around with his proverbial TV stardom," Laurel said. "Prima donna."

"I had an idea worth exploring if you want to talk about it. But I wanted to see if Jacob made any progress on the furniture." CJ appeared hopeful that she'd give him a break.

She noticed that Ellie had ended her phone conversation and was waiting expectantly to see how this played out between Laurel and CJ.

"Anything I should know about?" Trevor asked.

"Not really. I just had some notion where we could look next," CJ said. "Hey, by the way, have you experienced anything ghostly in the attic room?"

Trevor straightened and said, "No, nothing. Why?"

CJ nodded, but he was smiling just a little bit. Laurel took CJ's hand and pulled him in the direction of the sunroom and the back door. He immediately tightened his hold on her hand, and she appreciated that he wanted to make amends, despite how she had reacted earlier.

"I'm sorry about last night." CJ looked down at her with such compassion, she knew he was being honest about this.

"You did what you thought best. I'm sorry the skeleton was there, but I'm glad it wasn't my aunt. What did you have in mind?"

He smiled down at her as they walked outside into the brisk, cold breeze.

"About the investigation," she reminded him.

His smile broadened.

She chuckled, freed her hand, and wrapped her arm around his waist to get closer. "I think my sisters were mostly irritated with me for being upset with you."

"Did I mention how much I love your sisters?" CJ wrapped his arm around her shoulders. "All of the boxes containing my dad's personal effects are stored in Eric's basement. I'll call him, and you and I can go through what we can, if you want. None of us ever looked through the stuff. Just boxed it up and stored it down there. I doubt we'll find anything of importance, but it's worth taking a look."

With tears in her eyes, Laurel pulled him to a stop. "This has to be really difficult for you. But yes, even if we can't find anything among his things, that will be one place we can cross off our list."

He lifted her face. "I want you to know I only thought of checking through my dad's things this morning when I was making breakfast. Then other business sidetracked us this morning."

"I understand completely." But Laurel knew going through his dad's stuff had to bother the brothers. They'd just boxed everything up instead of sorting through and getting rid of some of it, while keeping treasured mementos at their homes. CJ's words spoke volumes. The brothers hadn't been able to deal with their father's belongings or his betrayal.

"Thank you. You can't know how much that means to me."

"We might not find anything. I don't want to get your hopes up."

That wasn't what made the gesture so incredibly important to her. "Thank you."

They walked into the house, and Jacob shook his head. "I've checked both pieces of furniture thoroughly. I couldn't find any hidden compartments. They don't have any."

Disappointed, Laurel thanked him.

"Did you want Jacob and me to move the furniture someplace else?" CJ asked, since the chest and highboy were just sitting in the middle of their living room and in the way.

"The guest room, if you don't mind." Laurel hugged Meghan, who gave her a warm embrace back.

"We'll learn the truth," Meghan assured her.

"We're going to Eric's house to look through some boxes of stuff," Laurel said.

"Boxes?"

"Sheridan's personal effects."

Her expression sympathetic, Meghan glanced at CJ. "Okay. What did you want me to do in the meantime?"

"Look through all those photos again and see if you recognize our aunt in any of them. But show CJ and Jacob where to put the furniture first. I need to pack a couple of bags."

Meghan smiled brightly. "You're staying with CJ tonight?"

"That's usually the way it goes."

Meghan was still smiling when she went with the men to show them where to take the furniture.

Laurel saw CJ's pleased expression before she ran up the stairs and entered her bedroom. She had nearly finished packing the second bag when she heard footfalls on the stairs and looked up to see CJ entering her room.

"Can I help you with packing?" The tension in his

body gone, he looked relieved that she was packing some of her things so she could stay with him. She had to admit that moving out felt weird when her sisters were staying behind.

"No thanks. I've got it. Did you get ahold of Eric?"

"Yeah. He's going to meet us there and help us sort through the stuff."

"It's not going to be too upsetting for you both, is it?"

"No. It's way past time to do this. Brett and Sarandon will be by a little later. We're going to discard what no one wants, and if anyone wants any of it, we'll sort it out."

"All right." She finished packing and CJ took the bags.

"Meghan sure seemed glad to see that you are moving out."

Laurel smiled. "Only because I'm not fighting with you and I'm not going to uproot them again. But I have to say that each of my sisters has always been delighted about moving. Until we settled here. It just feels like home. Like we belong. I don't know how it could when our aunt went missing from here."

"It's the pack."

"Yes. And the town. But especially you."

CJ put her bags down and pulled her into his arms. "I'm sorry for not telling you about the skeleton last night. I love you, Laurel. I don't want anything to come between us."

She hugged him tight. "I just want to learn the truth and put this behind us. Especially if someone in the pack murdered her, and he or she is still here."

CJ kissed her mouth. "Agreed."

"After we look through the boxes, would you mind if we visited the pit where you fell?"

"We can do that. We haven't eaten yet. Did you want to do that first?"

"Okay, we can drop my bags at your place…"

"Our place."

She smiled a little. "Haven't gotten used to that idea yet. Or I could make something here."

"My place."

She suspected he wanted a little privacy.

"What are you thinking concerning the pit?" He carried her bags downstairs, and she followed him.

"I don't know how to explain it. But ever since I learned that you'd been injured there, then the skeleton was found, and the white wolf had visited you as if to see if you were all right, I've had this compelling urge to go there. What if the white wolf is hanging around the area?"

"If we manage to fall into the pit, he might come check us out. But I seriously doubt, as elusive as he is, that he'll freely come to us. He didn't even howl for help."

"That could be because no one would know his howl. Don't you think?"

"Could be."

They found Meghan in the dining room, sifting through the photos. "Did you pay Jacob for his time?" Laurel asked, realizing he'd already left.

"No need. He's gone, but he said he wished he could have found a false bottom or something to help us. He said if we have any trouble with any electrical wiring, just give him a call and he'll be right over."

"Thanks, Meghan. I'll call you later if we locate anything."

"Same here."

Laurel hoped they'd find something in Sheridan's effects to help them, and yet she hoped they wouldn't if it proved he had anything to do with their aunt's disappearance.

Chapter 19

CJ HAD EVERY INTENTION OF MAKING UP TO LAUREL for last night and this morning after he'd burned their breakfast. He wanted to make a fresh start.

When they got to his house, he turned off the security alarm right away. Before he could even carry her bags up to the bedroom, Laurel began removing her clothes. She was only ditching her coat, gloves, and hat—winter weather gear—but the way she was doing it had him intrigued and smiling.

She dumped them on the carpeted living room floor, piece by piece, not hanging her hat or coat on the coatrack. She yanked off one snow boot and then the other as she continued on her way upstairs to the master bedroom.

He thought she might just be planning to change into her cute, fuzzy slipper boots while they ate lunch. But something about the way she was moving, her hips swaying a bit, and the way she was tossing her clothes in a flirtatious manner indicated she was being her playful self again. Only this time with sexual overtones.

Carrying her bags, he followed behind her, stopping when she paused to pull off one sock and then the other, tossing them over her shoulder in a come-hither way. One bounced off his chest, the other off his crotch, his cock already swelling with interest. "Are you leaving a trail for me?"

She glanced over her shoulder. "If you hurry, you might get something."

He had planned to make love to her after they had something to eat and before they went to Eric's house. But this worked even better.

When they reached the bedroom, he dumped her bags on the floor and pulled out his phone.

She yanked off her sweater and threw it at him.

Grinning, he caught it, got hold of his brother, and said, "Hey, Eric, we'll be there a little later than we planned."

"Gotcha."

CJ ended the call, tossed the phone and Laurel's sweater to the foot of the bed, and tackled his playful mate, pinning her to the mattress before he began kissing her. He loved this. She was still too dressed in her jeans and bra, but he loved her playfulness and wanted to draw out the fun. He was glad they were back to this stage in their new mating.

Her heart was beating faster, her green eyes dark and sultry, her mouth curved in a half smile as she began yanking his shirttail out of his jeans. And all that sexy she-wolf was his. His mate. His love.

The room was cool, but rubbing his body against hers, his jeans against hers, with the heat building between them, he felt like every cell was on fire. He breathed in the tangy, citrusy scent of her, the sweetness and spiciness.

Her breasts rising and falling, she breathed him in just as eagerly. Her hands fumbled with his buttons, while he rubbed against her jeans-covered mound, wanting to savor the sensation of all her softness pressed against his hardness.

Burning desire flooded every bit of him as he ached to fill her with his cock, but he took it slowly, unfastening her bra—glad it unsnapped in the front—and pulling the lace aside so he could ply her nipples with his tongue.

When he mouthed her, she groaned a little. She tried to yank his shirt off. He quickly pulled it off and tossed it aside.

She slid her hands up his chest, her touch warm and tender. She ran her palms over his nipples. He groaned a little at how sensitive they were with the silky contact.

She smiled wickedly, then wriggled her hand between them to stroke him through his jeans. Not to be outdone, he moved a little off her so he could do the same through *her* jeans, the fabric molding to her clit.

But with his move, she started to tackle his belt, trying to unfasten it. He rolled off her and unbuckled it. But then he realized he hadn't even taken off his boots and let out a frustrated groan.

She laughed and removed her jeans and her bra, then got on the floor and began untying his bootlaces.

He tangled his fingers through her satiny red hair, loving the soft feel of it. She made him hot just with her fingers untying his laces, the anticipation killing him. He wanted to help, but he wanted to savor this too.

After she tugged off his boots and socks, she slid her hands up his jeans-covered thighs, a wickedly devious smile playing on her lips and in her eyes. Her thumbs stroked up his cock, already rock hard and ready for action, the erotic sensation making it throb with pent-up need. She peeled his jeans down, and he rose from the bed so she could finish pulling them off.

And again she ran her hands over his erection

straining against his briefs. "Hmm," she said and began stroking.

He quickly slipped his hand inside her panties and began to rub her sweet spot, which made her melt against him. It was time. He slipped off her panties and she did the same with his briefs, admiring his cock as it sprang forward. Smiling, he pulled her onto the bed and began to stroke her in earnest.

Enough foreplay; he was ready for the whole, sweet deal. Her mouth opened to his, their breaths mingling, before he pressed his lips against hers. Deepening the kiss, he continued to stroke her, enjoying the way she moaned at his touch, arching her back and pressing against his fingers. She was so tense, so wet and ready for him.

"Oh, CeeeJaay," she said in a half groan, half whisper.

He pushed his cock into her wetness, deep, plunging, pulling out nearly to the end and lunging in again. Her hands ran over his arms, his waist, her body supple and soft and welcoming.

He was glad they had this time together, to love as mated wolves loved each other. They needed this. He needed this.

She jacked him up, made him crave her touch, and sent him rocketing to the ends of the earth, and then he released deep inside of her and felt his wolf half collide with the moon, his human side sizzling in the sun.

He continued to pump into her until he was spent, drained, and so happily satiated. Collapsing on top of her to give her a hot embrace, he said, "You're everything to me."

She wrapped her arms and legs around him, kept him

seated to her, and smiled up at him in a dreamy, sexy way. "Do…you think your brother will mind if we take a little longer?"

CJ smiled at her, loving her.

After a nap and another quick bout of lovemaking— they were "newlyweds," after all—they finally dressed and headed downstairs to the kitchen.

"Okay. Do…you want me to make us lunch and you can work on the pan soaking in the cold water?" she asked, her hand on his.

"Sure, I can do that." They shared another blissful tongue-tingling kiss, and then he began to scrub the burned crepe off the pan from the morning's breakfast disaster.

She made them tuna sandwiches and pulled out of a jar of pickles. "I was so disappointed that we didn't find any hidden niches in my aunt's furniture." She paused as she forked some pickles onto their plates. "I wonder if we could find the cabinetmaker."

CJ finished scrubbing the pan and rinsed it. "Possibly someone else in the pack would know who the initials belonged to. Maybe he made furniture for some others."

"I'll have one of my sisters take a picture of it and send it to Darien, Peter, and you."

CJ smiled a little at her.

She knew what he was thinking. This was the first time she was asking the pack to search for clues. She had finally accepted that she was part of the pack. Though she thought that had been obvious when she had mated CJ. Still, contacting Darien and not doing everything on her own definitely signaled a change.

CJ set the pan on a board to dry, then poured some chips onto their plates.

She sighed, wrapped her arms around him, and kissed him. "Okay, let me get this done, then we can eat." As soon as she texted her sisters, Meghan sent back a picture of the cabinet that Laurel then forwarded to Darien, Peter, and CJ.

Before CJ could pull out his phone and look, Darien called her. "Thanks, Laurel. I believe that belongs to Elroy Summers."

"Is he related to Jacob Summers, the electrician?" She was about ready to tell Darien how Jacob had already looked over the furniture and hadn't located anything.

"His father, yes. That's why Jacob knows how to create furniture, but he really didn't care to do it and instead went into the electrical business, to his father's dismay."

"Okay, so can we speak with Elroy?"

"He's deceased, I'm afraid."

Figured. "Thanks."

"You're welcome. If you come up with any other ideas, feel free to run them past me."

She ended the call and she down to eat with CJ.

"No luck?" CJ asked.

"Darien said it was Jacob's father's work. But that he's deceased."

CJ rose from his chair, surprising her, then pulled her from her chair and hugged her tight, and she loved him for it. "We'll learn the truth sooner or later."

<hr />

For hours, Laurel, CJ, and his brothers combed through all their dad's stuff in the boxes—piles of clothes and knickknacks, books, kitchen stuff—all sitting around the basement, each sorting carefully through everything.

Laurel so appreciated them for it, for taking the time and caring when they could very well find something that implicated their father in her aunt's disappearance.

Eric was sifting through every article of clothing, checking all the pockets and folding the clothes neatly in another stack in one corner of the basement after he'd finished with them. "If no one objects, I'm donating all his clothing to charity once we're through with it."

"Agreed," Sarandon said.

Brett and CJ concurred.

Brett was sorting through kitchen items and stacking them in another pile. "I suggest we dispose of all this stuff in the same way."

Everyone agreed.

"I wonder if Dad's old furniture had any secret compartments," Brett added.

Everyone stopped what they were doing and looked at him.

"Probably not. Just a thought," Brett said.

"We sold all of Dad's furniture at auction because none of us had room for it or any interest in hanging on to it," Eric said. "Besides, it was new stuff. I doubt any of it would have had secret compartments."

"Except for that old chest with all the drawers that belonged to our grandfather. I kept that," CJ said. "I'll check it out tonight."

Laurel found a picture of what looked like the boys with their mother and father. They were all smiling, and that made her smile. She set it aside and had begun sifting through men's jewelry—tie tacks, an old pocket watch, and cuff links—when she came across a locket. At once, a chill raced up her spine.

What were the odds that Sheridan's mother, or maybe his wife, had owned a locket just like the ones her mother and aunt owned, with a tree of life etched into the metal? Though most wolves didn't wear jewelry because they didn't want to lose it if they had to shift and leave their clothes behind, her mother and aunt had always kept the pictures of each other close to their hearts. She realized then that CJ had never talked about his mother. Nor had she discussed hers with him.

Barely breathing, her fingers trembling, she prayed it wasn't her aunt's locket as she opened it. And saw what she feared she'd see—her mother and aunt's pictures when they were sixteen. Suddenly Laurel felt light-headed. She gasped. The room had been quiet, so the brothers must have heard her. CJ was on his feet in an instant and headed for her. Tears filling her eyes, she stared at the picture of her mother and aunt. Though they were twins, they looked so different. She couldn't believe Sheridan would have her aunt's locket, and she felt sick to her stomach.

"Laurel." CJ rubbed her back as he saw the color completely drain from her face and knew she'd found something that belonged to her aunt. But when he looked down at the pictures in the locket, Laurel's hand trembling, he was confused. "Ellie?" The one woman was the spitting image of her.

"Clarinda and my mother, her twin sister, Sadie," she whispered. "Ellie looked just like Mom when she was that age." She looked up at CJ with tears in her eyes, and his heart went out to her. She was worried how *they* would feel about going through their father's things. And now this. "Why would your father have this? My aunt always wore it. My mother had a matching one, and when she died, she was wearing it when we buried her."

CJ swore under his breath. If his dad had anything to do with Laurel's aunt's disappearance, he'd have wanted to kill the bastard himself, if he'd still been alive.

His brothers had stopped sorting through their father's effects, red-faced and looking as angry as he felt.

"I want to go for a run." Laurel stood.

"We'll keep looking through his stuff," Eric assured her.

"Yeah," Brett said.

Sarandon nodded.

"I'll go with you." CJ knew where she wanted to run. And he suspected she had to get away from anything to do with his father for the moment. Did she believe the white wolf might come to them? He didn't think it would.

They grabbed their coats, and he walked her out to his truck. "I'm so sorry."

"Don't be. It…it was just a shock to find it there. That's all. I don't want to speculate on why. I…I don't want to think about it."

CJ couldn't imagine one good reason why his father would have had her aunt's treasured possession. "I'm sure we won't find anything in the area of the pit, if you're thinking we'll locate any clues. We've had tons of men out there searching for any evidence."

"I just want to see it."

"All right." He didn't want to get her hopes up. And he wanted to talk to her about how she was feeling about things—the necklace, his father, him. He didn't want anything to come between them over this.

She zipped the necklace into a pocket of her coat, and then they drove as close to the pit as they could and parked. Then they stripped, leaving the clothes in the truck, locked it, and shifted.

CJ had planned to lead the way because he thought he could find the pit again.

But she suddenly veered off in a different direction. A couple of years back, some of their teens had survived a fall from the cliffs that were located in this direction, and he sure as hell didn't want her getting anywhere near them.

He chased after her to head her off, until he saw what she must have seen—wolf tracks in the crystallized snow. He smelled the air—crisp, clean, fresh, pine-scented air. A rabbit, deer, no other wolves except for the pack members' scents. How many had come after him? Dozens.

The tracks could have been from any of the wolves searching for clues. Except for one thing. These were fresher tracks. Still, anyone could have come back and began snooping around.

Then Laurel stopped and was staring at something in the woods. He looked to see what she saw. A wolf. White. And female, he thought, because of her smaller stature. She was a long ways from where they were.

They chased after her, but when they reached a snow-covered dirt road, they witnessed a blue truck taking off, the windows so tinted that they couldn't see the driver. But this time CJ got the license plate number and smiled a little.

Chapter 20

As soon as CJ ran the license plate number and got the name of the vehicle's owner, CJ and Laurel headed for Green Valley, where Ryan McKinley and Carol, his mate, ran the wolf pack. Green Valley wasn't wolf run, but Ryan and Carol were working on that, modeling it after Silver Town. When CJ learned who the truck belonged to, he called Ryan, putting the call on speakerphone so that Laurel could hear everything that was being said as they drove to Green Valley. Ryan was a private investigator, so he could help them clear this matter up if they couldn't on their own.

"Okay, so you're saying the sweet little lady who owns the local candy shop, Pamela Houser, has been running through your territory as a white wolf? Yes, she's white. Not Arctic though. I don't understand the trouble," Ryan said.

Good leaders stuck up for their pack members, and CJ expected as much from Ryan. "She's been hanging around an area where we found a skeleton—a male who fell through a deadfall. We want to question her to see if she knows anything about Warren and Charity Wernicke's disappearances while they were operating the Silver Town Inn. Can you hold her there for questioning? We've got a lot of unanswered questions, including some concerning the disappearance of Clarinda O'Brien, aunt of the MacTire sisters who now run the hotel."

"Will do. Call you back as soon as I have confirmation. We'll meet at my house. She really is the sweetest woman."

"Thanks, Ryan. We owe you big-time on this."

"You're welcome. Anything we can do to help."

When they arrived at the McKinleys' house, Ryan's sister, Rosalind, invited them inside. Lavender candles on the spruce-decorated mantel scented the air as a warm fire glowed.

"Would you like some peppermint mocha?" Rosalind asked, smiling cheerily.

"We don't want to put you out any," CJ said at the same instant that Laurel said, "I'd love it."

He smiled at Laurel, glad she was not overly anxious about this. Or, maybe she was and this was a way for her to relax a little.

Rosalind asked CJ, "Are you sure? It's as easy to fix one as it is two."

"Sure, thanks."

CJ and Laurel took a seat on the blue-and-white couch and waited for Ryan to arrive with Pamela.

His mate, Carol, was at the clinic working as a nurse. Rosalind brought them cups of peppermint mocha decorated with red, white, and green candy canes while they waited. "They'll be here shortly," Rosalind said, looking concerned. She motioned to the greenhouse out back. "I've got some orders to deliver, if you don't mind me running off."

"No, go ahead," Laurel said, then took a sip of her drink. "And thanks so much for the peppermint mocha. It's delicious."

"You're so welcome. Season's been busy. Have to

deliver some more poinsettias." Then Rosalind grabbed a coat and gloves and disappeared out back.

CJ took Laurel's hand in his, but it was ice cold. He wrapped his arm around her shoulders, assuming she was nervous about what they'd learn.

She studied the tree near the fireplace, decorated in huge bows, with a red wood-beaded garland, blue and white ornaments, and sparkly blue lights.

"You don't have a Christmas tree up in your house," she suddenly said.

Given the circumstances, he was surprised when Laurel brought it up, but he was glad she was thinking about happier subjects. "Um, no. It seemed kind of silly to put one up just for me."

"We'll have to put one up now."

He smiled. "Sure. I'd love to." Anything to please his mate. He hadn't even thought about waking up with her on Christmas morning. He knew just what he was going to get her for Christmas though.

She kept drawing in deep breaths, and he squeezed her against his body with reassurance. "It'll be all right."

"Right."

But he knew it wasn't really. He was trying to be her rock, but he was just as worried about what they'd learn.

As soon as they heard Ryan unlocking the door, CJ stood. Laurel remained seated on the couch. Ryan entered with a spry, white-haired woman, her hair done up in a bun, her blue eyes taking in Laurel and CJ. She looked stern, probably just as anxious to get this over with.

CJ hurried to welcome her, his hand outstretched, wanting to put her at ease. Her hand was as cold as Laurel's had been.

"Did you want something to drink?" Ryan asked Pamela.

"No, thank you."

"Unless you need me for anything, I'll be in my office working on some business," Ryan said, also trying to put everyone at ease.

"Sure, thanks. We're fine." CJ was glad the McKinleys were letting them handle this on their own. CJ took a whiff, trying to smell the woman's scent. She-wolf and sweet, as if she'd been working in a candy shop—vanilla, sugar, maple, oranges.

"Pamela? I'm Laurel MacTire," Laurel said as the woman took a seat on a blue-and-white floral chair perpendicular to the couch.

CJ rejoined Laurel and sat as close as he had before, bodies touching to show her he supported her totally.

For a long moment, the woman just considered Laurel. Then she finally said, "Yes." But her voice hitched and her eyes filled with tears. Her spine was tense, her knuckles white as she fisted her hands in her lap.

"Pamela Houser isn't your real name, is it?" Laurel asked, her words gentle as if she was trying to coax the truth out of the woman.

CJ hadn't thought that. More that the older woman knew the man in the pit and had been close to him.

The woman didn't say anything, but her jaw tightened.

"You're...you're Warren Wernicke's sister, Charity, aren't you?"

A couple of tears rolled down the woman's cheeks. Her lips were pinched, and she nodded.

"We found his skeleton in the pit where I fell, didn't we?" CJ asked, needing verification that the remains were those of Warren Wernicke.

"Yes," she said so softly that if he hadn't had wolf hearing, he might not have heard her response. "I'm… Charity. Though Warren called me Chair for short. But he was the only one who called me by that term of endearment."

"Your brother, Warren," Laurel said, getting clarification.

The older woman nodded and looked down at the floor.

"How did he end up in the pit?" CJ asked.

She shook her head.

"You don't know?" Laurel asked.

"No." Again, the word was spoken so softly that it was hard to hear. He thought she was telling the truth.

Laurel took the discussion in a different direction. "My aunt Clarinda was living with you in the house behind the Silver Town Inn, wasn't she?"

CJ understood Laurel's need to learn about her aunt, though he still wanted to know if Charity knew anything more about her brother's death.

The woman's face was already tight with emotion and grew even more so at the mention of Clarinda's name. "She was living off my brother's generosity and seeing another wolf. That's what she was doing."

Laurel clenched her teeth a little but didn't say a word.

"Who was the other wolf?" CJ took hold of Laurel's hand. He wanted to give her support, but not treat her like she couldn't deal with this on her own. Yet, anything the woman said could be untrue. After all, she'd been living under a false identity. Then again, some wolves changed their identities because of the trouble with their longevity and humans growing suspicious of someone who didn't age as quickly as they did.

"How do *I* know?" Charity sounded annoyed.

Laurel stiffened a little beside him. "You knew she was seeing another wolf, you said," she reminded her.

"My brother was so angry with her. He knew she was seeing someone else. But he wouldn't say who."

CJ narrowed his eyes. "Because he didn't know, or he just imagined she was and she wasn't really?" CJ realized that they had a hostile witness on their hands where Laurel's aunt was concerned. He hadn't expected this.

"The woman didn't do anything. She didn't work for him. He didn't want her to. He wanted to care for her. He loved her. Treasured her. Doted on her. He wanted to mate her, but she kept putting him off. And what did she do in return? Used him. Free room and board, smiled sweetly when it was convenient for her, and that was it. He kept broaching the subject of mating her. He adored her, no matter how she treated him. I tried to get him to see what she really was. I did all the household chores—cooked, cleaned, and kept the books. I adored my brother. The two of us had always been close. Until the night that *she* arrived."

Thinking back on what Stanton Wernicke had said, CJ prompted, "So Warren took her in because he had no room at the hotel for her and—"

"Who said *that*? Of course, there was room for her. Only she didn't have money to pay for a room. And my brother, who didn't want to give up a good room to a nonpaying guest, decided to make other arrangements. I objected, but my brother just ignored me. She was a perfect stranger. What did we know about her? Nothing. And we needed another maid. Not that she would have been a good choice. She was spoiled rotten. Never lifted a finger around the place. Didn't know how to cook. Didn't want to learn. I doubted she would have done a good job as a maid."

"What did she do while she was staying with you?" Laurel asked, her tone cool.

"Nothing!"

"She sat on the couch and stared out the window? Read books? Left the house each day? She had to have done something." Laurel sounded totally exasperated.

CJ knew that the woman held a major grudge against Clarinda and everything she said was tainted by that hate. Was she jealous? He wished they could hear Clarinda's version of the story. "So your brother disappears—"

"Right. And I had to take over the hotel."

"And my aunt?" Laurel asked.

"Oh, she disappeared the night before that. I figured my brother had gone after her. And then he never came back. At first, I thought he had caught up with her, decided not to return, and they went off together. But he loved the hotel. And she just wasn't mating him."

Laurel took a deep breath and let it out. "Why wouldn't she mate him? Did she say?"

"No. And my brother kept asking her. They started having arguments. I wasn't supposed to be privy, but you know how it is with our wolf hearing. I was in the kitchen making supper so I wasn't all that far away. They were loud. She started crying, and then she left. I heard my brother pacing across the floor in the living room. I came in to check on him.

"He growled at me to stay the hell out of his business. He knew I didn't like her, so I guess he felt I'd say something bad about her to him, and he didn't want to hear it. But I hadn't planned to. He was angry and distraught, and I had no intention of making it worse. I was trying to lend him a sympathetic ear."

CJ didn't believe it. "When did he leave?"

"He was up most of the night, pacing or cursing. He managed the hotel through the next day, but when she hadn't returned by nightfall, he went out looking for her." Even though Charity's words were spoken with annoyance, her eyes clouded with tears again, and he assumed she still grieved for the loss of her brother.

"Wearing a suit and his diamond stickpin?" Laurel asked.

"I guess. He was dressed that way for work, and he hadn't changed when he went out."

"You came to the pit when I had fallen down there. You visited him, didn't you?" CJ asked, his tone reconciliatory. He knew she had to have realized her brother had died there, and she was drawn to the place, mourning him. No matter how much she hadn't liked Clarinda, she must have still loved her brother.

"It was the anniversary of his disappearance. I always visit him at his grave and wish him well. I always wished I had gotten through to Clarinda. Done something differently so I wouldn't have lost my brother."

The thing CJ couldn't understand was why Charity had also vanished. "Why didn't you report this to the sheriff? To the pack?"

"I reported it to Sheriff Sheridan Silver." She gave CJ an annoyed look. "And your father said he'd look into it. He said he never knew that some woman named Clarinda O'Brien was living with us since she never was involved in the pack, and she never showed her face in town. He acted like I had made the whole thing up! Like I was crazy. Even like I had something to do with my brother's disappearance.

"Once Warren was gone, I could run the hotel the way I wanted to. But the truth was I hated the hotel. It brought in money, sure, but I was happy running the household. Some of the drifters that came through the hotel were not…respectable types. And it was way too much for me to manage on my own. Then I hired someone to do the books, and he ran off with the money."

The pack would have gone after the thief. "Did you report this?"

"No. My brother was gone. The money was gone. We had debts to pay. I would have lost everything. It just seemed…futile at that point. I'd begun to hate the hotel. I packed my bags and left. It was like once Clarinda arrived, we were cursed."

"Why didn't you stay and ask the pack for help?" CJ couldn't understand why she hadn't gone to Darien's father, the pack leader at the time.

"I did when my brother disappeared. Fat lot of luck that did me."

True, but she could have gone to the pack leader if she felt the sheriff wasn't doing his job. "What was the fight between your brother and John all about?" he asked.

Her white brows shot up and she looked thoroughly confused, although he swore he saw a faint hint of panic. "John?"

"Your triplet brother." CJ hadn't thought he'd have to remind her she had another brother. Maybe they had all been estranged, but he didn't expect that kind of reaction.

"What triplet brother?"

Was she kidding?

"Warren and I were twins. We didn't have any other siblings. Well, wait, yes, years later Mom did mention she had a baby that was a stillbirth. So I guess we started out as triplets. But we never thought of ourselves like that. Maybe she named the other baby John. I don't remember if she ever told us even. But she didn't have any other living children. Just Warren and me."

CJ glanced at Laurel. She quickly said, "There are three brothers staying in Silver Town who are claiming they are the sons of John Wernicke."

Charity was silent for a moment. Then she said, "Maybe they are."

Laurel looked so exasperated. "You just *said* your mother didn't have another living son."

"She *didn't*. But it doesn't mean that the three brothers don't have a father named John. However, he wasn't related to *us*."

CJ sat back on the couch. "Well, hell. How did they know about Clarinda and a supposed love triangle?"

"Maybe they're related to the man who was her lover? How do *I* know? Are they new wolves or old?"

"Now that I don't know," CJ said.

"We're new wolves. Not royals. Our bloodlines haven't been *lupus garou* forever. Our parents were humans turned. If the brothers are several generations *lupus garou* and can hold their human form during the call of the full moon, then they're not related to us by any stretch of the imagination. They could be distant cousins. Our dad did have one brother. He was killed in one of the wars, but never had a mate or any offspring as far as we knew. But it's possible, and that would make his offspring fairly new wolves like us. It will show another hole in the brothers' story, if they're royal wolves. Full moon tonight." Charity smiled. "Good time to check."

Somehow, CJ had to convince Darien to lock the Wernicke brothers up and then watch them. If they didn't shift, good chance they were royals.

"Is this going to take much longer? Unless you think I killed my brother, I've got to get back to the candy shop. I have a new girl there, but she's rather hopeless."

"Just a few more questions we need answers to. Why did you come and check on me when I fell in the pit?" Though CJ suspected Charity wouldn't have killed her brother, she might have murdered Clarinda, as much as she seemed to despise her.

"I was curious if one of Sheridan's sons would really investigate the disappearance of my brother and reveal the truth. When I left Silver Town, I left for good, figuring my brother and Clarinda were enjoying running a hotel somewhere else, having gotten rid of me, and had found their happily ever after. It angered me to think that, of course. Yet another part of me hoped that's what had happened and that my brother hadn't met with foul play."

Charity let out her breath. "I stayed away for a good decade, mated, and lost my mate, but in all that time, I couldn't quit wondering what had become of my brother. I kept looking for him, searching for clues. I even did Internet searches, hoping I'd find him somewhere. As you know, we often change our identities over the years because of our longevity."

"How did you find him in the pit?" Laurel asked.

"I was taking a run out there. Still searching for clues that my brother hadn't left the area. I kept thinking he wouldn't abandon the hotel and not me either. I smelled something dead, an elk, and curious, I came to see what had killed it. The smell was coming from a pit. The deadfall had fallen through. It was winter and the sun was shining brightly. But it was still too dark in the pit to see clearly, as deep as it was. You know how things can keep nagging at you? Well, that pit kept nagging at me. Why would someone cover up a pit, then catch an animal for supper, and not come and remove the beast? Why would it be rotting down there?"

"The hunter was long gone?" CJ asked.

"Could have been. Still, I had to know. I left to get a rope and a lantern. I didn't have any way to climb in there, without being afraid I couldn't get back out. So I just lowered the lantern into the pit. And what I saw horrified me. A skeleton, and the light reflecting off my brother's diamond stickpin. So who killed him? Someone in your pack. I couldn't approach anyone. I didn't know who had done it."

CJ looked at Laurel. She had worried about the same thing.

"I heard that Sheridan had died. Thinking he was the one who had been involved with Clarinda, that he killed my brother and she ran away, I decided it didn't matter."

"Yet you continued to come here. To visit the area," CJ said.

Charity brushed away a tear. "Yes. If my brother had been killed, and Sheridan had done it, Clarinda might have run off, fearing for her life. But what if she didn't? What if I came across her body next? So I kept looking—to find closure."

CJ thought about how his father had Clarinda's locket. He felt his stomach knot again. But what if his father had only found the locket? What if he didn't know who it belonged to and never followed up on it?

The truth was, as sheriff, his father was too methodical to let something like that go. He would have investigated the case until he learned the truth.

"I understand. One other thing. Before I fell into the pit, the deadfall was covering it up."

"Yes, someone did it every time something fell in the pit."

"Why?"

She gave him a sly look. "That was another reason I kept going back to the area, watching, waiting for—him."

"Then it has to be someone still in the area."

"Or someone covering for someone else. I always wore hunter's spray so he wouldn't smell my scent in the area. But so was he."

"Hell, you should have let the pack know," CJ said. "We would have looked into this."

"Like Sheridan did? No, thank you."

CJ shook his head. "All right. Well, we'll damn sure look into it now. I want to thank you for all your help, Charity. Will you be staying in the area?"

"Yes. I own a successful candy shop here. I enjoy Green Valley and don't have any plans to leave. Stop by there anytime, if you like."

"We will," Laurel said, and this time she offered a small smile.

"I'm sorry about Clarinda's disappearance. If I knew what happened that day, I'd share."

"Thank you," Laurel said.

"Can we drop you off at your store?" CJ asked.

Charity hesitated, then nodded. "Thank you."

"Hey, Ryan, we're going to drop Charity off at her shop," CJ called out. He knew that even if Ryan hadn't been purposefully listening in, he would have heard some of the discussion, so he probably heard she had another name.

Ryan came out of his office and said, "Okay. Just let us know when you have those gift boxes of chocolates ready to pick up and I'll drop by. Did you want to go by Charity or Pamela?"

"Pamela." The woman's whole outlook seemed to brighten when Ryan mentioned the candy order, and she smiled at him. "I'll give you a call."

After they said their good-byes, CJ drove them into the town of Green Valley. Charity's candy store was simply called the Candy Store. It was housed in an old Victorian house painted purple with white trim, the inside bright and white to emphasize the carousels of displays, colorful suckers hanging from the ceiling, jars and barrels filled with neon-colored candies, and gift boxes of chocolates displayed for every occasion.

"I know where I'm going to start *my* Christmas shopping," Laurel said, and Charity's expression softened a bit.

"I'll give you a discount," she offered.

Laurel laughed. "You have a deal."

"Oh, and take this," Charity said, pulling a card off her counter. "It has my number on it if you ever want to talk. If…there's anything else you think of and need to know. And…if you learn what happened to your aunt, I'd love to know too."

"We'll let you know," Laurel said, and then she gave Charity a hug.

Both women's eyes were filled with tears, and CJ was at a loss as to what to say.

But then Laurel started to shop for candy for gifts, and everything seemed fine.

After spending over a couple hundred dollars on boxes of special candies for everyone who had helped Laurel and her sisters, she and CJ thanked Charity again and headed out.

"I think that was a step in helping Charity to heal," CJ said as they drove back to his place, the truck filled with the fragrance of sweet treats.

"I was glad to. And I really was delighted to get so much of my Christmas shopping done in one fell swoop." Though she was wondering what she was going to get for CJ. "So what do you think? About everything Charity said?"

"It's hard to say. She held a real grudge against your aunt, so some of the things she said were colored by that. It happened quite a number of years ago, so that will make a difference memory-wise. As to whether she had a triplet brother named John—one who fathered Stanton Wernicke and his brothers? I don't think she had reason to lie. Which means that the brothers just coincidentally had the same name and thought they'd try to take advantage of the situation by claiming kinship. They probably suspected Warren and Charity were dead and couldn't come back to tell the truth concerning their supposed kinship. Or, the brothers weren't named Wernicke that far back. It's just a name they've used more recently."

"But Darien said he found that John did exist and had died where and when the brothers said that he had."

"Agreed. But if they've been wolves for a long time, they might have changed their identities at some point. I need to take you home, and then we'll see if my grandfather's chest of drawers had any secret compartments that my dad might have known about and hidden something in."

Laurel was glad to know Charity was among the living. That she was happily running her own candy store and not the hotel she had loathed. Laurel wished they had found Charity's brother alive. But she still hoped her aunt might be.

"I'd forgotten all about your grandfather's chest." Laurel hoped they wouldn't find anything to confirm that Sheridan had something to do with her aunt's disappearance.

Chapter 21

ON THE WAY HOME, CJ CALLED DARIEN. "WE DIDN'T learn much new, but here's what we have." He explained everything and then added, "Can you have Peter arrest the Wernicke brothers on some charge? Have them locked up and watched to see if they shift during the full moon tonight? We just need one in jail to prove whether they're royals or not."

"I'll see what I can do."

"Another thing, we don't want the word to get out about Charity running the candy store in case someone killed her brother and wants to get rid of her too. She's going by Pamela Houser, and I figure we'll keep her real name under wraps."

"Understand."

"Okay, well, we're looking into another matter and then taking off the rest of the night."

"Sounds good, CJ. I'll let you know about the Wernicke brothers later. We'll be questioning them about what Charity said. We'll just say we have a source of information that proves it, without identifying her. We're having the meeting with the elders tomorrow night in the conference room."

"All right. Let me know how it goes with the brothers." They ended the call, and when they reached CJ's home—and now Laurel's, CJ thought with a thrill—he asked her, "How are you feeling?"

"Exhausted."

"I'll fix us some hot cocoa if you'd like, and then we'll see if we can find anything in my grandfather's chest." He motioned to an old oak chest, tall with thirty drawers.

"CJ, I hate to bring this up, but why would your father have a locket with a picture of both my mom and my aunt in it? He told my mother when she came looking for her sister that Clarinda had never worked at the hotel. So that proves he lied about it."

"Maybe."

She frowned at him, and he pulled her into his arms and kissed her. "We can't know for sure. We have to consider every possibility. What if he found it and kept it, hoping to find the owner? She could have shifted, left, and then was never seen again. Anything could have happened. We just don't know."

Laurel let out her breath in exasperation, hating to admit CJ was right.

"You've never talked about your mother." Not that she'd mentioned her own either. But maybe Sheridan's relationship with his wife would give Laurel a clue.

"She died when we were six. A hunter killed her when she was taking us out to the woods to run as wolves."

CJ had to have been traumatized to see his own mother shot and killed like that, and Laurel felt terrible about it. "As wolves?"

"No. None of us had shifted yet. He said he thought she was a deer."

"God, I'm so sorry, CJ. Was he human?"

"Yeah. Darien's dad was the leader at the time. Dad wanted the man dead for killing his mate. But Darien's dad had to find the man not guilty of murder. It wasn't a case of premeditated murder. Just an accident."

She stirred the chocolate around in the milk in the saucepan. "Was your dad angry about it?"

"Yeah. Not only did he love our mom, but he had four six-year-old boys to raise on his own. Though everyone in the pack helped to raise us, including Darien's mom."

"Did Sheridan ever take another mate?"

"No. He didn't let that stop him from having affairs, but he never took a mate again."

"I hate to ask this…" Laurel hesitated.

"Ask. Any question that can lead us to solving this case is worth asking."

"Did your father take a token after he committed the murder?"

"No."

Laurel sighed with relief. "Then why would he have my aunt's locket?"

"Your guess is as good as mine, I'm afraid."

"What if—and I know this is really far-out—but what if your father was romantically involved with my aunt? What if she was referring to your father in the postcard?"

"Why would he have her locket? And deny she had been here?"

"I don't know. What if she went for a run in the woods and vanished? And Sheridan discovered her clothes and necklace?"

"But he would have reported it. He wouldn't have ignored it. Not if he felt something for her."

"And if he didn't?"

"Then you're back to the notion that my father had something to do with her disappearance."

She hated to admit he was right. She poured the heated cocoa into mugs.

He added marshmallows, then took her in his arms and hugged her tight. "No matter what we find—"

"It doesn't reflect on you or your brothers, CJ. I just want to know the truth."

He kissed her mouth. "I know. I do too."

She loved him and was grateful he was taking all of this in stride.

They each grabbed a mug of cocoa and walked into the living room to start searching the old chest.

"I guess we'll just begin pulling out drawers and see what we can find," he said.

They drank their mugs of cocoa, then set them on the coffee table and began to pull one drawer out at a time to examine.

"Wait," she said, feeling something move as she slid her fingers over the bottom of the drawer. "Maybe the joints are no longer as secure, but…if it has a secret bottom, wouldn't there be a trigger to release the cover?"

"Can you use one of your fingernails to lift the panel, if that's what it is?" CJ asked, drawing closer, his breath warm against her hair as he peered down at the drawer.

"No. Do you have a fingernail file?"

"Turn it upside down."

She did and it rattled a bit, which she figured was the loose panel or the bottom of the drawer no longer fitting snuggly against the sides.

"Okay, let me see what I can find."

She kept trying to slip her fingernail between the panel and the front of the drawer without success.

"This is a long shot," CJ said, returning with a thin screwdriver and a magnet.

He used the magnet first and it immediately grabbed hold of the panel and lifted it. "Well, I'll be damned." A piece of metal glued to the underside of the panel had attracted the magnet.

But they didn't find any secret items or documents. Just lots of big, green bills—ten-thousand-dollar bills. Ten of them.

"Ohmigod, CJ." She turned to pull another drawer out. "Why would he have all this money hidden in here? And such big bills?"

"Grandfather Silver didn't trust the banks. We found around five hundred thousand stuffed in his mattress. I'm surprised Dad didn't come across the false drawers. Then again, each of the drawers was stuffed with stationary supplies—pens, ink, envelopes, notepads, paper clips, scissors, and the like. Dad never emptied them.

"Before I brought it home, I dumped all the stuff in the drawers into one of the boxes we searched through. And everything was rattling around so much in the drawers, I never considered they might have false bottoms." He smiled again. "Man, are my brothers going to be surprised. None of them wanted this old chest. But I'd always loved it. Grandfather built it himself. Now I know why."

"Where did he get the money?"

"He worked hard all his very long life. Made some wise investments in land and ended up having property with a gravel pit. Gravel made a mint for him."

"Wow. Are you going to share? Or turn the bills over to a museum?"

"I'll ask my brothers what they want to do with the money, though since you're my mate…"

"It's your family's. You and your brothers need to decide."

She rattled the second drawer. "He can't have had false drawers in all of these."

CJ was grinning his head off as he watched her use the magnet on the second drawer. Up came the panel. And more greenbacks. Ten more.

"I've got to call Mason, the owner of the bank. We need to put these in the safety deposit box tonight," CJ said.

"They'll open the bank for you?"

"Hell, yeah. It's pack run and we do things for each other like that. Banker's hours don't count if we've got a real issue to deal with."

"I love it." As if the money didn't mean anything, she grabbed for another drawer. This time so did CJ.

Thirty drawers. A mix of money—from one-hundred-dollar bills to piles of the granddaddy of them all, the ten-thousand-dollar green note. CJ stared at one of the big notes. "I wonder who Samuel P. Chase was."

Laurel was busy counting the money, stacking the bills in like denominations, then counting the stacks.

"Two hundred and fifty thousand dollars."

CJ shook his head. "Let me make this call and get this money to the bank, and then I'm taking you to bed."

She laughed.

"What?"

"We've been mated how long and money is the priority?"

He smiled and took her in his arms. "You'd rather we made love first?"

"No. Really, just teasing. It would kill me if someone broke into the house and stole all that money. Go call and make the arrangements. I'm going to take a nice, warm bath and see you when you return."

"If you go to sleep on me, I'm waking you."

"Promises." She kissed him, then hurried off to the bedroom.

He got on the phone, wishing he didn't have to take care of this right now. "Hey, Mason? I need to make a nighttime deposit."

"What's going on?"

"Remember when my brothers and I found all that money Granddad hid in his old mattress? I just found more. But let's keep this just between you and me—and my mate, of course."

Before Laurel took a bath, she wondered if anything as simple as a magnet could locate false bottoms to the drawers in her aunt's furniture. She called Ellie. "Ellie, I don't think we have any, but we just found a secret hideaway in CJ's grandfather's old chest, using a magnet to lift the false drawer bottom."

"Oh, cool. Um, I don't think we have any magnets in the house. And I'm on a date right now."

Shocked that her sister would start dating as soon as Laurel mated a wolf, she realized just how much her sisters had put their lives on hold because of her. "Who?"

"Brett. We're at the tavern. I'll see if he has a magnet, but we're going for a moonlit run tonight first."

"I'll call Meghan."

"Can you call her a little later?"

Suspicious, Laurel asked, "Why?"

"She's got company."

Laurel smiled. When the pack leader was away… "Who?"

"Peter."

Laurel chuckled. "All right. I'll check with her later."

After that, she climbed into the warm water in the tub and had nearly dozed off when she heard her phone ringing in the bedroom. She groaned and climbed out of the tub. Seizing a towel, she wrapped it around herself, then hurried into the other room. When she grabbed the phone, she saw it was Meghan. "What's wrong?"

"We just had a break-in."

Laurel heard CJ in the living room and wondered when he'd gotten home from the bank.

"I just had to call and let you know that we were broken into. Peter had already left and said CJ was at the bank and was closer. CJ's here now and wanted me to let you know we're all right, and he'd be home soon."

If CJ was with Meghan… Her heart racing to the moon and back, Laurel hurried to the bedroom door, shut it, and locked it. "Someone's in the house," she whispered. "I'm shifting."

"Ohmigod," was all Meghan said before Laurel dropped the phone on the bed, leaving the line open in the event something happened to her. Then her sister shouted, "CJ, someone's broken into your house!"

Laurel had already shifted into her wolf form and had been staring at the door for a second when she heard footfalls headed toward the bedroom door. Her heart in her throat, she didn't know what to do. She didn't know if CJ had another gun in the house, but she'd never used one anyway, so she figured her teeth were a better bet. Still, if someone in the house had a gun, she wouldn't be any match for him.

She shifted back into her human form, ran to the window, unlocked it, and then slid it open, hoping whoever it was wouldn't realize she was trying to escape that way.

The doorknob twisted. She shifted and leaped through the window as a wolf. She suspected many of CJ's neighbors were wolves, but she didn't know for sure.

Then she wondered why anyone would have broken into her sisters' home and now CJ's. What was the man—as she was certain it was a man—looking for?

But she figured running outside in the snow would be a safer bet, and she headed for the hotel, hoping she'd encounter CJ, who would be driving back here at once.

If the Wernicke brothers had been taken in for questioning, they'd be in jail, not out breaking into homes. Unless Darien had incarcerated only one of them. Yet, she wondered how the person had broken into the hotel's guest house. They had an alarm set. Maybe it had gone off and that's why they knew someone was breaking in.

She raced along the wide front yards of the homes in CJ's development, the houses all looking cheerfully Christmas-like in their holiday finery, many of them having icicle lights that dripped off the eaves, simulating real icicles, though they all had some of those too.

She headed south through the treed area that had been set aside as a park with fountains and walking trails that were dark at night, perfect for the wolves living closer to town. The full moon was shining off the white snow collected on the fir branches and the path when she heard movement in the trees to her left.

Then she saw the green glow of eyes—wolf eyes. The wolf's coat was white. A smaller female wolf, about Laurel's size. And she instantly thought of Charity. What was she doing here? Still trying to catch the wolf who killed her brother? Or had Charity had something to do with it?

Laurel hesitated, not sure what to think, when she heard a van parking at the lot used for visitors to the park. She turned and listened. A door slid open. It sounded like a panel van, like the one the Wernicke brothers owned. If she'd been near when they had opened the door or had driven by her in that van, she would have recognized the sound of the vehicle.

Whoever it was, he was coming this way as a human, his boots crunching on the crusted snow.

Laurel glanced back at the wolf. She was gone. Laurel was just as glad because if the person following her was bad news, she didn't want the older woman to be hurt. The problem was that if the man was a wolf, he could follow Laurel's scent, shift if he wanted, and come after her.

"Laurel?" Jacob called out.

Their electrician? She frowned. Then she melted into the woods, wanting to go to him, but unsure about exposing herself.

"CJ said your house was broken into. I was over at your sisters' place, trying to determine why the alarm hadn't gone off, when we learned someone was at CJ's house. CJ and I immediately headed for his place in separate vehicles. But then I saw you running as a wolf in the direction of the park. CJ was going to try to catch up to the men who had broken into his house. We figure it's the same ones who broke into the other house. I headed in the direction you took off in since he has a gun and I don't. I'll take you home before anyone sees you running out here as a wolf."

CJ wouldn't have gone home to apprehend the house breaker. His priority would have to search for her and protect her.

"Shit!" Jacob cried out at the same time that a wolf's vicious growls rent the air.

Laurel raced to the scene and saw Charity's wolf teeth clamped on Jacob's arm, clinging for dear life as Jacob tried to beat her off with his bare hands.

Laurel lunged at him, slamming her front paws into his chest and bringing him down hard against the crusted snow. She clamped her teeth on his left arm and bit hard enough to force him to hold still, praying that she hadn't just injured an innocent man. But he had to have lied to her about CJ.

Then she let go and lifted her chin and howled.

Chapter 22

At the clinic, Darien, CJ, Laurel, Jake, and Doc Weber gathered around Jacob, who had been treated for minor wolf-bite wounds. But for now, he was strapped to the table so they could question him before he was released.

"You're wearing hunter's spray," Darien accused.

"I didn't do anything wrong. They came out of nowhere and bit me. They should be up on charges of attempted murder."

"You lied to Laurel and said I was going to the house when everyone knows I would have gone to protect her."

"I didn't want her to think I was out there to harm her. She was frightened enough."

"How come you broke into her sisters' home and then mine? Were you looking for something in the false bottoms of the drawers? You knew the furniture your father made for Clarinda had false bottoms and how to get into them, but you couldn't with Meghan watching. You set up the alarm system in the house, so you knew how to disable it. The same with mine. Peter's checking the furniture, and when he finds what's hidden in the drawers, the jig will be up. What were you trying to find?"

"I didn't break into anyone's place."

Unfortunately, they had no proof that he had.

"I tried to find the secret compartments when

Meghan was watching me and didn't find any. Every cabinetmaker has his own way of creating them. I told the MacTire sisters that."

"And you learned cabinetmaking from your father."

"Yeah, so? Find one piece of furniture I made with my initials on it that's constructed in the same way as my father's furniture and has a false bottom."

"What happened to my aunt?" Laurel asked, her voice soft, but CJ heard the steel behind it.

"I don't know what happened to your aunt, and that's the God's honest truth. Hell, as soon as she bit me, she took off."

"What?" Laurel said, suddenly looking so pale, CJ took hold of her arm and made her sit in a chair.

"The white wolf that bit me! Who did you think she was?"

"Charity Wernicke."

"Where did you come up with that idea?"

"She—Charity—said she was keeping house, and then my aunt came to live with Warren and her."

He gave a sarcastic laugh. "Hell, if Warren had a sister, she wasn't living there."

"She was running the hotel. After her brother vanished," Laurel managed to get out.

"She might have let on that she was his sister, but she was Clarinda O'Brien."

CJ rested his hand on Laurel's shoulder, ready to keep her in her seat if she suddenly passed out, she appeared so pale.

"How do you know this for certain?" she asked.

Jacob narrowed his eyes. "Because my father was seeing her, made her the furniture even. Free, because he loved her. But Warren did too. She was perfect for him, did all his housework and kept the books."

"Are…are you her son?"

"No. My mother had died two years earlier. My father hadn't looked at another wolf until he laid eyes on her."

Laurel swallowed hard. "So she mated Warren?"

"She wouldn't mate either wolf. She wouldn't say why."

"Did your father have something to do with Warren's death?"

"No. He died of a broken heart. He thought, like I did, that Warren left to set up another hotel somewhere else, somewhere that Clarinda was happier, that she managed this hotel, then took off and joined him."

"Oh, right," Laurel said, sounding like she didn't believe him in the least.

CJ got a call on his phone. "Yeah, Peter, what did you find?"

"It's not good. I'm emailing you a picture so you don't have to leave there and end your interrogation."

CJ waited with dreaded anticipation as the picture uploaded. A damn blackmail note? And it looked suspiciously like his father's handwriting. He was blackmailing Clarinda? For pretending to be Warren's sister? But Jacob just said she wasn't pretending.

Every eye was on CJ. "Darien, Laurel, can I see you in Doc Weber's office for a moment?"

Doc Weber nodded his okay for them to use it.

CJ took hold of Laurel's arm. She was so shaky, he was worried that she might be going into shock.

When they were in the doc's office, Darien shut the door. "What did Peter find?"

CJ helped Laurel onto the couch and sat beside her. "A blackmail note from my father, hidden in one of the drawers."

"Someone needs to catch Clarinda, Charity…whoever she is," Laurel said, sounding numb.

Looking sympathetic, Darien nodded. "While you were both questioning Jacob, I sent a text to Ryan to have her taken into custody, not as a murder suspect, but to help clear this matter up."

"Could Jacob be lying?" she asked.

"Could be. We can't take what either of them say at face value, it seems." Darien looked over the blackmail note. "It's Sheridan's handwriting, all right."

"If he was blackmailing her, maybe that's why she disappeared. But why did he blackmail her?" Laurel asked.

Darien glanced at his phone. "Hell, Ryan says they're looking for her, but she hasn't returned to her home or store in Green Valley."

"What if she runs again?" Laurel asked.

"I've already put out an alert for her truck. A third of the pack members are out searching in the vicinity where she ran." Darien's phone rang. "Yeah? Okay, so she's running as a wolf still. Good to know. Keep looking until you find her."

He ended the call and said, "Mason found her truck, and her clothes are inside. She might be headed for home. We're confiscating her truck."

"I want to go to my sisters' house," Laurel suddenly said.

"All right. Darien, we'll keep you posted if we learn anything more. Wait, what happened with the Wernicke brothers?"

"They're royals as far as we can tell. Stanton's one pissed-off wolf, but he hasn't shifted yet."

"Okay, we'll talk later." CJ helped Laurel leave the room. "Are you going to be all right?"

"Yes."

But her voice was toneless, and he had to know what she was feeling. "Laurel, don't shut me out."

"What was going on? I want to go to the pit."

CJ stopped her as they left the clinic. "Why there?"

"I think she loved Warren. I think she couldn't mate him for some reason. I think Jacob's father loved her too. And I think she was pretending to be Warren's sister because she was afraid of someone."

"But Jacob said—"

"I think Jacob just learned the truth of who she was. Or his father did before he died. And so Jacob knew who she was, but she was gone, so there was no need to say anything to anyone about it. So why wouldn't she mate either man?"

"Hell, she probably already had a mate! She couldn't mate Warren because she had a mate and she was scared. He took her in and kept her hidden at his house where she did the books and the household chores."

"That's why she loves her 'brother' so much," Laurel said. "She feels guilty that Warren died for loving her. Don't you think?"

"Yeah. Sounds to me like a good reason. So who killed Warren?" CJ drove her out to the area closest to where the pit was.

"Her abusive mate? And she took care of the hotel for a short while, still pretending to be Warren's sister after the threat was past, but she couldn't manage it on her own and probably hated the hotel because it represented the man she lost."

"So why do you think she's at the pit?"

Laurel looked out the window. "She goes there when she needs to be comforted. Maybe she feels his spirit there. I don't know. Maybe he gave her direction in her life and she loved him for it. I'm just grasping at straws here."

"Why was Jacob trying to find something in the houses?"

"To protect his father, maybe? Thinking that maybe his father did kill Warren? Or maybe he was trying to locate something that would prove his father didn't have anything to do with it. You know how bad you felt when you learned your father had committed murder. You left the pack. Jacob doesn't want to live with the pack knowing his father murdered one of its pack members. And he doesn't want to leave the pack. Just like you and your brothers didn't really want to."

"Yeah, okay. That makes sense. Then he would have opened the secret compartment right away, if he could have gotten away with it. He didn't know what we would find and was afraid it would condemn the memory of his father."

"Like with you and your brothers and your father."

CJ let out his breath. "We'll deal with it. We have before. And...I hadn't mentioned it because I didn't think it was relevant, but my father had been the mastermind of a blackmail scheme before."

"I'm so sorry," Laurel said, squeezing his shoulder as he parked.

"As soon as I saw the blackmail note, I realized he'd

done it before. Hell, maybe it's like you said, he murdered before too."

"He wouldn't if he was getting money from Warren. Once Clarinda took over the hotel, she lost all the money."

"And my dad might have threatened to expose who she was to her mate if she didn't give him more money."

"Or, she did give him money, and that's why she was broke, not that someone was doing the books and stole it from her."

"If that's the case, in a way, she hadn't lied, because the blackmailer would have stolen the money from her."

"No matter that she lied, I think she did so only to protect herself, and maybe even my sisters and me. What if her mate came after us, looking to catch up with her?"

"That's true. I hadn't thought of that. Do we go as wolves or humans?"

"I need to talk with her."

"Okay." They got out of his truck and trudged along the trails left earlier in the snow. Then CJ got another call. "Yeah, Darien?"

"While searching for the white wolf, Jake saw Vernon and Yolan Wernicke in their wolf forms. He thinks they're trying to chase her down."

"Hell, okay. We're on our way to the pit. Laurel thinks she might be there. We'll keep you informed. Is Stanton still in jail?"

"Released. We had nothing to hold him on. He didn't shift and—"

"Crap. I just saw him running as a wolf in the same direction we're going. I'm giving Laurel my gun. I'm shifting."

"Wait for backup," Darien said.

CJ handed Laurel his gun and phone and began ditching his clothes. "I'm going to head Stanton off."

"I should run as a wolf too. I don't know how to shoot a gun, but that way I can fight a wolf if I need to."

"Laurel." He frowned. "All right. Hurry."

They quickly buried their clothes and both shifted, then ran full out for the pit.

Laurel's heart was racing so hard that she thought she was going to have a heart attack. She still didn't know what to think—Clarinda was Charity, Charity was Clarinda? Why would the Wernicke brothers be after her? Because she could prove they couldn't lay claim to the hotel, Laurel suspected.

When they reached the cordoned-off area, the yellow tape stating it was a crime scene, Laurel saw flower wreaths circling the pit. From wolf pack members? Her eyes filled with tears at the thoughtfulness. And then she saw the white wolf, nearly blending with the snow, standing among the pines. Laurel approached her cautiously, not wanting the wolf to run off. CJ hung back, letting Laurel attempt to win the wolf over.

Laurel had just reached her, the wolf not leaving, thankfully, and they'd touched noses and licked each other in greeting, when Stanton came loping into view.

CJ immediately raced to intercept him. The two faced off against each other. But Stanton didn't do what CJ thought he would. Instead of fighting, he lay down on his belly, a modified beta move. To be truly subservient and show no animosity, he would have rolled over and exposed his belly. CJ waited for him to do so.

Stanton wouldn't.

CJ stayed where he was, eyeing the wolf with

suspicion. But when he saw Stanton's brothers join him, CJ growled at them to do as Stanton was doing. No way could he fight three male wolves. The white wolf and Laurel couldn't help in the matter.

At first, the brothers stood next to Stanton, staring CJ down, challenging him. Finally, Stanton snapped at one of them, who let out a low growl, then sat down. Stanton turned to his other brother and snapped at him too.

He grumbled back and sat down, then they both lay down on their bellies.

What the hell was going on? CJ stayed alert, though when Laurel lifted her chin to howl, the white wolf joining in, he was glad to have Laurel as his mate.

He didn't want to lift his own chin to howl. He was keeping his eyes trained on the three male wolves, any of whom could suddenly attack him. If that happened, he'd be dead, along with his mate and the older white wolf.

An answering howl called back. Brett. And then several more. His other brothers and others. Darien must have gotten word to them somehow, though CJ remembered him saying that Brett was chasing after two of the brothers. So his brother must have just followed them here.

And then the wolves from the Silver pack began to gather around the pit. The three Wernicke brothers were still lying on their bellies in a submissive way, though CJ suspected that all three were alert and ready to jump up and fight. The women were standing near the woods, tense, waiting, and watching.

Lelandi walked through the snow to reach them, escorted by Trevor and Peter in their wolf forms for protection.

"Darien's on his way." She glanced at Laurel and the white wolf. "I need the two of you to come with me."

Laurel licked the white wolf's face and then moved a little, watching to see if the white wolf would follow her.

She hesitated.

"Come on," Lelandi said, half an order, half an entreaty. "I've got to get back to my toddlers."

Laurel began to walk toward Lelandi, and the white wolf joined her. Some of the wolves watched them as they left, but most of them kept their focus on the Wernicke brothers.

CJ and the others waited another half hour until they heard some others crunching through the snow on their way there. Darien and five other men finally appeared. "You're coming with us. Dead. Or alive. Your choice," Darien said to the Wernicke brothers. His patience was shot to hell.

CJ smiled a little at his cousin. But he knew the pack leader meant it, and he'd shift right then and there to prove it.

Stanton reluctantly stood. His brothers followed his lead. And then they moved toward Darien, who turned and headed back the way he'd come. The wolves of the Silver pack flanked the Wernicke brothers and a few followed behind. If the brothers did anything that appeared threatening to Darien or anyone in the pack, the rest of the wolves would tear them apart.

CJ didn't know what Darien planned, but he figured they were back to questioning the brothers. CJ stopped where he'd left his clothes and found Laurel's were gone but his still there. He quickly shifted, dressed, and ran after the wolves. He thought Darien would haul the brothers to his house in the back of a police car, but instead, he opened the door to CJ's truck and said, "Stanton, you and your brothers will ride with CJ. He'll bring you to the house."

CJ thought Darien was crazy! He sure as hell hoped his cousin knew what he was doing.

Even so, Brett and Eric got in with them as wolf backup. His whole truck smelled like wet wolf.

"Why did you lie to us about who Charity was?" CJ asked, not that anyone could answer him as a wolf.

Stanton shifted. "We've been looking for our mother for years."

Chapter 23

By the time everyone arrived at Darien's place, a couple of the men had retrieved the Wernicke brothers' clothes so that they could shift and dress, and then they all met in the outdoor hall reserved for larger pack events.

Maybe thirty wolves were in attendance, the rest going home to their families at Darien's request. Most everyone had shifted and dressed. Ten were still in wolf form, providing wolf muscle if things got out of hand.

It seemed strange meeting in the Silver Hall when it was all decorated for Christmas. The business at hand seemed too onerous to suit the occasion.

Laurel and the white wolf were in the house, CJ figured when he didn't see them. "I'm going to check on the women."

"All right, CJ. We'll wait while you ask them to join us," Darien said.

CJ stalked out the door and headed along the path to the house. When he walked inside, calling out to Lelandi to let her know he was there, she replied, "We're in the sunroom."

He hadn't made it two steps before Laurel ran out of the sunroom, raced across the living room, and threw herself into his arms. She was crying tears of joy. The only way he could tell was that she was smiling at him.

He hugged her tight, suspecting the white wolf was her aunt, and Laurel was glad to know Clarinda was alive and well. "She's my aunt," Laurel confirmed, choking on the words. "Ellie and Meghan are on the way."

"Happy, I take it?"

"Ecstatic."

"I figure she had hidden her identity from an abusive mate."

"Yeah. John Wernicke."

CJ's brows lifted. "Warren's brother?"

"Yeah. John really was Warren's brother. They had a sister named Charity, but she died from a fever the year before Clarinda arrived. Charity had never lived with Warren, so no one knew that Clarinda wasn't his sister. Warren and John had had a falling-out about his treatment of his mate—my aunt. When she managed to run away, she took refuge in Warren's home, praying he would take her in and that John wouldn't find her."

"She left three young sons behind."

Laurel frowned up at CJ. "What? Oh God, no."

"She knew her husband would kill her if she took his sons with her, so doing the worst thing she could imagine, she left them behind and pretended to be Charity."

"Stanton and his brothers…" Laurel looked ill.

CJ didn't blame her. "Come on. Let's get your aunt, and we'll all go to the meeting Darien's having."

They headed for the sunroom, and Laurel said, "I don't want them as my cousins."

CJ chuckled. "To get into the Christmas spirit, I thought we could have them over for Christmas dinner."

She scowled at him.

He smiled and kissed her lips. "We'll do whatever you want to do."

"I want my aunt to have Christmas dinner with us. My sisters. Your brothers. And your cousins and their mates."

"Deal. But if your aunt wants her sons to have dinner with us?"

Laurel growled. "Under coercion, I'll agree. But against my better judgment."

He smiled at her and tucked her under his arm as they walked together to join her aunt and Lelandi.

When they reached the sunroom, Lelandi was talking about the pack Christmas celebration and New Year's party they were having and how much they wanted Clarinda to be there.

They grew quiet when Laurel and CJ entered the room. "Lelandi, Aunt Clarinda, Darien wants us to go to the hall to discuss the Wernicke brothers' situation," Laurel said. "Are they really your sons?" she asked her aunt, sounding as if she still didn't believe it.

"I didn't know they were here looking for me."

CJ didn't believe the brothers had been either. They were here to get what they thought was theirs: the title to the hotel. Instead, it had belonged to John's mate until the pack took it over.

"Why didn't you tell us who you really were?" Laurel asked.

"I didn't know John was dead. He was a brutal man. I was certain he wouldn't have changed how he acted toward me. I couldn't risk involving you or your sisters, or your mate either. It was just safer that way. Had I known he was dead, I would have told you the truth."

"I'm so sorry for all that you've suffered," Laurel said.

"It's in the past. Now I'm reunited with my sons and my nieces, and I don't want that ever to end."

"Agreed."

But CJ didn't think it would be an entirely happy family reunion.

As soon as Meghan and Ellie arrived, they walked into the hall, where everyone turned to watch them. Darien joined Lelandi and pulled her into a hug, and Laurel loved how affectionate he was with his pack leader mate in front of the pack.

Clarinda took a seat, but everyone else remained standing, tense and alert as Darien said, "Ladies first. Clarinda O'Brien?"

"Wernicke," Clarinda said. "I was mated to John Wernicke. He beat me so badly the last time, I miscarried our next set of twins. I did the only thing I could do. I abandoned my three four-year-old sons, whom John adored. I knew he'd never hurt them. I found refuge with John's brother, Warren, knowing they were estranged. I assumed John would never look for me there. Warren loved me and wanted me for his mate, but we couldn't be, not while John was still alive. Warren had a heart of gold. Elroy Summers was new to the area, and he thought to woo me, believing I was Warren's sister.

"She had died in another city before I arrived in Silver Town, so I took on the role of his sister, pretending to have just arrived to help Warren by taking care of the household and budget. We made up this far-fetched story about how Clarinda O'Brien had lived there and run off. No one had ever 'seen' her, so we figured if John learned someone was living with Warren, he wouldn't suspect it was me. Just their sister. As long as he didn't come and see Warren and me. I wanted so badly to get in touch with my sons, but I was afraid John would learn of it and kill me for it."

"What about Elroy Summers?" Darien asked.

"He made me the furniture—free of charge, which upset Warren since he loved me. He hated to pretend I was his sister. And he hated that I couldn't mate him. Then Sheridan…" She glanced in CJ's direction. "He somehow learned I wasn't who I said I was. He sent me a blackmail note. I showed it to Warren, but I didn't want him to pay Sheridan. I was certain Sheridan would keep asking for more money to maintain my secret. Then everything fell apart at once. Warren disappeared, and though I went in search of him, I couldn't find him. I tried to manage the hotel, but then Sheridan sent me another blackmail note. I tucked it into the secret compartment in the highboy and ran."

"Why would Elroy's son think something was hidden in your chest that would cause problems for his dad?" Laurel asked.

"I suspect one of the two men—Elroy or John— killed Warren," Clarinda said.

"Our father didn't do it," Stanton said. "You ran off and it had nothing to do with Dad being abusive. He never was abusive."

"Not with you. But with me, he was," Clarinda said gently.

"You lie. Dad said—"

"Your father told you what he wanted you to hear. That I was a bad mother. That I abandoned you because I didn't want children. All lies. I loved you. Leaving you was the hardest thing for me to do. I wanted to die. But I wanted to live too, hopeful that someday I could hold you again in my arms as a mother would. I knew if I had taken you with me, I wouldn't have gotten far. He would have killed me for sure.

"He adored the three of you. I knew he would raise you well. He poisoned you against me. I never could return to see you. And now he's dead, but you've decided to believe what he said about me. I had hoped it would be otherwise. Despite not wanting to have to let you go, I've come to terms with this."

"By rights, the hotel is still ours," Stanton said.

"It would go to John's mate, since he's deceased, if she had paid the taxes, although we would have made arrangements to resolve the situation to everyone's satisfaction if the MacTire sisters hadn't already bought and renovated it," Darien said. "That means Clarinda Wernicke would have owned it."

"If I had owned it, I would gladly have given you the hotel, if my nieces hadn't bought it with their hard-earned money and renovated it so beautifully. Not only that, but they had every intention of learning what had happened to me and bringing my murderer to justice. And so, the hotel is theirs. I didn't know John had died recently or I would have already revealed who I was to them."

"Our mother didn't know what had happened to you," Laurel said.

"No, dear. I couldn't even tell my beloved sister or hug my nieces one last time."

"I don't believe this. You're a habitual liar," Stanton said. "Father told us you'd say anything if we ever saw you again so that you'd look like the innocent in all this. I can't believe you'd drag his name through the mud.

For what? Just so you looked like the sweet, adoring mother who was fighting for her life?"

"Give it up, Stanton," Vernon said, sounding so angry, Laurel knew it was going to get physical between the brothers. Stanton was their leader, and he wouldn't take any guff from his brothers.

Stanton turned on his brother and growled. But Vernon's fist shot out so fast and connected with Stanton's jaw so hard that he knocked Stanton on his ass before he could react.

Everyone looked as shocked as Laurel felt, not expecting Vernon to win the confrontation. But she was damn glad he had.

Vernon swallowed hard, rubbing his hand that had to hurt like hell after hitting his brother's iron jaw with so much force, and then he stalked toward Clarinda. Everyone was watching him closely, ensuring he didn't attack her, but he got on his knees in front of her, laid his head in her lap, and hugged her. "Mom," he said in a choked sob.

Laurel swore there wasn't a dry eye among all the wolves gathered. Family meant everything to them. CJ offered his hand to Stanton to help him up, and the hard-headed wolf accepted it, stood, and then waited while Yolan gently pulled his mother to standing and gave her a hug.

Looking like a teen with attitude, Stanton stalked across the floor to join them. Everyone was still tense, just in case, as Yolan stepped back to allow Stanton time with their mother. "I'm sorry." With tears in his eyes, he kissed his mother's cheek and pulled her into his arms to give her a hug.

"The fault is not yours," she said softly to him, but Laurel was close enough that she heard.

"The hotel is my nieces', your cousins', but when I die, the candy store, which is very profitable, will be yours."

"It doesn't matter," Stanton said and hugged her again. "We'll make it up to you—for what our father did to you and to us by forcing you to run."

Laurel joined CJ. He immediately took her into his arms and held her tight, making her feel warm and well loved.

She whispered, "When we're done here, I want to get a tree and decorate for Christmas. I want to have a Christmas celebration with your brothers, my sisters, the Silver cousins and their mates, my aunt, and the Wernicke cousins, if they want to join us."

He smiled. "We've got our work cut out for us."

"But it's good work for a good cause."

Three days later, Laurel and CJ were enjoying a grand celebration. The Christmas tree was clothed in Victorian style with burgundy velvet garland; gold, silver, green, and burgundy balls; and twinkly lights—and her sisters were helping to prepare the main meal of hickory-smoked ham and potatoes.

Aunt Clarinda had made all the heavenly chocolates that their mother fixed when she was alive, and Laurel realized it was a family tradition that she and her sisters had to carry on. Lelandi helped bake some special bread; Tom's wife, Elizabeth, was fixing mistletoe margaritas; and Jake's wife, Alicia, was preparing the greens for the meal.

Laurel hoped the men were getting along. At first, it was quiet, and then they began to talk about guy kinds of things—hunting, fishing, boating, camping.

The women talked about all kinds of things—babies, the hotel and the sisters' plans for it, like renovating the basement and turning the maids' quarters into more rooms.

Laurel paused while carving the ham and turned to face her aunt. "Aunt Clarinda, you never told Mom about your mate or that you had three sons."

Her aunt shook her head. "It was a whirlwind romance and mating. But he was a brutal man. I tried to run away twice, and he caught me and beat me for it. At that point, I was pregnant and afraid I'd lose my babies. So I 'behaved.' When I gave him three adorable little boys, I thought he'd be happy with me." She snorted.

"It didn't work that way. I learned later, too late, that he'd had an abusive father. Not toward him, but toward his mother. He wouldn't let me get in touch with your mother. I sent a letter, and then that postcard was the second time I'd been able to send her a note. I was so happy with Warren, but..."

Laurel set down the carving knife and fork and gave her aunt a hug. "We're so glad you're alive and well and part of the family again."

"You don't know how glad I am."

Ellie asked, "Do you know anything about the stencil-type letter on the wall in the main lobby area of the hotel?"

"That's Chrissy's doing. She was a maid who died from a raging fever, and she still hangs around the place. She created a beautiful quilt with the letter *C* on it, and

I thought her talents were wasted on working as a maid at the hotel."

"We saw it in one of the pictures," Meghan said.

"It was beautiful, wasn't it? Chrissy's harmless. But sometimes people can see her peering out the attic window after she's cleaned the room, wishing for a mate and a different life," Aunt Clarinda said.

"That's so sad," Ellie said.

"She seems content," Aunt Clarinda said. "She just flips the light on and off every once in a while."

Laurel exchanged glances with her sisters.

Ellie smiled. "So, it's not an electrical short in the light switch."

Laurel wondered if Chrissy was the woman that Carol, the psychic, had seen peering out the window during the grand opening, and not a premonition of someone else staying in the attic room.

"The painting was moved from the hotel to the house," Laurel said.

"No ghost did that. My son Stanton said he moved it."

"Why?" Laurel asked.

"Trying to scare you into believing the ghosts haunting the hotel had a lot of power. The same thing with painting the X on the ceiling and moving the paint and ladders. They had planned to do a ghost show that showed how terribly haunted the place was if they couldn't find a way to get the hotel legally. But then you stopped them by denying permission."

"How do you know all this?" Ellie asked.

"CJ told me all that had been going on, and I asked Stanton. He told me what they had been doing. But he said it was because he really believed the hotel belonged to his family—and at the time, he didn't know that you were family. The boys never knew my maiden name. John hated my first name, so he called me Claire instead of Clarinda. So I could see why they wouldn't make the connection. And they had no idea that I was alive."

"What about Elroy, the cabinetmaker?" Laurel asked.

"I felt so bad about him. He was a good man, but I was already mated and I couldn't tell him the truth. Elroy thought Warren didn't think he was good enough for his sister. I just couldn't let him know. His son was so upset with me, knowing his father loved me, and I really cared for the son, but everyone's life that I touched would have been in danger if John Wernicke had learned the truth. It was heartbreaking for me, yet I could do nothing about it. After his father died, Jacob learned who I was, but he never said anything because what did it matter at that point? I was gone, and so was everyone else involved in the affair—John, Sheridan, Elroy, and Warren."

"Who replaced the deadfall? You thought the murderer had done it to hide the body," Laurel said.

"Whoever killed Warren at first. When another animal fell through, Jacob told me he did it. He was afraid his father had killed Warren, and he wanted to keep the pit covered up."

"Who really killed Warren?" Laurel asked.

"I suspect John did. When I talked to my sons, we tried to piece together the sequence of events. Their father disappeared for a while, and they learned he had gone to see Warren and said he had reconciled with him. He didn't. I saw John arrive in front of the hotel, and Warren told me to leave. So I did. When I returned,

Chapter 24

EVERYONE HAD SUCH A WONDERFUL TIME, LAUREL vowed they'd do it again next year.

Once everyone had said good night and left, she was ready to slip into bed with her wolf. She wondered what he had gotten for her for Christmas. She had wrapped presents and placed them under the tree for him, but he hadn't put one gift under the tree for her.

She hoped he hadn't forgotten and ordered them too late. Despite knowing she should be in the Christmas spirit, she felt like withholding his gifts until hers arrived. "Tell Jake, if he's agreeable, that we'd love to hang one of his beautiful photos of the Rocky Mountains on the wall where the letter *C* was. Ellie told me the letter is back."

CJ shook his head as he turned out the downstairs lights and followed her up to bed. "I'll tell Jake that you'd love to showcase one of his photos. He'll be pleased. I have a question. You hired only men outside the pack to work on the place. Later, we learned it was because you were worried that one of the pack members might be guilty of your aunt's disappearance. But why did you hire Jacob then?"

"He gave us such a great bargain on his electrical work, after we had gotten other estimates, that we just couldn't hire anyone else."

"Ah, okay."

"And we still have to schedule our special dinner for winning the snowman competition."

"A couple of days after Christmas?"

"Okay."

"I saw Stanton slip a present to you. What was it?"

Laurel chuckled. "The first season of their ghost busters show."

CJ laughed and pulled the covers back. "And your aunt?"

"A year's subscription to a chocolates box-of-the-month club. She really is devious. She knows that will never be enough, so she'll get me into the shop to see her more often. And buy. She also gifted the highboy and the blanket chest to my sisters to keep in the house where Clarinda had loved Warren."

"I'm glad you have her in your life again."

"Me too. She was so pleased to have her locket back with the picture of her and my mother in it."

"How had she lost it?"

"She said it had disappeared when she went to run as a wolf. When I told her that Sheridan had it, she said it figured. He probably planned to use it as evidence to prove to John she was there, if she didn't pay up." Laurel began stripping out of her clothes. "Hmm, talking about sweets and subscriptions, and not having enough…"

As soon as CJ was naked and had climbed onto the mattress, waiting for her, she tackled him. She wasn't sure why she felt compelled to launch an assault. Maybe because of the lack of Christmas presents for her under the tree. Or maybe because he'd beat her to it the last two nights and tackled her *first*.

He laughed as she took charge, licking and nibbling on

his taut nipples, rubbing her naked body against his, arousing him fully. She ran her hand over his cock and said, "This is the only thing I ever want to come between us."

His grin couldn't have stretched any further.

Her hair dangled about his head as she leaned down to kiss his mouth, his hands cupping her breasts, massaging. Her knees speared the mattress on either side of his waist as she deepened the kiss.

One of his hands pulled her closer. Not expecting what came next, she was startled a bit when he moved his hand between her knees and started to stroke at the apex of her thighs. Straddling him made her feel more exposed, the craving for completion greater. With a hand on her thigh, he continued to stroke her. She arched back and gave into his fondling, coming unglued, ready to howl at the moon. To her shock, she was so close, so hot and wet and ready, that when he plunged two fingers into her, she screamed with release.

He quickly re-situated her on his cock, pushing in, penetrating deep, then guided her as she rode him hard. He smelled like musky, male wolf: her wolf, her mate, powerful, hot, and lovable. She couldn't have chosen a better mate for herself, and she loved him with all her heart.

"Beautiful," he said on a groan, and she didn't know if he meant she was or this was, but it didn't matter.

He was beautiful to her.

He pumped into her hard, and she saw the tension leave his face. She laughed when he growled and turned her so that she was on her back, and he was still connected, still thrusting until the end.

"I love you." She wrapped her arms around him and held him tight. "Forever and always."

He smiled and kissed her mouth before he rolled off her and took her into his arms to snuggle. "You are the love of my life. I knew it that first time I greeted you and mispronounced your name."

She laughed. "Who would be named after a tire?"

He smiled and kissed her again. "You were cute when your green eyes narrowed, and then they lit up and you bowled me over with that beautiful Irish lilt to your voice. I knew I was in love then."

"I have to admit, when you turned fifty shades of red for mispronouncing my name, I had a devil of a time keeping my distance from you."

"I know."

She laughed. "You did *not*."

"Yeah, I did. How would we have gotten here if it wasn't so?"

"Hmm, your private ski lessons? I can't decide if that's when it really hit me, or when we were making the snow sculpture, and just in sweet fun, you kissed my nose. Or when we fell asleep on the couch watching *A Christmas Story*. But I knew then that keeping my distance wasn't going to happen."

He sighed. "I'll second that. We were meant to be together. Merry Christmas, honey."

"Merry Christmas, CJ." She couldn't sleep though. Well, maybe she dozed. She kept waiting for CJ to get out of bed and put her packages under the tree! But he didn't.

Instead, he made love to her two more times.

CJ felt the mattress move, again, as Laurel slipped out of bed early the next morning.

"Where are you going?" As if he didn't know.

"To see what Santa brought."

"I've got a present for you right here."

She glanced at his erection tenting the sheet and smiled. "You can give that to me later."

He smiled as she slipped on a soft, robin's-egg-blue robe, her red hair cascading about her shoulders, and then headed out of the bedroom. He couldn't believe how many times she'd left the bed in the middle of the night to see if he'd tucked her presents under the tree. He'd thought she'd never fall asleep, though making love to her two times during the night hadn't helped him carry out his Santa mission.

He groaned when he saw it was still dark out, then climbed out of bed, put on his navy blue robe, and padded down the stairs.

She was poking around at the presents he'd finally managed to put under the tree. Well, except for one.

She was crouched in front of the brightly colored packages, grinning. "What is this? It weighs a ton."

"Open it and see."

She opened the package and beamed at the blue-and-white ski boot. "You're taking me skiing again, but this time I have my own boots."

She was just like a little kid, and he loved seeing her excitement. Christmas had never been quite like this— and it was the best.

Then she rummaged through the packages to find the other. Inside the second ski boot was an envelope. She tore it open and smiled. "Free private and personalized ski lessons for a lifetime."

He hadn't even opened his first present from her

when she came over to thank him. She leaned over to kiss him, her robe gaping enough for him to see her mouthwatering breasts. In the next instant, he was pulling her down on top of his lap; then she was pushing him onto his back, untying his robe, and spreading it wide like a blanket.

He was still fully aroused and she smiled. "I love you, and this is the best Christmas ever."

And it had barely begun. She untied her robe and tossed it aside, then lowered herself onto his cock and began to ride him. With the lights sparkling on the tree, two packages unwrapped, and a hot she-wolf making his dreams come true, he couldn't have loved Christmas more.

"Forget waiting for this Christmas present. I didn't give you yours yet."

"This is the best one yet," he said, and then there were no more words as he brought her to climax and gave her yet another Christmas present before she collapsed on top of him and hugged him tight.

"Here I was looking for presents under the tree when I could have just found them in bed."

He smiled.

Then she hurried to get off him, pulled on her robe and belted it, then handed him some of his gifts. When she gave him his first present, he pulled her onto his lap to open it, because it wasn't the gift, but the giver that made his Christmas so special. He opened the package and saw the picture of him, his brothers, and their father and mother at a happier time in their lives, and he looked up at her with tears in his eyes.

"I found it in your father's things. I had Jake take the

original and refinish it and then framed one for you and each of your brothers."

He kissed her soundly. "Thank you. I'll cherish your gift to me always."

"I…I hope your brothers will love it too and won't be upset that I did this. I worried about it the whole time I was getting them ready."

"They'll love it. Thank you."

Then she gave him another present, and he said, "Your turn next."

"I opened two."

He chuckled. "Two ski boots."

"And skiing lessons for a lifetime."

He smiled and was starting to open the present when she found one of the ten-thousand-dollar bills in her next present. "I thought you put them all in the bank."

"I did. Until right before Christmas."

"You gave some to your brothers, didn't you?"

"Yeah. They're sure to be surprised. I usually don't spend that much on them."

She laughed. "I bet they'll be shocked." She stared at the bill, not believing it.

"You can do whatever your heart desires with the money. Fix up the basement of the hotel, redecorate the house—whatever you'd like."

"Take you on a trip to Ireland."

"I thought they got rid of wolves over there," he said, smiling.

"They don't know about us."

"It's a deal."

He finished opening his present. "A book on how

to create snow sculptures." He laughed. "Planning this early to win next year's competition, I see."

"Absolutely. I'm all ready for a winning streak. And we have lots of snow so we can practice. But we'll have to do it in the backyard so no one sees what we're working on next."

"Speaking of snow, do you want to look outside and see if it snowed last night? Maybe we can get in a snow-fort building contest and have a snowball fight later."

She laughed. She got up, crossed the living room to the back door, and peeked out the blinds. "Ohmigod, CJ. You got me skis and poles!"

Standing upright in the snow, her skis sat in front of his taller ones, their pole straps looped around the skis, indicating they were together, now and forever.

He joined her at the door and wrapped his arms around her, pulling her tight against his body and nuzzling her neck. "I don't know about you, but all this Christmas is wearing me out. Did you want to go back to bed for a while?"

She turned and slipped her arms around his waist. "This is the best Christmas ever." And with CJ in her life, she knew it would only get better. She was glad to have found their aunt alive and well, and that her sisters were even beginning to date. She thought a friendship with her cousins had promise. But most of all, she loved the pack, Silver Town, and CJ.

She broke free and said, "Let's take a break from Christmas." She headed for the stairs, but he began to chase her and the thrill of the hunt had her squealing and bounding up the stairs before he could catch her.

He did anyway, swinging her in his arms in their

bedroom and collapsing with her on the bed. "You really didn't believe I'd forget about your presents for Christmas, did you?" he asked, smiling at her.

"You are such a tease. Just remember this next Christmas."

"I'll be ready. Next Christmas and beyond."

She laughed and kissed him, and CJ was glad he'd convinced Laurel they were meant to be together. Haunted hotel and all.

Read on for a sneak peek from

SEAL Wolf in Too Deep

FEELING USELESS, PAUL CUNNINGHAM PROPPED HIS broken leg on a few more pillows as he and his partner Lori watched from the deck of their lakeside cabin. Their best friend Allan Rappaport headed down the dock with his temporary police dive partner Debbie Renaud, both ready to do some more practice diving with each other. Paul's leg was casted all the way up to his hip after a freak accident on a dive rescue mission.

"I still think Allan should ask the sheriff to make new assignments. You and Allan were raised as brothers, you're SEAL team members, although you've left the Navy, and you're used to working with other men, not women. And you're both wolves, not that anyone on the force knows that, but it makes it easier to work together. This business"—Lori motioned to Allan and Debbie as they talked to each other on the dock—"is bound to cause problems."

"Allan respects her work too much. It would look like he's having trouble with her on a professional level. He won't do anything that might jeopardize her career."

Looking cross, Lori folded her arms over her expanding belly. Paul reached over and she slipped her hand into his. "They'll be all right. Allan's smart enough to know the boundaries between *lupus garou* and humans," Paul said.

Lori squeezed his hand. "Watch the way she looks up

at him. They've been together for only two weeks and she is so enamored with him. All smiles and sweetness. She adores him. He's a SEAL and women just fall all over themselves when they learn that."

Paul raised his brows at Lori.

She shook her head at him. "I know the two of you too well. Your SEAL status doesn't affect me in the least."

He chuckled. "As far as Debbie goes, she's a smiley, sweet woman, Lori. You worry too much."

Lori frowned and settled back in her chair. "You make light of this and it's dangerous. He hasn't dated any of the eligible women in our pack, and we have several. Sure, he's nice and polite, but he's not interested in any of them. Look at the way he helps Debbie with her dive checks. They look like they're lovers."

Paul smiled. He knew it wasn't that Lori didn't want Allan to care about a woman, but the woman *had* to be one of their kind, or it would cause all kinds of complications they couldn't afford. "Come here."

"Your leg—"

"Come on the other side." She moved to his chaise lounge, and he snuggled with her. "He'll be okay. We're talking about Allan. In all our years of wolf longevity, how many times has he fallen for a human woman and not been able to let go of the notion?"

Lori relaxed then. "Never."

"Right. Never. So they're just working together, doing practice dives as a team so when they have risky dives to make, they'll be working in sync with each other. And look, they didn't have to dive here in front of us, knowing we're observing every move they make. He could have taken her anywhere to practice diving with her."

"True. But they won't always be here under our watchful supervision."

Paul chuckled. "Lori, you are a worrywart."

—᲌᲌—

The day was nice and hot, perfect for practice dives, if that's all that was going on between Allan and Debbie. But Lori knew she wasn't just paranoid. She knew Debbie was interested in Allan and he returned the interest right back. What was not to like about Allan anyway? He was sexy and fit and loved to do what Debbie loved to do—dive. They had an easy way with each other, like they already knew each other intimately, not like people who had just started to work together. No formality between them. No getting to know each other.

Paul was trying to calm her fears, but he too worried about Allan. How could he not?

Debbie was a lovely brunette, vivacious, something that totally appealed to Allan. She was definitely an alpha, ready for adventure. She loved the police work, loved saving people and animals, just like Allan. Worst of all, she was single.

"You need to talk to him," Lori told Paul.

"He's a grown man and knows what he's doing."

"He's human, well, and wolf, and both are going to get him into trouble."

"I'll talk to him—but he's going to wonder what all the fuss is about."

Lori was certain he'd know just why they were concerned.

—᲌᲌—

Allan was just as concerned about working with a human woman as Paul and Lori were, but he knew he could handle this. It sure was a hell of a lot different going on dives with Debbie than with Paul.

He was so used to working with Paul over the years that they just did everything in perfect sync—the hand signals, body movement, the awareness of their partner. Though some signals were universal, he and Paul, along with the other members of their SEAL wolf team, had developed some over the years that were distinctive to them.

Allan knew Paul and Lori were warily observing them. He had to admit watching Debbie swim was a hell of a lot more attention-grabbing than watching Paul. And when she smiled at him, she made him feel as though he was dating her and not just working a job. He had to remind himself to act professional and get the training done. On an assignment, they had to concentrate on the mission so they could get the results they needed—evidence from a crime scene, people or animals to safety—while ensuring they came out of it unscathed.

If he'd been assigned to a human male dive partner, no problem. But working with a single female, one who fascinated him like she did, he could see it would take a lot of diligence on his part to keep his mind on business and not on Debbie. If he could just become interested in one of the new single females in the pack, that would solve all his problems.

But when he swam next to Debbie in the clear blue lake, she fired his testosterone sky-high. That didn't happen when he was around the single women in his pack. He hoped he could deal with this without getting them both into dangerous waters.

Chapter 2

Four months later

THE TIRES OF ALLAN'S HATCHBACK SLID ON A PATCH of ice on the bridge just as he spied tires sticking up out of a deluge of water in a culvert. A rush of adrenaline poured through his veins, readying him for the frigid conditions and a rescue mission. In the cold of winter in Northern Montana, he and his dive partner were the first to arrive on the scene of the accident and had to act quickly.

Debbie was requesting emergency backup and an ambulance as she held on to the dashboard, looking just as alarmed when the tires lost traction on the ice. He worried that they'd end up down the embankment, crashing into the upside-down SUV.

Frantically, a woman jerked at the back door of the SUV without success.

As soon as he saw who it was, his heart took a dive. It was Franny White, wife of the new chef at their wolf-run Italian restaurant, Fame da Lupo. She didn't go anywhere without her daughter. But the baby wasn't in her arms and Franny was trying so hard to get into the backseat, he knew little Stacy had to be buckled into her car seat and submerged underwater.

"Cancel the call for the ambulance!" he said to Debbie, knowing that this was a risk he had to take. "Call this number!" He gave her the number for the medical clinic that catered to his kind, though Debbie would be clueless. "I know the woman—her baby is in the car. Just...call it." He didn't have time to make up a cover story.

Debbie hesitated, and he knew she had to be thinking his request was a dangerous mistake. That precious time could be wasted. But lots more was at stake if the human-run hospital's ambulance picked up Franny and Stacy and they shifted. Debbie quickly called for the other ambulance and canceled the one for the main hospital in Bigfork.

As soon as he could safely brake the car and stop, Allan and Debbie were out of the vehicle, dashing down the steep incline on the crunchy snow and ice. Debbie had grabbed the emergency medical kit on the way out.

Seeing Allan and Debbie, Franny screamed, "My baby's in there! She's in a car seat in back." She was soaking wet, her tearful words were slurred, and she was stumbling around as if she were drunk. She was wearing just a sweater and jeans, standing in the nearly waist-deep water. Allan was certain she was hypothermic. Confusion and the natural instinct to warm herself could cause her to shift too. Between that and rescuing the baby, they were in a hell of a fix.

"She's only three months old!" Franny added, as if she didn't recognize Allan—another sign she had hypothermia.

"Get the mom out of the water," he said to Debbie as her boots crunched in the snow and ice behind him.

She slipped, her boot kicking the back of his. He swung around and grabbed her arm to keep her from falling.

"Thanks," she said, looking a little embarrassed.

"It's slippery." He was having a difficult time staying

on his own two feet, but with bigger boots and more weight than Debbie had, he was managing better.

When he reached the moving water, he waded right in. The icy cold sent a jolt of adrenaline straight through him, and he wished he were wearing a wet suit.

The driver's-side door was open where Franny had managed to get out. Allan pushed through the strong currents to the SUV, while Debbie went after Franny. When he reached the car, he tried to get the back door open, but couldn't. He scrambled into the driver's seat and squeezed through the front seats to access the baby's carrier. Upside down and buckled firmly into her carrier, the baby was unconscious. The cold water covered her, and Allan feared the worst.

He shined his light inside the vehicle to give him more illumination in the dark, though he could see well enough with his wolf night vision in most conditions. But this was so precarious, and with a life hanging in the balance, he didn't want to make any mistakes.

Praying he could revive the unconscious baby in time, he yanked out his knife. The icy water made his hands so stiff and numb, he feared he would drop it as he cut away the straps to the car seat, careful not to injure Stacy. He yanked at the straps until they gave way. Pulling the baby free, he cradled her against his chest and backed out of the vehicle. He held the lifeless infant close as he waded through the icy water toward the snow-covered shore.

Debbie was still struggling to guide the mom out of the water. Franny was stumbling, shivering—though they all were—and instead of moving briskly out of the water like Debbie and he were doing, Franny kept stopping and turning. Debbie kept reassuring her she was taking her to her baby, holding the woman close to share body heat, and trying to rush her out of the water as fast as she could.

If he could have, he would have given Debbie the unresponsive baby and carried Franny from the water. But he had to resuscitate the baby pronto. Every second counted.

"I'll get the blankets," Debbie said as she left Franny on the shore and ran up the incline to the vehicle while Allan administered CPR on baby Stacy.

The infant suddenly coughed up water and let out a weak cry. Allan swore his stopped heart came back to life. She wasn't out of danger yet. She was lethargic and her skin was bright red and cold.

Franny was trying to pull off her wet clothes in the frigid weather. He was afraid she was planning to turn into her wolf.

"Franny, hold on. We'll get you and Stacy to the clinic as soon as we can. The ambulance will be here any minute. Dr. Holt will take care of you both." With one arm, he held the baby against his wet chest, holding Franny close to him with the other, trying to keep her from stripping out of her clothes. They needed to, but not as a prelude to shifting. He moved them up toward the hatchback to get them out of the stiff, cold wind, but Franny was struggling to get free.

Slipping a bit, Debbie hurried as fast as she could back down the hill with blankets and some dry clothes.

"Let's get them up to the vehicle. You can remove the baby's clothes inside the car, and I'll take care of Franny," Allan said.

"Okay," Debbie replied, and Allan gave her the baby, then lifted Franny's trembling body into his arms and trudged up the hill.

"Need…to…turn," Franny bit out.

Yes, their double coat would help warm her, and even just the shift would warm her, but her baby would turn too. He could just see Debbie dropping the baby-turned-wolf-pup and scream out in fright.

"When you're in the ambulance, Franny. Just wait." He spoke firmly, as a pack sub-leader would, encouraging her but at the same time commanding her to do his bidding.

At the car, Debbie climbed into the backseat and pulled off the baby's sopping wet pink fleece jumpsuit and wrapped her in a dry blanket, while Allan struggled to remove Franny's wet clothes. She was shaking badly from the cold, which was better than if she wasn't shivering at all, but her skin was ice white, her breathing abnormally slow.

Sirens in the distance told them the cavalry was coming. Thank God. He just hoped it was *their* ambulance and not the regular one.

"What happened?" Allan asked Franny. He had to keep her talking and alert, keep her from shifting unexpectedly.

"Red car—no accident."

Allan paused as he was trying to get a wool ski hat on her head, but she kept removing the blanket. She was either thoroughly confused or she really wanted to shift. Maybe a little of both.

Franny looked on the verge of collapse as he pulled the wool knit cap over her head and removed the rest of her wet clothes. Then he wrapped her tightly in the blanket, lifted her into his arms, and set her inside the hatchback. At least inside the vehicle, she was protected from the bitter wind. Debbie was holding the baby close. Both he and Debbie were suffering from hypothermia also. He felt his speech slurring, and he was having a time concentrating on what *he* needed to do next. But he had enough presence of mind to know not to shift.

"Your daughter's breathing and her heartbeat's steady," Allan reassured Franny, though he couldn't know for sure about her overall condition until the EMTs took her to the clinic and had her checked out.

Debbie frowned a little at him, and he realized he'd made another mistake. The problem was his wolf hearing was enhanced enough that he could hear, smell, and see things that humans couldn't. She probably figured he was just soothing the mother over with a story. The truth was he could hear the baby's heartbeat, and it was steady, which gave him a modicum of relief.

The ambulance pulled up and the medics took over from there. Allan should have asked Franny more particulars about the accident, but he wasn't thinking as clearly as he normally did in an emergency. Not that Franny could have responded with any real mental clarity, but it was something he should have done in a case like this.

He and Debbie were shaking as hard from the cold, but the EMTs had already given them blankets too.

"My...purse," Franny said, her teeth chattering.

"Anything else you need from the car?" Allan wished he could put on his wolf coat or his wet suit. He was afraid she had something damning in her purse with regard to being *lupus garous*, though he couldn't imagine what. He didn't want to jeopardize their situation if anyone else were to get it for her later. So he made the decision to get it for her, despite how chilled he was.

"Just…purse," she managed to get out. "Front…seat."

"I'll get it for you," he reassured her.

Debbie took hold of his arm. "You're already suffering from hypothermia. Let someone else do it."

"I'll be fine. I'm already wet. We'll get warm and dry real soon." Their wolf pack didn't have wolves working for the sheriff's department, except for Paul and Allan as contracted divers. So they had to take care of their own. Not that he could let on to Debbie why that was so.

At the edge of the culvert, he dropped the blanket on top of the snow.

Despite already being soaking wet and chilled to the marrow of his bones, he felt even colder when he entered the water. But his faster wolf healing abilities would help him overcome this more quickly, than if any human responders had to deal with it.

He waded out, then dove into the submerged SUV, glad Debbie had returned to the hatchback to protect herself from the chilling wind. He pulled his flashlight out, just in case he needed it and to ensure no one would question how he could find the purse in the dark if anyone happened to be watching. He was certain Debbie would be, to ensure he would return safely.

He located the black leather bag resting on the roof of the upside-down SUV and pulled it out. Clutching the purse against his chest, fearful he wouldn't be able to hold on to it in the fast-moving water, he waded through it until he reached the shore. On the shore, he grabbed up the blanket and wrapped it around himself, then trudged slowly up the slope to the waiting ambulance. He felt as if he were wearing wet cement shoes.

"Thank you," Franny said, taking her sopping wet bag and holding it tightly to her body, as if it was her baby too.

With the ambulance doors now shut, but before the ambulance took off for the clinic, a bark came from inside. Then with its lights flashing and siren blaring, the ambulance headed for the clinic as some of the sheriff's men arrived at the scene.

Debbie was staring at the ambulance as it drove away. "Did you hear a dog bark inside the ambulance?"

"No." A wolf, yes. Dog? No.

"You should have let someone else get her bag, Allan. You're not invincible," she said, shaking hard as they sat inside the vehicle with the heat blasting, a cold north wind sweeping across the area as they waited to speak to the police officers who had arrived.

"Well," said Rowdy Sanderson, a homicide detective, his blue eyes considering the two of them, "why don't you get into something warm and dry before both of you need hospitalization too. I'll handle this until you can file a report."

"What the hell are you doing here? No dead bodies," Allan said. He knew Rowdy was here because Debbie was.

"Could have been," Rowdy said, glancing at Debbie.

"Thanks, we're out of here," Allan said. They had to get into dry clothes pronto.

Allan and Debbie were always on call if something came up. They had been finishing up some paperwork on a murder case—a car buried in water in one of the area lakes. The driver had contusions that were probably not due to the car accident. More likely, the victim had been beaten and the car accident had been staged. He and Debbie were just on their way to get some lunch when they had seen the SUV upside down in the culvert.

"I want to drop by the clinic as soon as we can change and get warmed up." Debbie leaned down to pull off a boot, and then the other. She slid off a wet sock, dropping it on the floor, then struggled to get the other off.

"Agreed. I can drop you off at your place, let you get a hot shower, dry your hair, and dress. I'll pick you up, and we'll head on over there."

The clinic took only *lupus garous* in for long-term care. In an emergency, they would provide care for humans, stabilizing the patient so they could be sent off to the hospital in Bigfork. That meant human visitors rarely came to the clinic. They would have to be on alert when Debbie dropped by to see Franny and her baby.

"Thanks, sounds like a good plan," she said.

Debbie pulled off her sopping-wet sweater and dumped it on the floor. This was the first time in the four and a half months they'd worked together that they'd had a situation like this, where they needed to get warm and dry pronto, and were too far from anywhere to do it quickly. He hadn't expected Debbie to start stripping though. It was a good idea, but he just hadn't predicted it.

Next, came her black turtleneck. He was trying to concentrate on the ice and snow-covered road, but out of the corner of his eye, he saw that her bra was purple and white polka-dotted silk. He smiled a little, never figuring her for wearing bright and fanciful underwear.

She unfastened her bra and dropped it on the floor. He nearly missed his turn to the main road that would take him to Whitefish. He *really* was trying to be a gentleman, but, hell, he'd worked with her for months, and lots of times he'd envisioned what she would look like naked when she was wearing a skintight diving suit. Now she was stripping next to him?

Not that this wasn't essential to their, well, *her* good health, but it was wreaking havoc with his libido, despite how cold and wet he was. He was a wolf, after all. But he was going to have a damn accident if he wasn't careful.

She used one of the towels they kept in the car when they went diving to cover her waist and another to dry herself off.

Thankfully, she was concentrating on pulling on a dry turtleneck and then a sweater, too cold to notice him glance at her. They always kept a couple pairs of clothes in backpacks in the car for diving and emergencies. She struggled to get her jeans off next, and then wiggled out of her panties, which matched her bra.

As soon as she'd pulled on the rest of her dry clothes, zipped her parka up to her throat, and tugged her ski hat on, she said, "Pull over. You've got to get out of your wet things too."

"I bet you say that to all the guys you dive with." He pulled onto the shoulder and they switched places, the cold outdoors feeling even icier.

She laughed. "If I were diving with Lou Messer, probably not. His brand-new wife told the sheriff if he paired Lou up with me, he'd be leaving the police dive force."

Allan smiled. "I heard she checks up on him all the time, wanting to know where he's at, what he's doing, is he safe. I'm glad I don't have to deal with her. If I did, I'd probably say something and get myself into trouble."

"Yeah, but everyone needs your expertise, so they're stuck with you."

He laughed. "Stuck with me, eh?"

"It can be a good thing. I still can't believe you went back for Franny's purse. They could have gotten it when they pulled her SUV out of the culvert."

"You know how women are. She was probably afraid of losing her credit cards, cash, driver's license, no telling what. Maybe a special keepsake she was afraid might be lost."

Then it was Allan's turn to remove his wet clothes. He moved the passenger seat as far back as he could to give himself more leg room, and began the tedious project, his fingers numb with cold, and the shivering impeding his progress.

"Well, it was sweet of you, but too risky."

After he got a dry flannel shirt and wool sweater on and had yanked a wool ski hat over his head, he finally felt relief. Then he tugged at his boots, socks, and jeans. When he got down to his black boxers, Debbie said, "I figured you for white briefs."

"I figured you'd wear white lacy bikini panties and bra."

"You looked!" But she was smiling when she said it.

He chuckled and pulled on a pair of blue briefs, jeans, socks, and a pair of dry boots.

All dry now, he was feeling a hell of a lot better. His hair was cut short, but Debbie's was long. He was certain her wet hair was making her cold still, but the hat she wore would keep the heat from escaping in the meantime.

He got a call on his cell and fumbled to get it out of the console, realizing then he was still feeling some of the effects of the hypothermia. The call was from Paul. He and the rest of the SEAL wolf team members still did contract missions together, but they'd put that part of their life mostly on hold while they raised families. The shared responsibility of raising *lupus garou* pups was all too important to a pack like theirs.

Now wasn't the best time to call because Allan was with Debbie, but Paul would know that. Which meant Allan was probably needed for a pack-related emergency, and he worried that it had to do with Franny and her claim that the accident she had been involved in hadn't been an accident. With Paul's broken leg still incapacitating him, Allan was taking up the slack.

"Allan, we've got a problem."

"Okay. Just a sec. Debbie and I were just on a case, and we're suffering from a mild case of hypothermia." Which Paul would be aware of, as the EMTs who rescued Franny would have told him. But Allan couldn't let Debbie know that Paul was aware of it. "We're dropping by her place so she can dry her hair and get warmed up a bit and I'm headed over to my cabin. Can I call you back?" Allan didn't want to have to watch what he was saying.

"Call me as soon as you can. We have a minor emergency."

"Will do." Allan was dying to know what the emergency was all about, if it was related to Franny or something else, but he really didn't want to ask in front of Debbie and then have to make up some story about it later.

They ended the call and he phoned the clinic. "How are Franny and Stacy doing?" he asked Dr. Christine Holt.

"They're in stable condition. Your partner didn't suspect anything?" Christine asked him.

"No."

"Good. Are you all right? The EMTs said that you went back in the water after her purse."

"Yeah, in case she had something important in there."

"Well, she pulled a piece of paper out of her purse, sopping wet, the ink all gone, but she said it wasn't important anyway. She was so out of it, she just knew she had to have her purse with her. Both Franny and her baby will be fine. Her husband is here with them now."

"Good to hear. Debbie and I will be dropping by later as soon as we can get dry and warm."

"Give us a heads-up when you're on your way. We don't have any other patients at the moment, but you never know when we might, and we need to make sure that Franny remains human."

"Will do."

"Take care."

Allan told Debbie about the condition of Mom and Baby, but not about the purse. He didn't want her reminding him how he shouldn't have gone after it.

He was tasked with ensuring all the new wolf pack members worked well together, but he also helped with any trouble the pack was having. He should have been interested in one of the lovely single she-wolves, but he couldn't get his thoughts off a certain sexy, kick-ass human. Some of it was because they worked together, but they also had a lot in common: they both loved to dive as a hobby, loved thrillers, Italian food, and read some of the same fantasy books.

"I'm glad to hear Franny and her baby are doing well. Is there a problem at home?" Debbie asked.

"Not sure. Probably some minor family issue." This was the part Allan hated. He'd told her about his family, as far as he could say. That his mother and sister had taken Paul in. That he was like a brother to them. But Allan hadn't been able to say much more than that. Certainly nothing about their wolf pack, and their increased longevity, though that had changed and they were aging nearly the same as humans now, but they hadn't figured out why. He and his family had lived for many years, though they didn't look it.

Trying to explain how eons ago he had run through a forest that once was on dry land and now buried underwater in Lake MacDonald, and other such things, wasn't an option. He had gone diving with her there just for fun, and wished he could have told her about the time Paul and he had a very close call with a bear, when the forest *wasn't* underwater. She would never have believed him.

"Hope everything's all right," she said, sounding genuinely concerned.

The problem was she had a cop's way of thinking. She was curious and had good instincts. She could tell something was going on. He knew the longer they worked together, the dicier it would get. Paul had warned him, but what could Allan do? He couldn't very well ask for another partner when he really loved working with her, and how would he explain why he could no longer work with her?

Anything he said might hurt her career. And he wasn't about to do that.

He sighed. Somehow he would just have to keep up the facade. That meant not letting on that he could smell things that humans couldn't. She'd already commented on his remarkable eyesight when it was getting to be dusk and dawn.

Yeah, working with her was great…and dangerous. Not only because of what he was, but because he totally had the hots for her. And that was a no go in this business. He told himself it would be easy because partners didn't date, normally. If he just kept it on a professional basis, he should have no problem.

His focus turned to Paul's phone call. He knew the situation wouldn't be some minor issue. He was anxious to learn what the trouble was this time.

Chapter 3

DEBBIE REALLY LOVED WORKING WITH ALLAN, THOUGH
he was…different. Maybe that's why she loved working
with him so much. She could tell he really wanted to see her
after hours, and did sometimes—to talk more about a case.

They would keep working on cases no matter the
hour, have dinner together, work on them some more.
Get up early, start on it again. They'd rescued four
people who had fallen through ice while ice fishing,
saved a baby moose that had fallen through ice, and
rescued two accident victims due to icy road conditions
this month. Not only that, but they'd been working on
this murder case too, and though the vehicle and body
had already been removed from the lake, they planned to
see if they could find anything else in the water around
the site of the accident.

She glanced at him, trying to read his expression. He
had one of those faces that made her think of a really
nice guy, but she knew Allan could be all business when
it came to taking someone in hand.

He appreciated her training and often remarked
on what a great partner she was. She knew he wasn't
saying it just to be nice. He truly meant what he said,
and she really respected him for it. She felt the same
way about him.

"Are we still on for pizza?" she asked, wanting to
check on the baby and mom at the clinic to see for

herself they were okay, but she was also dying to have a pizza. She hadn't had one in ages, and it was a nice way to take a break once she dried her wet clothes and her hair. At least the car heater was now warming her up.

"You bet." His eyes always lit up when his gaze caught hers. He was seriously sexy, muscular and in great shape and that appealed too.

She'd always wanted to hear his SEAL stories, the ones that he could share with her. He'd told her about a couple of rescues he and his team had performed for private contracts. They'd been in the Amazon a number of times on dangerous missions. She found him to be the most fascinating man she'd ever met.

Some of her fascination was because his family was so important to him. She was estranged from her own. Her father had been the town drunk, and her mother, the perfect enabler. Good thing Debbie was an only child so only she'd had to suffer the consequences of a dysfunctional family like theirs.

"When you were getting Franny's purse, she said a red car nearly hit hers, slid on the ice, and she turned to avoid it. That's how she ended up careening down the hill and sailing into the culvert. She said he did it on purpose, but she doesn't remember the SUV being upside down. Just that somehow she managed to get out and then couldn't get to her baby. So I suspect she just imagined the driver had caused the accident on purpose."

"Hell, I thought she was mistaken. The driver didn't stop to help? Call it in or anything?"

"It wasn't technically a hit and run, and he might have been afraid if he tried to brake on the ice he'd be where she was."

"If it was a woman or someone elderly, I'd give the driver the benefit of the doubt, but her baby could have died. And Franny could have also."

"Agreed. She said he was wearing a camo cap and his hair was cut short, but that's all she could see before she swerved to avoid him. He was about our age."

"Then he should be strung up."

She wasn't surprised at the way Allan felt. She had thought the same thing, though she had tried to see it from the other driver's point of view too. But she had to agree with Allan.

When he drove into her duplex driveway, he finally said, "Uh, about lunch, yeah. I'll give you a call in just a bit."

Then he dropped her off, and she knew as distracted as he was, whatever was the matter had to be really important.

He pulled out of her driveway, a frown marring his temple as he talked to someone on his cell. She wondered again just what the trouble was and if she would be going alone to the clinic.

She realized she really wanted to be part of his life, to be there for him if he needed someone to talk to about family stuff. Not in a boyfriend/girlfriend relationship, particularly, but just as a friend. That had been something she had trouble with growing up. She had had no one to talk to about her parents. Better to just leave home and stay away. As a kid, that had meant spending hours at the library after school and immersing herself in books until the library closed for the night. Often a police officer would drive her home.

She'd gotten to know nearly everyone on the police

force that way. One of the officers had rescued her
father from his submerged truck when he'd gotten
drunk and crashed it through the bridge. The officer
had only delayed the inevitable, though. Her dad killed
himself a year later in another accident, one with a con-
crete bridge column. But the officer's dedication as a
diver, and her love of the water and subsequent scuba
diving certification, had made the decision for her. She
had become a contracted police diver just like Officer
Hardy Monroe.

She knew Allan had chosen to be one so he could
work closer to home and spend more time with his
family, though he had told her when he was needed for
a mission, he would have to take a leave of absence and
deal with it. She was surprised he would continue to
do missions away from home as close as he was to his
family. In the four and a half months he'd been working with her, he hadn't gone on any assignments. She
was glad because she really enjoyed working with him.
Trying to train with a new diver would mean learning
his or her idiosyncrasies all over again.

Paul Cunningham was the same way as far as continuing to do contract work out of country, though he'd
set aside that business because his wife was pregnant.
Debbie had felt bad when he'd broken his leg and hoped
it would mend just fine. He was out of the cast now, but
he was still using a cane. When he was fully recovered,
would he go back to being partnered with Allan?

That made her feel a little blue.

After washing up, getting dressed, and drying her
hair, she was hopeful she could have lunch with Allan
and head over to the clinic. When she checked her

phone, Allan had texted his regrets: *Need to deal with some family issues. Talk to you soon. Allan*

No "sorry for lunch." No "wish I could see Franny and the baby." Debbie knew whatever it had to do with had to be bad news or Allan would have said something more. He was always good about that. And he was always conscientious about personally seeing victims they'd rescued to learn how they were faring.

She wished she could help in some way. She put in a call to the clinic as she headed over there, hoping when she saw Allan again, he'd feel comfortable sharing with her this time.

"We don't know who she is?" Allan asked Paul, angered that a *lupus garou* had come into their territory, maybe looking for protection, and had been murdered.

His countenance stormy, Paul stared out the window of his cabin overlooking the lake, his arms folded across his chest. "No. Since she was naked and one of our kind, we presume she was trapped and killed as a wolf. Your sister and my mate were out running as wolves before dawn's first light and came across her body in the woods near the cabin. Whoever did it caught her in an animal trap and shot her. The ladies saw burn marks on the bullet wounds. Though ballistics haven't come back to confirm it yet, the rounds had to have been silver. The ladies smelled the sweet, subtle scent of pure silver. She had lots of defensive wounds where she was trying to get loose from the trap and bite at her attacker."

"Did she bite him?"

"Yes."

"What about DNA samples from his blood? Skin?" Allan considered the ramifications further. "What if her bites transferred the *lupus garou* genetics into his bloodstream and he turns into a wolf? He won't have much control over it for some time. He won't be able to shift for another week—not while it's the phase of the new moon right now."

"The forensics lab is testing the blood and tissue samples. But you know it takes a while for the lab work results to come in. If he hasn't committed any crimes, or even if he has, he might not be in the database. An autopsy is being done as we speak. If we find the bastard soon, he'll be wearing some hefty bite marks and scratches. But if he's been turned, that's another story. That means we have a week to catch him before the half moon appears. What's worse is someone anonymously reported the murder. If he was a wolf, we'd have to handle it on our own. But now the police are involved."

"The killer did?"

"Possibly." Paul let out his breath. "Probably. Neither Lori nor Rose saw, smelled, or heard anyone. Rowdy Sanderson is the homicide detective in charge of the investigation. Because the killer used silver rounds, whoever murdered the wolf had to have known she was a *lupus garou*."

"He didn't try to remove her body to claim he'd killed a werewolf?"

"No. I'm declaring that no one in the pack shifts until we can learn who did this and take him down."

"Good idea. Any clues?"

Paul shook his head. "I suspect the woman was

coming here to meet with us so she could join the pack. I want you to check out the crime scene. I've got Everett trying to track down who she was. I've asked Lori's grandma to discover if the woman had any contact with any member of our pack, asking to join, since Emma and your mother have been involved the most in asking single female wolves to join the pack."

"Sounds like we have a werewolf hunter on our hands, don't you agree?" In all the years of their existence, they had never had to deal with such an issue.

"It sure as hell sounds like it. On the other hand, what if it is a *lupus garou,* and he covered his tracks by making it *look* like a werewolf hunter was after her? If that's the case, his victim wouldn't have turned him."

"Yeah, I was just thinking that too. And if he's not recently turned, that can be good and bad. Good, because he won't shift unexpectedly around humans and give our kind away. And bad because he'll be harder to track down."

"Either way, we have to stop him. But if he hasn't been turned, we need the police to handle this." Paul headed into the kitchen and got them both a bottled water. Then they moved to the living room and took a seat on the couches.

"Agreed." Allan noticed Paul's cane leaning next to the couch, but he wasn't using it today. "How's your leg?"

"It's fine. If one more person asks…"

Allan nodded. He knew how much that had to bother Paul. "But you're getting around without the cane, and I don't see you limping."

"Inside buildings, I'm fine. Plowing through snowdrifts or walking on ice…" Paul shook his head.

"Besides, I get enough coddling from Lori, Mom, Rose, and Grandma. I don't need it from you also."

"*Me* coddle *you*? When have I ever done that? It's not in my SEAL or wolf nature. Hell, any of us, broken leg or not, can have trouble on ice unless we're in our wolf form and have better traction. It'll get better."

Paul grunted, then took a swig from his water bottle. "There was a *lupus garou* pack that had to deal with a werewolf hunter group. They successfully turned one of the men, and he works for the pack. The others had to be put down. They couldn't have the men arrested and tried for murder—they had to deal with the threat permanently, because the men wouldn't give up their quest to destroy the wolves and to convert new wolf hunters. They hadn't even been looking for werewolves initially. They were searching for Bigfoot, but saw a *lupus garou* shift. The same could have happened with this case. I could be mistaken, but I suspect the shooter is someone who possibly had prior military service or is a hunter. I can't imagine the average man would take up a gun to hunt werewolves."

"All right, so that's a possibility. That the hunter didn't know about our kind until the woman shifted and he saw her. I would agree with you about being a hunter or prior military." Allan set his bottle on the table.

"Here's another thought, though it's even more far-fetched," Paul said. "After seeing the murdered woman, Rose told Lori that she had looked into one of those live action role-playing game, LARP, groups in southern Montana: werewolf versus villager werewolf hunters. She wanted to see if it was just a game or if any of the players were real wolves while we were away on a mission."

"Hell, Paul. Why would she even do that?"

"She had been corresponding with one of the players online, thinking he was one of us. She had no one to date in the area, and she had discovered his website where he talked about werewolves and being one."

"Which should have clued her in that he wasn't."

"I agree. But no *lupus garous* had passed through our area in months, and she was lonely. When she began to talk to him, she had convinced herself he really was a *lupus garou*. So she went down to see him. This was a month before she met Everett. Which shows we were right to stay here and take over the pack."

"Sounds like it."

"When Rose arrived in Helena, she had lunch with the man, Guy Lamb, and discovered he really was a wolf."

Allan's jaw dropped, then he shook his head. "I never would have believed it. And by the name of Lamb?"

"Yeah, it was his parents' idea. Everyone teased him about being a lamb when he was a kid, so he had fun with saying he was a werewolf on his website."

"A wolf in sheep's clothing."

"Right. Anyway, he liked Rose, but once she met him, she wasn't interested in getting to know him further. She said he was too weird for her. Loved horror stories, music she didn't care for, books she wouldn't read. He was such a big horror fan that he loved to act in plays of that nature and visit horror conventions. They just didn't have anything in common. But she did want to check out the game for curiosity sake, in case one of the other players was a real wolf also. Someone she might connect with more. Rose did manage to meet with the group: eight werewolf hunters, one seer, and two wolves. Though who was playing which roles was a mystery. She said no one smelled like wolves. But when she and Lori came across the woman's body, Rose was pretty rattled and told us about the group, just in case it had any bearing on this situation."

"Okay. I can't think of any other scenario offhand. The notion the killer saw the *lupus garou* shift and then eliminated her has my vote."

Paul finished his bottle of water and set the empty container on the coffee table. "After viewing the wounds inflicted on the woman, I really think something deeper was going on. The murderer attacked her in a rage. It wasn't just a case of killing a random person—passion was involved—anger."

"Maybe he was a former lover and discovered what she was?"

"Now that could be."

"Why would he leave her like that? Why not hide the body?"

"Lori and Rose's arrival might have stopped him."

"Why would he call the police to warn them about the killing, if he was the one who called in anonymously?" Allan asked.

"Because he's proud of the kill? Maybe he thought the coroner could prove she's a werewolf through DNA. Then he could brag about killing a werewolf."

"Then he had to know or believe the woman *was* a werewolf. She had to know him, probably trusted him." Thinking of an even worst-case scenario, Allan ran his hands through his hair. "What if he was watching when Rose and Lori arrived? And when they left, followed them?"

"That's what I'm worried about. The police were at

the crime scene while you were at work this morning. And I've told the homicide detective in charge of this that you'll be looking into it also since it was so close to our cabin and we might have more trouble because the two ladies found the victim."

"Good. What was said about how Lori and Rose located her?"

"They were taking a hike through the woods. There's a trail near there. They were headed up to the lookout over the lake. Anyway, that's the story. In truth, they smelled blood and lots of it. So they headed that way to locate the wounded wolf and help it, if they could. When they discovered the woman, smelled she was one of us, they hated to have to leave her body behind, but they didn't have any choice. They went to the cabin, shifted, dressed, called me, and then headed back to the killing site to 'find' her as humans."

"They didn't wait for you though?"

"No. It would have taken me too long to get there. I was at Lori's dojo, working out some of the stiffness in my leg. Lori called me to make sure she and Rose were doing the right thing. Of course, I didn't want them returning to the scene in case the bastard was still in the area. But understandably, they wanted to call it in before the body happened to vanish, if the murderer decided to dispose of it."

"Hell. Which means if the killer was watching the women arrive as wolves and then return as humans, he could have put two and two together, tracked them back to your cabin, learned you're Lori's mate, and well, hell, just everyone related to them: Lori's grandmother, Mom, Rose's mate, and his mother and sister. And that's just the few of us from the original pack."

"You and me. Yes, very possibly. Which means we have to catch this bastard pronto. Rose contacted everyone on the roster to let them know they need to avoid seeing any of us for the time being. We don't know if this guy has any way to track the rest of the pack members, but if we cut off seeing them in person, that might help." Paul pointed to a map on the wall showing the whole area: lakes, parks, trails, even elevations. "Here's where the woman was found."

"I'll let you know if I discover anything further."

His blood cold with anger, Allan left the cabin and drove to the logging road closest to the location of the crime scene.

On the way to the site, Allan made a call to Debbie, wanting to know how she was doing and how Franny and her baby were faring. He had already called ahead to let the staff know that Debbie would be arriving to check on them on her own, but he learned from them that she had already called ahead. He felt bad that he hadn't been able to go with Debbie to see to Franny and the baby, that he'd had to break his lunch engagement with Debbie, and that he hadn't been able to discuss this other business with her. "How's the baby and Franny doing?"

"I'm still at the clinic and the doc is keeping them overnight. They're going to be just fine. Thanks to you."

"And you. Hell, you saw the vehicle first."

He mentioned that only because she'd commented on his keen vision too many times to count, and he didn't want her to find that odd. "I'm sorry about lunch. I'll make it up to you later."

"No problem at all, Allan, but I'll certainly take you up on it. Is everything all right?"

He couldn't lie to her and say everything was fine. Everything wouldn't be all right until they caught this maniac. "It's a small family crisis." Which was the truth. Anything that affected *lupus garous* in their territory affected them. So it *was* a family crisis. "I'll be back tomorrow to help investigate the Van Lake accident scene." It was located fifty-three miles from where Allan lived, so not too far.

"Can I help in any way?"

"No, thanks. I'll...I'll call you later tonight." He hated this part of their relationship, where he couldn't be completely honest with her. He could imagine just how well telling her the truth would go over. That he even considered such a notion bothered him. Normally, he never gave it any thought when he was around strictly humans. He and his kind were what they were and it was their own business.

"All right. I'll fill out the accident report on the mother and baby. I'll...talk to you later."

He knew she wasn't happy with the way he always shut down about his family when there were issues. She'd told him about her alcoholic father, and he suspected it bothered her that he wouldn't come clean with *his* family "issues."

"Talk to you later, Debbie." He hung up as he reached the area where the killing had taken place.

He hated that tens of thousands of leghold traps and snares were legally set up on Montana's public lands and along waterways. Reportedly, fifty thousand wild animals were trapped a year, but trappers weren't required to check traps regularly or report numbers. People and pets could be the victims, as well as any other animal the hunter wasn't interested in capturing. One of the former vice presidents of the Montana Trappers Association had agreed that trappers cause pain and suffering to animals, but would apologize to no one. Really a sad state of affairs.

Allan found the victim's blood splattered all over the fresh snow. Tracks were everywhere, from the wolves who found the victim and humans who had come to retrieve her body. He looked around at the thick pine forest and where the trap had been set near a tree, buried by the snow. He tried to sense if the murderer was in the area. The trappers were a danger to them all. But this guy, even more so.

So many people had been in the area, it was hard to say who might have done this. Allan followed boot tracks in the snow for over a mile, then went back and followed another set of tracks. None of them led him to anything suspicious. Tons of tire tracks were on an old logging trail nearby too—the ambulance and police vehicles for sure. So again, nothing that could help him there.

Once he climbed back into his vehicle and shut the door, he called Paul. "I didn't find anything that stood out to me."

"I just got the preliminary report on the autopsy. She was shot five times and all the rounds were silver."

"He has to be a werewolf hunter then."

"You know, we've been thinking it's a he, but it might have been a she. Some of her wolf fur was stuck to the blood on the jaws of the trap, though the coroner believes that a wolf had been caught earlier. Rose and Lori smelled it was the woman's fur. So the victim couldn't have been a new wolf or she couldn't have been in her wolf form."

"We need to put this guy down."

"I'd like to also, but as long as the killer might be human and the police are involved, we have to let the homicide detectives working the case deal with it. We've got to catch the guy before they do to determine if he's one of our kind now. If we catch him and he's still human, we turn him over to the police. I've let everyone know to be extra vigilant if they think they're being followed. I don't want anyone to see our families except for you and me. I don't want him to identify anyone else as a pack member so no one else will be put in harm's way."

"Agreed." Allan couldn't believe what a nightmare this could be for all of them.

"We have another situation that arose. Lori went in to see Franny and she wants to speak with you about her car crash. Lori thought maybe she had been confused, but Franny was adamant it wasn't an accident."

"That's what she told me and she talked to Debbie about."

"Franny knows you're the only one in the pack available to investigate it right now, but I think there's something else she's hiding."

"From Lori?"

"Yeah. If you're going to investigate this, she'll have to tell you what she knows."

"All right. I'll drop by the clinic next." What *else* could go wrong?

"Hey, Debbie," Rowdy said, meeting up with her as she headed to the clinic lobby. She was ready to get take-out somewhere close by and then work on the accident report back at the sheriff's office. She was relieved Franny and baby Stacy were doing well.

She was surprised to see Rowdy here, since he was a *homicide* detective.

"Hey," she said, disliking the speculative gleam in his eyes.

He glanced around the lobby and seeing it was empty, said to her, "I heard you were here by yourself and wondered where your partner had gone."

She shrugged it off. "Yeah, he had a minor family crisis."

Rowdy raised his brows.

She suspected then that he knew something she didn't and it wasn't good news. *Especially* when he was a homicide detective. But if someone in Allan's family had been murdered, she was certain Allan would have told her. "Well, spill."

"Allan's twin sister and Paul's wife were hiking in the woods when they came across a body—near Paul's cabin. Didn't he tell you?"

About the Author

USA Today bestselling and award-winning author Terry Spear has written more than fifty paranormal romance novels and four medieval Highland historical romances. Her first werewolf romance, *Heart of the Wolf*, was named a 2008 *Publishers Weekly*'s Best Book of the Year, and her subsequent titles have garnered high praise and hit the *USA Today* bestseller list. A retired officer of the U.S. Army Reserves, Terry lives in Crawford, Texas, where she is working on her next werewolf romance, continuing her new series about shapeshifting jaguars, loving to share her hot Highlanders, and having fun with her young adult novels. For more information, please visit www.terryspear.com, or follow her on Twitter, @TerrySpear. She is also on Facebook at www.facebook.com/TerrySpearParanormalRomantics, and her *Terry Spear's Shifter* blog on Wordpress at www.terryspear.wordpress.com.